Praise for Elmer Kelton

"One of the best of a new breed of Western writers who have driven the genre into new territory."
—*The New York Times*

"[Kelton] never shrank from bending the rules of the genre. . . . He devoted himself to explaining and defending the cowboy's way of life."
—*The Wall Street Journal*

"[A] masterful Western author."
—*Lubbock Avalanche-Journal*

"Voted the Greatest Western Writer of All Time by the Western Writers of America, Kelton creates characters more complex than L'Amour's."
—*Kirkus Reviews*

"Kelton's writing is absolutely authentic, and he is a master at spinning that wildly expressive species of dusty idiom that makes good Western writing so gratifying. Add to that some stern, if flexible, morality and tight plotting full of tense, finger-twitching a͟ ͟ ͟ ͟ ͟ ͟tstanding Western far ͟ ͟ ͟ ͟ ͟ ͟ ͟ ͟ ͟ ͟ ͟ ͟ ͟-*Booklist*

"Next to L ͟ ͟ ͟ ͟ ͟ ͟ ͟ ͟ ͟ ͟ d Larry McMurtry, ͟ ͟ ͟ ͟ ͟ ͟ ͟ ͟ ͟ ͟ o find a better Wester ͟ ͟ ͟ ͟ ͟ ͟ ͟ ͟n. . . . A true master of the Western literary form."
—*American Cowboy* magazine

FORGE BOOKS BY ELMER KELTON

DONOVAN

AND

DARK THICKET

Elmer Kelton

A TOM DOHERTY ASSOCIATES BOOK • NEW YORK

NOTE: If you purchased this book without a cover, you should be aware that this book is stolen property. It was reported as "unsold and destroyed" to the publisher, and neither the author nor the publisher has received any payment for this "stripped book."

This is a work of fiction. All of the characters, organizations, and events portrayed in this novel are either products of the author's imagination or are used fictitiously.

DONOVAN AND DARK THICKET

Donovan copyright © 1961, 1986 by the Estate of Elmer Kelton

Dark Thicket copyright © 1985 by the Estate of Elmer Kelton

All rights reserved.

A Forge Book
Published by Tom Doherty Associates, LLC
175 Fifth Avenue
New York, NY 10010

www.tor-forge.com

Forge® is a registered trademark of Tom Doherty Associates, LLC.

ISBN 978-0-7653-7045-7

First Edition: November 2012

Printed in the United States of America

0 9 8 7 6 5 4 3 2 1

CONTENTS

DONOVAN

1

Even before his horse's ears suddenly pointed forward, Webb Matlock was becoming uneasy. He had slipped his saddlegun out of its scabbard beneath his leg and had lifted it up across the pommel, on the ready. He pulled the dun horse to a halt and raised his left hand as a signal to the riders with him.

"Easy, boys. We don't want to be in no hurry about this thing."

Webb Matlock wore a sheriff's badge. With him rode five men from the Box L cow outfit, hurriedly deputized to help him run out the trail of some would-be cattle thieves. Johnny Willet and another Box L hand had come unexpectedly upon a half a dozen men hazing seventy or eighty of Old Man Jess Leggett's good cows south toward the Rio Grande. Rather than tackle the rustlers themselves, they had pulled back unseen and spurred to the ranch headquarters.

For several years now, Old Man Jess had been bringing in good Durham bulls to breed out the Longhorn strain. He was proud of these halfbreed cows and didn't want to lose any of them. Over and above that, he held a deep and abiding hatred for thieves. In olden times, before there had been law to look to, he had shot or hanged them himself. This time he had sent for Webb Matlock. Then, instead of waiting, the impatient old man had taken his cowboys and set out in pursuit. They fought a running battle that forced the thieves to give up the cattle. But Old Jess had fallen with a bullet in his shoulder. That had stopped the pursuit until Webb got there.

The last thing Jess had hollered at Webb as they had hauled him toward town in a wagon was: "You get 'em now, you hear?"

This was the Texas border country, and *ladrones* out of Mexico sometimes still came over the border to hit and run, steal and carry off whatever they could get away with. In many people on both sides of the river, old hatreds still burned. To some on the south side, the Texas revolution and the Mexican War had meant nothing. To these this land still rightfully belonged to Mexico, and so did everything that walked upon it.

Webb had asked Johnny Willet, "Mexicans, Johnny?"

Johnny had been riding in a strange, thoughtful silence. He shook his head. "Mostly it was *gringos*. Odd thing about one of them, he . . ." Johnny broke off. "Forget it, you wouldn't believe it."

"Believe what, Johnny?"

"Nothin', it was a crazy notion." He changed the subject. "I'm pretty sure we hit one of them. He slumped over, nearly fell off his horse. Got away into the brush, though, and that was the last we seen of him."

A mile or so back they had come upon a blood-crusted handkerchief lying amid the fresh horsetracks, and they had known for sure.

Now Webb sat rigid in the saddle, squinting into a brushy header where in rainy times the water would come rushing off the sides of the rocky hills to spread out down a silty mesquite draw. Webb Matlock was a medium-tall man in his early thirties, a little on the stocky side but without any fat on him. He had a square face, a strong jaw that showed the dark stubble of two days' whiskers. His gray eyes were habitually squinted a little, for this was a land of harsh sunlight, dust, and wind. He was a sober, serious man for the most part, so much so that people who didn't know sometimes guessed him to be much older than he was. He had toted his own load since before he was fifteen.

The black-tipped ears of his dun horse were still pointed forward. Looking around him, Matlock could see that a couple of the other horses were the same.

Something ahead of us yonder, he thought. *Pity a man can't be as smart as a horse.*

He made a sweeping motion with his hand. "Fan out, boys. Couple of you work up the hill on one side of that header, a couple on the other. Better go afoot. Ollie Reed, what say you hold the horses."

Ollie Reed, fifty now and bald as an egg, was glad enough to accept that chore. He was not the contentious kind.

Halfway out of his saddle, Johnny Willet stopped himself and asked, "Webb, what *you* aimin' to do?"

"You don't flush quail by ridin' around them. Somebody's got to go on in."

The sheriff swung to the ground to make himself

less of a target. He stood behind his horse for cover and peered across the saddle, looking for signs of anything in the brush. He waited then, giving the men time to work up the hills on either side of the header. Once they were there, they should have a good view of whatever might be below them. They could provide cover for Webb when he moved in.

Ollie Reed's voice was thin with excitement. "I don't like this, Webb, don't like it atall. Puts me in mind of the days when Clabe Donovan and his bunch was runnin' loose."

"Clabe Donovan's dead, Ollie."

Ollie nodded, shivering. "That don't keep me from rememberin'."

Not many years ago, Clabe Donovan and a wild bunch that ran with him were cutting a wide swath through the border country, jumping back and forth across the Rio Grande, stealing what they wanted, killing when someone got in their way. Donovan caught the blame for just about everything bad that happened in those days. Likely it wasn't all justified, but he had gloried in it anyway, perversely proud that he was becoming a legend while he still lived.

In death, the legend had kept on growing.

Webb's horse nickered. An answering nicker came from within the thorny tangle of mesquite. Limbs crackled. A riderless bay horse broke into the open, moving in a long trot. He came straight toward the possemen's horses and stopped among them.

Webb saw blood splotches on the saddle.

He glanced at the wide-eyed Ollie Reed. "There's probably a rustler lyin' in yonder dead."

"And again, maybe he ain't," Reed observed nervously. "Wounded animal is the most dangerous kind."

"A man's different from an animal."

"Some of them ain't."

Webb handed Ollie his bridle reins. "We'll find out pretty quick." Holding the saddlegun ready, he started toward the brush afoot. He moved cautiously from one mesquite to another, keeping himself behind cover of the green leaves as much as he could. A cold tingle ran up and down his back. His sweaty shirt clung to him.

A bullet whined by his head. Leaves drifted down from a mesquite where the slug had clipped them. He threw himself to the ground, breaking his fall first with his knees, then with the butt of the rifle. He snapped a shot in the direction from which the report had come. A second bullet buzzed angrily overhead.

Six-shooter. Webb could tell by the sound. Six-shooter must be all the man had. If he had a rifle he would have used it. At this range, only the rankest kind of luck would score the man a hit. The sheriff levered another cartridge into the breech, pushed to his knees, and sprinted again. This time he saw the flash. The saddlegun was nearly torn from his hands. Splinters drove searing hot into his skin. The bullet had glanced off the wooden stock.

He saw a depression ahead, with a bush beyond to help hide him. He dived, sliding in the loose rocks, ripping his clothing, tearing his flesh. He knew he was bruised blue. Breathing hard, he paused to wipe sweat from his forehead onto his sleeve. He listened, hearing movement as the gunman tried to shift position. Webb called:

"This is Sheriff Matlock. We got you surrounded. No sense in you fightin' anymore. Throw your gun out and raise up where we can see you."

Another shot sent more mesquite leaves showering down.

Webb called again: "You're playin' the fool. If you're wounded, you need doctorin'. Don't just lay there and die."

He heard a cough. A weak voice said, "You'd never get me to town. You'd hang me."

"Nobody'll molest you, I give my word on that."

Johnny Willet was cautiously working his way back down the hillside. The cowboy paused tensely and caught the sheriff's eye. He held up one finger. Just one man, that was all.

The sheriff tried reasoning again. "You haven't got a chance, so why keep on with it? Don't make us have to kill you." He held his breath, waiting for an answer that didn't come. "There's already been enough blood spilled. We don't want any more."

Johnny Willet was moving in closer.

"Last chance," Webb called. "What do you say?"

The outlaw squeezed off another shot. It kicked dirt into Webb Matlock's eyes. The sheriff blinked desperately to clear away the burning, the momentary blindness.

He could hear Johnny's voice. "All right now, mister, how about it?"

Webb heard a desperate cry as the outlaw flopped over to see the man who had crept up on him unseen.

The pistol cracked. Then Willet's rifle roared. Webb heard a groan. The pistol fell, rattling upon the rocks.

Webb stood up rubbing his eyes, blinking away the sand. He could see the cowboys closing in. Johnny Willet stood slump-shouldered, the smoking rifle held slackly in one hand. He glanced up as the sheriff reached him.

"Sometimes, Johnny, a man's got no choice. Did he hit you?"

Eyes bleak, Johnny shook his head. "Missed. Scared, I reckon. Took a wild shot."

"Next one might not've been so wild. You had to shoot him."

Willet's mouth twisted. "That don't make it no easier." He walked off into the brush to stand alone, his back turned.

The gunman lay twisted, face to the ground, legs drawn up in dying agony. Breath still struggled in him, but it wouldn't last long. Gently Webb turned him over. His heart went sick.

Gray-haired Uncle Joe Vickers, the Box L foreman, took a long look and cursed softly. "A button, Webb, not a day over twenty! Just a slick-faced kid is all!"

Webb knelt beside the dying youth. "Can you hear me, boy?"

The youngster tried hard. He managed a weak "Yes."

"They just threw you away, kid. They left you to cover for them, and they ran off. Who was it?"

The boy didn't answer.

Webb said, "You don't owe them a thing now, son. Tell us, who was it?"

His lips painfully attempted to form the word. "Dono . . . Donovan."

Webb looked quickly up at the perplexed faces around him. He said, "Boy, that can't be. Donovan is dead."

The youngster started again. "Don . . . Don . . ." The voice trailed off and he was gone.

Webb stayed on one knee. Despite the heat, a chill played up and down his back. Presently he said, "That's the strangest thing I ever heard. Everybody knows Donovan is dead."

Uncle Joe Vickers' face had turned as gray as ashes. "Sure we know. It was me that killed him!"

Webb Matlock closed his eyes, remembering the violent night Clabe Donovan's wild border-jumping career had suddenly been brought to a close. Donovan had had a brother named Morg, a salty young hellion a few years younger than himself. Morg had been a reckless rider, a good shot, a headstrong desperado of Clabe's own stripe. One thing he had lacked had been Clabe's shrewd judgment. Trying to pull a robbery on his own, Morg had gotten himself into a jackpot he couldn't get out of alone. Clabe had come to his rescue. Morg had escaped, but Clabe's horse had been hit. Left afoot, Clabe was tracked down like a wild animal.

His trial had been short, the verdict certain. And the sentence: to hang by the neck until dead.

Morg had made a big effort one night to free his brother. He had sent part of the Donovan bunch to one end of Dry Fork to set up a diversion and draw much of the guard away from the jail. Then he had moved in with the rest of the men. They stormed the jail and broke Clabe out. But spurring away, they rode into a deadly barrage of bullets.

Clabe Donovan's trademark had always been a black Mexican hat with peaked crown and wide brim. Uncle Joe Vickers had seen that hat and had stepped out into the dusty, dark street with a double-barreled shotgun. He had triggered both barrels at once. His target had rolled in the dirt, face blasted away. He had been dead before he hit the ground.

The people of Dry Fork never doubted the man's identity. They buried him and put up a marker: *Clabe Donovan*. The Donovan gang disappeared. Some said Morg had tried later to rob a mint deep down in Mexico and had been cut down by the *rurales*. Nobody worried much about Morg. Main thing was that Clabe was dead, and this section of the border country had comparative peace for the first time in years.

Sure, there were stories, persistent stories that came from God knows where, rumors that Clabe Donovan still lived down in Mexico. Those kinds of stories arose about every well-known outlaw. Always, after a passage of time, there were some who claimed the man had never really died. There were those who claimed to have seen him alive, long after the man had been buried.

At Dry Fork, men shrugged off such stories. They knew, for Uncle Joe Vickers had killed Clabe Donovan, and nearly everybody in Dry Fork had gone down to the cemetery to watch the outlaw's wooden coffin lowered into the grave. In time, souvenir hunters had whittled away so much of the simple little cross that the county had had to put up a new one.

Donovan, the young rustler had said. *Donovan!*

Johnny Willet had heard. Slowly he came back and stood looking down at this youngster he had killed. Voice unsteady, he said, "Webb, that's what I started to tell you while ago, only the more I thought about it, the crazier it seemed. I remember seein' Clabe Donovan in his prime. I'll never forget the way he looked, tall, straight, broad-shouldered, with that big black Mexican hat."

He looked around at the other men and said shakily, "I got in pretty close to them cow thieves today. If I hadn't known better, I'd have sworn one of them was Clabe Donovan, black hat and all!"

No effort was made to go on with the chase. In the first place, no one had the spirit for it now. In the second, tracks showed the rustlers had been gone a long time. They had simply left the wounded boy to die because they knew he would anyway, and he would slow them down. They probably had hoped for him to delay pursuit. That he had done.

"Not much use goin' any farther," Webb said. "They'll be across the river before we can catch them anyhow."

Beyond the river lay the wild and brushy sanctuary that was Mexico. There the *gringo* lawman was never welcome. Decades of border warfare had left in much of the Mexican population a mortal hatred for the *rinches*, a term they applied to Rangers and all other *gringo* officers. There the *gringo* lawbreaker could find safety, even a welcome of sorts, so long as he spent good money and did not unduly disturb the people.

Webb Matlock looked down at the body. "It'd take us till this time tomorrow to get him to town. We better not wait that long."

Uncle Joe Vickers said, "There's a Box L line shack back yonderway. I expect we could find a shovel."

All they found for identification was a letter, carried in the shirt pocket so long that the envelope was beginning to wear through at the edges. They rolled the body in a slicker and tied it across the bay horse the young outlaw had been riding. At the line shack they found a shovel but no Bible. They dug a grave, and Webb Matlock stood over it with bared head, repeating the Twenty-third Psalm by heart.

Afterwards, the grave covered and a mound tamped over it, the gray-haired foreman said, "We'll put up some sort of a marker. Ordinarily I'd be inclined to leave a cow thief lay where he fell. But this one bein' just a kid and all . . ."

Webb nodded. "It's a long way to town, Uncle Joe. I expect I'd best be gettin' started."

"We'll go with you," said Vickers, "me and Ollie Reed. We're anxious to see how Jess Leggett's gettin' along. That old man's a way too ancient to be carryin' a slug in his shoulder . . ."

For the first time, Webb had to suppress a smile. The worried foreman lacked only three or four years being as old as his boss.

Camped on the trail that night, Webb kept remembering. The dying outlaw's words came back to him again and again. *Donovan. Donovan.*

"Uncle Joe," he said, "is there a chance you could've been mistaken? Is there a chance the man you shot *wasn't* Clabe Donovan?"

Fiercely Joe Vickers responded, "No sir, there ain't. I seen him!"

But the old man stared into the firelight, doubt coming into his eyes.

And Ollie Reed murmured wonderingly to himself, "Clabe Donovan, come back to life. Now, ain't that somethin'?"

2

Dry Fork was an unplanned, unpretty scattering of lumber and adobe houses, most of them better called shacks. A rock courthouse and a few solid-looking business buildings put up in the last few years revealed a hope that better times waited somewhere ahead. At the south end, by coincidence on the side that lay nearest Mexico, was the town's sizeable Mexican settlement. It looked even poorer than the unassuming Anglo side.

Tired and much-sweated in the afternoon sun, three riders stirred a flurry of interest as they rode their flagging horses down the wagon-rutted, hoof-scarred street. It was not the men themselves so much as the riderless horse they led, a gunbelt hanging from the horn of an empty saddle. They stopped first at the doctor's house near the head of the street. Webb tarried only long enough to reassure himself that Jess Leggett was going to make out all right. In fact, Jess was already raising cain because two of his men had come to see about him. One, he maintained, would have been plenty.

"I ought to dock your wages," he told Ollie Reed, "because you sure can't claim you're workin'."

Old Jess didn't mean it, for attention really pleased him. That he felt like hell-raising was a good sign. He never spoke kindly except when he was sick.

Webb swung back into the saddle and moved on down the street toward Quince Pyburn's livery stable. At the little Dry Fork Cafe, Ellie Donovan stepped out onto the small shaded porch to watch silently as Webb rode by. Webb raised his hand, and she nodded to him, a fleeting smile crossing her face. Her gaze fell upon the led horse, and it stayed there.

What am I going to tell Ellie? Webb asked himself darkly. *What can I say?*

Quince Pyburn stood in the stable's big open door. He was a tall, gaunt man with a slight stoop to his shoulders, the look of hard years in his squinted eyes. He watched Webb Matlock ride in and dismount. The liveryman's gaze drifted over the led horse, but he was a patient man, not given to probing questions. He knew Webb would tell him when he was ready.

The sheriff said, "I got a saddle here to sell, Quince. You interested?"

Pyburn shrugged. "Man can always use an extra saddle around a barn like this. The gun too?"

Webb nodded. "It won't be of no use to *him* anymore. The money might be of some use to his mother."

Pyburn's eyebrows lifted. "Mother?" He looked at the horse again, frowning. "Forty dollars for the saddle and gun." That was overgenerous. "How about the horse?"

Matt shook his head. "Got a Rafter T brand on his

hip. I'll take him home tomorrow." His mouth was set grimly as he wondered how the young rustler came to be riding a Rafter T horse in the first place.

Quince said, "I guess Bronc Tomlin will have some explainin' to do."

"He'll just say the horse was stolen. I couldn't prove different. But I'm goin' to talk with him anyhow. Might throw a scare into him."

Webb unsaddled his dun horse and turned him loose in a corral behind the barn. He left his saddle, blanket and bridle on a rack that had long since been considered his own. Quince was turning the Rafter T horse loose and examining the saddle he had bought. In the barn Webb paused, face dark in thought. "Quince, you were helpin' us the night Clabe Donovan was broken out of jail. You saw him after Uncle Joe brought him down."

Quince nodded.

Webb said, "Would you say there was room for any doubt that it was Clabe Donovan we buried?"

Quince's eyes narrowed. "What're you gettin' at, Webb?"

Webb told him the whole story. Quince listened unbelievingly. "Webb, it can't be. And yet . . ." He was silent a moment, calling up old memories. "You know, his face *was* shot away. All we really had to go by was the size of him, and that black Mexican hat. And Uncle Joe swore it was him."

Webb said, "It was dark in that street. There was plenty of excitement. As for the hat, maybe one of the others picked it up in the jail. *Quién sabe?*"

"If Clabe Donovan had lived, why would he have

stayed out of sight all these years? It wasn't his nature."

"Maybe he saw a chance to fade away, to get himself a fresh start."

"Then how come he would turn up now, outlawed again?"

"Could be he couldn't make it straight."

Quince Pyburn paced back and forth on the dirt floor of the barn, scowling in disbelief.

Webb said, "I don't want to believe it either, Quince. But we can't ignore what's happened. There's got to be an explanation."

"If we didn't kill Clabe Donovan, then who's that buried out yonder?"

Webb shrugged. "One of Clabe's *compadres*. Maybe even his brother Morg. They always looked a lot alike."

Quince dropped his thin frame upon a bale of hay. For a while he sat nervously flexing his hands, his face twisted. "If it *is* Clabe—and mind you, I'm not sayin' it is him come back to life—there's a bunch of us around here got to start watchin' our step. There's a bunch of us he swore he'd kill."

"Includin' you, Quince. And *me*!"

Most of the buildings on the street had low wooden porches, but between them there was only the dirt. Webb walked in the edge of the street itself, preferring that to stepping on and off the porches.

His living quarters—what there was of them—were in the long, narrow rock jail building beside the courthouse. He walked through the office into the small room where he kept his cot. He gathered up a change of clothes and walked out again. The doors of his two cells were swung open, the way he had left them. The only prisoner he had had was one *vaquero* arrested for fighting, and Webb had turned him loose before starting out toward the Box L.

He angled across the street to the barber shop, pausing in front of its peppermint-striped sign to glance at the Dry Fork Cafe. He didn't see Ellie Donovan. It was just as well, he thought.

What he had to tell her was going to floor her, he knew. He would put it off awhile. Maybe later he would know what to say.

"Got some hot water, Syl?" he asked the barber. "I sure do need a bath."

The barber nodded. "Got a kettle on the stove in the back."

Webb enjoyed a long, leisurely soak in the shop's cast-iron tub. The warm water seemed to draw out some of the fatigue that weighted his shoulders. Finished, he put on clean clothes, transferring his badge to a clean shirt. He walked out front again and dropped into the barber chair. Without having to ask, the barber began whipping up a lather and applying it to Webb's face. Syl was bald, or almost so. It seemed to Webb that most of the barbers he had known didn't have much hair, and he idly wondered why.

Webb could tell that curiosity was burning a hole in the barber. Webb waited until Syl was through using the razor, then gave him a brief account of the chase and gunfight. He left out any reference to Clabe Donovan. There had to be some kind of explanation, he was sure. No use getting people stirred up.

Changing the subject, Webb asked, "Syl, have you seen anything of my kid brother?"

Syl was slow in answering. "Yes, I seen Sandy."

Webb didn't like the tone of the reply. "He been into somethin' again?"

The barber shrugged. "Just a little scrap last night. Young rooster like that, he plays rougher than us older folks."

Finished, Webb paid Syl and rolled up his dirty clothes. "Syl, what did Sandy do this time?"

"Nothin' too bad, really. It's apt to cost a little, though. Him and that Augie Brock kid he's always runnin' around with, they had a scrap with a couple of gamblers over at the Longhorn Bar last night. There was some furniture and windowglass broke. And I think maybe a gambler's head."

Webb groaned. There was always a gambler or two over at the Longhorn, and most of them needed their heads broken. But it wasn't Sandy's place to do it, he thought with irritation.

The sun was getting low. Webb glanced again at the cafe, then carried the bundle of clothes across the railroad tracks to an adobe house where the widow Sanchez had a misspelled sign posted: CLOTHS WASHING. The old woman made a fair living washing for some of the town's unattached Anglo men. That done, Webb walked back down the street to the Longhorn Bar. It was an adobe building about twenty feet wide and some forty feet long. Lanterns, not lighted yet, hung on either side of the door and one more out at the edge of the porch roof's overhang. Webb noted that one of the front window glasses was missing.

A Mexican swamper pushed the swinging door open and swept dirt out into the street. He held the door for Webb and dropped his head slightly in deference. Inside, Webb paused to look around. The twelve-foot mahogany bar stood to the front, parallel to the left-hand wall. A big mirror with ornate wooden frame hung behind it. The bar and mirror had an expensive appearance out of place with the plastered adobe walls and the hard-packed dirt floor. The story was that Jake Scully had won them from another saloonkeeper in San Antonio in an all-night poker game.

Behind his bar, Scully polished glasses on his white towel apron and frowned at Webb. "You hear what that brother of yours done in here last night?"

Cautiously Webb said, "I heard there was some kind of ruckus."

"Ruckus? More like a gangfight between a bunch of Irish railroaders. Them two boys, Sandy and Augie Brock, they came in here nosin' around. I could tell right off that they was trouble lookin' for a good place to happen. Things was kind of slow, and a couple of gamblers was sittin' back there havin' a quiet little game between theirselves. The boys, they asked to get in, and the gamblers said, 'Sure enough.' After a while Sandy jumped up and accused a gambler of pullin' a card out of his sleeve. It was hell amongst the yearlin's there for a little bit."

"Who won?"

"Them boys, I reckon you'd say. They was younger

and a mite the liveliest. I finally had to cool that Brock button with a bung-starter. This mornin' both gamblers left town." Jake frowned deeply. "I sure did hate to see them go. They was payin' me a right nice percentage for the use of the place."

Webb pulled out his wallet. "How much you figure the damage comes to, Jake?"

Jake looked hungrily at Webb's money. "Well, they busted up a table, but I can fix that. It's been busted before. No charge. Then there's three chairs, gone beyond recall. Two dollars apiece—they wasn't plumb new. Boys, they busted four bottles of good whisky back there behind the bar, throwin' chairs. Two dollars apiece for them—all I'll ask is wholesale. Then there's this here mirror. They busted a corner out of it, and it'll never be as pretty as it was. I expect twenty dollars would be fair for the mirror. And, oh yes, the front window."

"I reckon they tossed a chair through that?"

"No, they threw out one of them gamblers, right through the glass." Jake frowned. "He never did come back in. Come to think of it, he owed me for a couple of drinks. But I reckon it ain't fair to charge you for that."

Webb shook his head. "No, I don't guess it is." He counted on his fingers. "Jake, I'll take you at your word on this, all except about that mirror. I happen to remember that corner bein' busted out before. I'll give you twenty-five dollars. That ought to cover it."

Jake Scully grimaced. "Now, Webb, I was kind of figurin' it would run more than that."

"I oughtn't to pay you anything, you tryin' to get

by me with that mirror. But I'll give you twenty-five dollars if you'll call it square."

Scully took the money, grunting as he counted it. "Don't hold it agin me, Webb, me tryin' to get you to pay for that mirror. It was broke by a couple of drunks in here a while back. It was really your fault in a way. You're supposed to keep the peace."

Webb said, "When they get to drinkin' that stuff you sell, they're bound to bust somethin'."

Webb started toward the door. Jake Scully said, "Sheriff, mind if I give you a little advice?"

"Shoot."

Scully fingered the money. "That boy has come of age, Webb. It's time he found out a man's got to pay for his own breakage. You keep on payin' him out of scrapes, he'll keep causin' you trouble."

Webb said, "I'll take care of Sandy."

Dusk was settling over Dry Fork, bringing a fresh and pleasant coolness. As Webb left the saloon, the Mexican swamper was lighting the lanterns to have them aglow before darkness came. Jake Scully wouldn't want thirsty riders to pass by and miss seeing his place.

From down the street Webb heard someone start picking out a Mexican melody on a guitar, and he heard a thin voice begin to lift with it. He stopped in front of the cafe and glanced through the window to see if Ellie Donovan had any customers. She didn't.

He stepped inside. "Hello, Ellie."

She turned, her face lighting as she saw him. She was a woman of thirty, or perhaps a little less. Like Webb, she had seen much of trouble, and it had left its stamp in her face, its mark in her eyes. She had been beaten and crushed but had risen again to stand upon her own feet with a stoic dignity. To Webb, she was still one of the prettiest women he had ever seen.

Ellie moved out from behind the counter. She gripped Webb's arms and tiptoed to kiss him. He started to put his arms around her but caught himself. Ellie was instantly aware that he was troubled.

"What is it, Webb?" She peered intently into his face. He avoided looking into her eyes. She said, "I saw you bring in a saddled horse." It was meant as a question.

"We had to kill a man," he replied.

She nodded soberly, looking away a moment. "No wonder you've got trouble riding on your shoulders. Sit down, Webb. I'll bring you some coffee. Want me to pour something extra into it?"

He shook his head and sat at a table. Ellie set down a steaming cup of black coffee. She moved around to stand beside him, her hand on his shoulder. "Been a long time since you've had to do that, Webb. I know you wouldn't have done it if it could have been avoided at all. You shouldn't let it get you down."

He glanced up at her a moment and was grateful for the gentle understanding in her eyes. Yet, there was a lot she didn't know about this, not yet. There was so much more he had to tell her. How could he say it?

Not long ago Webb had asked Ellie to marry him, and she had said yes. He was in the process of buying a house from a merchant who had sold out his business here and was moving to San Antonio.

Now . . .

Webb's mind drifted far back into memory. He had come to this part of the country when he was only about fifteen, hunting a ranch job. His father, a sheriff farther east, had been killed while trying to make an arrest. Webb had figured his mother would have a hard enough time trying to earn a living for herself and his five-year-old brother Sandy. He had gotten the ranch job, and he had sent most of the money home. Life had seemed terribly hard to him in those days.

He remembered the first time he had met Clabe Donovan. Clabe was a couple of years older than Webb. He still had both parents, but he had run off and left them. Now he was hanging around with a wild bunch along the river. He always seemed to have plenty of money without showing much sign of having to work for it. Webb had liked Clabe in those days, and he had been sorely tempted to follow Clabe's example. Ranch work was long and hard and didn't pay much for a kid.

It had even reached the point that Webb was supposed to meet Clabe one night and ride off with the bunch on some mysterious expedition. Webb hadn't known then just what the plan was, but he had known it was something lawless. Webb's father and mother had taught him a strong sense of values, had pounded into him their solid belief that it was no disgrace to be poor if one was honest and of good conscience. Webb had ridden to the rendezvous point with those voices of old ringing in his ears. And when Clabe had come, Webb had pulled back into the shadows and hidden from him.

Days later, Webb heard of a bank robbery seventy miles away, a robbery in which a bank teller and an outlaw were killed. The outlaw had been a kid holding the robbers' horses.

That, Webb had realized, would have been his job if he had gone.

When Webb was about twenty, his mother died. It became Webb's duty to take his little brother under his wing. Because Webb had been a level-headed youth and a crack shot, the sheriff had offered him a job as deputy. Lawing paid better than cowboying. With a brother to care for, Webb had accepted. He had worn a badge ever since. He had tried to take good care of Sandy and teach him the lessons his mother would have taught if she had lived.

As for Clabe Donovan, he had slipped irretrievably beyond the pale. He had become an expert border jumper, keeping himself out of the hands of the law on both sides of the river. Most of his depredations were on the Texas side, where he could go back across to sanctuary. True, there was law in Mexico, too, but it was a big and wild country across there. Its law-enforcement agencies were not so well developed, not well equipped, nor did they have much incentive to go against Clabe. After all, Clabe caused little trouble on their side, and he *did* bring back considerable amounts of money which he spread around with complete abandon. Easy come, easy go. And money was not easy to come by in Mexico.

Like Webb Matlock, Clabe Donovan had had a younger brother. While Webb had been trying to teach Sandy to ride a straight road, Clabe had taught

Morg Donovan the twisted ways of a crooked trail. It had not been hard to do, for by natural bent Morg took to the lawless ways like a duck to water.

The brothers' daring had brought them a grudging respect, if not a liking, among many of the border settlers—those the Donovans had not yet bothered.

It had been significant to Webb that the people who spoke with sympathy of the Donovans had never been their victims. And those who did feel some admiration for them usually changed readily enough when they had seen the outlaws in a new light—say, over the muzzle of a gun. That took the romance out of it.

Once Clabe and Morg had dropped out of sight for more than a year. Rumor had it that they had been cut down while trying to steal golden ornaments from a cathedral far down in Mexico. But it turned out later they had simply gone west under assumed names. Clabe had taken a notion he wanted a simpler life. He had found Ellie and married her, the girl having no idea what he had been. Before long, the old restlessness came over him again. One night he and Morg had spurred home on sweat-lathered horses, anxiously watching their backtrail. They had dragged the dismayed Ellie Donovan with them back to this part of the country.

Sickening of a hideout life across the river, her dreams and illusions shattered, she had ridden away one night while the Donovans were gone. She had wound up in Dry Fork. Here she had found hostility from some but sympathy from many more. Among the sympathetic was Webb Matlock.

Webb had fallen in love with Ellie a long time ago.

Lately, with Clabe Donovan thought dead and that nightmare gradually receding into the past, Ellie had begun to return Webb's love.

Now . . .

"Ellie," Webb said regretfully, "I got somethin' to tell you. It may not be true . . . I can't believe it is. But *if* it is, I want you to hear it first from me, not from the gossip of the street."

He told her what had happened. As she listened, Ellie's face drained of color. Both hands went up over her eyes. When finally she brought the hands down, Webb could see that her eyes brimmed with tears.

"Clabe, alive?" Her voice quavered. "How, Webb? How?"

He shook his head. "Like I told you, Ellie, it may not be true. For my sake—and for yours—I hope it's not."

She lowered her chin. A tear ran slowly down her check. "But if it is, I'm still married to him."

"You could get a divorce, Ellie. There's not a court in the country wouldn't give it to you and say you deserved it."

She clasped her hands together. "When I married him, I made a promise—for better or for worse."

"He broke all the promises he ever made to you."

"I made my promise to God, not to Clabe Donovan." Pushing to her feet, she took a handkerchief from a pocket in her apron. She turned her back to Webb, but he could see her shoulders tremble. She touched the handkerchief to her eyes. Webb put his hand on her shoulders and turned her around, pulling her to him so that her bowed head touched his chest.

"Ellie . . ."

She pulled away. "Webb, this changes a lot of things."

"What do you mean?"

"Until we know for sure, we can't see each other the way we've been doing. Our marriage is off, Webb. It *has* to be. And you'd better not visit me at home anymore. It wouldn't be proper."

Regretfully he said, "All right, Ellie."

She sat down at one of the tables, her body stiff from shock, the handkerchief gripped so tightly that her right hand was almost white.

"Pull down the shades for me, Webb. I don't feel like serving anybody else tonight."

He pulled down the shades and paused a moment at the door, looking back at her with his heart aching. She dropped her head into her arms and began to cry.

"Good night, Ellie," he said.

She couldn't answer and didn't try. He pulled the door shut and walked down the street, his shoulders slumped.

In his office Webb lighted a lamp, rolled up the top of his desk and sat down. From his shirtpocket he took the worn letter he had found on the dead boy. He smoothed it out and laboriously copied onto a fresh envelope the smudged return address. It was in such poor condition that he had to work it out letter by letter:

On a sheet of white paper he began to write:

Dear Mrs. Brill:
  It becomes my most painful duty to write and inform you of the death of your son James. He was working on the Box L Ranch when a horse fell on him. He lived only long enough to ask us to write and tell you he loved you. Your son had not been here long, but he was well liked. He was a hard worker.

Webb took out a few bills he had found in the boy's pocket and placed them with the money Quince had given him for the saddle and gun. It was not very much, he thought. Remembering his own mother and her constant need, he opened his own wallet and removed most of the money he had left in it. He placed these bills with the others.

  Your son had some wages due him, and his employer asked me to forward them to you. Also, we took the liberty of selling his saddle. The proceeds are enclosed herewith. My deepest sympathies to you in this time of bereavement.
                    Your most sympathetic servant,
                    Webb Matlock, sheriff.

Webb had started to write the words "and gun" after "saddle" but caught himself. He folded the letter with the money inside it, stuck it into the envelope and sealed the flap. He put a stamp on it so it would be ready to mail as soon as he got over to the postoffice.

He blew out the lamp and sat awhile in the darkness, thinking about Clabe Donovan, wondering why a boy like this James Brill would have gotten himself tied up with a wild bunch, why he had to die just when his life should have been beginning to reach its fulfillment. Webb knew the answer, for he had heard the same wild call himself once. It was the call to which Clabe Donovan had responded years ago, a call to which he had hopelessly abandoned himself.

Once over the edge that way, it was hard ever to come back. A majority of them never wanted to.

Brooding to himself, Webb didn't hear the girl come silently into his office. She spoke, and he jerked himself aright. "Birdie! You gave me a jolt."

Birdie Hanks, just turned seventeen, apologized. "I didn't mean to scare you, Webb. I just wondered if you've seen Sandy."

He shook his head. "Not since I left here day before yesterday."

She said worriedly, "He hasn't been around. I wondered if I'd done or said something to make him mad."

Another time, Webb would have smiled. He liked this slender, guileless girl with her honey-colored hair done in braids, the bloom of womanhood just beginning to touch her. An older woman would not have asked so directly. She would have taken ten minutes in working around the question, asking it but at the same time not asking.

"He's at an ornery age, Birdie," Webb said. "He's just commenced to feel his manhood, and he's not right sure what to do about it. He doesn't know what he wants to make of himself, whichaway to jump.

Most boys go through it, and they come out all right. Don't you worry."

"I heard about that fight he got into last night. It caused a real commotion over at my house. Dad says Sandy's too wild for me, wants me to stop seeing him."

Webb frowned, placing his fingertips together. Sandy *was* getting a reputation. Webb didn't know what to do about it. Talking didn't seem to help much anymore. He figured the boy would just have to thrash it out for himself—with a little helpful push here and there.

"Birdie, Sandy has had to grow up without the guidance that most boys get. I've had to try to be both daddy and mother to him, and I really wasn't either one. Some of the lessons, I've pounded into him. Some of them, though, I never have been able to make him take. Maybe someday a woman can teach him the rest. You might be that woman."

Birdie sat sideways in a cane-bottomed chair, one arm over the back of it, her chin resting on the arm. Wistfully she said, "I'd like to be."

He rolled a cigarette and licked the edge of the paper to make it stick. "I hope you will. You're a good girl, Birdie. I like you."

"I like you, too, Webb. I wish Sandy could be more like you."

Webb felt a glow of pride in the compliment. "He'll be all right, Birdie. We've just got to have patience."

She nodded and stood up. As she started toward the door, Webb said, "Glad you came by. I'll tell Sandy you were here."

She shook her head. "Don't. I don't want to give him that satisfaction."

It was warm in his office. With so much on his mind, Webb knew it would be futile to try to go to bed and sleep. He pulled a chair out onto the little wooden porch and leaned back in the darkness to feel the south breeze that had cooled with the night and to listen to the lulling night sounds of the town. It was a quiet town, a low murmur of talk coming from one of the bars. From another came the plaintive picking of a Mexican guitar. Somewhere a baby cried, and a cow bawled for a calf.

At length Webb heard footsteps. He could recognize Sandy by his way of walking as the young man approached the front of the jail. Sandy didn't see Webb until the sheriff spoke.

"Hello, Sandy."

Sandy jerked in surprise and stopped to stare. "That you, Webb?"

"It's me. Got back this afternoon."

"Heard you did. Heard you got one of them." Webb felt a hint of resentment in his brother's voice.

"He was a kid, Sandy, no older than you are. Even a little younger, I'd say."

"I wanted to go. I tried to get you to take me." The resentment was bold and open now.

"I told you *no*. That's all there was to it. Just be glad you weren't there." A testiness crept into Webb's tone. Seemed almost any discussion he had with Sandy anymore worked into an argument.

Sandy demanded, "Why? Tell me why you won't let me go with you. Tell me why you won't deputize me when you've got somethin' like that."

Tiredly Webb said, "Sandy, I've told you before. You know, so why keep on askin'?"

He stared at his brother. He couldn't make him out in the night, but he could let his imagination fill in what he couldn't see. Sandy was almost as tall as Webb but lighter in weight. He had the quick, easy movement of the very young, an erect stance and walk that bespoke a fierce pride. He had a self-assurance that with a little coaxing could almost become arrogance. He was quick to laugh, quick to flare into anger. As a boy he had sometimes said things in the heat of argument that he later regretted. But rather than apologize or take them back, he would fight to uphold them. Even now, he probably had more fist fights than anybody in Dry Fork.

Up to now this quick temper had made it hard for him to hold a steady ranch job. Sooner or later he would swell up and come to blows with one of the other hands and either quit or be sent back to town. Most of the time he did "day work," temporary jobs at roundup time or on short cattle drives. A good hand with horses, he picked up some money breaking and training broncs.

Sandy stubbornly pressed the issue. "All right, Webb, tell me again how come you don't want me along as a deputy?"

Pushing back a grating impatience, Webb said, "In the first place, you're my own brother. I couldn't hire you steady because people would say I was usin' my office to put my family on the county payroll."

"All right, so you can't hire me steady. But you could occasionally swear me in when you need extra help, like the other day. I could at least be gettin' the experience."

"Experience for what? What could it lead to? I don't know a single job where posse experience would be worth two cents Mexican money to you."

"I want to be a lawman, Webb."

Webb let his leaned-back chair tip forward, the front legs thumping solidly on the porch. "Boy, we've been through that before. It's foolishness. A lawman's life is no damned good. I'd sooner see you out with a wagon, gatherin' up cow bones."

"*You* haven't done so bad at it. You haven't been killed yet."

Webb started to say *I'm still young*, but he didn't feel that it was exactly true. Young in years, perhaps, but not in experience. And tonight he felt old. He said, "It killed our father, Sandy. It's a dirty business sometimes, a dirty, bloody business. Like yesterday, us havin' to shoot that kid. I got enough on my conscience already. Do you think I want to see you have to go carryin' things like that around? Stick to your cowboying."

Sandy said, "I'm gettin' too old for you to keep on tellin' me what to do."

"You're not near as old as you think you are."

"I'm already older than you were when they first pinned a deputy badge on you."

Webb felt a compulsion to say, *Then for God's sake act like it!* But he held it down. "Sandy," he said evenly, "some people just take a lot longer to grow up than others do. You haven't got there yet."

Times he wondered if Sandy ever would.

Sandy argued, "I can take care of myself—always did. You just try me one time, that's all I ask. Just one time. I heard who-all was on that posse from the Box L. Men like Uncle Joe Vickers, so old and stiff he can't hardly get on a horse anymore. And Ollie Reed. If there's anyone who's got less business on a posse than Ollie Reed, I'd hate to see him. I sure couldn't be any worse than some of that bunch."

Impatience needling him, Webb responded, "They're all grown men, and they've got grown men's judgment. Their bodies may move slow, but their minds are quick enough. They won't pull some sudden fool stunt and get themselves or somebody else killed."

Sandy began to bristle. "And you think I would?"

"I think you might. The way you act around here, I'd be afraid to trust you."

Sandy's fists clenched. Webb knew that if it had been anyone besides himself, Sandy would have been ready to fight. They'd had plenty of arguments, but they had never fought each other.

Sandy said, "I'm no baby, and one of these days I'll prove it to you." He strode past Webb and went into the office. He lighted a lamp, the yellow glow spilling out the open door onto the porch. In a couple of minutes he was back with a roll of blankets under one arm, his war-bag of clothes and belongings in the other.

Webb demanded, "Where you goin'?"

Sandy glared at him. "I got a job breakin' some colts. I had figured on goin' out in the mornin'. Now I think I'll just ride on out tonight."

"Don't act like a six-year-old kid who's had his cookies taken away from him! There's no sense startin' out in the dark."

"Then maybe I'll sleep in Quince's wagonyard. I sure don't aim to stay here."

"Cool off, Sandy. Show some sense."

"*You* show some." Sandy stepped off the porch and stomped down the street, quickly passing beyond the weak glow of the lamp. Webb stood up and watched him go, wanting to call him back and try to reason with him. But what was the use? He couldn't reason with Sandy much anymore. The boy had a head as hard as that of a freighter's mule.

They had argued like this before, and other times Sandy had left in anger. He always came back.

But what if one day he left and didn't come back?

3

Sometime that night Ollie Reed got to drinking and unhinged his tongue. By morning the story about Clabe Donovan was all over town. A dozen people came into Webb's office while he was trying to finish some paperwork. For each of them he had to tell all over again what he knew, what he believed and didn't believe.

"I'm not satisfied yet that it is Clabe," he said. "Don't stand to reason that a man would come back after all these years when everybody thought he was dead. But then, Clabe never was a reasonable sort of a man."

The interruption Webb really hated to see coming was Judge Upshaw. The judge was a pompous, middle-aged man who in this hot weather was wearing a black vest with a golden watch chain hanging across his ample belly. He stopped in the door and looked down his nose at Webb.

"What's this foolishness going around town about Clabe Donovan?" he demanded.

Coolly Webb said, "I don't know what you've heard."

"You know. And I think you ought to arrest any man who gets drunk and goes around telling tales like that to scare people. There isn't a word of truth in it!" He paused, eyebrows lifting hopefully. "Is there?"

With forced patience Webb told him what he had told all the others.

"Preposterous!" the judge snorted. "Preposterous!" but doubt seemed to crowd into his eyes. "What if it *were* true, though? Think of all the people Clabe Donovan threatened. He even threatened *me!*"

Webb nodded. "That's right, judge. He sure did. You said some mighty hard things about him when you sentenced him to hang. And he said some hard things back at you."

The judge had only been in the county a couple of years when Clabe had been tried. At that time he and Webb still got along fairly well. But they had drawn apart since. Upshaw had tried to use his office to do some personal land grabbing. Webb had stopped him by throwing his hired toughs in jail or by escorting them to the county line. Webb had no use for the man now. But the judge had gotten himself re-elected. He still had that much political power, although he hadn't been able to beat Webb with one of his own hand-picked candidates for sheriff.

It was a stand-off, the way it looked now.

Upshaw said sharply, "Matlock, it's your job to find out if Clabe Donovan *is* alive. If he is, it's up to you to bring him in. And I hope you bring him dead!"

By the time Webb got started for the Rafter T ranch, much of the morning was gone. At the livery barn he slipped a rope halter on the bay horse the young outlaw had been riding. He headed south, leading the horse in a steady trot.

The summer sun bore down with uncompromising hostility. Not even a cotton-puff cloud was in sight to promise a moment's shade and relief. But Webb Matlock had been born to this kind of country, raised in it so that he hardly knew any other kind of country existed. He was aware of the heat, but he took it in stride and did not waste time or emotion cursing it. He soon started to sweat, and now and then a breeze came searching across the rolling prairie to make the wet shirt feel cool against his skin.

For such little favors he was grateful, but his mind was on things more important than the heat.

The rolling prairie broke off into rough, rocky hills, crisscrossed by draws and rough headers. Some of these draws were wide and covered by knee-high grass. The grass was brown now from summer heat, but it had made good growth earlier, and though brown it had considerable strength. Fall rains, if they came, would put green back into the grass in time to rebuild its value for winter grazing before frost came. This thick grass would lie there all winter, cured and strong, like hay on the ground.

Good country for a horse outfit. Or cattle. Webb had a few cattle of his own grazing on free range north of town. He wished he had some land like this, bought and paid for. This was Bronc Tomlin's country, paid in cash. Nobody ever knew where Tomlin got the money. When he had come here fifteen years ago he hadn't seemed the kind to have earned so much honestly. But he had it, and nobody thought it judicious to ask questions. His money spent as good as anyone else's, when he spent any. Most of the time Bronc Tomlin stayed home and minded his business.

Webb came upon a small band of mares with colts, and a stallion moved forward to look him over. Webb made a healthy circle, for sometimes these old studs could be mean. When the stallion came close, Webb took off his hat and waved it, hollering. The animal moved away, and Webb breathed easier. The stud and all the mares, he had noted, bore the Rafter T brand, same as this bay the young outlaw had ridden.

When he came in sight of the ranch headquarters, Webb stopped. He stepped to the ground and stretched a moment, for he had been in the saddle a long time. He reached into his saddlebags and brought out a couple of cans. One was a flat tin of sardines, the other a can of tomatoes. He opened them with a heavy blade of his pocketknife and squatted in the grass to eat. He would like to have had bread and coffee, but they weren't practical to carry on a ride like this. He could do without. A man could make out on sardines and tomatoes now and again. It was well past noon. Even if it hadn't been, Webb didn't want to ask or accept any favors from Bronc Tomlin.

Sitting there, he studied the ranch layout. There weren't any womenfolks on the Rafter T, at least not on a steady basis. Once in a while old Bronc found himself a saloon girl who thought she wanted some fresh air, and he would take her out there a little while.

Most of them didn't stay long. Tomlin's ranchhouse was built of rock, solid but not designed for looks. As far as Webb could remember, none of the windows had ever seen a curtain. He couldn't make it out from here, but Webb could remember the junk pile of rusted tin cans and whisky bottles just back of the house. Bronc Tomlin had strung wire around it to keep his horses from straying in and cutting their feet. That made it no less of an eyesore. Bronc had an eye for beauty in horses, but he wasn't particular about the place he lived in. Anything with a roof over it suited him. Like many another old open-range man who had spent years sleeping out under the stars, Bronc Tomlin was easily satisfied in that respect.

Riding in, Webb had to get down and open a wire gate leading into a small horse pasture where Tomlin could keep several horses within easy reach. Most of his horses ran on the unfenced range. The bay Webb was leading nickered at some young horses nearby, and the horses came up in friendly curiosity.

Webb could see activity in a circular corral, where dust stirred restlessly. He could see the outline of a man bobbing up and down, riding a pitching bronc. Webb could hear shouts of encouragement and knew other men were in the corral afoot. He started to ride that way, then reined around. He spotted Bronc Tomlin standing on the front porch of the rock house. Webb touched spurs to his own horse and rode over to Tomlin.

Tomlin leaned lazily against a porch post, rolling a cigarette. He nodded at Webb but devoted most of his attention to a horseman's appraisal of the sheriff's mount. Then his gaze drifted back to the bay Webb was leading.

"By George," he exclaimed, "that there's one of my horses."

Dryly Webb said, "It sure is."

The rancher pushed himself away from the post and stepped down to look the horse over. Tomlin was well into his fifties, a freckle-faced, heavy-moving man with a soft belly sagging over his belt. His clothes were dirty. His graying hair bushed out from beneath a greasy old hat. He hadn't had a haircut in months, nor had he shaved lately. No woman out here right now, Webb would bet.

Tomlin walked around the bay, patting the animal, lifting up one forefoot and looking at it. "Has a tendency to lame easy, this one does. Been limpin' any?"

"Not that I could see," Webb replied, waiting to hear what kind of explanation Tomlin would have. He figured the man was stalling for time, thinking up a good story.

"Been missin' this horse for three or four weeks now. Him and six others, they just disappeared. I ran onto a cowboy who'd seen them—said he'd accidently ridden onto some tough-lookin' hombres camped down on the river with my horses. I decided I didn't really need them very much. Man can't figure on keepin' them all."

Webb studied the man's face. "They stole those horses, did they?"

"I sure didn't give 'em away!"

"How come you didn't report it to me?"

Tomlin shrugged. "Look, sheriff, I'm off down here

toward the river, a long ways from town. Any of them border outlaws really wanted to, they could wipe me off the map in one good sweep. I ain't a-lookin' for no trouble with them. If the worst they do is pick up a horse now and again, I don't figure I'm bad off. I'll just look on that kind of like a tax and leave things be."

Webb eyed him narrowly. "You don't appear to me to be afraid of an occasional outlaw, Bronc."

"I ain't afraid, exactly. But what's the sense in a man goin' out in the dark with his lamp lit, huntin' trouble? I go my own way, mind my own business and don't cause nobody any worry."

Webb said dryly, "You cause some worry, all right." He didn't believe Bronc, but what could he prove? "Sometimes a man who stands by and does nothing can be as much help to an outlaw like Clabe Donovan as somebody who really pitches in with him."

Tomlin looked up sharply. "What do you mean, Clabe Donovan? He's been dead a long time."

Webb watched the man closely for any betrayal, any loss of composure. "Has he, Bronc?"

Suddenly ill at ease, Tomlin said, "Sheriff, I got no idea what you're hintin' at."

"I think you do, Bronc."

Tomlin said, "I ain't done nothin' illegal, sheriff. And if I had, you couldn't prove it on me."

"I'm not accusin' you of anything, Bronc. I just came to bring you your horse." *And*, he thought, *to look around a little*.

Bronc Tomlin usually kept from six to ten hands around. Webb could see sign of only three right now, the three in the corral where the broncs were being worked.

He stepped down from the saddle and handed the halter rein to Tomlin. "Halter belongs to Quince. I better take it back."

Tomlin nodded, pushing aside any resentment he might have felt. "We'll go turn him into a corral." They walked side by side. Tomlin said, "Sure do thank you, sheriff, for bringin' me my horse. Maybe some of the others will turn up eventually."

Webb didn't pay much attention because he was sure Tomlin was lying anyway. He listened to a murmur of talk out in the circular corral and a pounding of hoofs as a bronc broke into pitching. Webb decided to see what Tomlin's helpers looked like. He thought he could still recognize a couple or three of the old Donovan bunch on sight.

A man never knew until he tried.

Several young broncs were haltered and tied along the fence outside the circular corral. Inside, a brown horse pitched with a saddle. The men were letting him work himself down before they mounted him. Webb could make out two men in the center of the pen, their backs to him. A third leaned against a fence so that Webb could see nothing of him but the color of his clothes between the planks.

One of the cowboys half turned and said over his shoulder, "All right, Sandy, let's see you top him."

Webb stopped in midstride. Sandy?

He climbed up on the fence for a look. He saw Sandy's friend, young Augie Brock, working up the taut rope and grabbing the bronc by the ears. In panic the bronc tried to paw him, but Augie held himself close to the horse's body and swung with agility. "Come on, Sandy," he said, "hurry it up."

Sandy Matlock strode confidently out into the stirring dust. The bronc tried to kick him, but Sandy stepped quickly aside. He stuck his left foot into the stirrup, gripped the reins up short and swung aboard. "Let 'er rip!"

Augie Brock turned loose and jumped back out of the way. The bronc humped its back and lunged forward. Leather popped as the brown jumped and twisted. The hoofs raised clouds of dust. Sandy Matlock sat in full control, swaying with the violent motion, keeping the hackamore rein loose, and giving the bronc all the freedom it wanted. He wasn't spurring, for it would only make the horse pitch harder. That might have been good for a show, but it wasn't worth much in training a horse for useful purpose.

Webb watched with pride, for he knew Sandy was one of the best bronc riders in this part of the country, a better one than Webb had ever been. Each man to his own talents.

Sandy let the bronc pitch until it began to tire. Then he started drawing up the hackamore rein, firmly pulling the pony's head higher. With its head up, a horse cannot do a good job of pitching. Once the brown had gotten its fill and found the rider unshaken, it began to run aimlessly around and around the corral. Sandy let it run awhile, then began pulling the rein first one way, then the other. The horse did not respond well to the rein, but that would come. It was part of the training.

Finally Sandy stepped down and walked away laughing, his legs wobbly from fatigue. It was hard work handling one of these broncs.

"I'm goin' to need me some coffee before I climb on the next one," he said to Augie Brock.

Webb and Tomlin had watched without saying anything to one another. Sandy had had his hands too full to notice Webb. Now, walking toward the gate, he saw him. He stopped, his grin turning quickly into a frown.

"What're you doin' here, Webb?"

Webb said, "I was fixin' to ask you the same thing."

"I told you I had me a job breakin' some broncs."

"You didn't tell me it was here."

"No reason I ought to've."

Bronc Tomlin said, "This boy in some kind of trouble, sheriff? I sure don't want no trouble out here."

Webb shook his head. "He's not in trouble. And he's not goin' to stay here and get in any."

Belligerently Sandy said to Webb, "I don't know as you've got any say about it."

Tomlin squinted at Sandy Matlock, "You know, boy, I don't believe Augie ever told me your name. Who are you?"

Webb answered the question. "His name is Sandy Matlock. He's my brother."

Tomlin's eyes widened for a second. "Your brother?" He peered intently at Sandy. "I ought to've known it, but its been so long since I saw the button, and he's growed a right smart." Tomlin glanced at Augie Brock. "Why didn't you tell me this here boy was the sheriff's brother?"

Augie shrugged. He was a tall kid with a crooked-toothed grin and a heavy shock of reddish hair pushing out from under his hat. "Never thought about it. Didn't know it would make any difference."

Tomlin said, "It don't, to me. But seems like it does to the sheriff."

Webb nodded at Sandy. "Get your stuff together. You're goin' back with me."

Sandy flushed. "Not this time."

Webb stiffened. "Sandy . . ." The one word was enough, the firm way he said it.

Bronc Tomlin watched, a flicker of malice in his eyes. He asked Sandy, "How old are you, boy?"

Sandy replied, "Old enough!"

"Then stay if you want to. This ain't no sheriff matter, and Webb's got no more rights over you as a brother."

This, then, was a challenge from Tomlin, a challenge to be met only through Sandy. Webb knew he could not hesitate. He took Sandy's arm and pulled his brother forward. "Come on!"

Sandy hauled back. For a moment he glared at Webb, then Webb saw the intention flare in the young man's eyes. Sandy crouched, his fist suddenly coming up. Webb swung aside, taking the blow on his shoulder. Sandy was strong. Webb staggered back, thrown off balance.

Well, he thought, *it's been a long time working up to this. Now we'll get it over and done with.*

He didn't want to fight Sandy, but he knew he had to, now. He just wanted to get it finished the quickest way he could. He stepped in close and swung hard. His fist struck Sandy a glancing blow across the ribs, for Sandy had twisted away. Grunting, Sandy drove a hard right into Webb's chin. Pain hammered through Webb's brain. He staggered again.

Sandy was stouter than he had thought.

Sandy followed up with a vengeance, trying again to connect with Webb's chin. Webb warded off the blow with his left arm and put his whole weight into a hard right to Sandy's stomach. Sandy grunted as the breath went out of him. Webb struck him again, this time with the left.

They stood toe to toe and swapped blows, each man putting all he had in it. It was a cruel beating for both of them. They wore themselves down in a stubborn stand. Neither tried very hard to duck what the other had to give him. Each attempted only to hit harder than the other.

Sandy's youth had given him endurance, but Webb's weight gave the sheriff power. Even as he himself tired, Webb sensed that Sandy was wearing faster.

Webb tried to keep from hitting the kid in the face. He drove his fists into Sandy's body, swinging, punching, pushing, and punching again. Sandy was gasping, the breath almost gone from him. He swayed, he staggered, and at last he sank to his knees. He knelt there with his head down, struggling hard for breath.

Breathing hard, swaying too, Webb reached down for his brother's arm. "Come on, Sandy."

In a last rush of anger, Sandy pushed up off his knees

and swung again at Webb. Webb stepped back. The blow missed him, and Sandy flopped belly down on the ground.

Webb knew it was over.

He stood a while, fighting to get his breath back. His shirt was torn half off, the sleeve hanging down from the elbow. He was soaked in sweat, and dust clung to him. The salty taste of dust and sweat and blood was on his lips.

When he was able, Webb stepped behind his brother and helped him to his feet. "We're goin', button. Make up your mind to that."

Tomlin watched, frowning but keeping hands off. "That boy come within an inch of whippin' you, Webb. He's grown but you won't admit it."

Webb wanted to tell him to mind his own business, but he had no breath yet to waste in talking.

Tomlin said, "Some day, Webb, you got to cut the cord."

Webb found Sandy's horse and saddled him. Silently Augie Brock brought out Sandy's blankets, still rolled up the way Sandy had carried them here. Webb tied them behind Sandy's saddle. He glanced at Augie. "How about you? You goin' in with us?"

Augie gave him a hard, challenging grin. "You're *his* brother, not mine."

Webb shrugged, seeing no point in arguing with him. He turned to Sandy. "Can you get up by yourself, or do you need help?"

Sandy glared, one eye beginning to darken. He put his foot in the stirrup and painfully pulled himself up without accepting assistance.

Tomlin stood with hands shoved deep into his pockets, his eyes unfriendly. "What's the matter with us out here, sheriff? We got smallpox or somethin'?"

Firmly Webb said, "You know what the matter is. I don't have to spell it out for you."

The dirty, bewhiskered old horseman stood and stared Webb in the eye. Finally he turned aside and spat a stream of tobacco juice. To Sandy he said, "Boy, any time you want to come back out here and work, you just do it."

Webb pulled away. Sandy followed along behind him.

For a long time they rode like that, Sandy trailing in a surly mood. Finally Webb turned in the saddle and looked back at him. "What are you, an Indian, that you've got to ride single file?"

Sandy touched a spur to his horse and pulled up even with his brother. His jaw was swelling a little. It jutted in a smouldering anger. At length he demanded, "When you finally goin' to leave me alone? I was goin' to get good pay for ridin' them broncs."

"That's an outlaw bunch yonder, Sandy. You don't want to have nothin' to do with an outfit like that."

"I didn't see nothin' that looked shady to me."

"You would have if you'd stayed long enough, I expect. And you might've got yourself mixed up in it so you couldn't get out."

"I got two eyes of my own, and I got a brain, too. I can figure out what's best for me. I don't need your help."

"I wish I could believe that was so."

They rode in silence again, Sandy plainly doing

some deep thinking. Finally he said, "I think you're all wet about that place. But if it *was* the truth, what did you leave Augie Brock out there for?"

Webb said grimly, "Augie's in just the kind of place where he belongs. If you haven't seen through him yet, I guess you never will."

4

Ellie Donovan daubed at the reddening abrasions on Webb's face, with a clean cloth wet with antiseptic. Webb flinched, breathing in a hissing sound between his teeth.

"At least you had the wounds cleaned," she said.

"We stopped at the creek and washed the dirt off."

"The creek?" Her voice was incredulous. "Probably let your horses drink out of it first, too. It'll be a wonder if you don't both get these place infected and die from it."

"We'll be all right."

Her scolding tone disappeared. Her voice became sympathetic. "It's a terrible thing, having to fight your own brother that way."

"I didn't want to, but I guess it's been a long time comin'. Now at least we got it over with."

She looked critically at a cut place. "Well, I hope he doesn't look any worse than you do. Where is Sandy, anyhow?"

"I don't rightly know. He cut away from me quick's we hit town."

"Why don't you hunt him and send him over here? I'll fix his face, too."

"He'll probably go to Birdie Hanks. She'll take care of him. Anyway, he's not in bad shape. I avoided his face as much as I could."

Ellie went on quietly with the work, flinching each time Webb flinched, biting her lip when she caused him pain. Finally done, she leaned back and said, "I guess that will hold you. It's not the worst fight you were ever in, I suppose."

He said evenly, "It's the one I least wanted. But I couldn't let him stay out there, not in that outlaw bunch."

Ellie looked nervously at her hands, wanting to ask him a question but plainly dreading the answer he might give her. "Webb, did you . . . did you find out anything?"

He shook his head. "Not for sure. I fished for information, mentioned Clabe Donovan without any warning just to see if anything showed up in Bronc Tomlin's face. It surprised him, all right. But I couldn't tell if it was just that he hadn't thought about Clabe in a long time, or if he was surprised that I knew about Clabe bein' alive."

"Webb, are you sure he *is* alive? Are you sure we haven't all been jumping to some wrong conclusions?"

"I'm not sure of anything, Ellie. Nothin' at all." He took Ellie's hand. "Even if he *is* alive, you don't love him anymore. You couldn't."

Miserably Ellie said, "How can I answer you, Webb? I only know that when I left him I was still in love with him. I knew in my mind that I should hate him, but I couldn't. I left him because I couldn't stand the kind of life we were living, not because I didn't love him. Once I was away from him, I could tell that I was beginning to change. And after he was killed—or we *thought* he was killed—I finally had to close my mind to him, had to let him go. Now things are different again. Maybe I wouldn't love him anymore—probably wouldn't. But how can I know? Unless I really see him again, how can I ever know?"

Webb turned away, avoiding her eyes. Silent a while, he finally said, "I oughtn't to come here at all, Ellie. It'd be better for both of us if I didn't even see you till this thing was settled for once and for all. But I don't think I could get up the will power to stay away. I still want you as much as I ever did. Whatever happens won't change that."

He walked down to the doctor's house and knocked. Uncle Joe Vickers opened the door.

"Howdy, Uncle Joe. Came to see how Jess Leggett is gettin' along."

Joe Vickers answered loudly enough so he was sure the wounded rancher in the back room could hear. "The old reprobate's in better shape than he's got any right to be. The weller he gets, the meaner he is. If he was much meaner, he'd just bite himself and die. Come on in. Doctor's off on a call. Mexican woman sick the other side of town."

From the back room Webb could hear Jess Leggett call: "That you, Webb Matlock? You git yourself in here!"

Sitting up in his bed, the crusty old rancher scowled, "Where the hell you been?"

There hadn't been much today to smile about, but now Webb Matlock began to let himself go. "Your temperature must be all right, because your temper's back to normal. The better you feel, the harder you are for a man to get along with."

Jess Leggett said crisply, "I didn't ask you in here to insult me. I got men here who can do that better than you, and I'm payin' them." He nodded his chin toward Joe Vickers and the pleasant-faced young cowboy, Johnny Willet. "What happened to your face, Webb? You look like you came out second in a two-dog fight."

Webb shrugged it off. "I guess I did." He didn't tell Jess any more, and the old man seemed to sense that he wouldn't. The rancher asked, "What've you found out about them cow thieves?"

Webb told about his visit to the Bronc Tomlin place, but he left out his fight with Sandy.

Leggett demanded, "What about this foolishness bein' spread around town that Donovan's back in circulation? It's a lie, ain't it?"

Soberly Webb said, "I wish I could say for sure that it was. I'm not convinced yet that it's true. But it could be."

"Hogwash! I was there when they nailed the coffin shut."

"Could you see Clabe Donovan's face?"

Leggett frowned. "No, old Joe yonder did too good a job with his shotgun for that. But hell, everybody knew it was Clabe. There wasn't anybody had any doubt."

"Could be we were all wrong, Jess."

Gray-haired Joe Vickers straightened his bent shoulders. "I wasn't wrong, Webb. I swore it then and I'll swear it now: I shot Clabe Donovan!"

Webb shrugged. No use in a man arguing with somebody who was that sure about something, especially when Webb didn't want to believe it anyway. He changed the subject.

"That shoulder hurtin' you much, Jess?"

"A slug in the shoulder won't kill me. I fought in the Mexican War, and I've lived on the border the biggest part of my life. Takes more than a little skirmish with a few mangy cow thieves to knock me out of the saddle. Now I want you to take me home."

"Jess, I can't take you home till the doctor says so. And then you've got Joe and Johnny here to do that for you."

"No I don't. I fired them two."

"You told me while ago that you were payin' them."

"Well, I've fired them now. They won't take me home."

Webb smiled again. "I'm afraid you can't fire me, Jess. And I can't take you home."

Jess roared, "Dammit, if you're not goin' to help a man, git out of here!" Still smiling, Webb turned to go. He got as far as the next room when the cranky old rancher called to him, "Where do you think you're goin'? Come back here!"

"Got work to do, Jess."

"You sure do. You go catch them cow thieves before they git into my cattle again. If *I* catch them, I'll hang them."

"Better let *me* catch them, Jess."

"Then you get busy. I'll be back on my horse in a day or two, and I'll sure be a-lookin'."

Joe Vickers followed Webb to the door. They stood together in the darkness on the front porch. Webb asked, "He really gettin' along all right?"

"He's an old man, and an old man heals slow. He'll make it all right, though, if we can keep him down long enough. Us old brushpoppers are hard to kill."

Webb turned to leave. Vickers said, "Webb . . ." The sheriff paused. "Webb, I still think it was Clabe Donovan I shot. Sure, I know what's happened, but I can still remember how things was. I don't nowise see how I could have made a mistake."

Webb made no reply.

"It ain't that I take any pride in killin' him, Webb; I don't. But I hate to see people gettin' themselves all nervous thinkin' he's back amongst them like a wolf in a flock of sheep. He's dead and gone; I'd stake my life on that."

"I never said different, Uncle Joe."

Walking back into his office, Webb lighted the lamp. The lamp chimney was still warm. He knew of no one else who would have had business here, so he figured it probably had been Sandy.

He glanced at Sandy's cot, expecting to see his brother's blanket roll and his warbag there where Sandy would have pitched them when he came in. They weren't. Some clothes that had been hanging on a nail weren't in sight either. Webb strode across and pulled out the top drawer of an old bureau they had used together. The drawer was empty. Sandy had taken everything he owned and had left.

"Hard-headed kid!" Webb breathed impatiently. "Won't listen and won't learn."

Webb leaned his shoulder against the steel bars of a cell and pondered what to do. He'd had his fight with Sandy, the only one he ever intended to have. He had said his piece and brought the boy in. He might go hunt him down again now and try to reason with him, but, if it came to the point of another fight, Webb wouldn't do it. A man could go only so far. Beyond that, it would be up to Sandy.

Quick footsteps pounded on the porch. Webb turned and saw Judge Upshaw stopping to lean heavily against the desk, shoulders a-heave with his hard breathing. The judge's face was flushed with excitement. He turned to look at Webb, and Webb could see the grip of fear in the man's eyes. Wordlessly the judge held up a piece of rope for Webb to see. He dropped into Webb's chair, his hands trembling.

Webb picked up the rope and felt a shock. It had been formed into a noose, with a hangman's knot.

"Where did you get it, judge?"

The judge was shaking so he could hardly answer. "Found it hanging on my door. I went down to the . . . went out on a legal matter. When I got back to the house I found this."

Webb fingered the knot thoughtfully. "Could be some kind of a joke."

"It doesn't look at all funny to me, sheriff. I want you to do something about it."

"First I'd have to have some idea who put it there."

The judge swallowed. "It was Clabe Donovan! It had to be him!"

"Judge, there's no use gettin' panicky. Frankly you've done some things here that have made some strong enemies for you. Could be one of them is usin' this Donovan talk to throw a scare into you."

"It's Donovan. I know it is. And he's going to kill me!"

Webb frowned and stared out the open door into the darkness. It made sense if Donovan *was* alive. The things the judge had said in the courtroom would have been enough to make Donovan hate him this much. It would have been like Clabe to want to make the judge eat his own words. Donovan was a man who could hate hard.

The judge said, "Webb, you've got to give me protection."

"How, judge? The county budget only allows me one deputy, and he's placed way off in the upper end of the county."

"Send for him."

"Donovan swore to get revenge on lots of other people, too. I can't guard them all."

"I'm the county judge. You can certainly protect *me*."

"Bein' judge don't make your life worth more than anybody else's. If I had to tie myself to your apron-strings, I couldn't get out and hunt for Donovan."

"Webb, you've *got* to . . ."

It was then that Webb heard the shot. The blast

echoed through town and stirred a dozen dogs into a frenzy of barking.

Judge Upshaw nearly fell out of his chair. For a second Webb thought the man was shot. Then he saw that the judge was gripped by panic.

Even before he heard a man begin calling for help, Webb sensed that the shot meant trouble. He was off the porch in two long strides and went running up the street. He saw people looking out of their doors. A few men began shouting. The shout was taken up quickly by others, both up and down the street.

"Where's the sheriff?" someone yelled. "Get Webb Matlock!"

Webb shouted, "Here I am. Where's the shootin' at?"

A cowboy appeared from between two buildings, pointing behind him. "Thisaway, Webb. Hurry." As Webb reached him, the cowboy turned and ran beside the sheriff, pointing the direction. "Over by Quince's corral. It's an awful thing, Webb, an awful thing."

Ahead of him, by the fence behind the livery barn, Webb could see men gathered, some of them gesturing excitedly, some standing in shocked silence. Webb pushed his way through. "Let me in there, boys."

Someone held a lantern. On the ground lay a man. As the lantern holder extended his arm, bringing the light over the body, Webb felt a chill run through him. Involuntarily he turned away.

"Uncle Joe Vickers, isn't it?" he asked tightly.

Quince Pyburn stood with his shoulders slumped. "Not much left to go by, but it's him, Webb. Caught a shotgun blast full in the face."

Webb made himself look again. A sickness welled up inside him. Over by the corral he could hear a man retching. In the pale glow of the lantern he recognized Johnny Willet. "What happened?" Webb asked Quince.

The liveryman shook his head. "Can't rightly say. Johnny was there. He saw it, but he's been shook too bad to talk."

The men stepped aside so Webb could walk over to Johnny and put his hand on the cowboy's shoulder. "How about it, Johnny? What can you tell us?"

Johnny turned, his body trembling a little, his face paled from shock. "Webb, it was . . ." His voice broke. He looked down a moment, clenching his fists in an effort to regain strength. "We was on our way to sleep in Quince's wagon-yard. We got right here when a man suddenly rose up over yonder." Johnny pointed off into the darkness. "He wasn't more than twelve, fifteen feet away. He says to Joe, he says, 'Is that Joe Vickers?' Joe stops and says, 'Yeah, I'm him. Who are you?' Without a word, this feller raises up a shotgun and lets Joe have a full blast. Joe never knew what hit him. Me, I was petrified. I just stood there waitin' for him to kill me too. Then this feller says to me, he says, 'Tell the rest of them around here that Clabe Donovan owes a lot of debts, and they're all goin' to be paid.' "

Johnny shuddered and looked down at the old ranch foreman who had so long been his friend.

Webb could feel cold sweat. It had to be true, then. To question the fact any longer was idle. Clabe Donovan was alive and seeking vengeance!

Joe Vickers had said he would stake his life on the

fact that he had killed Clabe Donovan. And Joe Vickers was dead.

Webb said, "Johnny, which way did Clabe go after the shootin'?"

Johnny frowned, trying to remember. He rubbed his hand against his cheek. "I think he had a horse tied back around at that corral. I remember hearin' some horses go off in a lope."

Quince Pyburn said, "I expect he's right, Webb. I was the first one here. I heard the shot and came runnin'. I heard horses headin' east."

Someone shouted, "Let's go get him!" Some of the crowd surged away.

Webb yelled, "Hold on, boys. No use goin' off out there now."

Men protested. Webb held up his hand for silence. "Boys, you couldn't find him in that dark. Go ridin' off now and all you'll do is mess up his tracks so nobody can trail him."

Johnny Willet was getting his composure back. "What're you goin' to do, just let him get flat away?"

Soberly Webb said, "It may be the hardest job we ever did, but we've got to make ourselves wait till daylight. Then we'll track him. He'll have a long start, but he's got to stop someplace and rest. Once we start, we don't stop. We'll stay on his trail till we've got him run back to his hole. We'll get him."

The men talked it over among themselves and grudgingly admitted that this was the only course which really made sense. Johnny Willet said grimly, "Just tell us what time to meet you, Webb. You'll have a-plenty of help."

Webb nodded, satisfied. "Right here at Quince's barn. We'll ride at the first light. Everybody bring along enough food to last him a couple or three days. Now go get yourselves a good night's sleep, because you may not get much more rest for a while."

The men scattered into the night, talking quietly among themselves. In the cold gray of dawn some of them would change their minds about going. But Webb knew he would have enough men for the job.

Quince Pyburn said, "No use goin' after the doctor for Uncle Joe. Guess he needs the undertaker instead."

Webb nodded. "Go get him, will you, Quince?" Then to Johnny Willet he said, "We better go break this to Jess Leggett."

Old Jess sat in grieving silence. Johnny Willet stood looking out into the darkness while Webb told about it. "Clabe must have found out that Uncle Joe had been sleepin' in the wagonyard the last couple or three nights, and he knew to wait for him there."

Eyes glazing, Jess blew his nose. "Why Joe? Why not me or any one of a dozen others? The time we tried and convicted Clabe, he swore he'd get loose and pay off a lot of us—you because you was the sheriff; Florentino Rodriguez because he tracked Clabe down; me because it was mostly me and my men who hounded Clabe to the end; the judge and the jury because they condemned him to hang. How come he picked Joe to start on?"

Webb sat with his hands clasped tightly together, his grief a dull ache because he had regarded Uncle Joe Vickers almost as blood kin. "Man on the dodge can't always be figured out, Jess. He does crazy things sometimes. For years now, everybody has thought Clabe Donovan was dead. Joe Vickers got the credit for killin' him, blastin' him off his horse with both barrels of a shotgun. When Clabe decided to show he was still alive, maybe he thought it would be appropriate to kill the man who was supposed to have killed *him*, and do it the same way Uncle Joe was supposed to have done."

"Sounds crazy to me."

"Maybe Clabe *is* crazy now, Jess. That makes him all the more dangerous. It's all the more reason we got to get him!"

Webb knocked on the door of the little frame house where Ellie Donovan lived. He could see a lamp burning inside. He saw her shadow fall across the curtain that covered the oval glass in the door. Then she stood framed against the lamplight.

Webb said apologetically, "Ellie, I know I told you I wouldn't come to your house anymore, but this time I had to. I . . ." He broke off to stare at her. "You look like you'd seen a ghost. What's the matter, Ellie?"

She stepped back into the room, and he followed her. She said in a trembling voice, "That shot . . . it had something to do with Clabe, didn't it?"

He nodded. "Yes, Ellie, it did. How did you know?"

"He was here."

"You saw him? You talked to him?"

She shook her head. "I was sitting here sewing a dress. All of a sudden I got the feeling someone was watching me. I went to the window and looked out.

That's when I saw him, standing in the shadows. I ran to the front door and called to him, but he was gone."

"You're sure it was Clabe?"

"I didn't see him close, but I could make out the Mexican hat, and I could recognize the way Clabe had of standing. I could feel his presence, Webb. Somehow, even before I saw him, I sensed that it was Clabe, and he was watching me."

Webb stood with his hands shoved deep into his pockets. "That was before you heard the shot?"

"A little while."

Webb bit his lip. It all added up. He told Ellie about Joe Vickers. She listened incredulously. "He was bad in lots of ways, Webb, but it wasn't like him to stand there and kill a man that way."

"He did though, Ellie. He's changed." He stared at her in a swelling of sympathy, wanting to take her in his arms but knowing now that he couldn't. He could never do it again so long as Clabe Donovan lived. "Ellie, we're goin' after him in the mornin'. One way or another, we've got to stop him. If it comes to that, we might even have to . . ." He frowned. "It may be me who has to fire the shot."

She buried her face in her hands.

Webb said, "I hope you won't hate me, Ellie."

She didn't reply. He waited a moment, hoping she might. Then knowing she wouldn't, he turned and left the house.

He crossed into the Mexican settlement afoot and moved down a dark, dusty street. Lanterns glowed in front of cantinas, and lamplight shone from the sometimes-glassless windows of adobe houses. Not recognizing him as the sheriff, a woman in a shadowy doorway spoke softly to him in Spanish, and he ignored her. A happy Mexican song drifted to him on the cool night breeze, its verses lusty and ribald.

Webb walked around a small adobe general store to the living quarters in the rear. The door was wide open, and Webb could see most of the inside. But it would be impolite to enter or even to look in without first announcing himself. He called, "Florentino!"

A man got up from a rawhide chair and limped to the door. "*Si?*" Squinting into the darkness, he smiled as recognition came. "Mister Webb." He motioned with his hand. "*Pase, pase.*" Florentino was still a young man, not past thirty.

Webb took off his hat and bent a little to enter the low door. A Mexican woman sat in an oversized old rocking chair. She arose, and Webb saw that she was heavy with child. "*Señor* sheriff, please to sit down."

A young man stood up from a bench in the corner. This was Aparicio Rodriguez, Florentino's cousin.

Florentino and Aparicio had worked on the ranches. They could speak and understand English well enough, but Florentino's wife had only meager knowledge of the language. Webb shifted to Spanish, which he could handle with fair ease if not with accuracy. "Please, Consuela, keep your chair. I'll sit on this bench." A little girl, a yearling-past, sat on the bare dirt floor, looking up suspiciously at Webb. He knelt and stuck out his hand as if to pinch the girl's chin. The baby backed away from him. But she didn't back far. It wouldn't take her long to warm up, Webb thought. If he had a lump or two of that brown *piloncillo* sugar from Mexico . . .

By the look of Consuela Rodriguez, Webb knew it wouldn't be many days before the little *muchacha* had a new brother or sister to share the adobe house with. She was a handsome woman, this Consuela, but like most of her people in that time, she faced a life of hard work and privation. Already it had begun to show on her. By the time she was thirty she would look forty. When she was forty, she would look old.

Webb said, "I came to ask a favor of you, Florentino. Whether you choose to do it or not is up to you, and you alone. Because of your family . . ." he glanced at the woman and the child ". . . you may want to think about it a little."

He told what had happened tonight, and about his plan to take out a posse in the morning. "Florentino, you're the best tracker in the county. There's not a *gringo* can touch you. Without you, we might find Donovan and we might not. With you, I think we could track him clear to Mexico City. But there's a hazard: the tracker is always the one out front, the one easiest to kill. That's why you'll have to make up your own mind. I won't try to pressure you."

Florentino frowned darkly, studying his little family a long time. "I have heard the talk about Clabe Donovan, but I thought it was only talk." Mouth tightening, he said, "He spoke of old debts, did he?"

Webb repeated what Johnny Willet had said.

Rodriguez recalled, "Never will I forget what he promised when I tracked him and led you to where he was hiding. He shot me in the leg, remember? After he was caught, he called me a greaser, this Clabe Donovan. He looked at me as if he could kill me with his eyes. He said, 'You dirty Mex, someday I'll get you. Next time I'll kill you so dead that even the buzzards will leave you alone!'"

Webb nodded. "I remember. He threatened a lot of people. But he's gone all these years without carrying out any of the threats."

Florentino said pointedly, "He has begun now."

The Mexican slowly walked back and forth across the small, lime-plastered room, thinking. One leg was board-stiff because of Donovan's bullet. Walking was not easy for him. He stopped and looked again at his family. "Mister Joe was a good friend of mine. I worked a long time for him and Mister Jess. When my leg was ruined, they helped me buy the store so I would have a way to live. They came when Consuela and I were married. My boy's name is going to be José, for Mister Joe." Florentino turned, saddened. "Another time, I would gladly help you find the man who killed him. But any day now, Consuela's time will come. I cannot be away when my first son is born."

Webb was disappointed, but he felt no blame for Florentino. "I know how it is. Thanks, anyway." He turned toward the door.

Young Aparicio spoke quickly, "Wait, Master Webb. I have no baby coming. I can go."

Webb said, "You are not Florentino."

"I am his cousin, and Florentino has taught me how to track. No man can do it better, except Florentino."

Webb saw concern in Florentino's eyes, worry for

Aparicio. Family ties were strong among Mexican people. Florentino said, "He is good, Mister Webb. But he is also young and a little headstrong."

Webb could see Aparicio's eagerness. "You'd have to take orders, Aparicio. You'd have to do whatever I say, or I'd send you home."

The young man said quickly, "Anything you say, I will do. Mister Joe was good to me. I want to help find the man who killed him."

Not sure, Webb hesitated. But he knew he needed the youth. Webb was no tracker for a job like this. He didn't know a *gringo* in Dry Fork who was.

Finally he nodded. "All right. Daylight, then. I'll send a man with a horse."

The lamp was burning in Webb's office when he returned. He walked in with a sense of relief, expecting to find Sandy. Instead he saw Birdie Hanks, sitting in the chair by the roll-top desk. She arose.

"Birdie," he said, surprised. "I sure didn't expect to find you here."

"Sandy's gone," she blurted. Looking closer, Webb could tell she had been crying.

"Gone where?"

She shook her head. "I don't know. Did he leave any word here for you?"

"No, all he did was gather his gear and ride off while I was out of the office. Took everything he owned."

Near crying again, the girl said, "It was the fight that capped it, I suppose. He said he had argued with you lots of times, but you'd never actually fought before."

Soberly Webb said, "It wasn't my choice. I didn't want to."

"Sandy told me he was on his way out. Told me he was going to live his own life and let you be shed of him. Said he'd be back to see me someday. Then he kissed me goodbye and rode off."

"Didn't even tell you whichaway he was headed?"

"Not a word."

Back out to Bronc Tomlin's I'll bet, Webb thought angrily.

He took a handkerchief and touched it to a tear rolling down Birdie's cheek. "Don't you go cryin' over him. He's young and so are you. He'll get to thinkin' about you, and he won't be able to stay away. You watch, he'll be back."

"You really think so?"

"Bet you anything."

She tried to force a smile. "He's a hard man to put up with sometimes. But I guess I couldn't forget him if I tried."

"Have patience, Birdie. He'll come back."

The girl left. Webb's smile left with her. Soberly he blew out the lamp, undressed, and flopped down on his cot. He lay there a long time, unable to sleep. In his mind he kept seeing Ellie Donovan and Clabe Donovan and Uncle Joe Vickers. Most of all, he kept seeing Sandy Matlock.

He knew he didn't really believe what he had told Birdie.

Maybe this time Sandy wouldn't come back.

5

⁓

Arriving at the livery barn well before daylight, Webb found Quince Pyburn feeding the horses. Quince already had one saddled for himself. The livery-man said, "I got Juan Obregon comin' over directly to take care of the place for me. I'm goin' with you."

"You don't have to, Quince."

"I knew Joe Vickers a long time. Wasn't no squarer man ever walked the streets of this town. Thinkin' of myself, too. I was foreman of the jury that convicted Clabe Donovan. I'd rather be lookin' for him than have him lookin' for me."

Webb nodded approval. "I don't know anybody I'd rather have ride with me, Quince. Come along, and welcome."

One by one the other men began gathering. Webb picked a horse for Aparicio Rodriguez and had a rider lead the animal across the town, bareback. Aparicio would have his own saddle. Before long the puncher returned, the young tracker beside him. Rodriguez rode a big-horned Mexico saddle but wore a plain

Texas-style cowboy hat instead of a wide-brimmed Mexican sombrero. Good judgment, Webb reflected. With Donovan wearing a sombrero, and with men being excitable the way they were in the confusion of a gunfight, somebody might make a mistake.

"How is Florentino's wife this mornin'?" Webb asked.

"Consuela, she is having the pains. Pretty soon now is time, she say. But for that, I think Florentino make me stay home and he go instead."

Webb nodded. He had rather have had it that way. Aparicio was still an unknown quantity. Likely the boy would prove to be as good as Florentino had said. But Webb liked to play the safe game when he could.

Johnny Willet showed up, dark-eyed and grim. It was evident he hadn't slept. Webb said, "Don't you want to stay for the funeral, Johnny? They'll be buryin' Uncle Joe today."

Johnny shook his head. "I'd rather bury the man who killed him."

The eastern sky began to glow pink. First daylight crept across the prairie. Webb glanced at Aparicio. "Reckon it's light enough to commence followin' tracks?"

Rodriguez nodded with the confidence of youth. "You bet."

Judge Upshaw came hurrying from the direction of his house, greatly disturbed. He was breathing hard when he stopped by Webb's horse. "Sheriff, what do you mean, taking all of these men?"

"We're goin' after Clabe Donovan."

"But those of us in town need protection. Who are you leaving here to make sure Donovan doesn't come back and kill us all?"

Evenly Webb said, "The only way to get Clabe Donovan is to go where he's at, not wait for him to come and pick us off one by one."

Upshaw was trembling. "But what if you miss him? He could come back and kill me. You know he said he would."

Badly as he disliked the judge, Webb felt a momentary pity for the man. "You can go with us if you'd like to."

The judge stepped back. "I . . . I have court business here."

Webb nodded. "Well, then, good luck." He motioned to Aparicio. "Let's be gettin' at it."

The judge called after him, "Matlock . . ." Then Upshaw gave up. He turned his back and started hurrying toward his house.

Quince Pyburn remarked, "Did you see that gun he's got shoved into his waistband? Liable to kill somebody with it."

A cowboy said, "I walked by his house last night. He was hangin' blankets up over the windows so nobody could see in. I expect he's bolted the doors."

Quince said, "God help the first poor Mexican who steps up onto that porch. Judge is liable to shoot anything that wears a sombrero."

The possemen held back while Aparicio examined the sign around back of Quince's corral. The Mexican looked a minute or so and gave his verdict:

"Four men here. Three stay with the horses while

one, he goes afoot to the corner of the corral. This one, I think, is Clabe Donovan. After he is shoot Mister Joe, he run back to the horses. All four men, they ride away."

Webb never had claimed to know a lot about tracks, but it seemed to be as Aparicio said. He could see the stubs of cigarettes lying around where the three men had waited. He turned in the saddle. "Boys, we'll stay off to one side of the tracks. Aparicio will be the only one who rides in close. Time comes we have to check back on them, we don't want them rubbed out."

Rodriguez took the lead eagerly, like a young hound turned loose on a scent. The posse strung out behind him and a little to the left, moving in an easy trot. It was not a difficult trail to follow. It had been made in darkness, with little chance for cover-up. With daylight, Donovan might start hiding his trail. Then would come Aparicio's real test.

For a while the tracks led the posse east. A thought began needling Webb. After upwards of an hour he called a halt, signaled the Mexican back and waited for the men to circle in around him.

"Boys, I think they're headin' east to lead us astray. Ten to one, Clabe figures sooner or later to strike south for the Rio Grande. Likely he'll go east till he gets to a creek or a gravel bed where he can lose his tracks. Then he'll cut south, countin' on us to waste a lot of time tryin' to pick up his trail somewhere to the east. Looks to me like we can gain time if we drop south now, bearin' east a mite. If I'm right, we'll eventually cross his trail. Short-cuttin' him, we could gain some hours. And we sure do need them."

If I'm right? And if I'm wrong . . .

Webb could simply have made it in the form of a command, but he wanted the men's approval. He was no army officer, expecting blind obedience, and these were not soldiers to give it. He saw no sign of argument.

Quince Pyburn said, "It's a gamble, Webb. But then, what in life ain't a gamble? Lead the way."

Gratified, Webb nodded. "We'll fan out and watch the ground. Can't afford to miss those tracks when we cross over them."

They rode in a steady trot, Webb occasionally giving his horse a gentle touch of the spurs, putting him into an easy lope for short stretches to gain on Donovan. Daylight broke full across the land, and the sun began its climb in a sky from which the thin morning clouds slowly dissolved. By midmorning the sky was clear and the sun already hot. Though impatience prickled him, Webb no longer allowed himself the time-gaining runs in which he had indulged during the cool hours of early morning. Now the horses had to be held in, had to be spared.

There had been no sign of tracks leading south. A couple of times the riders crossed suspicious trails, but Aparicio pronounced them to have been left by loose horses, meandering in the devious patterns which grazing animals make.

As noon came on, Webb's face lengthened with worry. It had been a risk, striking south instead of staying with Donovan's actual tracks, but it had seemed a reasonable gamble. Now Webb began to suffer doubt. What if Donovan hadn't gone south? What if he had intended all along to go east? Worse, what if he had doubled back? Clabe Donovan had always possessed a fox's cunning. He might purposely have led the pursuit astray so he could slip back into town.

Joe Vickers might have been only the beginning.

It seemed to Webb that they should have come across the southbound tracks by now if there were any. The specter of failure rode on Webb's shoulder, but he didn't turn back. He had made his decision and would stick with it. Too late to stop Donovan now if the man *had* outwitted him. Webb could only go on with his plan as he had started it, gambling all the chips on one card.

Aparicio still rode out front, his dark brown eyes intently studying the ground. Watching him, Webb had come to feel confident the youth wouldn't miss much. Young, maybe, but in his veins flowed the same blood as Florentino's.

The sun was about noon high when Rodriguez reined up suddenly. He lifted his hand, and the other riders stopped. Aparicio swung to the ground, legs stiff from the long ride. He knelt and fingered a set of tracks. When he stood up, his white teeth were shining.

"You call him right, Mister Webb. These are the ones, the same four." He pointed. "South they go, straight like a shot."

Relief lifted Webb's shoulders. Without meaning to, he let his mouth crack open in a broad grin. He breathed a long sigh as he looked back at the men behind him and saw them perk up. Doubtless the same worry had nagged them all. Probably they knew how it had plagued him, but they hadn't said a word to add to his own self-doubt.

"Aparicio, can you tell how old the tracks are?"

The Mexican pointed his chin downtrail. "From the sign, I say this trail she is not very old. Two, three hours. Maybeso these men think they are safe, and they stop to sleep a little in the night. We have make a pretty good gain, looks like."

Quince Pyburn eyed Webb Matlock with appreciation. "Man who don't ever gamble nothin' don't ever win nothin'. But it had me boogered a while, Webb."

Webb said, "We better stop and eat us a bite; let the horses blow a little."

The men ate hurriedly from the food they had brought along. Finished, they swung into their saddles and rode again. Excitement began to build in Webb. He fought down a strong impulse to run the horses awhile, to try catching up faster. The sun was hot. Sweat was beginning to stick the shirt to his back. He could sense that the horse was tiring beneath him. A man could expect only so much from an animal.

They had ridden into the rough country that was Bronc Tomlin's Rafter T land. Ahead, Webb saw a scattering of trees. Aparicio, up front, reined in and looked at the ground. Webb touched spurs to his horse and caught up to the tracker.

"Here," Rodriguez pointed to the ground, "they change horses. See where ropes rub on the trunks of those trees? They stake horses here yesterday and leave them. While ago they come by, saddle those horses and turn the others loose."

Webb studied the sign. From the close-cropped grass

and the droppings, it was easy to tell that four horses had been staked here a long time.

Aparicio said, "Donovan, he is ride south again. And on fresh horses. The loose horses, they drift off yonderway."

Gritting his teeth, Webb glanced back at the possemen who had caught up and gathered around him. "Bronc Tomlin's headquarters. Donovan used Rafter T horses, I'd bet my bottom dollar."

Quince Pyburn swore. "We ought to bring Bronc out here and stretch his neck from one of these here trees."

Webb said, "That'd make us as bad as he is. There's somethin' we can do, though. We'll go down there and make Bronc lend us some fresh horses."

Quince clenched his fist. "I hope he says no."

"He won't. He'll act surprised that Donovan used his horses, and he'll say he's real glad to be of help to us."

Riding toward the ranchhouse, they came upon the four horses the outlaws had ridden. The animals were slowly drifting in the direction of water, grazing as they went. Sweat had dried on their hides, and not long ago.

Bronc Tomlin walked out from his corrals to meet the possemen, his hand up in a thin semblance of friendliness. "Howdy, fellers. Git down and we'll fix us some coffee." He looked innocently at Webb Matlock. "Never figured to see you so soon after the last time, sheriff. You huntin' that brother of yours?"

The way the man said it gave Webb a start. "Is he here?"

"Any reason he ought to be?"

That was no answer. Webb frowned, his teeth digging into his lower lip. He hadn't had much time today to let his mind dwell on Sandy. Now he would have to admit there was a good chance the boy had come back out here last night. Angry as Sandy had been, it would be a logical way for him to show his defiance. "You didn't answer my question, Bronc."

The rancher smiled dryly, showing brown-stained teeth. "You're welcome to look around."

Webb glared at Tomlin a moment, then switched the subject. "Bronc, we came to borrow some fresh horses."

Bronc was on the point of putting up an argument. "Now, sheriff . . ."

"Before you say another word, listen! Clabe Donovan did a murder last night in Dry Fork. He and three others got away on Rafter T horses. There's a lot of folks believe you let them have them, and they'll be real put out if you act like you don't want us to catch up with him."

Tomlin's gaze flicked from one man to another, and he seemed to sense their hair-trigger temper. He began to backtrack. "Sheriff, I wasn't goin' to say you couldn't have no horses. Sure, you just help yourself to anything you want. I'll do anything I can."

Webb suggested blandly, "You could go along and help us."

Tomlin quickly shook his shaggy head. "I would, only I got some broncs here that I couldn't just ride off and leave."

The possemen quickly changed horses. Starting out

fresh, Quince Pyburn looked darkly back over his thin shoulder. "I still say we ought to stretch his neck a foot or two."

"We can't prove anything on him," Webb said. "Just give him plenty of rope. Someday he'll strangle on it."

Rather than go back where Donovan and his men had changed horses, the posse cut south, angling just enough to intercept the Donovan trail farther down. Eventually they found it. With the fresh horses, Webb no longer feared to spur into a lope.

"We still got distance to close up," he said, "and it's not far to the river."

From sign, they could tell they were gaining. Evidently feeling sure of himself, Donovan had slowed down. But Webb could soon see that even with this advantage, the posse wouldn't catch up before it reached the river. Donovan had beaten them there.

At last Aparicio rode through the thick maze of green brush that screened the edge of the stream. He stopped his horse on the silty bank of the muddy, slow-moving Rio Grande. He didn't have to point down at the tracks in the mud. They were plain for all to see. Squinting, Webb could see where the tracks came out on the other side of the river. Even from here, he could tell they were still fairly wet. Probably not an hour old.

Webb glanced around at Quince and the others. "Well, boys," he said, "here we are. Wouldn't surprise me if Clabe's across yonder in the brush, snickerin' at us."

Quince Pyburn swore, a task at which he was proficient. Johnny Willet said grimly, "Ain't nothin' but just another river. I've swum many a river on the trail to Kansas."

Webb fingered the badge on his shirt. "Not like this one. Across yonder is a different county, a different law. This badge don't mean much when we cross over."

Johnny said, "But you got a .44 on your hip and a saddlegun under your leg. They means a-plenty no matter where they're at."

Webb glanced at Aparicio. "You game to go across?"

"Ready when you say."

Webb drew the saddlegun and held it in his right hand to keep it from getting wet. "All right, let's see if these Bronc Tomlin horses can swim."

It was the dry season of year, and the river was running low. The horses had little trouble because their feet were on the soft bottom most of the way across. The only mishap came when Johnny Willet's horse lost its footing and plunged the cowboy into the river. The other men moved in quickly to help. Shifting the rifle to his left hand, Webb grabbed Johnny beneath one arm and pulled the cowboy up against his saddle. Johnny sputtered but held on until they got across the river. On the far bank he dropped to his knees and coughed up some of the muddy water.

Concerned, Webb asked, 'You goin' to make it all right, Johnny?"

Johnny blinked away the eye-burning river sand. "All right. Just didn't figure on a bath, is all."

Someone brought Johnny's horse. The cowboy

swung up, his clothes dripping. He said, "Let's don't be losin' no time on my account."

Webb started to lead out but pulled up when he heard Quince Pyburn grunt, "Uh oh, we got company comin'." Webb turned his horse and saw soldiers riding along the edge of the river, moving up on them in an easy lope.

What a time, he thought, *to run into the Mexican cavalry?*

There were upwards of a dozen soldiers mounted on scrubby little Mexican ponies that had never seen enough feed a day in their lives. The lieutenant was easy to spot, not only because he rode out front but also because he had the only good horse in the bunch. It was a handsome sorrel that stood two hands taller than any other animal in the lot.

The sand finally blinked away, Johnny Willet remarked, "I know that sorrel horse. He's Old Jess Leggett's Big Red, stole a couple of months ago by some horse thieves from this side of the river."

Webb knew how it was with these isolated Mexican border detachments, serving under only a modicum of real military law. Each officer ran things pretty much to suit himself, sometimes taking bribes or receiving stolen property in return for protection to those who preyed on the rest of the Mexican populace, or on the *gringos* across the river. Some of these officers demanded tribute from the poor people they were supposed to be protecting. Sometimes they falsified purchases and charged up artificially high prices to their government while they lined their own pockets.

Under little supervision, corrupt officers could rule as virtual dictators within their own areas of command, holding even the power of life and death.

An ugly picture, but who was to tell? It was a long way to Mexico City.

The lieutenant halted his patrol. On command, the soldiers fanned out on either side of him, as if they meant business. To Webb they looked like mercenaries of the worst kind, dregs of the border towns, their faces tough, their eyes brutal. The officer looked grimly over the Texas posse, seeking the man in charge. He spotted Webb's badge, and his cold dark eyes lifted to Webb's face. In passable English he said, "You have come to invade Mexico? Your army is small."

Webb had met some Mexican officers he liked and some he disliked. He had classified this one on sight. "We're on the trail of some outlaws who crossed the river ahead of us."

"I see no outlaws."

Webb pointed. "That there's their tracks."

The officer didn't look. "I see no tracks."

Then Webb knew. The lieutenant was in league with Donovan.

The officer's gaze roved once more over the possemen and settled on Aparicio Rodriguez. Resentment coloring his voice, he said in Spanish, "What sort of Mexican are you, riding with these *gringos?*"

"The outlaws we seek are not Mexican, they are *gringo*. They killed a man."

"A *gringo?*" the lieutenant asked. When Aparicio nodded, the man said, "What we need, then, are more *gringo* outlaws. Let the *gringos* kill off each other."

His eyes narrowed as he studied the young tracker. "If you lived on this side of the river, I would teach you a lesson about riding with these men. You are a traitor to your own kind!"

The quick temper of youth flared in Aparicio. "And you are a dog, to wear the uniform and be in league with killers. You are worse than they are because they claim to be nothing else. You are supposed to be a soldier."

Anger leaped in the lieutenant's eyes. "Careful. On this side of the river I am the master. When I speak, everyone jumps."

Aparicio stiffened. "I am not jumping. I say you are a dog!"

The lieutenant's arm streaked, and a sword flashed into his hand. "You are only a *peon*. No *peon* speaks to me that way." For a second it appeared he would drive the sword into the boy. But he caught himself and lowered the blade. Fire crackled in his eyes. "Go back, *peon*, and stay. If I ever catch you on this side again . . ."

The officer's gaze cut back to Webb. He reverted to English. "You go now, back *al otro lado*." His voice was sharp with command.

Sullenly Webb said, "We came to get those outlaws."

The lieutenant waved the sword point at Webb. "You are here against Mexican law. By right we could shoot you, all of you. But the heart of Tiburcio Armendariz is kind. We let you go, *this time!*"

"You're protectin' murderers and you know it."

"You go to Mexico City, *gringo*. Get papers from *el presidente*. Then perhaps Armendariz lets you look for your outlaws. Now go!"

Face flushed, Webb clenched his fists in helpless anger. He muttered under his breath to the men around him. "They got us dead to rights."

Johnny Willet said stubbornly, "Between us we could whip the whole bunch."

Quince Pyburn replied, "And start a sure-enough border war? Webb's right, we got no legal status here. If we hadn't got caught, fine. But we did get caught, and we better get ourselves back across the *rio*."

Webb reined his horse toward the water, frustration boiling in him. Johnny Willet hung back. "We could take them, I know we could."

"Come on, Johnny," said Webb.

The lieutenant hailed Webb, halting him at the river's edge. "*Gringo!* We watch this river. You try to come back, we shoot you before you are out of the water!"

They swam across to the Texas side. Looking over his shoulder, Webb could see the patrol remained where it was, watching them. He swung down. "We best let the horses blow a spell." His trousers were soaked, his toes squishing in water-filled boots.

All eyes watched the Mexican soldiers. Webb could sense the men's simmering anger.

Johnny Willet felt his shirt pocket, then said thinly, "Webb, you got the makin's? All my tobacco was soaked when I took that fall."

Webb handed him a sack of tobacco. Johnny rolled himself a smoke while his angry eyes fastened on the distant patrol. "You ain't aimin' to let the thing lie the way it is, are you?"

"We did the best we could, Johnny. We couldn't

have known there'd be a patrol to stop us the minute we got across."

"We could ride up or down the river a ways and try again."

"They'd pick up our tracks and come a-huntin' us. I'd hate to have the thing come to a shoot-out because in the eyes of the law we'd be in the wrong. Across yonder we're trespassers."

"That Armendariz has got some kind of agreement with Clabe Donovan," Johnny said bitterly.

"Sure he has. But you'd have to go all the way to Mexico City to get anything done about it."

Johnny Willet leaned against his dripping horse and stared across the saddle at the men on the far bank of the Rio Grande. "I intend to do somethin' about it. One way or another, old Joe Vickers is goin' to have the account settled for him."

"We'll do somethin', Johnny," Webb promised. "But I don't reckon it'll be today."

"There's too many of us," Johnny agreed. "One or two might be able to slip across there and make it."

"Forget it, Johnny."

But Johnny didn't forget it. They camped for the night a couple of miles north of the river to rest and dry out. At daylight Webb was awakened by distant gunfire. Jumping to his feet, he found that Johnny Willet and Aparicio Rodriguez had gone. Their tracks led south.

Webb and the others saddled quickly and spurred toward the river, following the plain tracks. At the bank they pulled up in dismay.

On the near edge, Johnny Willet sat hunched in the mud, breathing hard from exhaustion. His right hand gripped his left shoulder, and crimson edged slowly out between his fingers. Aparicio lay crumpled where Johnny had dragged him out of the river. A dark red stain drained off into the water. Without touching him, Webb knew the young Mexican was dead.

Looking across the river in helpless fury, Webb could see the Mexican patrol, guns in their hands, the lieutenant in the center of the soldiers. Webb also saw someone else: a broad-shouldered man wearing *gringo* clothes and a black Mexican sombrero. Even from here, he knew that shape, that stance.

Donovan!

6

ᔕ

One of the possemen fired a vengeful shot in the direction of the Mexican patrol, but it didn't hit anybody.

"No more shootin'!" Webb ordered sharply.

With Quince Pyburn's help he picked up Johnny Willet and half-dragged him back into the brush beyond the river bank. Someone else brought the young Mexican's body and carefully laid it out in the shade of a mesquite. Shade would help the boy none now, but it still seemed the thing to do.

Webb tore Johnny's sleeve for a look at the wound. Johnny protested weakly. "I'm all right, it's just a scratch. How about Aparicio?"

"Dead."

Johnny's head drooped. "I thought he was. Couldn't tell for sure. So winded there wasn't much I could do after I drug him out of the water."

Webb knew he should reproach the cowboy, but it would serve no useful purpose now. The harm was done. The stricken look in Johnny's eyes showed that nothing Webb could say would hurt half as much as what had already happened.

"It was a stupid thing to try," Johnny spoke tightly. "It was my idea. Thought the two of us could get somethin' done, him trackin', me along for an extra gun. We never got halfway across the river. They must have seen us the minute we came out of the brush. But they laid back and waited. They let us get way into the water before they came out and opened up. The man in the sombrero—Donovan, I guess it was—shot the horse out from under me. That Lieutenant Armendariz, he was the one that got Aparicio. Hit him in the shoulder first, knocked him out of the saddle. Boy was cryin' and chokin'. Armendariz just kept on shootin', puttin' bullets into him. Seemed like it pleasured him to do it."

Webb examined Johnny's wound. "Deep gash, but clean. Bullet went on through. It'll get sore as sin, but it'll heal. Quince, I brought a bottle of whisky along for a case like this. It's in my saddlebag."

Quince said, "I'll get it."

Johnny didn't seem to care about himself. "He was a game little Mex, that Aparicio, game as ever I seen."

Webb said, "It's done now. Won't help to cry over what's already done."

Johnny's teeth clenched as Webb poured a little of the whisky over the wound. "Webb, I took him into that scrape. It was my fault. I'm goin' to see to it that he didn't die for nothin'."

With a stirring of impatience Webb asked, "Don't you think you've done enough already?"

"I ain't even started!"

"You've started and you've finished. You're goin' home, Johnny."

Johnny shook his head. "I've dealt myself into this game to stay. I'll play it out to the last hand."

Webb sat on his spurred heels, wrapping a cloth around the cowboy's wound and studying Johnny's face. He saw a stolid determination there and knew argument was useless. "What do you think you could do?"

"I'll think of somethin'."

"You can't go back across that river. None of us are goin' to, at least not yet awhile."

Johnny nodded grimly. "I know. I learned my lesson there. But there's bound to be another way." He sat a while, sorrowfully staring at the body of the young Mexican. "Florentino's goin' to take it hard, Webb. They were as close as brothers, him and Aparicio. If it hadn't been for me . . ."

"Don't keep beatin' yourself over the head, Johnny. Maybe it *was* your idea, but he went of his own will, same as you did."

Johnny pushed onto his feet, wincing a little and gripping his burning shoulder. He glanced from one to another of the men scattered around him as if he were looking for some sign of blame. He found none. At length he turned back to the sheriff. "Webb, you ain't got a deputy, have you? I mean, a full-time deputy in Dry Fork?"

Webb shook his head. "Been several years since the county needed one."

"You need one now. And I'm it."

"Johnny, you've got a good job with Jess Leggett."

"I got a bigger job to do right now."

Webb knew a moment of exasperation, but he also knew by looking at the cowboy that argument would be wasted on him. "Takes more than just wantin' the job to make a man a deputy."

"I'll do the job, Webb, whether you hire me or not. So you'd just as well put me on the payroll and make it legal."

"What about Jess?"

"He's got enough help to take care of his cows."

"Have you figured out just what you could do, Johnny?"

Johnny's jaw was set firm. "It's a long ways to Dry Fork, Webb. You got to stay around there most of the time. You can't be down here a-ridin' this river. But somebody needs to." He frowned. "Way I see it, Donovan has got to cross the *rio* before he can make a raid on anybody. He can't cross without leavin' tracks.

"This is a long old river, but Donovan always did it in the same general area, every time. Now, supposin' I was to stay here and do nothin' but ride that river up and down, day in and day out. Unless he goes a long ways upstream or down, Donovan can't cross without me either seein' him or cuttin' his sign in a matter of hours. With a fast horse, and knowin' whichaway he's headed, I got a good chance of beatin' him there."

Webb rubbed his chin, uncertain. "Johnny . . ."

"I'm goin' to do it whether I got a badge or not, and whether you pay me or not. I'd just a little rather you made it legal, is all."

Webb gave in, knowing he had just as well. "Then I'll make it legal, Johnny."

Webb didn't want to ride down the main street, leading Aparicio's horse with the young Mexican's tarp-wrapped body tied across it and getting the town all stirred up. He circled Dry Fork, entering by way of the Mexican settlement. He was dusty and bearded and felt as badly as he looked. He reined up in front of the small adobe store run by Florentino Rodriguez. He glanced back at weary, slump-shouldered Quince Pyburn as if to ask him for support. But this was a job that wouldn't improve, even with help.

Stiffly Webb swung to the ground. Saddles creaked as other riders did the same. Webb looped his reins over a rail, swallowed, then stepped through the front door out of the heat, into the deep shadow behind the thick adobe walls.

Florentino limped out from behind the counter. "Mister Webb, you catch Donovan, maybe?"

Webb shook his head and dropped his chin. "Almost, Florentino. He got to the river ahead of us."

Florentino said solemnly, "Too bad." He paused. "How about Aparicio? He's one good tracker, si? Did he do you a good job?"

Webb looked at the hard-packed dirt floor. "He did us a fine job."

With pride the Mexican said, "I told you. He's one good boy, that Aparicio." He looked over the men's silent faces. "Where is he? Did he not come home?"

Webb's hands flexed nervously. "He came home. He's outside." Florentino moved toward the door. Webb caught the Mexican's shoulder, stopping him. "Florentino!" He looked the man in the eyes, and he saw sudden alarm in Florentino's face. Webb said sorrowfully, "I hate to tell you. He's dead."

The Mexican stood in shock, his dark face unbelieving. Stiffly then he limped out the door into the sunshine. He stared dry-eyed at the body tied across the horse.

"Who is kill him? Donovan?"

"A Mexican officer did the shootin'. Donovan was the cause of it." Quietly he recounted the events that led up to Aparicio's death. Florentino listened with a deep sadness in his eyes.

"A good boy, Aparicio," he said finally. "But very young, and maybeso a little foolish. Please, you will help me take him into the house?"

Carefully they untied Aparicio and carried him into the living quarters behind the store. Webb heard a cry and saw Florentino's wife, Consuela, sit up in bed, staring in horror. Florentino said to her, "*Es Aparicio.*" She began to sob. For the first time Webb saw the tiny bundle lying beside her. Her movement awakened the newly-born child, and it began to whimper.

Webb said, "I see the baby got here."

Florentino nodded grimly. "One is born, another dies."

"Named it yet?"

Florentino shook his head. "We could not decide. Now, I think, there is no question." He looked bleakly at the baby. "We will call him Aparicio."

From there they rode on to Quince's livery stable and unsaddled. Juan Obregon, a gray-haired Mexican who had been watching the place for Quince, took care of the horses as the men released them. He put out some grain for them—not too much, for this was summertime, and grain made for heat.

Webb said to Quince, "Juan's some kin to Aparicio and Florentino, isn't he?"

"An uncle, I think. I better break the news to him."

Webb nodded. "Boy died in the line of duty. Tell Juan I reckon the county will pay his buryin'. If it don't, *I* will. He deserves more than just bein' wrapped in an old blanket and covered over with dirt."

Quince said, "We'll *all* help pay for it." He paused, his face clouding. "And Donovan will pay for it too, one of these days."

From the livery barn it wasn't far up to the hill where the town's cemetery was. Drawn there, Webb stood awhile among the crosses and leaning headstones, staring at the small mound where they had buried someone and called him Donovan, so many years ago. He looked at the wooden cross with the words CLABE DONOVAN printed across it in peeling black paint.

"Clabe," Webb said quietly, absently, "if it's not you down there, then who in hell is it?"

He wanted desperately to see Ellie Donovan, but to do so now would only cause pain, and for no good reason. He gathered clean clothes from his office, noting that nothing had been touched while he had been gone. Sandy hadn't been back. Well, Webb hadn't really expected him, not this soon. Maybe not at all.

He walked down to the barber shop to clean up. Afterwards he carried his dirty clothes across to the widow Sanchez, as was his custom. He could tell by the old woman's manner that she already knew about Aparicio. By now the word had had time to spread all over the Mexican settlement. There would be much grief down there, for the boy hadn't had an enemy.

Looked like, sometimes, the good ones died young while the Donovans of the world lived on forever.

Walking back, Webb took a long look at Ellie's Dry Fork Cafe, wishing . . .

He shook his head. Idle to think about it. No need in a man punishing himself like that.

To his surprise he found Ellie pacing the floor in his office, waiting for him. After staring a moment, speechless, he finally said, "Never expected to see you here, Ellie. Figured you'd be at the cafe, gettin' supper ready."

"It can wait," she said thinly. From the dark hollows beneath her eyes, he could tell she hadn't slept much lately. A brooding anxiety showed in her face. He took a step forward as if to take her in his arms, then stopped. She said, "I heard a little of the rumor that worked down the street a while ago. You didn't catch Clabe."

He shook his head. "No."

She dropped her chin. "I don't know whether I'm glad or not. I wish I *did* know." She paused. "I'm sorry about that Mexican boy. Folks say he was a nice boy."

He nodded, studying her face, an ache twisting inside him like a knife blade. He said, "That makes another thing Clabe Donovan will have to pay for. Sooner or later we *will* catch him, Ellie. You've got to prepare yourself for that."

She didn't reply. She was in misery, yet she didn't cry. Probably she had cried herself out.

He went on, "Long as he stays out loose, more people are goin' to die. First was old Joe Vickers—as good a man as ever drew a breath. And then that Rodriguez boy, shot for no reason. No, not by Clabe himself, but on account of Clabe. It won't end there. The only way to stop it is to stop Clabe." He hesitated, wishing he could avoid what he was about to say. "Ellie, even if you do still love him, you're bound to see that he's got to be brought in, else there'll be others. You could help."

She raised her eyes to him. "How?"

"Clabe used the same hideout down there all the time you lived with him, didn't he?"

She nodded.

He said, "It stands to reason he's likely usin' it again. Now, we can't go into Mexico and search him out. The Mexican cavalry wouldn't allow us that much time. But if we knew right where to go, we might cross at night, grab him and bring him back across the river before that trigger-happy Armendariz knew what had happened. You could tell us, Ellie."

Ellie Donovan had been standing up all this time. Now, suddenly, she sank into a chair. "Webb, do you know what you're asking of me?"

He nodded soberly. "I do, Ellie. I'm not sayin' you have to, not even sayin' I *want* you to. But it's a way to put an end to all this. You'll have to make up your own mind. I don't aim to pressure you."

For a long time she sat there, her face in her hands. When finally she looked up, she was still dry-eyed. She shook her head. "Whatever he's done, however bad he's become, he's still my husband. I'd do anything else—even go down there myself and plead with him. But this . . ." Again she shook her head. "I couldn't do it, Webb. Please don't ask me."

He studied her gravely. "All right, Ellie. Forget I said anything."

She stood up to go. Again he felt a desperate yearning to take her into his arms. He put his hands behind him and turned half around, away from her. "I wish there was somethin' I could do, Ellie, somethin' I could say."

She replied quietly, "There isn't, Webb. I suppose this is as hard for you, in a way, as it is for me. You coming over for supper later?"

"No, I thought it'd be better if I took my meals over at the Dutchman's awhile. Be better for both of us, Ellie."

"It would, Webb. Goodbye."

She stepped out into the street and was gone.

She hadn't been out of the place more than a couple of minutes when Judge Upshaw arrived, nervous as a condemned man. One look and Webb knew he was in for a wrangle.

"You let him get through your fingers, didn't you?" Upshaw exclaimed.

Seated at his desk, Webb didn't stand up or offer the judge a chair. "If you've heard that much, you've heard enough to know the cards were stacked against us. We couldn't stay across the river."

"Maybe you didn't really want to catch him."

Webb's teeth clamped together. "You're workin' up to somethin', judge. Say it plain."

"All right, I will. Maybe you're afraid of him. Or maybe it's something else. A long time ago, you were friends with Clabe Donovan. Even now you share a common interest . . . perhaps a more common interest than we've supposed."

Webb stiffened. "Watch out, judge."

"I saw her leave here just now. Didn't waste much time getting together with her after you came in, did you? Did she promise you anything if you wouldn't catch up with her husband?"

Webb pushed to his feet and took a step toward the judge, his fist clenched. "Call me anything you want to, judge; you've already done it often enough. But say another word about Ellie Donovan and I'll drag you through that street on your face!"

The judge shrank back and swallowed, but he had a deeper fear of Clabe Donovan than of Webb Matlock. "Dammit, man," the jurist said, "you know what Donovan swore to do. You ought to know better than anybody why he's got to be brought in."

Webb loosened a little. He realized that the tight grip of fear was on the judge, making him say things he probably wouldn't otherwise. Even the bravest man might lose sleep over the thought of an outlaw coming back from the grave to carry out a promise of vengeance, made years ago. And Judge Upshaw was not a brave man. A shuddering dread had eroded his reason.

"We'll bring him in, judge," Webb promised. "Somehow, we'll get him!"

7

For a time then, nothing was heard of Donovan. So far as anyone at Dry Fork knew, he made no effort to cross the river. With a grimly single-minded purpose, Johnny Willet had begun a one-man patrol on a long section of the river. He put in a hard ride from his starting point at daylight each morning, stopping at noon where he had kept a few extra horses in a little valley that had some decent grass. He would eat a cold meal, carried with him all morning, put his saddle on a fresh horse and start back, covering the same ground twice a day, diligently watching for tracks. At night he slept in a tiny abandoned rock house built long ago by a venturesome Mexican family which finally withdrew because of Indians and never came back. The house had only half a roof, but at this time of year it didn't rain much anyway.

One day the mail brought cryptic letters to several people in town. Webb got one of them. His was simply a piece of paper with a skull and crossbones penciled on it, and the word SOON scrawled beneath the picture. Quince Pyburn received a similar one. Judge

Upshaw staggered to Webb's office and with trembling hands gave Webb the one he had received. It bore a picture of a hangman's knot and noose. The judge's face had turned almost as white as the paper.

"It's from Donovan," he croaked. "He's going to kill me, Matlock. He's going to kill me unless you give me protection. I *demand* protection."

"Several people got letters like that today," Webb told him. "Every one of them deserves protection. But the only way I could guarantee it is to put all of you in a jail cell together where I could keep watch on the whole bunch at one time."

"It's your duty to protect me. I'm an officer of the court."

"It's my job to protect everybody, but there's a point where I can do just so much and no more. Everybody's got to help take care of himself."

Tears showed in the judge's eyes. "You're going to let him kill me, Matlock. You're just going to stand there and let him come to kill me!"

He weaved out the front door, braced himself a moment on a post, then made his way down the street toward his house.

The judge had left his letter behind. Webb studied it, face twisting as he looked for something he could put his finger on. Far as he could tell, it had been drawn by the same hand which had prepared the others Webb had seen. Postmark was the same on all of them—Rio Escondido. That was a railroad town forty miles northeast, much farther from the Rio Grande than Dry Fork was. Unlikely that Donovan had been up there himself. Probably he had had someone do the task for him.

Webb became certain of it when Bronc Tomlin came through town, headed toward his ranch with a fresh suit of clothes, a shave, haircut and a red-haired saloon girl folks said he had just brought from Rio Escondido. That was a larger and busier town than Dry Fork. It was where Bronc usually went periodically when he wanted feminine company to share his ranchhouse a while. It afforded more selection. Besides, the few Dry Fork girls who would even consider the type of proposition Bronc made knew Bronc's place by now. They wouldn't go for love or money.

Webb was almost certain Bronc had mailed the letters. After checking with Ellie and learning that the writing was not Clabe Donovan's, Webb decided Bronc had even done the drawings himself. He had no doubt that the work had been done at Donovan's request, though.

"You ain't goin' to arrest him?" Quince Pyburn asked incredulously as the two of them watched Bronc's buckboard roll dustily down the trail toward the Rafter T.

Webb shook his head. "What could I prove on him? When I put Bronc Tomlin in that jailhouse, I want to know I can keep him."

One afternoon Johnny Willet rode into town on a sweat-lathered horse so exhausted it stood and trembled at the hitchrack while Johnny sprinted onto the porch and into Webb's office. Webb looked up in surprise. Seeing the excitement in Johnny's eyes, he wasted no time in foolish questions.

"Donovan?"

Johnny nodded and braced himself against Webb's desk. He was too worn out to stand steady. "I think so, Webb." He weaved across the room to a water pitcher. Thirstily he emptied the dipper twice, then poured another dipperful over his head, letting the water run off into a tin washbasin. He sank into a chair, breathing a long, weary sigh.

"I think he's fixin' to come across the river. May already be over, headin' for Rio Escondido. Yesterday three men swam the *rio*, two white men and a Mexican. All of a sudden I got the idea they were Donovan men. I took and followed them all the way to Bronc Tomlin's. I laid up on a rise and watched them through my spyglass. They gathered a bunch of horses. Then, with a couple of Bronc's men to help them, they commenced pushin' the horses to the northeast. I followed, a good ways back. About twenty miles from Tomlin's, they dropped off six head. One of the Tomlin men stayed to loose-herd them on grass around a hole of water. Another twenty miles or so, they done the same thing again. When I left to come here, they had six horses left and was pushin' them on in the direction of Rio Escondido.

"It come to me, Webb, that they was settin' up a relay of fresh horses. Does that mean to you what it meant to me?"

Excitement began to rise in Webb. "A raid on Rio Escondido! Bank, most likely. When they're through they can head south and have fresh horses all the way back to the Rio Grande."

Johnny nodded. "That's what it looked like to me."

Standing up, Webb glanced toward his gun cabinet. "I sure wish we had a telegraph line from here to Rio Escondido." He unsnapped the padlock that held a bar in front of the guns. "Only way to get a message there is to take it. Think you're up to another ride?"

"For a chance at Donovan? I'd go bareback, plumb to the Mississippi River."

The rifles were loaded. Webb kept them that way, even though they weren't used much anymore. "Take your horse over to Quince's, Johnny. Tell him what's up. Tell him I'm goin' to gather some men and be over there in a few minutes. May need to use some of his horses."

Tired though he was, Johnny Willet stepped out of the office in long strides. He mounted and urged the weary horse up the street.

Webb sat at his desk just long enough to pen a short note. He knew it might take hours to round up a large posse such as he ought to have. He must settle for what he could get. He walked up the street, looking in every place he came to for men he had confidence in, men he felt were stable enough for the job. He avoided any he feared might be trigger-happy. They were even worse than the gun-shy kind. By the time Webb reached Quince's, he had picked nearly a dozen men. Some who had horses handy went to fetch them. Others hurried to Quince's afoot to see what the stableman could offer.

Among the people gathered at the livery barn was

Quince's sixteen-year-old nephew. Webb didn't want any kids along on a mission like this. "Billy," he said, "I got a mighty important job for you." He took out the note he had written. "Ride to Rio Escondido as fast as you can. Don't kill your horse, but don't hold back any more than you have to. Find the sheriff and tell him we think Clabe Donovan is fixin' to pay him a call. Give him this note. He knows my handwritin', and he'll know you're tellin' him the truth. Tell him we know where the relay horses are posted, and we're goin' to try to stop Donovan before he ever gets to Rio Escondido. A gunfight in town is too risky to women and kids. But tell him he better be ready in case we miss."

A little disappointed, the boy nodded. "If you want me to, Webb. Only, I was sure hopin' . . ."

"This is a serious responsibility I'm handin' you, Billy. You're light and can make a fast ride. I wouldn't give the job to just anybody."

The compliment paid off. Beaming, Billy swung onto his horse and left town in a lope. He sat straight and proud in the saddle.

Johnny Willet came back from the general store with a pack of supplies tied across the back of a led horse. "Ready whenever you are, Webb," he said. The deputy was tired, but he wouldn't back down.

Webb said, "Let's go."

It hadn't been half an hour since Johnny had arrived in town. Now he and Webb were heading out again with Quince Pyburn and nearly a dozen men following in an easy lope. Off to meet Clabe Donovan . . .

* * *

The second group of Donovan relay horses had been placed at a fairly well-known landmark, several grand old cottonwood trees marking a spring that had not been known to go dry in even the droughtiest years. It was a logical place because Donovan, possessing an old familiarity with the country, would not have trouble finding it, even hard pressed by pursuit.

A mile from the spring, Webb held up his hand and told the possemen to dismount so they would not easily be seen. To Johnny he said, "Let's me and you go scout the situation."

Circling the spring, they came up from the hilly side where they wouldn't be spotted. The tops of the cottonwoods showed above the hills where the two men tied their horses to set out afoot. Webb removed his spurs and hung them on the saddlehorn so they wouldn't jingle while he walked, or trip him as he climbed the hill. Johnny followed suit. Webb slipped his saddlegun out of its scabbard and started to climb. Again Johnny followed his example. The cowboy was a fair shot with a rifle, but with a pistol he couldn't hit a barn from the inside with all the doors shut.

The top of the hill was almost bare of vegetation. Grass and weeds had burned to a brittle brown in the sun. Webb took off his hat which might show conspicuously against the skyline. He dropped to his hands and knees, easing in behind a small clump of hardy *guajilla*. Johnny inched up beside him. In both men had lurked an unspoken fear that they might have arrived too late, that Donovan might already have passed this way.

Johnny had brought his spyglass with him, but there was no need for it. They could see readily enough that six hobbled horses grazed near the spring. One man waited down there in the shade of the cotton-woods, a rifle across his lap and his hat down over his eyes. He appeared to be dozing in the summer heat.

"We could slip down there and take him," Johnny suggested.

Webb shook his head. "We'll leave things alone. When Donovan rides in, we want to have everything lookin' natural. We'll catch them while they're unsad-dlin', maybe set some of them afoot."

Johnny said, "From here, if the breaks come right, it'll be like shootin' fish in a barrel."

Webb saw an eagerness in the cowboy's eyes. He remembered how Johnny had sickened after having to kill his first man—that young rustler who had been wounded while running off some of Jess Leggett's cows. Johnny had hated the thought of killing, then. Now he had had reason enough to change. He had seen two men die because of Donovan—Uncle Joe Vickers and Aparicio.

Webb thought fleetingly of Ellie Donovan, and he wished things could have turned out some other way. "I hope when the time comes, Johnny, it isn't me who has to kill Clabe."

From the hilltop he had a fair command of the sur-rounding countryside. He could see fairly clearly to the south across the scattering of mesquite, the stunty green *guajilla*, all the way to where the horizon line shimmered in the sun. He whispered, "You stay here and keep your eyes peeled, Johnny. I'll go back and fetch the rest of the boys in closer."

Using the roundabout approach, out of sight of the lone man who took care of the horses, Webb brought his posse in behind the hill. From his position he could make out Johnny, still bellied down. Johnny shook his head as if to say he had seen nothing yet. Webb nodded and turned to the possemen. "We'd just as well settle down for a wait. No tellin' when Donovan is liable to show up."

He expected the outlaw to appear before long. It didn't stand to reason Donovan would send these horses very far ahead of him; too much chance of somebody coming across them and getting suspicious. But the minutes stretched into hours, and Webb saw no sign. He and Johnny Willet remained on top of the hill, watching. At intervals Webb took Johnny's spyglass and carefully swept the horizon, looking for sign of dust or of moving figures. Nothing.

Night came. The man at the spring built a small fire and began to boil coffee in a can. The pleasant smell of it drifted up and set Webb's stomach to stirring. He said, "Johnny, ease down and tell the boys they can fix some coffee if they want it. Just a small fire, though. That feller couldn't smell it over his own."

Johnny said with gratitude, "Sure suits me. I got a terrible cravin'." He hesitated about moving down off the hill. "Webb, I figured they'd get here before now. Reckon somethin' went wrong?"

Webb could see worry in Johnny's eyes. The same worry had begun to gnaw at Webb, too. "All we can do is wait. He might've figured on hittin' Rio Escondido at night, maybe to blow the safe. You never can tell what a man like Clabe Donovan is liable to do. You just have to wait and be ready."

Johnny left. Before long Webb could see the dim flicker of a small fire where the possemen waited. They had dug a hole and built the fire in it. From ground level, it wouldn't be visible very far. After a long time Johnny came back, and Webb was able to go back down the hill. The men at the bottom sat around silently sipping hot coffee. Webb could hardly see them in the darkness. Quince Pyburn had kicked sand over the small fire once it was no longer needed. Now there was not even a glow. Quince handed Webb a cup. He said nothing, but Webb could sense in the tall man the same plaguing doubt that he felt in himself.

"Quince, you're thinkin' we might've made a wrong guess."

Quince shook his head. "I don't know how we could have. A blind man could see what Donovan sent these horses for. But . . ."

"But what?"

"Maybe somethin' changed Clabe's plans. Maybe somethin' boogered him." Quince finished his coffee. He let the dregs and the last drops drip out into the dirt.

Webb said, "You never can be sure of anything, Quince. You just use your judgment and take your choice and hope it works out. No man can do more than that." He stood up. "I'm goin' back up that hill.

You fellers try to get you some sleep. Could be a long night."

It *was* a long night, a terribly long night. Webb stayed atop the hill with Johnny, dozing occasionally when he knew Johnny was awake. But even dozing, he was never far from consciousness. He heard every stamp of a horse's foot, heard the thin snore of the lone man who waited at the spring. When the first flush of dawn spread in the east, he opened his burning eyes and squinted across the rolling land to the south.

He saw nothing.

Below, the man with the horses awakened and rebuilt his burned-out fire. In a little while he had coffee going and was frying bacon in a small skillet. The smell of it stirred hunger in Webb. It also awakened a strong doubt.

Donovan should have been here before this.

On the other side of the hill, the possemen moved with caution, making no noise. Webb sent Johnny down to eat. Later, when Johnny returned, Webb went down.

Webb had only half finished his coffee when Johnny signaled him excitedly. Webb dropped his cup in the grass and hurried up the hill. Lying flat on his stomach, Johnny pointed. Webb saw a single rider moving toward the spring, coming from the southwest. He took out the spyglass and focused on the man. He thought this was another Tomlin rider.

The horseman drew up at the spring and swung down with a wave of his hand. The man who had kept the horses was standing, waiting. He motioned the newcomer to the fire and poured coffee for him. Webb could hear the low murmur of their conversation, but he couldn't make out a word of it.

The rider ate a little. He caught a fresh horse, leaving his own, then waved to the other man and started out again, heading northeast.

"Goin' toward the place where they left the next bunch of horses," Johnny observed.

"I'd give a lot to know what kind of message he brought with him."

"We could catch him and find out."

"No, best we let them play out the string their own way."

The man by the spring began leisurely gathering up what little camp gear he had. He rolled his blanket and tied it behind his saddle. He caught one of the horses, saddled him, then began removing the hobbles from the others. Moving slowly, as if he had the rest of the year to do it in, he swung up and began pushing the horses southwestward.

Incredulous, Johnny exclaimed, "Webb, he's takin' them horses home!"

Webb swore. "There's a skunk in the woods someplace. Come on, we'll find out what it is."

Moving down the hillside, he signaled the possemen to their horses. By the time he and Johnny got there, the men were tightening their cinches and getting ready to ride. Excitedly Quince Pyburn asked, "Donovan?"

Webb shook his head. "Feller's leavin' with the horses. Somethin's gone wrong, and I want to know what."

He led out in a hard lope that soon had the men

spurring to catch up with him. Johnny Willet rode half a length behind, the other possemen followed in a ragged pattern. The man with the loose horses had a quarter-mile head start, but it didn't last long. A mile from the spring, Webb Matlock overtook him. The rider looked back and drew rein. He faced around and waited, letting his horses work on ahead. They moved along in a steady trot as if they enjoyed being free of the hobbles and moving toward the home range they knew. Horses, like many people, had a powerful homing instinct.

Webb stopped. The rider who faced him was in his early twenties, shaggy-haired and needing a shave. Webb had seen him in town with Bronc Tomlin. Clinch, his name was. An insolent amusement played in the cowboy's pale eyes. He glanced at the pistol on Webb's hip and at the saddlegun.

"You're sure packin' the hardware, sheriff. Goin' to a shootin' match someplace?"

"Where you takin' those horses?" Webb demanded.

"Home, sheriff, that's all. Back to Bronc Tomlin's. Bronc's broncs, these are."

The other possemen began to catch up. They formed a half circle around the Tomlin man, their faces grim. Webb caught a momentary flicker of fear in the young rider's eyes, a lapse quickly corrected. The cowboy managed somehow to grin. It was plainly forced, but a grin nevertheless.

Webb asked harshly, "What were you doin' out here?"

"Any law against a man travelin', sheriff?"

"Depends on where he's goin' and what he figures

on doin' when he gets there. How come you to hold those horses at the spring?"

"Because that's where the water was. Some grass too." Clinch seemed to enjoy his innocent answers. "Wouldn't want me to camp where the horses couldn't get no feed or water, would you?"

"You know that's not what I meant. What were you here for in the first place? Doesn't make sense, bringin' horses all the way here from the Rafter T and then takin' them right back again."

"Ain't no law says a man has got to make sense all the time, sheriff."

Angered, Webb said, "*You'd* better start makin' sense!"

For a minute Clinch sat there, his grin fading, his eyes turning hostile. Then, silently, Quince Pyburn loosened his hornstring and took his rope loose from the horn. Coolly he built a small loop in it and looked toward Clinch. He spoke not a word, but his eyes carried a strong message.

The rider swallowed. He began to break. "Now look, sheriff, you know I ain't done nothin'. All I done was to bring them horses out here, just like Bronc Tomlin told me to. Said a buyer might show up, wantin' them. Nobody did, and while ago one of the boys came and told me Bronc said bring the horses home." He looked around nervously. "Ain't nothin' wrong in that. I'm workin' for wages and I do what I'm told to. Any complaint you got, you go take it up with Bronc Tomlin."

Webb sat rigid in the saddle, leaning forward on

stiffened arms, his hands on the horn. He glared in helpless anger. Finally he jerked his head abruptly. "Go on, then. Get out of here!"

Quince Pyburn protested, "Webb, you lettin' him go?"

"Have to. We can't show that there's been a law broken."

"We know they figured on it."

"It's not what we know to our own satisfaction that counts; it's what we can convince a jury of."

"It's a hell of a note, that's all I can say."

"Quince, the law's written so that the guilty ones slip through sometimes. But it's got to be that way to protect the innocent. If we go stretchin' it to get at those we know are guilty, it can someday backfire against those who are innocent. Better to let a dozen badmen get away than to hang one man who didn't deserve it."

He reined his horse around and headed him toward Dry Fork.

A vague prescience came to him like a cold hand across his throat long before the posse got back to town. For no solid reason, a terrible feeling grew in him that something had gone badly wrong. When he reined off the trail and into the dusty street, he knew. He could see it in the silent faces that stared at him and his posse.

The word of their arrival preceded them up the street. Ellie Donovan stepped out onto the porch of her restaurant. As the riders neared, she walked into the street and stood waiting for Webb.

Webb swung stiffly out of the saddle. He looked down into her anxious eyes. "What is it, Ellie? What's happened?"

"Trouble, Webb. Some of it's already over with, and some is waiting for you. The bank was robbed late yesterday afternoon."

Stunned, Webb let his lips move in an oath that didn't come out loud. He glanced down at her again, hating what he had to ask her.

"Clabe?"

"They said it was."

Webb clenched his fists futilely. How could he have figured wrong? It didn't make sense.

"Anybody hurt?" he asked.

She shook her head. "They fired bullets into Judge Upshaw's house but didn't hit him. He came out later with lint all over him. He'd been under the bed."

"You didn't see Clabe yourself? He didn't even ride by your place?"

She said, "No."

Clabe had changed a lot, Webb thought. Strange the man would ride into the town where his wife lived—a wife like Ellie—and not even try to see her. *In his place*, he told himself, *I'd even have taken her with me, whether she wanted to go or not.*

He said, "Thanks, Ellie. I better get on down to the bank."

She looked as if she had something else to say but was afraid to bring it out. Finally: "Webb, there's something else . . . something I can't tell you. Don't you believe it. Don't let yourself believe it."

She turned quickly away. He called, "Ellie . . ." She

didn't stop. She entered the small restaurant without looking back at him.

Now that cold feeling lay like a chunk of lead in the pit of his stomach. A little sick with dread, he swung back into the saddle and moved on toward the bank. In front of it, waiting for him, stood Judge Upshaw, banker William Freeman, and half a dozen others, all prominent in business or politics. All were gravely silent except the judge. Upshaw said caustically, "Well, sheriff, you finally got here. Almost a day late."

Webb wished he had a good answer, but he didn't; so he kept his mouth shut and tried to hold down the resentment that flared in him against the judge.

Banker Freeman gazed at Webb with no evident ill will. Almost, there was sorrow in his eyes. "Some of us got up a posse of sorts, Webb, but we didn't do much good. The best men in town were with you."

Webb said regretfully, "I did what looked like the best thing at the time. How bad was the damage?"

"Not as bad as it could've been. They hit late in the afternoon. They rode into town firing their guns to scare people off of the streets and out of the way, the way they say Jesse James used to do it. I knew what was coming. I had half a minute to grab up most of the money and shove it away in some desk drawers. I told them they had come too late—that I'd just sent a shipment of money to the big bank in Rio Escondido. They believed me. They took what they could find and left with it. Twenty-five hundred—maybe three thousand dollars."

Webb asked, "It *was* Clabe Donovan?"

Freeman nodded. "They wore masks, Webb, all of them. But the leader of the bunch had all the old

Donovan trademarks—the build, the voice, the black sombrero. It was a little eerie, like seeing a ghost."

"An awfully live ghost," Webb gritted. "They got across the Rio Grande, I expect."

Freeman said, "They were headed in that direction. We trailed them a while, but they fired on us, and we knew we weren't the kind of posse that could stop them. No use getting somebody killed. We gave up and came back."

"You did the right thing," Webb said. "I wish I had been here."

Freeman frowned darkly. "Webb, in a way you'd best be glad you weren't."

"What do you mean?"

Freeman had trouble framing the words for a reply.

Judge Upshaw said, "Where's that brother of yours, sheriff?"

"I don't know."

Upshaw snorted, "You don't know, but *we* know."

Flame came in Webb's cheeks. "Stop talkin' in circles, judge. What's this about Sandy?"

The banker cut Upshaw off with a sharp look. "Let me handle it, judge. You've got about as much tact as a black Mexican bull." He turned back to Webb, his face heavy with regret. "Four of them came into the bank—Donovan and three more. One stayed at the front door, and the last one held the horses. They had just gotten the money and were fixing to go when the mask slipped on one outlaw's face. I got a good look. So did Jake Scully, who happened to be in here at the time. It was Augie Brock, the kid who always pals around with your brother Sandy."

Webb felt the rest coming. "Sandy and Augie haven't been together in a good while."

"Can you say for sure, Webb? You haven't seen Sandy lately." Freeman's chin dropped and he added slowly, "One of the other outlaws stayed right by Augie during the holdup. He wore a mask and didn't say a word, but I could tell he was young, about the same age as Augie. About the same age as Sandy too, Webb. Same age, same height, same build. Jake and I compared notes after the ruckus. Neither one of us could get on a witness stand and swear to it, but we agreed that other boy could have been Sandy!"

Webb swayed.

The banker said, "I'm sorry, Webb. I can only tell you what I saw."

"But you didn't see Sandy. You couldn't have!"

Freeman said evenly, "He's always been a wild sort of a boy. Even you will admit that."

"Wild, sure, but not an outlaw. You know he's not an outlaw!"

Freeman looked down. "I'd be pleased to find out I was wrong, Webb. I'm sorry."

He turned with slumped shoulders and walked back into the bank.

Webb took a deep breath, but there was nothing to say.

Judge Upshaw said, "One more thing you ought to know, sheriff. I've sent for the Rangers. We've got to bring this thing to an end."

He turned and walked away, leaving Webb to stand alone.

8

Webb saw little to be gained in taking a posse out on Donovan's trail, or even in following it himself. Donovan had surely gone across the river hours ago. Moreover, Webb's possemen were already tired from their fruitless mission.

Webb was still puzzled over that mission. It seemed unlikely the outlaw had gone to all that trouble just in hope he could lead the sheriff astray. If Johnny Willet hadn't elected to follow the Bronc Tomlin horses, Webb wouldn't have been out of Dry Fork when the raiders hit the bank. Any number of things could have gone wrong if this had been an actual plan of Donovan's. Webb felt sure the man had really intended to use those horses in a ride to Rio Escondido. Somehow at the last minute he had switched his plans.

Why? That question kept nagging Webb as he slumped exhausted in his chair at the office and stared absently at a crack in the wall.

Preying on his mind even more was the question of Sandy. That was something else that didn't make sense.

Granted that Sandy had always been hard to handle, more prone than most to take the bit in his teeth and run with it. Granted that it was in his nature to be a rebel. He still wasn't an outlaw, not a thief, not a robber of banks. Webb conceded that he hadn't understood his brother. Still, he thought he knew him this well. He thought he had pounded at least that much of his own and his parents' ideas of right and wrong into the boy's head.

Webb hadn't realized how weary he was, having ridden so far, having only dozed occasionally through last night. Sitting still, he dropped off to sleep in the chair. He didn't awaken until he felt someone's hand lightly touch his shoulder. Startled, he jerked himself erect, blinking. He was surprised to find that night had come. The office was dark. Outside, lamps glowed in the buildings up and down the street.

"Didn't mean to drop off to sleep," Webb said, still a little loggy. "Can't see you in the dark. Who is it?"

"It's me, Quince." Quince Pyburn struck a match and held it. Webb reached to his desk and removed the glass chimney from a lamp. He held the lamp out for Quince to light. He trimmed the burning wick to suit him and set the chimney back in place. Then he rubbed his eyes.

"I feel like a fool, Quince, goin' off to sleep like this when I ought to be out doin' somethin' about Donovan. Only, what could I do?"

Quince pulled up a rawhide chair. "Nothin'. You'd just as well catch up on your rest. At least *that* will do you some good."

Webb stared somberly at the dancing shadows cast on the wall by the flickering lamp. "You've heard what they said about Sandy?"

Quince frowned, taking a long time before he came up with an answer. When he did, it was straight and honest. "I've heard. I'm not sayin' it was him. I *am* sayin' it *could be*. He's always been a little on the salty side, Webb. He may have looked like you, but he never did think the same way."

"He wasn't *that* different, Quince."

"Remember, he left here mad, wantin' to show you he was his own man. Boy with that kind of attitude is liable to make a mistake just out of orneriness."

Webb blinked his burning eyes and kept his gaze away from Quince. Quince paused a long time, then added, "Keep on hopin' it wasn't him, Webb. But be ready to take it in case it was." He placed his hand on Webb's shoulder. That's more or less the reason I came over here. Thought you ought to know the talk that's been goin' on up the street."

"Talk?"

"Well, a little. Most of it's comin' from one man, and I don't have to tell you his name. His initials are Judge Upshaw."

Webb swore. "That fathead! What's he been sayin'?"

Quince shrugged. "Without me havin' to tell you, I think you can pretty well guess what he's been sayin' about Sandy. Johnny Willet and me, we went into Jake Scully's place while ago for a drink. Kind of felt like we needed one. The judge was there talkin'—he's always talkin', seems like. Talkin' about Sandy some, sayin' things had come to a pretty pass when the sheriff's own brother would go to the bad like that. Said a man who would let a brother grow up and take to the back trails didn't deserve no badge.

"Well, mostly it was like that for a while. Didn't seem like the boys was payin' him much mind anyway, so we just sat and kept our mouths shut. Then he commenced to talk about Ellie Donovan."

Webb straightened in anger. "That foul-mouthed . . ."

Quince held up his hand. "Now, just wait a minute before you jump out there and make a racket. Let me tell you the rest of it." Webb sat down, his face burning. Quince said, "He pointed out that Ellie is Clabe Donovan's wife. Said all these years we thought she was a widow, he would bet she knew different. He would bet she'd been sittin' here spyin' on us, waitin' to tell him when the time was right for him to come back. Even stringin' the sheriff along, pullin' the wool over his eyes, which wasn't hard to do. Man like Webb Matlock could be easy swayed by a fetchin' woman, the judge said."

Webb stood up so fast that the chair fell back against the wall. He reached for his hat. Quince Pyburn caught Webb's arm. "Now, hold on. Johnny and me, we took care of the judge. When he said what he did about Ellie, we decided he'd gone as far as any right-thinkin' man could allow. You remember them wooden pegs Jake Scully has driven into his walls for people to hang their hats and coats on? Well, me and Johnny, we picked the judge up and hung him on a peg by his collar. We told Jake Scully if he lifted the judge down we would put *him* there in his place. Jake just grinned and said he never bothered anything his customers hung up."

Webb said grimly, "I wish *I* had been there . . ."

"Better that you weren't. A man belittles himself to get mixed up in a barroom argument thataway. You might've caused a lot of smoke and made some folks begin to think maybe the judge had a point. Way it was, everybody got a big laugh out of it—everybody but the judge."

Webb stood and fumed and flexed his hands. But finally the first flush of anger passed, and he could see Quince was talking sense to him. "I thank you, Quince. You did right. But I reckon I still better do some talkin' to the judge."

Quince looked at him questioningly, and Webb shook his head. "No smoke, Quince. Just a little talk."

"Promise?"

"I promise."

He was still weary, and his steps were short as he worked his way down the lamp-lighted street, pausing to glance inside each saloon. When he came to Jake Scully's, he stopped and peered over the swinging doors, looking first at the row of pegs. Somebody had taken the judge down from the wall. Jake, wiping the bar, spotted Webb standing outside. Sensing Webb's mission, he slowly shook his head and pointed on down the street. Webb gave him a short wave of his hand and went on.

Jake's was the last bar. The judge must have gone home. Webb walked across to Upshaw's house. At first he thought the place was dark. Then he could make out a faint glow of light at the bottom of the door. Webb remembered someone telling him that the judge had nailed blankets over the windows after the first Donovan scare.

Must have been insufferably hot in that house with the windows covered and the doors closed, Webb reflected. Summer wasn't this country's most comfortable season even with the windows open. But the judge was more interested in preservation than in comfort.

Webb knocked briskly on the front door. He heard a sudden noise, a chair sliding back across the floor. He had probably frightened the judge half out of his wits. "Judge," Webb called, "open up."

He hadn't tested the doorknob, but he was sure without doing so that the door was firmly locked. It was probably also barred from the inside.

A quavering voice asked, "Who is it? Who's out yonder?"

"Webb Matlock."

There was a moment of silence. Then: "What do you want with me, sheriff?"

"Just want to talk a little, is all."

"Go away. Go away."

"I'm not goin' to hurt you, judge. I just think it's time we did a little talkin', you and me. I'm goin' to do it even if I have to break that door down."

Another moment of indecisive quiet, then footsteps sounded on the floor. Webb heard the clink of a key in the lock and the sliding of a bar from its place. "Come on in, then," Upshaw said.

Webb pushed the door open. The judge stood back out of reach, leaning with his left hand on a table while his shaking right hand gripped a pistol. It was pointed vaguely in Webb's direction. "Step inside and shut the door," the judge said. "Don't want anybody to be able to get a shot at me in here. Then you just stop where you are. Don't you come one step closer to me."

Webb glanced around him, almost sickening at the hot, foul air, the closeness of a room shut up for days in the stifling heat of summer. He caught the strong smell of whisky. Webb could see a bottle and a half-empty glass on the table, near Upshaw's hand. He knew then where the judge got what little courage it took for him to stand and hold the pistol.

Webb said, "You can put that cannon away. I don't aim to dirty my hands."

Warily the judge lowered the pistol. He held onto it a moment before he finally laid it on the table. He picked up the glass and swallowed in one gulp the whisky that remained in it. Then he sank into his chair. The man was trembling. In the flickering lamplight Webb could see the dark hollows beneath the judge's eyes, the sallow color of his cheeks. Upshaw hadn't slept much lately. Mostly he had kept himself locked in this fetid room, eating too little, drinking too much, letting his mind run riot with all manner of dark fears.

Webb stared, and slowly most of the things he had intended to say lost their importance. He could almost feel sorry for this wretched little man who slacked here in fearful misery.

"Judge, I came to scorch your hide for the things you've said about Sandy, and about Ellie Donovan. I came to tell you that if you said them again, I'd make you wish you was dead. But you *are* dead. You're a dead man on your feet, livin' in your own private hell. I couldn't make it any worse than this; I won't even try."

He turned his back on the judge and walked out the door.

Weary though he was, he couldn't sleep now. That unintentional nap broken up by Quince seemed to have taken the edge off. He lay tossing on his cot, trying to keep his eyes closed, knowing how bone-weary he was and how badly he needed rest. But through the night in a nightmarish half-sleep he kept seeing the rebellious face of Sandy Matlock. He could imagine Sandy riding beside Clabe Donovan, proud and straight in the saddle, taking the outlaw trail that once had come so near claiming Webb himself.

Webb rejected the picture. Once he heard himself cry out, "No!" He sat up on the edge of the cot and rubbed his face. He rummaged around in a bottom drawer of the desk for a bottle he had taken from a drunk and had forgotten to return later when the man was sober. He drank from it, shuddering at its bite but hoping it would drive away the image. It didn't. The picture was still there—Sandy and Donovan, side by side.

It didn't fit. It couldn't be . . . mustn't be! Sandy wasn't like that!

Webb finally dropped into a fitful sleep, awakening before sunup. He had to find out about Sandy, one

way or the other. He went to Quince's livery stable.
Quince was still sleeping soundly, snoring a little. The
long ride had taken a lot out of Webb's old friend.
Webb moved quietly to keep from waking him. He
caught up a horse he sometimes borrowed and threw
a saddle on him. Quince would know, when he saw
Webb's saddle gone, that Webb had taken the animal.
Before most of the town ever began to stir, Webb was
on his way out toward Bronc Tomlin's Rafter T.

He knew he ought to have taken someone with
him—Johnny Willet, perhaps, or even Quince. But this
was a thing Webb had to do for himself. Sandy was *his*
brother.

Hunger caught up with him, for he hadn't been eating much the last couple of days. As he rode, he ate
from a can of sardines he had brought along, and drank
from a can of tomatoes. When finally he reached the
Rafter T headquarters, he didn't stop for a look around.
He rode boldly up to the house. He shouted, "Bronc!
Bronc Tomlin!"

He heard a movement and looked around to see a
cowboy step up onto the little porch from somewhere
around at one side of the house. It was the man named
Clinch, the one Webb had surveyed so long from the
hilltop near the cottonwood spring. Clinch still hadn't
shaved. He slouched across to stop directly in front of
Webb. "Bronc ain't here. Too bad."

"I've come to see him. Where's he at?"

"Gone off gatherin' horses. Won't be back for quite
a while. You come again some other time."

Webb swung slowly down from the saddle. His

hand close to his gun, he said firmly, "I reckon I'll go look for myself."

The cowboy stiffened. "Bronc give me orders to watch things. Ain't nobody goin' into that house without he says so."

"You better just step to one side, Clinch. I'm huntin' Bronc Tomlin, and I won't leave here till I've had a talk with him. You reach for that pistol and I'll have to use mine."

Webb dropped his reins and started toward the porch. The cowboy watched him indecisively, retreating a step. Just before Webb reached him, Clinch suddenly decided to act. He crouched and rushed. Webb stepped to one side, bringing up his pistol as he moved. He swung it and struck the barrel across the back of the cowboy's head. The felt hat cushioned the blow, but the man sprawled out flat on the ground, dazed. Webb reached down and took the pistol out of the cowboy's holster.

"Just to prevent temptation," he said. "Now I'm goin' in. I'd be much obliged if you wouldn't cause me no more trouble."

Half expecting Tomlin's bachelor house to smell as badly as the judge's did, he was a little surprised to find it well-aired and even to have a vague wisp of perfume about. He remembered then the saloon girl Bronc Tomlin had brought out from Rio Escondido. She was probably still here.

A closed door opened cautiously, and a frightened face looked out, a feminine face surrounded by long red hair that had missed a brushing.

Webb removed his hat. It was an old habit of his in the presence of women, and the fact that this was a saloon girl made no difference. "I'm lookin' for Bronc Tomlin," he said. "You got him in that room yonder?"

She shook her head, squinting for a better look at him. She must have seen Webb's badge, finally. The door opened wider, and she stepped into the front room. "You're a lawman? A Ranger or somethin'?"

"Sheriff."

She sighed in relief and moved toward him. She was not much over twenty, and she still had a pretty face. That face held a deep fear. "I didn't know if you'd find out, sheriff, but I'm sure glad you came. I want you to take me out of here."

"If I'd find out what?"

"Sheriff, he's not goin' to let me leave this place alive. I bribed a horse-breaker to take a note to town for me. Didn't you get it?"

Webb shook his head. "I didn't. Likely he just took your money and threw the note away."

"Money?" she said. Then she shrugged. "It doesn't matter, now that you're here. Please, just get me away from this godawful place."

Webb frowned. Maybe she knew a lot about what had happened—so much that Bronc Tomlin couldn't afford to let her get out of his hands. For a long time Webb had known to his own satisfaction that Tomlin was implicated with various border jumpers. He had never had enough proof to take action. Maybe this girl was what he needed to wrap Tomlin up tight.

"All right, Miss . . ."

"Smith. They just call me Blossom."

"Blossom, you get your things together. I'll take you to town."

She paused to look out the window worriedly. "I hope you're not by yourself."

"I am."

Some of the fear came back into her eyes. "Bronc Tomlin won't let us get away from here that easy. Not when you're just by yourself."

"I can handle Bronc Tomlin."

A voice spoke behind him. "Don't be making no bets, sheriff!"

Webb hadn't heard Tomlin ease up onto the porch. Now the man stood in the doorway, a gun in his hand. It wasn't pointed directly at Webb, but it wouldn't take Bronc the blinking of an eye to bring it up into line. The cowboy Webb had pistol-whipped stood behind Tomlin, peering over the horseman's shoulder. A thin trickle of blood had dried on the side of Clinch's face.

Tomlin said, "I got lots of patience, Matlock, but I don't like a man to abuse my hospitality. Clinch here told you I was gone. That ought to've been enough to satisfy you."

"But you weren't gone, Bronc. Not very far."

"If I'd of felt like visitin' with you, sheriff, I'd have come when I first saw you. I'm busy. Now you better just ride on back to town."

Webb watched Tomlin and weighed his chances of drawing his gun before Tomlin could shoot him. The chances weren't good.

"The young lady wants to go with me, Bronc. I'm takin' her."

Bronc shook his head. "I paid her to come out here awhile and keep house. She's goin' to stay."

Some housekeeper, Webb thought. "She'll go if she wants to."

Bronc's eyes narrowed. "She been tellin' you lies, sheriff? Man don't want to believe all these dancehall floozies tell him. They're great little liars, all of them, and this here gal is one of the best." He glared at the girl. "Now, you git ridin', sheriff. I don't want no trouble with you."

Webb Matlock stood his ground. He glanced at the trembling girl and saw desperation in her eyes. He said, "Bronc, I came here to find out somethin'. Did my brother Sandy ride with Clabe Donovan on that raid into Dry Fork?"

Blandly Tomlin said, "Raid? I don't know nothin' about no raid."

Grimly Webb replied, "You know plenty about that raid. I believe Sandy may have come back out here after I had that row with him. I want to know if you sent him ridin' with Donovan."

Tomlin shook his head. "Like I told you, I don't know nothin' about Donovan, or about no raid."

The girl cried, "That's a lie, sheriff. He knows all about it. Those outlaws were here, and they talked with him. He got a cut out of the money after it was all over."

Tomlin brought the gun up and trained it at Webb. But he cut a quick angry glance toward the girl. "Now you done it, Blossom. I never shot a woman in my life. I been tryin' hard to figure out some way to keep from havin' to shoot *you*. Now you've fixed it so I got to kill you *and* the sheriff."

Webb licked his dry lips. "Better think on it, Bronc. They won't hang you for bank robbery. They *will* hang you for murder."

"Not unless they find out. Now come on, sheriff, and slow. You too, Blossom. I don't want to do this in the house. Clinch, get the sheriff's gun."

The cowboy said shakily, "God, Bronc, you really aim to do it?"

"I got no choice. I didn't want to."

"But a woman . . ."

"A dancehall girl, that's all. There won't nobody even miss her."

"Bronc, runnin' horses for a bunch of border jumpers is one thing. Killin' is somethin' else, especially a woman. You just check me out of this."

Webb saw a glimmer of hope. "You're too late, cowboy," he said. "Even if you leave now, you're mixed up in it. The truth'll come out, and they'll be after you with a rope."

The cowboy pleaded, "Bronc, we can leave them afoot and ride for the border. We can be across the river and safe before he can get halfway to town."

Bronc said, "You can run because you got nothin' to lose. All you own is the clothes on your back. I got this ranch and all my horses. I'm not givin' that up for a long-nosed sheriff and a two-bit wheeligo girl."

The girl sank to her knees. She cried, "Please, Bronc, please. I promise you I won't ever say a word, not a word."

"Too late for promises now. You ought to've thought of that when you was makin' threats. Now come on, or I'll have to do it right here."

She surrendered completely to her terror. She grabbed hold of a table leg and clung to it hysterically. "No! No!"

Her screaming made Webb's hair feel as if it were going to stand. It seemed to unnerve Bronc, too. This wasn't making a bad situation any better to him. Basically the man was not a killer, Webb knew. But in this case he had been forced into it against his will. For a second Bronc turned toward the girl, distracted. "Blossom . . ."

In that instant Webb took a wild chance. He dived headlong across the floor toward Bronc, grabbing at his gun. In reflex Tomlin whirled and pulled off a quick shot that splintered the floor almost where Webb had landed. Webb brought his pistol up and fired point blank just as Tomlin's hand tightened again. The slug hurled Bronc back against the wall. Bronc's fingers stiffened as he tried desperately to hold onto the gun. The pistol slipped free and clattered to the floor. Bronc slumped and lay gasping. The fabric smouldered where the close-fired bullet had burned through his shirt, just above the heart.

Webb rolled over onto his knees, smoking gun still in his hand. He trained it on the cowboy. "How about you, Clinch? You through?"

Clinch stared in shock, his hands shoulder high. "I didn't even start."

Webb said, "I ought to take you in, but I expect I'll have enough to worry about. You saddle up and ride out of here. Don't ever let me see your face in my county again."

Clinch nodded and started to back away. Then he paused. "Bronc owed me some wages."

"Take a good horse. That ought to even it up."

The cowboy left the porch in a strong trot.

Tomlin's shirt still smouldered. Webb touched it with his hand to put out the fire and found that Tomlin still lived. But he wouldn't for long.

"Bronc," Webb said quickly, "tell me now, before it's too late. Was Sandy with Donovan?"

Bronc coughed. He tried once to speak but couldn't. He took a short, painful breath.

Webb said, "Tell me, Bronc! Tell me!"

Bronc whispered, "Go to hell!" and he was dead.

From outside, Webb could hear a commotion. Through the open door he saw the handful of cowboys and Bronc riders who worked for Bronc. They were gathering in front of the porch. Clinch wasn't among them. He was probably already picking his horse and getting ready to ride. Webb stepped to the door and surveyed the group, looking for any threat. He saw none, but he held the pistol in his hand anyway.

"Boys," he said, "Bronc Tomlin is dead. I'll tell you what I told Clinch: saddle up and ride out. Don't ever come back or you'll wind up in jail. And don't ride south to Donovan, either. His day is about done."

Slowly the stunned men pulled away from the house and headed toward the bunkhouse and the barn. In an hour or less, they would all be gone.

Webb had almost forgotten the girl. He turned to find her and saw that she had pulled herself to a chair at the table. She sat slumped over, her face buried in her arms. Her shoulders heaved. He could hear her quiet sobbing.

Sympathy moving in him, he touched her arm. Right now it didn't matter who she was or what she had been. She was simply a helpless young girl who had just gone through the most terrifying experience of her life.

"It's all over with," he said gently. "You'll live to be ninety."

Regaining control of herself, she began trying to wipe the tears away with a handkerchief. Webb could see she was making a conscious effort not to look toward the still body of Bronc Tomlin.

"Thank you, sheriff. I'll tell you anything you want to know."

"With Bronc dead, a lot of what I was goin' to ask you won't matter now. What did he mean when he said you were makin' threats to him?"

"They sent a man with Bronc's share of the money. I told Bronc I wanted part of it for keepin' my mouth shut. That's how I made my mistake, gettin' greedy. I put him in a spot where he almost had to kill me." She pointed to a chest at the far side of the room. "That's where he put the money, sheriff. You can take it back to that bank."

Webb said, "Did you see Donovan?"

"No, he never did come by here himself, just sent messages. Bronc looked over the Rio Escondido bank for him. They even went so far as to set up a relay of horses for Donovan to use on his way back after robbin' the bank. But one of Bronc's boys was in Dry

Fork when you and your posse pulled out. He headed Donovan off. Donovan decided not to go back to Mexico empty handed. With you and the town's best fightin' men gone anyway, he decided to take the Dry Fork bank instead."

Webb nodded. He had figured it had been something like that. He never had believed Donovan would go to all that trouble just to set up a ruse. Dry Fork had been a second choice, then, half a loaf taken instead of none.

The girl touched the handkerchief to her eyes. "You goin' to put me in jail, sheriff?"

He shook his head. "I don't see where it would help anybody. You did a wrong thing, but you came awful close to dyin' for it, and I don't expect you'll ever forget that. I'll see if I can rustle up a buckboard or somethin' to get you back to Dry Fork. Then, if you'll tell me all you know about Donovan, you'll be free to go wherever you want to."

Her chin stiffened. "I want to go home, sheriff. Back to my folks."

That sounded fine to him. "You sure?"

"I don't know why I ever left them. Stupid, I guess. It hasn't been an easy life, sheriff. I've done things and seen things . . ." She broke off a moment. "I'll live a clean life from now on, I promise you. I don't ever want to see another saloon."

Webb said, "That's fine, Blossom, sure fine. Now, just one more thing. You *did* see a few of Donovan's men. Was one of them young, about twenty-one, a good-lookin' kid with sandy-colored hair? They might've called him Sandy."

She thought hard, then slowly shook her head. "There were several young ones. A couple of them might have fit that description. I never did hear any names. Would you happen to have a picture?"

Disappointed, he said, "No, he never did go anywhere to have one made. We never were much for travelin'."

"Was he a partner of yours or somethin'?"

Webb said bleakly, "My brother!"

9

Webb took Blossom Smith to Dry Fork in Bronc Tomlin's buckboard. She studiously avoided looking at Bronc's body, blanket-wrapped in the back of the buckboard. The close brush with death had sobered her. Webb hoped she would stay sobered and live up to her vow to make a clean start.

Darkness came before they reached town. Webb was thankful for that. It should save him from having to make a lot of explanations, both about the girl and about Bronc Tomlin. He pulled up at the hotel and helped Blossom step down. The sleepy-eyed clerk waked up as he saw Blossom enter the small lobby. He looked her over from head to foot with obvious appreciation. He turned the register around to see what name she had signed. Taking a key from a hook, he spoke to Webb rather than to the girl.

"I'm givin' her room sixteen, sheriff. That's just down the hall."

Flushing a little, Webb said, "Tell her, not me."

The clerk shrugged, reappraising the situation. "Just thought maybe you'd want to know." He glanced at the girl. "Go ahead, miss. I'll bring your bags." The girl started down the short hall. As the clerk stooped to pick up the bags, Webb said, "Clarence, she tells me she wants to go clean. Don't you let anybody bother her."

He took the buckboard around to the back of the Hanks Mercantile and Hardware. Besides being the father of Sandy's girl friend, Birdie, Ashby Hanks was the town undertaker, such as there was. Selling hardware, it was only natural that he stock caskets. And stocking caskets, it was equally natural that he lay out the dead and prepare them for burial. One occupation seemed to fit in handily with the others. Webb knocked on the door of Hanks' adobe house. Birdie answered. Her eyes were red and swollen from crying.

"Hello, Webb," she said tightly.

He wished he could think of something to say to the sorrowing girl. He knew the anguish Birdie must be going through, defending Sandy when the town was condemning him. But what could a man say?

"I came to see your father, Birdie."

She turned half around and called, "Dad!" Then to Webb, "Any news about Sandy?"

He lowered his chin. "None. I'm sorry, Birdie."

"He didn't do it, Webb," she said fiercely. "One day they'll all find out they were wrong." He saw a stubborn faith burning in the girl's eyes and wished he had it himself.

"I'm glad you believe in him, Birdie," he said.

Hanks had been relaxing in his sock feet. He came to the door, his shoes still untied. Webb said, "I'm afraid I got a customer for you, Ashby."

"Kind of late, sheriff, but I'm always pleased to wait on a customer."

Webb shook his head. "Not one like this. He won't ever be back." He turned and walked to the buckboard. Webb lifted a corner of the blanket so Hanks could see Bronc Tomlin's face.

Hanks swallowed and asked, "How?"

Webb told him briefly what had happened. They carried Bronc into a small room at the back of Hanks' store, a room kept for just that purpose. They placed the body on a board. Hanks stepped back and gazed at it pensively. "Can't say I ever liked Bronc Tomlin much, but on the other hand it's hard to hold much reproach for a man when you see him like this. Makes you feel a little sad, somehow, no matter who he was or what he did."

Hanks began to roll up his sleeves. "Second time today I've had to do this job, Webb. Reckon you left town too early to know."

Surprised, Webb asked quickly, "Who died?"

"Judge Upshaw. Hanged himself, the judge did. Got so afraid Donovan was going to kill him that he just went and did it himself. Dutchman went over this morning to take the judge his breakfast. Found him hanging there. Empty whisky bottle on the floor. Judge must have drunk it all before he did the job."

Regret touched Webb, and he stared at the floor. This was a sorry way for any man to go. "I went over there and talked to him last night. I could tell he was in despair. It never occurred to me he would take that way out."

Hanks shrugged. "He wasn't the bravest man in the world, the judge."

Webb clenched his fist and stared out the open door into the darkness beyond the lamplight. "Donovan! Those he doesn't kill for himself, he reaches somehow else. One way or another, he gets them."

Webb wouldn't have expected to have any appetite after all that had happened today, but he found himself hungry. He hadn't eaten much lately. Out of long habit he walked down to Ellie Donovan's cafe without intending to. From the shadows he looked through the windows at Ellie. He stood and watched her and wished. Then he walked on to the Dutchman's for supper.

It was a dismal meal because the Dutchman insisted on giving him all the grim details of how he had come to find the judge. He didn't leave out a thing, so far as Webb could tell.

About the time Webb finished eating, Johnny Willet found him. Webb was thankful for the deputy's arrival because it shut the Dutchman up. Johnny drank a cup of black coffee while Webb finished his meal and smoked a cigarette. The two had little more than "Howdy" to say to each other. Finished, they walked out on the street together. Then Webb told him what had happened at Bronc Tomlin's.

Johnny asked, "Figured out what you're goin' to do next, Webb?"

Webb nodded somberly. "The only thing I *can* do,

Johnny. We can't just let this thing run on forever. I'm goin' down and get Donovan!"

"But he's across the river."

"I'll go across the river too."

Johnny chewed his lip. "You remember what happened the last time we swam the *rio?*"

"I remember. But that time we had a whole posse along, and we got stopped before our feet were even dry. A couple or three men, though, might slip across at night and not arouse too much suspicion."

"When do we leave, Webb?"

"We? I hadn't even asked you, Johnny."

"You don't have to ask. I'm goin'. You got anybody else in mind?"

Webb said, "One more, maybe. The big hitch is that we don't really have any clear idea where to look for Donovan. I thought I'd see Florentino Rodriguez. We might come up needin' a good tracker."

Johnny thoughtfully rubbed his chin. He glanced at Webb as if afraid Webb would take exception to the proposal Johnny was about to make. But Johnny made it anyway. "Maybe we wouldn't have to go there plumb blind. There's one person in town who might give us a good idea where to hunt."

Webb glanced sharply at Johnny. "You talkin' about Ellie?"

Johnny said defensively, "She *is* his wife. She knows the habits he used to have. Ain't likely he's changed them a lot. She could tell us, if she wanted to."

Webb said, "Johnny, I already asked her once. Like you said, she is his wife. It isn't fair to ask her again."

"Maybe this time she would see it different."

Adamant, Webb shook his head. "No, Johnny. I won't ask her."

He walked down into the south part of the settlement and made his way to Florentino's adobe. As he neared the door, he could hear Consuela Rodriguez softly singing a Mexican lullaby. He saw her in an old rocking chair, swaying forward and back, putting the new baby to sleep. Webb said quietly, "Florentino?"

Florentino appeared in the lamplighted doorway, squinting cautiously out into the darkness. He held a gun, but it was not in a position where he could readily have used it if Donovan had been waiting for him.

"It's just me," Webb said. "Can I talk to you?"

"Come in," Florentino said softly, looking toward the baby. Consuela found the child was asleep. She arose carefully and placed it in a handmade wooden cradle. Webb stepped over to look at the child. Its sleepy face was round and brown and totally at peace.

Webb said, "I'd give a lot to be able to sleep that way. No worries bearin' down—just lie there and sleep and let the world go by."

Florentino said wistfully in Spanish, "Only a child can do it. Once a person grows up and loses peace, it is gone forever."

Webb observed, "The baby is pretty. Favors you, Mrs. Rodriguez." Slow with English, Consuela had to have a translation from Florentino. Webb shifted to Spanish, "I'm afraid I didn't come to look at the baby,

Florentino. I came to tell you I'm going across the river after Donovan."

Florentino frowned. "You came to ask me to go with you?"

"I'm not asking you anything. I thought you would want to know when I went."

"But you would like to have me?"

Webb nodded. "We don't really know where to start looking for him. We may need a good tracker."

Consuela's eyes widened in anxiety. She warned, "Florentino, it is dangerous. Remember Aparicio."

Florentino cut her off with a wave of his hand. "I *am* remembering Aparicio." In Mexican families the woman was expected to accept the man's decisions without question or doubt. Often it didn't really turn out that way, but she was usually discreet enough not to argue with him in the presence of outsiders and cause him to lose stature.

Florentino stared down a while at his new son. "How many will go?"

"Just Johnny Willet and me. And you, if you decide to. It isn't many, but a big posse couldn't slip across that river. Three men might."

Memories kindled an anger that darkened Florentino's face. "I have much to settle with Donovan. This bad leg of mine, for one thing. Aparicio, for another. Except for Donovan, Aparicio would be alive and with us tonight." He looked at the baby. "Last time the child was due, and I would not go. Now my son is here, and there is nothing to hold me. Get a horse for me, Mister Webb. I will go with you."

Consuela Rodriguez voiced no protest. She turned

away, her head down, and silently made the sign of the cross.

Returning, Webb walked by Jake Scully's saloon. He heard a woman's laughter and stopped in surprise. Women were rarely seen in Jake's. The town's "good" women usually moved to the edge of the street or even crossed over when they passed. As for saloon girls, Jake never hired them. He had strong moral feelings, in his own fashion, and he kept his place strictly a man's establishment. A man went there to drink, gamble, or talk. If he wanted anything else, he went to some other place.

Peering inside, Webb swore softly. Perched on the edge of a table was Blossom Smith, her long dress pulled up just enough to show her trim ankles and high-laced shoes. Men had drawn chairs into a semicircle around her. Jake Scully, usually on the grumpy side, looked dangerously close to smiling as he eyed the girl and the rapidly-emptying glasses in the hands of the men. He saw Webb and gave him a nod, inviting him in.

Frowning, Webb pointed his chin at the girl. "What's she doin' here?"

"She's doublin' business, is what she's doin'. I got no idea who she is. She just come a-wanderin' in here while ago. Draws men like honey draws flies."

"You don't usually allow this kind of thing, Jake."

"She ain't done nothin' shady, if that's what you mean. Minute she does, I'll tell her to go."

Webb watched the girl. His first reaction was anger

and disappointment in her. But he could see the happy shine in her eyes, and he realized she was in her true element. She did this because she wanted to, and no amount of moralizing would change that. All her talk of reformation had gone for naught, a passing fancy born of fear and quickly forgotten.

Webb shrugged, a sense of frustration touching him, then fading. "You know, Jake, everybody has his own ways. You can't make one person be like somebody else. You try to change people, but you find they won't make themselves over into what you want them to be. You have to accept people the way they are."

Jake nodded, though he had only the foggiest notion what Webb was talking about.

Webb asked, "You goin' to let her stay here, Jake?"

"I'm not hirin' her. But as long as she keeps them turnin' their glasses up and don't take none of them out the back door, I don't reckon I'll run her off."

On his way back to the office, Webb noticed that Ellie Donovan's cafe was closed and dark. On impulse he stopped and looked toward her house. Maybe before he left he should tell her . . . But the house was dark, and he knew he shouldn't try to see her anyway. Getting so it was an ordeal for them both.

He stopped on the office porch to look back down the street and roll a cigarette. He stood there drawing thoughtfully upon the smoke, thinking ahead, wondering what would happen down yonder across the river.

He heard a movement inside the office and spun around, hand dropping instinctively to the gun at his hip. Dread gripped him, for ambush had become Donovan's way.

Ellie Donovan's voice came from the darkness of the room. "Webb, I came to talk to you."

"Ellie!" He swallowed, his heart pounding from the surprise.

She said, "I didn't intend to scare you."

"You didn't, exactly. It's just that here lately . . ." His hand flexed nervously, and he wiped cold sweat onto his pants leg. "I never expected to see you here, Ellie."

"I never expected to have to come here. But I'm told you're going after Clabe."

Webb peered toward her intently, wishing he could see her better in the darkness. "How did you hear that? I been keepin' it quiet."

"Johnny Willet came and told me. He said you wouldn't ask me to help you."

With a sudden impatience, Webb said, "No, I wouldn't, and he had no right to ask you either."

"He didn't ask me, Webb. He just said he thought I had a right to know what you were planning. And I think I do have such a right, Webb. Not only because of what Clabe used to mean to me, but because of what you have been to me, too."

"I wish you hadn't found out, Ellie. Knowin' won't help you any. It'll just cause you pain."

"There's pain either way."

He pulled on the cigarette, fist drawn tight. "It's been tough on you, Ellie. If I had my way . . ."

Abruptly she said, "I'm going with you, Webb!"

He dropped the cigarette. "Ellie . . ."

She didn't give him time to begin arguing. "Webb, you asked me once if I would tell you where you might be most likely to find Clabe. I said I couldn't do that to him because he was my husband. I still felt that much loyalty to him. Now I've changed my mind. People have died because of him, and even this town has begun to die a little. There is fear in the people here.

"He's done something to you too, Webb. You've changed since he came back. And there's that matter about Sandy. Some people have even hinted that you've held back on Clabe because of me, that you're in love with me and afraid that if you bring Clabe in you'll lose me. It's not fair to you to keep letting them point fingers. So I'm going with you, Webb."

"You can't, Ellie. No tellin' what we might run into."

"Without me you won't have any idea where to start."

"You could tell us. That would be enough."

"It's been too many years ago, Webb. I could find it myself, but I could never tell anybody else how to. The only way is for me to go." She placed her hand on his arm. "Please, Webb, I have to go."

Still doubtful, Webb took hold of her hand. "You know what's likely to happen if we find him. Are you prepared to be a witness to it?"

She leaned toward him, her face against his chest. "I know, Webb, but I've let it go too far already. It's time now to stop him, even if he is still my husband."

"And even though you still love him?"

For a minute she stood in silence, leaning against him. He reached up to touch her cheek and found it wet with tears. She whispered, "Even though I still love him!"

10

❧

Long before daylight they met in Quince Pyburn's livery barn and saddled their horses by lantern-light behind the closed doors. The fewer people who knew about this, the better. There would be that much less chance of word somehow getting to Clabe Donovan.

Quince finished lashing down a pack over a fifth horse which was to be led. Then he rechecked the side-saddle on Ellie's horse and complained because Webb wouldn't let him go.

Webb said, "Every extra man and horse we take cuts our chance of gettin' by."

"But just three men . . ."

"We don't aim to take on an army. We'll find out where Clabe is, sneak in and grab him, then run like hell."

"Supposin' he ain't keen on comin' along?"

Webb glanced at Ellie Donovan and refrained from making an answer. The answer was plain enough even unspoken.

Quince said, "You-all have a lot of guts to try this,

especially after what happened the other time. I only wish I could go with you. I still got a feelin' you'll be a-wishin' you had help." His gaze went back to Ellie, his eyes soft. "The most courageous one is you, Ellie. In your place, I couldn't do it."

Ellie dropped her chin and blinked quickly. Quince said, "It ain't too late. You could still back out."

She said, "Give me a boost up, will you, Quince?"

Gently he gave her a footlift to help her onto the saddle. Webb raised the bar that blocked the back door and led his horse outside. He opened the one remaining corral gate. In the east he could see the beginnings of daylight. Somewhere out behind Quince's haystack a rooster saw it, too, and proclaimed it with all the pride of his calling. Before long, people would be up and stirring. They arose early in a country town like this. Webb mounted and made a forward motion with his hand. Johnny Willet took the packhorse's lead rope from Quince. The horse was saddled, the pack tied down across the saddle. That would be for Clabe Donovan to ride . . . if they took him alive.

Eyes worried, Quince said, *"Buena suerte."*

"Thanks, Quince," Webb replied. "We'll need that luck."

They left Dry Fork, jog-trotting to put some distance behind them early. Later Webb slacked the pace because he knew the ride was going to be hard enough on Ellie even as it was. She hadn't been a-horseback much the last few years. They rode slowly because there was no need for haste, now that they were well clear of town. They would reach the river considerably before dark anyway, and they couldn't afford a daylight crossing. They would save the horses' strength for a time when it might be needed more.

Johnny Willet said, "Webb, mind if I make a suggestion?"

Webb hadn't said much to Johnny, for he had been angry with him for speaking to Ellie. Now the anger was gone. Webb was actually glad Ellie had been told, for it meant a better chance of finding Clabe Donovan.

"This isn't an army outfit, Johnny. Any suggestions are welcome."

"I've ridden up and down that river so many times lately that I know it pretty good. I know where there's a big gravel bar leadin' up on the Mexico side. Hoof tracks wouldn't show much if we crossed there. With a little luck, that bunch of Mexican horse cavalry wouldn't even see them."

"Sounds good to me," Webb said.

Late in the afternoon they came to a place where the land suddenly broke away before them into a chalky *guajilla* ridge. Beyond that, partially screened by a heavy stand of mesquite brush and catclaw, the surface of the river reflected the sun with a sparkling sheen that seemed to deny the ugly muddiness of it. Webb drew rein to keep from standing out against the skyline, where he might easily be spotted by anyone who happened to be across the river. He pulled back into the cover of the brush.

Johnny Willet said in satisfaction, "We hit it pretty good. That gravel bar ain't but a little ways upstream."

Florentino Rodriguez's eyes glittered with a grim resolve. He hadn't said much today. Now he asked evenly, "How far to where they shoot Aparicio?"

Johnny Willet looked westward. "Four or five miles. Pretty muddy on the Mexico side at that point. We'd leave tracks a foot deep."

Webb said, "It wouldn't help anything for you to see the place."

The Mexican shook his head. "It is not so important where Aparicio dies. It is important who kill him."

Webb turned his horse away from the river. "We'd best ease off a ways and find us a shady place to wait for night. We need to rest some anyway and cook supper before sundown so we can have the fire out by dark."

Not far from the river they found a few ancient, gnarled old liveoak trees growing along a near-dry creek that fed into the Rio. In the deep shade and the soft mat of rotted old leaves, they unsaddled and staked the horses at the ends of their ropes to graze. Ellie dug into the pack they had removed from the led horse. She began preparing supper.

Webb stood for a moment and stared at her. Ellie's face was dusty from the long ride, and dark lines beneath her eyes showed how tired she was. Probably hadn't slept last night, worrying about today and what was yet to come.

"Lie down and rest a while, Ellie," he said. "I'll take care of supper."

"Cooking is my job. I'll do it."

Probably wanted to keep busy, he thought. Couldn't say he blamed her. "I'll start a fire, then." He kindled a small blaze, took the coffee pot and fetched water from the creek. "Water's not the clearest I ever saw, but I reckon the coffee will cover up the mud."

They took their time eating supper and washing the utensils they had used. The fire had died down to embers; just enough to keep the coffee pot hot, and it was well hidden by the banks of the winding creek. Dusk came. This river country was at a lower altitude than Webb was used to at Dry Fork, and the daytime heat was oppressive. Now, with evening, the heat slowly gave way to a cool breeze drifting north from Mexico.

Ellie had spread a blanket on the soft cover of old leaves at the base of a liveoak tree so that she might lie down and rest. But she wasn't lying down. She sat with her knees drawn up under her chin, the long skirt spread out around her so that not even her feet were showing. She stared sadly into the darkness, immersed in thought, oblivious to everything around her.

Webb watched her a long time but left her alone until finally he saw her chin drop, her hands covering her face. He walked over to her.

"Ellie, you don't have to do it. Nobody would blame you if you decided to turn around now and go back to Dry Fork."

She looked up, but not at Webb. She kept staring off into the night. "I feel like some kind of a Judas. I'm betraying him. All the talk in the world won't change that."

"You haven't betrayed him. If you want to go home . . ."

"Want to? You know how much I want to. But I owe as much to the people of Dry Fork as I ever owed to Clabe. More, maybe. He has become a curse to the people who are my friends. Now, whichever way I go, I'm betraying somebody—either Clabe or my friends."

"You're not to blame, Ellie. There's no part of it that's your own doing."

"That doesn't make it any easier."

Webb touched her hand, then pulled back. His heart went out to her. But all he could do was hold his distance and look at the ground and endure the ache of denial.

"Whichever you decide, Ellie, I'll stand behind you all the way."

Her voice was unexpectedly firm. "I've already decided, Webb. I decided last night."

In the dark time before the rising of the moon they reined into the cool water and pointed their horses' heads toward the bar of gravel on the south side of the Rio. Webb rode close beside Ellie, ready to grab her if her horse had any trouble in the deep part of the river. They moved slowly, trying to make no more noise than they had to. There might not be a human being within miles on either side of the river. But again, the Mexican officer Armendariz and his patrol might be camped anywhere.

Halfway across, Ellie's horse began to flounder. The ground had dropped away from beneath his feet. Webb pulled in quickly and grabbed Ellie around the waist. She dropped the reins and threw both arms around his neck. The horse went under, splashing, but Webb pulled Ellie against him and held her tightly. His own horse never wavered. Soon Webb's dun found good footing and waded up onto the gravel bar. The river lay behind them, murmuring quietly. But for a long moment Webb continued to hold Ellie, and she held onto him. Not intending to, he kissed her, and her own arms seemed to tighten around him.

"Oh, Webb," she whispered, "Webb."

"It's all right now, Ellie," he said. "It's all right."

Gently he eased her to the ground. He swung off the horse and caught her hand again. "Scare you?"

She nodded, and he found she was shaking a little. "A bit, not bad. It's over now." She pulled her hand away and bowed her head. "Or maybe it's just started."

Johnny and Florentino brought back Ellie's horse. It was dancing around in eye-rolling panic, water running out of its mane and tail, dripping from its body. Florentino stepped down and began to pat the horse's neck, speaking soft Spanish in an effort to calm it down.

Webb said, "We better get off this bar and out of sight. Moon'll come up directly, and this gravel will shine."

They moved afoot into the cover of brush fifty yards from the river. It was the same brush one found on the Texas side, the same air. He heard the same birds singing. Hard to believe that short swim had put them into a different country. A different country, an alien land where he was no longer an officer of the law. Rather, he was here against the law. He reached down and unpinned the sheriff's badge from his shirt. He rubbed his fingers over it a moment, then shoved it into his pocket.

"Badge won't mean anything over here," he said,

more to himself than to anyone. "Might even make matters worse, if things go wrong."

The moon was beginning to rise. Looking back, the way the moonlight slanted across the gravel bar, Webb could see that the horses' hoofs had left pocks that showed patches of shadow. Johnny Willet saw them too. He broke a limb from a dead mesquite and walked back to the water's edge. He began raking over the gravel, smoothing out the pocks.

He was almost through when a Spanish voice cried, *"Quién es?"* Who is it? *"Qué pasa aquí?"* What's going on here?

The voice came from somewhere ahead, in the edge of the brush. Webb realized that Ellie had walked on in front, leading her horse. He drew his gun and sprinted toward her, his breath short from the sudden surprise. Ellie stood startled, her hand over her mouth. Webb put his arm around her and gently pushed her back. He had the pistol up and ready.

Then he saw they had walked into a small camp set up by an old Mexican man and a little boy. Dying embers glowed in what was left of a campfire, almost smothered now in ashes. The man stood uncertainly, his eyes large. The frightened little boy clung to the man's leg. A couple of fishing poles rested against a mesquite where a droop-eared burro was tied. Swallowing hard, Webb lowered the gun, then let it drop back into the holster.

The old man said in frightened Spanish, "We have nothing worth your stealing. We have no money."

Florentino Rodriguez made a gesture for the old man to sit down if he wished. "We do not come to harm you. We did not even know you were here. Do not be afraid of us."

The old man seemed slowly to decide Florentino was telling the truth. He began to relax. Finally he said, "We would offer you food, but we have none. The few fish we caught, we have already eaten."

Webb said, "We have had our supper. We are riding on." He frowned. "Have you seen anything of the Mexican cavalry patrol?"

A touch of fear came back into the old man's voice. "You are friends of Armendariz?"

Webb could tell that the *viejo* was not. "We are not friends. We want to be sure we do not come across him."

"*Bueno*. A while before dark he came with six of his men. They went down the river. They are probably camped at the home of the Gonzales family."

"How do you know?"

"This Gonzales, he has a young daughter. The lieutenant has a liking for girls."

"And Gonzales does not object?"

"No one can object to what Armendariz does. He has killed men who tried. There is hardly a village on the river that cannot show you the graves of men the lieutenant has killed. Even a woman or two."

Webb glanced at the clouding face of Florentino. He said, "There is at least one grave on the other side of the river, too."

Florentino said tightly, "It is time this Armendariz fills a grave of his own."

Sternly Webb reminded, "Florentino, we came after Clabe Donovan. That has got to be first."

Florentino clenched his fists. Regretfully he said, "I know."

"Providence has a way of takin' care of men like Armendariz."

Florentino turned toward his horse. "Providence is slow. Sometimes it is hard to wait."

Johnny Willet brought Ellie's horse. The animal had settled down now. Most of its fright was gone, although it might take a struggle to get the horse back into that river.

Ellie asked the old Mexican in broken Spanish, "Is this the right direction to the village of San Miguel, the one at the edge of the Rancho Villareal?"

The old man nodded. "*Si*, but a little more to the west. You have been there before?"

"Years ago."

"It has not changed much. It is no bigger, and a little the poorer."

Webb's eyebrows raised. "San Miguel?" He had never heard of it. But there were dozens of such tiny villages, virtually unknown except by those who lived there. "Is that where you think Clabe will be?"

She nodded gravely. "I think so. It is where we lived. We had a house at the edge of the village. It looked down on a pretty valley of little fields and green meadows where the cattle grazed. Clabe loved it there, Webb. He was not all bad then. No man could be all bad who could have so much love for a place. He used to say that someday when we had gotten all the money we needed we would go far away and try to find another place just like it. I would tell him we didn't need money, and we didn't need to go anywhere else. We had the perfect place right there, at the village of San Miguel. Times I thought he was about ready to agree with me, that he would quit the things he was doing. He did love that place. That is why now I think he would be there again."

"I guess the village has some wonderful memories for you, Ellie. It's a shame to have to go there now and spoil it."

She shook her head. "It was spoiled years ago. That was why I left. I realized he never would change. I knew someday he would ride out and not come back. Every time he did come back, I thanked God he was still alive, and yet I knew he had blood on his hands. I came to hate the village, the whole valley. I thought I even hated Clabe. You know how close hate and love can be. Finally I ran. It was all I could do, just as now this is the only thing I can do."

Webb placed his hand on her shoulder. "And we'd better be movin'. I want to get away from this river a few miles before we stop to rest." He gave her a foot-lift and helped her onto the sidesaddle. Her skirts were still wet from the crossing.

Florentino said to the old man, "*Por favor, amigo*, if anyone asks, you have not seen us."

The *viejo* shook his head. "We have seen nothing and heard nothing."

"*Bueno*. Good fishing."

"Go with God."

They were four or five miles south and west of the river when Webb took his pocketwatch and slanted it toward the moon to see the dial. "Well past midnight," he said. "I reckon we better rest."

"I am not tired," Ellie said.

"We got to think of the horses. We may be ridin' a right smart faster comin' back than we are goin' in."

In a dry grassy draw he found a spot where Ellie could spread her blanket and lie down in relative comfort. The three men moved away a short distance to afford her some privacy. Webb did not try to set up a guard shift. He thought it unlikely that anyone would ride up on them at this hour. Even if they did, he was a light sleeper. It didn't take much to bring him to his feet, wide awake.

He didn't really expect to sleep much, but several sleepless nights were catching up with him. He dropped off and didn't wake up until the rising sun caught him in the face. He sat up quickly, blinking in surprise. For a few seconds he didn't remember where he was.

The morning air was cool and fresh. The staked horses were beginning to move around a little, cropping the curing grass. Webb gathered some dry wood and kindled a fire. By the time he had filled the coffee pot out of his and Johnny's canteens, Johnny and Florentino were up and around. Breakfast wouldn't amount to much except a little fried bacon and some cold biscuits. But the coffee had a good smell. It brought Ellie up. She came with her blanket rolled under her arm. Her face was showing some burn from yesterday's sun, and dust still clung to it. But her hair was freshly brushed. Even out this way, a woman remained a woman, and Webb was glad for it.

They ate and rode on as the sun began rising and

building its heat in the cloudless east. With the passing hours they moved across a changing land, a thirsty land of mesquite and catclaw, chaparral and huisache, and prickly pear that stood hip high to a tall man, its spring blossoms long since burned away by the hot sun but still leaving a clinging remnant like black ashes.

Stopping on the crest of a hill, Webb made a sweeping motion with his hand. "Any of this look familiar to you, Ellie?"

She took her time. Finally she shook her head. "It's been a long time, Webb. Maybe a little farther on . . ."

About noon they came to a small creek, with a tumbled-down adobe house standing back a hundred feet from its sloping bank. In front of the house, their roots feeding from the soft mud of the creek, was a row of apple trees, alien to this dry land. The adobe hadn't been inhabited for some time, but it was obvious that this place was a favorite of travelers. A well-defined trail led to it and away again.

"I know this place," Ellie said suddenly. "At least, I think I do. A family lived here. Menchaca, I think their name was." They rode in so she could have a better look. The more she looked, the surer she became. "I passed by here when I was running from Clabe. These people fed me, I wonder why they left?"

Looking at the slope that climbed behind the house, Webb said, "I think I can see the reason." He rode up and looked at a mound and a cross. The paint was fading, and he could not decipher the date. But he could make out the words in Spanish:

Adolfa Menchaca, age 37. Murdered by Armendariz.

Webb's face twisted. "Armendariz. He's been busy."

Johnny Willet picked a few ripe apples and washed them in the creek. He carried one to Ellie. She looked at the cross and shook her head. "I don't know—I'd feel a little bad about it."

"These folks fed you the other time," Johnny pointed out. "I'll bet they'd want you to have some of their apples."

Ellie took one, rubbed it in her hands and bit into it. Her face lighted a little and she said, "Good." Then she began looking around again. A melancholy came over her. "They seemed like good people, happy people. Not the kind who would ever bother anybody."

Webb said, "It's usually the innocent who get hurt when a mad dog runs loose."

Ellie flinched. Webb realized how that must have sounded to her. "Ellie, I didn't go to hurt you."

She shook her head. "You didn't say anything that wasn't true. Let's leave this place."

The farther they rode, the more familiar the land became to her. Now she was retracing the tracks she had left years ago. She had some difficulty because the last time she saw it as she rode north, and it was natural that some of the landmarks appeared different when viewed from the opposite side.

At mid-afternoon Ellie drew up, her face tense. "Webb, I think when we cross the next hill we'll see it—the valley of San Miguel."

Webb considered the hill. "Not much brush cover up there. We better get off and walk as we get near the top. We won't stand as tall thataway."

They circled, moving around the sloping side of the hill rather than directly across the top of it. Webb watched Ellie with concern. She was dragging her feet wearily. She walked with her mouth open, breathing hard. For her sake, he hoped this search wouldn't take much longer. But even if it didn't, there would still be the ride out. Well, he philosophized, one did what had to be done. Before the mission was finished, she might prove as strong as the men were. Often a woman had more endurance than a man when stress demanded it. He thought Ellie Donovan was that kind of woman. She had endured much in recent years.

They moved down below the crest of the hill before they stopped. Ellie stared at the little valley which lay like an oasis in an irregular pattern along a winding creek. Her lips were tight.

"That's the one, Webb. That village is San Miguel!"

11

It was hardly a town. Even the smallest of Mexican villages was likely to boast a central *plaza* or square. This one didn't. San Miguel was really only a loose scattering of adobe houses, spaced out in an irregular manner along the creek which through countless centuries had built a fine-loam soil from the leavings of floodwaters sweeping down from the desert country around. Now this valley, small though it was, furnished sustenance for a number of families. It grazed their livestock and yielded small but fertile gardens which the people watered by means of small *acequias*, irrigation canals, zigzagging out from the creek.

Ellie pointed. Her voice was strained. "Yonder is our house, Clabe's and mine. Clabe bought it from the family which had built it. He could have just moved in and taken over, because these people aren't fighters. But he paid for it, Webb. He wasn't really a bad man, then."

The house was built a little higher off the creek than were most of the others. Webb thought it probably would give a good view over most of the valley.

That would have been one reason Clabe Donovan liked it so much. "A good place for a man who wanted to get himself lost," he observed aloud. "It's not a place a posse would be apt to come across by accident. They'd have to know where it was."

Johnny Willet said, "Not much of a place for a man who liked to have a good time, I'll bet. Don't look like there's even as much as a *cantina*."

Ellie said, "Clabe never did go for that sort of thing much. Some of his men did. There's a bigger village named Arroyo de Lopez about twenty miles from here. They used to go there and spend most of their time. Clabe seldom went there except to round them up."

Webb felt a prickling of excitement. "If he hasn't changed, then, he's likely to be down around that house right now. And most of his men could be over at that other town, Arroyo de Lopez."

Ellie nodded, her eyes downcast. "Could be."

The main problem as Webb saw it was that the adobe lay on the other side of the creek. To avoid the danger of being seen they had to ride far up the creek, cross over, circle way around and come in behind the place. To cross now in plain view would either flush the quarry or put him ready for a fight, depending upon how strong he might be.

Webb could see guilt and apprehension in Ellie's sad face. "Ellie," he said, "why don't you stay here? When it's all over, you can come on in."

She considered a moment. "I've come this far. I'll go the whole way."

"It may not be pleasant."

"It hasn't been, so far. I'm ready whenever you are."

It took them well over an hour to make the circle a-horseback. They stepped off their horses in a thicket a couple of hundred yards from the adobe. They looped their reins over branches. Turning away from Ellie in hopes she wouldn't notice, Webb drew his pistol and checked it. But he knew she had seen. Her shoulders were hunched in dread.

"Ellie," he said, "this time you've got to stay put. This is as far as you go. If Clabe's here . . ."

She nodded in resignation. "I won't argue with you. I'll stay here."

He turned to go. She said, "Webb . . ." He found her looking at him with tears in her eyes. "Webb, I just want you to know . . . I won't blame you for anything. But please, try not to kill him."

"I'll try," he promised.

He led the way, Johnny Willet hurrying to catch up with him, Florentino limping along behind, moving as fast as his stiff leg would allow him. Webb gripped his pistol. Johnny carried the short rifle from his saddle scabbard. Florentino, not particularly a good marksman, had a shotgun. If a man got close enough with one of those, he didn't have to be good.

They moved as near the house as they could without getting out of the mesquite and its covering foliage. Webb dropped to his stomach and studied the place. Johnny and Florentino knelt beside him.

"Somebody's been usin' the place," Webb observed. "See how the ground is packed? Horse tracks around it. I smell woodsmoke too. I expect somebody cooked dinner here."

They watched for a time but saw no sign of movement around the house. Down in the valley a Mexican worked a garden, and a small boy on a burro was driving a couple of cows.

Webb wished he could tell more about the place. It could be empty, or it could hold half a dozen of Clabe Donovan's outlaws. "We're about as close as we can get without steppin' out into the open. I say to shoot the works, make a dash for the house. It's liable to come as such a surprise to them that they can't get a shot at us till we're flat against the walls. Then they can't get out without comin' past us."

He glanced at the Mexican. "On second thought, Florentino, maybe you better stay here. That bad leg is goin' to slow you down—keep you in the open too long. You can cover us from here."

Florentino accepted Webb's logic. "This shotgun, it don't do much so far away."

Johnny traded with him, giving Florentino the rifle. Webb said, "Let's go."

They sprinted into the open. As he ran, Webb tried to watch the windows. With luck nobody would be looking.

The fifty yards hadn't appeared far before. Now that he was in it and running, it looked like a mile to the house. He wasn't used to running this way. The high heels didn't help. Still he saw no movement at the window. This was just too much luck . . . too much luck . . .

He made it to the wall and flattened against it, half expecting a shot to be fired even yet. Johnny reached the wall only a step behind him. They stood with backs against the rough, plaster-shedding adobe, breathing hard from the long run. Webb's heart beat heavily, and not altogether from the exercise. His mouth was dry.

He listened for movement, but these adobe houses with thick mud walls and dirt floors carried little sound.

They must have made it unseen, he figured. If they had been spotted, someone inside the house would have made a move by now. Webb motioned for Johnny to circle the house from the other side. They met at the front, still keeping themselves flat against the wall. They dared not speak. Webb hardly even dared breathe. Carefully he crept toward the door. He made sign talk to Johnny.

Inside. Me first, then you.

He took a deep breath, bracing himself. Then he leaped through the door. He saw a sudden movement near a corner of the room. Heart in his throat, he swung the gun around, finger tensed on the trigger.

He was prepared for anything but what he saw.

A young Mexican woman sat on a straight rawhide chair, rocking her body back and forth to put a baby to sleep. On a rough blanket spread upon the earthen floor lay a girl two or three years old, already asleep.

Webb heard Johnny vault into the room behind him. The woman had stared in terrified silence at Webb. Now, at sight of Johnny she screamed. The baby jerked in her arms and began to cry. The little girl rose up on the pallet, eyes big in fright. She saw the guns and began to wail.

"*Dónde está Donovan?*" Webb demanded. *Where is Donovan?*

The woman trembled, frightened too badly to speak.

She shrank back from the men, even after they holstered their guns to reassure her.

"We do not come to harm you," Webb told her in her own language. "Do not be afraid of us. We have come to find the man Donovan."

"There is no Donovan here," she managed. Then she broke down in fright and began to sob. Both of her children were crying too. It was something of a bedlam. Webb began backing toward the door, realizing he had upset a household for no valid reason. He glanced at Johnny and saw astonishment in the young cowboy's eyes.

"Looks like we just muddied the water," Webb said. "And the fish all gone."

He stepped outside and hailed Florentino. Webb stood in the open, his hands empty, to let the Mexican know the coast was clear. Florentino came in a run that was half hop, favoring the bad leg.

Florentino halted, breathing hard. "The place is empty?"

"Not quite. Listen."

Florentino's face twisted in confusion as he listened to the children's crying. "That is not Donovan."

Webb shook his head. "You can talk to the woman better than I can. See if you can find out what's happened here."

By the time they got the young woman calmed down, Ellie Donovan came in. She had decided for herself that there was no danger. She looked at the Mexican woman, who was scarcely more than a girl. Ellie's face warmed in recognition.

"María!"

The girl stared, and slowly she remembered Ellie. *"La Señora Donovan.* It has been so many years."

"Many years, María."

Before they had a chance to talk a young Mexican man rushed through the door, an ax in his hand as a weapon. He was looking for a fight until he saw Ellie and recognized her. He turned toward Webb and the other men, his eyes still hostile and demanding explanation. He held the ax where he could use it.

Without many details, Florentino explained the situation to him. He said they were looking for Clabe Donovan.

The young man, whose name was Pablo, shook his head.

"The Señor Donovan, he has not come here in many years. A while after the señora left, he left too, with all his men. Later we heard he was killed, in Texas. For years we heard nothing more. María and I, we married, and we needed a house. We thought no one would mind if we used this one."

Florentino said, "But Donovan is back."

Pablo nodded. "That is what we have heard, but he has not been to San Miguel. We hear he spends much of his time in Arroyo de Lopez. It is bigger, and a livelier place. *Cantinas,* gambling, women." He glanced regretfully at Ellie. "I am sorry, señora. I should not have said that."

Ellie's knowledge of Spanish was sketchy, but she understood that readily enough. She said, "He's changed. Like I told you, he never used to go there except when he had to. As for women . . ." Her lips drew tight. "Perhaps I should never have left him."

Webb said, "Strange he hasn't at least come back for a look at the place, if he loved it so much."

Ellie said, "Maybe he was bitter because I left him. Maybe this place has memories for him, like it has for me."

They stayed a while to rest. It didn't take long for the whole village to learn the Señora Donovan was back. It seemed the people all remembered her with affection. They came by twos and threes and half dozens to pay their respects, visit a while and go again. Ellie seemed to draw pleasure, now that she was here, in visiting with these old friends, recalling events so long forgotten or shoved aside in the dark corners of memory.

Pablo said, "We will move out of the house, señora. It is yours."

She shook her head. "No, keep it. I want you to have it. I would not have use for it, and I am pleased to know it is making a home for my friends."

Webb looked at his pocketwatch. He shook his head. "Gettin' late, Ellie. We better be on the move."

Florentino had stepped outdoors to look around. Now he rushed back, his face excited. "Mister Webb, something is happening down the creek. Looks like much excitement."

Stepping out the door, Webb saw a rising of dust, people running. A boy of eight or ten hurried toward the house, running as hard as he could.

"*Los soldados!*" he was shouting. "*Los soldados vienen!*" *The soldiers are coming!*

"Ellie," Webb shouted, "get out here quick! Run for the brush!"

The boy reached the house. Breathlessly he tried to

tell what was happening in the village. Lieutenant Armendariz had ridden in with six men. He was looking for some *gringos*, three men and a women. The people had told him nothing, so he ripped the shirt off an old man's back and was lashing him now. Armendariz, the boy said, did not stop lashing people until they gave him what he wanted . . . or until they died. And this man was old. He would not last long.

Webb's first instinct was to get their horses and ride. They could be making tracks toward Arroyo de Lopez while Armendariz was delayed here. He made half a dozen steps in the direction of the horses before he halted, his shoulders slumped.

"We can't run," he said dejectedly. "This isn't these people's fight. It isn't fair to dump it in their laps. Ellie, you do like I told you: run for the brush. Don't let him find you."

"And us?" Florentino asked excitedly. "We will get this Armendariz, no?"

Webb said, "We'll do whatever we have to. Back away if we can, or fight if it comes to that. Let's get our horses."

In a moment they were spurring into a lope down the trail worn by decades of hoof traffic and cart-wheels. They came around a pair of adobe houses and pulled up side by side.

An old man lay groveling in the dust, his shirt torn away, his back bleeding in streaks where the cruel lash had cut deep into naked flesh. Lieutenant Armendariz dropped the whip at sight of the three riders. They sat their horses in an even line some thirty feet from where Armendariz stood. In Webb's hand was the pistol, in Johnny's the rifle, in Florentino's the wicked shotgun. Armendariz stared in surprise. Then, slowly, a cruel grin crept across his dark face. He looked back over his shoulder where his six soldiers still sat on their poorly-fed horses. The men had held guns on the villagers who huddled fear-struck in front of the adobes. Now they swung the guns around to cover the Americans.

It was an impasse, a draw, for each side was ready to begin firing instantly. All that was needed was for someone to touch off the explosion.

The lieutenant spoke in Spanish, "Very effective, the whip. Usually it brings only information. This time it brings the *gringos*. If you will drop those guns, perhaps my men will not shoot you. Perhaps!"

Webb said, "We are as ready as they are. We can kill as many of you as you can kill of us."

The lieutenant's grin faded for only a moment, then came back, dry and mocking. "You are the same sheriff who tried to cross the river once before. Do you think I intend to let you get back again?"

"How did you find us so quickly?"

"This morning we stopped at a camp where an old man and a boy were fishing. We meant only to borrow a few fish. But we found horse tracks which led off a gravel bar. The old man did not wish to tell us anything at first. But the whip, it is good at persuasion."

Webb felt the rise of bitter anger. Florentino's jaw was set hard, his eyes a-glitter with hatred. He asked Webb, "Is this the man who killed Aparicio?"

Webb replied, "Yes."

Armendariz said, "Even with the guns in your hand, the advantage is mine. You are a man of conscience, *gringo*. Otherwise you would not have come to help one of so little value as this *viejo*, here in the dust. You can ride away from here if you choose. But if you do, I will take my vengeance on the people of this village. They have helped you."

He paused to watch the fury boil into Webb's face. "You do not like that, do you, *gringo*? You do not want these people on your conscience. That is why I have the advantage over you. I have no conscience. Believe me, I will do just what I say. I will come back, and the people here will answer for their help to you."

Florentino's voice was as quiet as the rattle of death. "No they won't. You are not leaving here!"

Armendariz saw the lethal intention in Florentino's eyes. Desperately he shouted at his men and reached for a pistol at his hips. He never touched it. Florentino's shotgun boomed. Armendariz reeled backward and sprawled in the dust of the street.

The soldiers' frightened horses began to rear and dance, and the men had their hands full. One soldier snapped a wild shot at Florentino but missed. The horse jumped, and the soldier landed on his shoulder, rolling in the dirt. He began clawing desperately for his dropped pistol. A villager grabbed it and jumped away. The soldier looked up in terror at the guns which faced him. *"No me mata!"* he shrilled. *Don't kill me!* "I am only a soldier. I do what I am told."

The other soldiers got their horses quieted down. Two of them had dropped their guns in the melee, and the others had lost their advantage. Seeing now that the fight was over almost without having begun, they let the guns drop from their fingers.

Webb asked them, "Any more guns?"

There were none.

"Go!" Webb ordered. "Never come back here. Understand? Never!"

"Never, *señor*," promised the one on the ground.

Webb knew they might not keep their word, but he doubted they could ever amount to much with Armendariz gone. Webb and his two men never relaxed their surveillance over the soldiers until the Mexicans turned their scrubby horses and headed out across the creek. Webb swung to the ground then. The villagers began to edge forward. Most of them formed a wide circle around the fallen Armendariz. A few began to pick up the weapons the soldiers had dropped.

Webb said, "Keep those guns. Hide them, because you may need them someday. If the soldiers come back, you can say the *gringos* took the guns."

Armendariz began to stir. He struggled for breath. Webb was surprised, for he had thought the blast had killed the lieutenant. But Florentino's aim had not been good. Only the outer edge of the shot pattern had struck Armendariz. That had been enough to knock the breath out of him and leave a bloody wound in his side. One of the villagers picked up Armendariz's gun to keep it out of the officer's reach.

Armendariz pushed himself into a sitting position, hands clasped painfully over the wound where blood was seeping out between his fingers. The people of San Miguel stared at him in a smouldering hatred.

Florentino gritted, "I did a poor job. I will finish it." He started to reload the shotgun. Webb reached out and pushed the barrel down. "No, Florentino. It's one thing to shoot him when he's standin' there reachin' for a gun. It's another thing to shoot him after he's helpless."

One of the older villagers stepped up with his hat in his hand. "Please, señor, we have suffered much from this man. We would be forever in your debt if you would leave him here."

Webb frowned.

The old man said, "*Señor*, we propose only to give him justice."

Armendariz's face had been defiant. Now defiance began to give way to fear. "*Gringo*, you must not do this. You are an officer of the law, just as I am. You cannot leave me in the hands of this rabble."

"What else could I do?"

"Take me with you."

Webb was sure that if they helped Armendariz the man would turn on them at the first opportunity like a vicious wolf released from a trap. "A few minutes ago you were going to shoot us."

"Justice, *señor!* All I ask is justice!"

"Justice!" Webb's mouth twisted in a bitter smile. "I doubt that you know what the word means. But I think you are about to find out." He turned away. "Come on, Johnny, Florentino. Let's ride."

They got on their horses. One of the younger men of the village reached up and pointed at Johnny's saddle. "*Señor, por favor*, your rope."

Johnny considered a moment, glancing toward Webb, then loosened the hornstring and dropped the rope into eager brown hands.

Armendariz cried out, "For the love of God, don't leave me here!"

Johnny said, "Webb, you know what they're fixin' to do?"

Webb shrugged and kept himself from looking back. "It's none of our affair. He brought it on himself. We've got no responsibility to him."

They spurred their horses into a trot toward the adobe house where Ellie would be waiting. Surrounded by the vengeful villagers, Armendariz kept crying out to the Americans. His pleading turned into a shrill screaming as the men began to send the women and children away. The screaming went on even after the three riders had gone out of sight around a bend in the trail.

Webb's flesh crawled, but he didn't slow his horse, didn't even turn around in the saddle to look.

12

They put San Miguel behind them a little while before dark, and Webb was glad to go. He didn't know precisely what the villagers had done to Armendariz, nor did he care to find out. The thought of it sent a chill down his back. Later on, if questions were ever asked, the villagers would say the officer had been killed by three unknown riders from *el otro lado*, the other side. Armendariz's own soldiers would back them in that. Perhaps the next officer sent to the river country would protect the people instead of preying on them.

Because Ellie asked him to, the young man Pablo caught up his own horse, one of the small-bodied, long-tailed Mexican kind, and went along to show the easiest way to Arroyo de Lopez. Webb wanted to be well away from San Miguel before night. He thought it unlikely that any of Armendariz's soldiers would come back, but just in case . . .

After riding in darkness a couple of hours, they stopped to rest. At daylight they arose and moved again, taking their time. It was only a short distance to the village they sought, and Webb had no intention of riding into it in broad daylight anyway, not without first keeping it under surveillance a long time.

They came upon a sluggish creek, where wild long-horn cattle broke into a run at the sight of them. Pablo said, "My friends, we are close now. Up this creek half an hour's ride is Arroyo de Lopez."

Webb asked, "Are you leaving us, Pablo?"

The young Mexican looked back at Ellie, who rode in the rear. "I have no quarrel with the *Señor* Donovan. But, if the *señora* wants me to stay, I will stay."

Often during the ride he had looked back over his shoulder, his troubled gaze studying the young woman. Loyalty to family was deeply ingrained in the Mexican people. It was hard for Pablo to comprehend how a woman could help in the tracking down of her own husband. She might kill him herself, perhaps, in a sudden flare of jealousy, but never help someone else to do it. In his limited experience Pablo had never seen the like of this.

"Donovan is no longer the same as when she married him," Webb said, trying to explain. "He has done much wrong, hurt many people."

"Has he hurt the *señora*?"

Webb pondered. "Yes, and no." Truly, Clabe Donovan had not done any direct wrong to Ellie herself, unless it was to have led her into a fugitive's life in the beginning. Webb said, "Pablo, if you had a faithful old dog, but he went mad and became a danger to other people, you would be obliged to kill him no matter how much you loved him."

Pablo observed, "A man, *señor*, is not a mad dog."

"He can be, sometimes. I think this one is."

Pablo turned back and pulled his horse in beside Ellie's. He asked her if she wanted him to stay. She replied, "Pablo, these are good men here. They may need help."

Pablo nodded. "Then I will stay."

They approached the village with caution. Although he could not see the whole place, Webb could tell it was much bigger than San Miguel. Pablo's eyes swelled, for to him this was a metropolis. It lay on a large north-south road, one that evidently carried a fair amount of commerce. They pulled off into the brush to avoid meeting a peddler who approached from the south in a hardware-laden two-wheel cart, drawn by a sharp-hipped mule. Webb could hear a multitude of mongrel dogs rushing to challenge the peddler. The man's whip cracked as one of the dogs moved too close to the gray mule. The dog yowled. A boy's voice cried sharp insults, but the peddler paid no mind.

From somewhere out of sight came the ring of a blacksmith's hammer, the ee-aww of a burro. Webb did not see much activity. But then, Mexican villages seldom had the constant shifting movement, the street-crowding foot and horse traffic that so often was found in towns on the north side of the river. Life was slower here, and the demands on it were less.

"Pablo," Webb asked, "do you have any idea where Donovan stays?"

Pablo shook his head. "I have been to this place only once before in my life. I was but a boy then, and I came with my father."

Webb had forgotten how little the average Mexican

traveled. A trip to another valley a few miles away might be the longest a man took in a lifetime if he was a farmer and had no particular reason to travel. Indeed, some looked upon people of other villages as foreigners. The state capitol was as far away for many of them as Europe might seem to an American, and Mexico City had as well be on the moon. This isolation manifested itself even in speech. Each town or village developed a slightly different dialect from that of its neighbors, with phrases and colloquialisms which indelibly marked a man's origin.

Webb leaned against his horse and stared across the saddle at that part of the village he could see through the green foliage of the mesquite. "No tellin' how many men might be with him in there," he said to Johnny and Florentino. "We'd be foolish to go a-ridin' in there in the daylight, not even knowin' where to start lookin' at. We'll just pull off aways and wait out the rest of the day. Come dark, we'll have to go in and try to nose him out."

Florentino dropped back beside Pablo. They talked a while in a fast-clipped Spanish that lost Webb somewhere along the line. At length Florentino announced in English, "Mister Webb, Pablo and I, we have decided. We two, we go down into the town when night comes. We are both Mexican. Who will notice us? We look, we ask questions. Maybe we find out where Donovan is."

Webb said, "Remember, Florentino, Donovan knows you. If he sees you . . ."

"It is many years ago. I have changed. But I will stay away from him if I can."

Although Webb didn't like the idea, he knew it made sense. And he had no ideas of his own. "All right, but promise me you'll be careful. Remember, you have a new son. You have to think of him and of Consuela."

"I will remember them. But I also remember Apari-cio, and Mister Joe."

This was rough hill country. Webb chose for their waiting place a hill which overlooked the town from the south. It had a fair covering of scrub brush and cactus. Webb decided to tie the horses on the off side and spend the day watching from the hilltop. Moving the long way around the hill, they pulled far off on a tangent, once to avoid meeting a couple of young boys who were picking up dry firewood and drop-ping it into a pair of large, dried-out, willow-switch baskets tied across the back of a gotch-eared, sleepy-eyed old burro. On the off side of the hill, where they left the horses, Ellie sat down in the thin shade of a mesquite. She hadn't said much this morning. She seemed to want to be left alone.

Johnny Willet built a small fire and put the coffee pot on to heat. He and Florentino and Pablo had staked the horses, loosening the cinches but not taking the saddles off. A stroke of bad luck might force the five to leave here in a hurry, and it might not give them time to resaddle.

Climbing the hill afoot, Webb disturbed a small string of multi-colored Spanish goats which were browsing around on the scattering of low brush.

Webb picked a shady spot which gave him a view over most of the town. The goats settled down to eat-ing again, although the strong-smelling old billy kept eyeing Webb with suspicion. Webb was glad for the company. He figured if he was seen from down in town, he probably would be mistaken for one of the goats. No one would pay him any attention. Through his spyglass he watched the two boys enter town with their burro and their load of firewood, the baskets bobbing up and down gently with the slow, lazy movement of the animal.

After a while *siesta* time came. Little movement remained on the street, and that little was therefore hard to miss. At each sign of movement Webb would swing the glass around for a look, hoping to catch sight of someone who was obviously *gringo*, someone who didn't belong. But if such *gringos* were here, they had adopted the Mexican custom of *siesta*. They weren't stirring about.

Johnny brought Webb a cup of coffee, some cold bread and bacon. "Man's got to eat, Webb, whether he wants to or not See anything?"

"Nothin' that'll help us any."

"Maybe they're not here. Maybe they went across the river on another raid."

Webb's face furrowed. "We'll sit here and wait if it takes a week!"

Through the long afternoon the still summer heat pushed down oppressively. Webb fought flies and the heat and the helpless impatience. Miserable as he felt, he knew how much more miserable the wait must be for Ellie. She remained below, asking no sympathy but keeping her own counsel and suffering alone.

Late in the afternoon a welcome breeze stirred from the south. It was not cool, but it served to carry away the flies and lift some of the still, intolerable heat. Down in town, people began stirring again. Women and girls carried vessels down to the creek to fetch water. Children played, an occasional vagrant scrap of their shouting and laughter reaching Webb on the hillside. Men appeared in the fields to do some hoeing amid the corn. Webb would watch through the spyglass until he had to put the instrument down and rest his eyes.

Discouragement settled over him, for all the people he saw appeared to be Mexican.

Suddenly he straightened, bringing up the glass and focusing. He saw two men on horseback. The horses were bigger and fatter than those which belonged to the people here. They were Texas horses, no mistake about that. And the men were *gringos*, Webb knew even at that distance. It showed in the clothes they wore, the cowboy-style hats on their heads. It was apparent in the heedless way they rode down the street, forcing even the women to move aside.

"Johnny," Webb spoke with a tone of excitement, "come look."

Johnny took the glass. A grim smile slowly came over his face. "I think we finally struck gold."

At nightfall Florentino and Pablo began tightening their cinches for the ride down into town. Webb laid his hand on the neck of the horse Florentino had been riding. He looked worriedly into the face of the Mexican who had so long been his friend. "Don't be takin' risks, Florentino. Don't hang around where the *gringos* are. Somebody might recognize you. And don't stay a minute longer than you have to."

He started to turn away, then stopped. "Florentino, if you see any sign of my brother . . ."

He broke off. It seemed disloyal even to entertain the thought that Sandy could be here. Yet the fear had tormented him ever since the day he had ridden back from his fruitless mission to find the Dry Fork bank robbed.

Webb hadn't finished what he was going to say. Florentino spoke, "If I see him, what?"

"If you see him, tell me. Don't keep it a secret."

Florentino said gravely, "If I see him, I won't lie to you."

The two rode away. Webb walked back to the camp where the cookfire was only hot coals. He poured himself a cup of coffee and glanced at the silent woman who sat with her knees gathered up under her, her face hidden in her arms. Webb's mouth twisted. Then he sat to sip the coffee and wait. Just wait, and wait . . .

It seemed hours before he heard the strike of hoofs. He sat stiffly, pistol in his hand. He heard Florentino's quiet voice: "Mister Webb."

"Up here, Florentino."

The two riders came on and dismounted. In the moonlight Webb could see victory in Florentino's face.

"He is here, Mister Webb. Donovan is here."

A flare of triumph came to Webb. It subsided, and he looked around for Ellie. She still sat where she had been all afternoon.

"Where's he at, Florentino?"

"Right now he is in the *cantina*. But we do not

want to try for him there. Too many of his men are with him. Six, seven men, I think, some *gringos*, a couple of Mexican *pistoleros*. *Ladrones*, all of them. Bad men."

Webb looked down, clenching his fist. "And Sandy?"

Florentino shook his head. "No, Mister Webb, and I do not lie to you. He is not in the *cantina*."

Webb's shoulders straightened a little. Maybe Sandy wasn't here at all. Maybe he never had been. Maybe the whole idea had been a mistake from the start.

He asked, "If we don't take Donovan in the *cantina*, where do we get a chance at him?"

"Pablo and me, we went among the people of the village. We ask many questions . . . not big questions, just little ones. Donovan, he has a house. He lives there alone." He looked around, evidently searching for Ellie and seeming glad she wasn't near enough to hear. "Almost alone. A girl of the village, she lives with him. She is in the *cantina* with him now."

"Did you see Donovan himself?"

Florentino nodded excitely. "I look through the window. His back is turn to me, but I see him. I know that back, for I have seen it many times. And the black sombrero, it was on the floor at his feet."

"You found out where his house is?"

Florentino glanced at Pablo and nodded. "*Si*. We find it."

A little coffee was left in Webb's cup, but suddenly it seemed cold and bitter. He flung it out upon the ground. A chill passed through him. "We'll go there, and we'll wait for him to come to us."

He turned to Johnny, who had come in time to hear

most of the conversation. "Johnny, will you go tell Ellie?" Then, thinking again, he said, "No, don't. I'll tell her."

Dogs picked them up as they rode down into Arroyo de Lopez, but no one paid attention because the dogs would bark at anything that moved. The riders themselves were as silent as the black shadows of night that they rode in. They kept away from the small open windows of the adobes, and the timid patches of dim candlelight that cautiously peeped out. To get rid of weight and to free the packhorse for Donovan, they untied the pack and left it near the door of a poor little brush-roofed adobe which looked as if its occupants could use the food. Moving away, Johnny brushed against a dry, tight fence made picket-style of the wicked, spike-edged stems of the *ocatillo* cactus. It was a lightweight fence, but its thorns would turn back a bull. Johnny squalled out in pain. He clapped his hand over his mouth after the damage already was done. They watched and listened nervously, expecting trouble. But nobody seemed to have heard. Nobody came.

They left the horses in a pool of blackness a hundred feet from Donovan's house. Ellie would stay with the horses, and Pablo was to stay beside Ellie. Webb had suggested the Mexican start home before any trouble began, but Pablo decided the good *señora* might need help. He owed her that in return for the house in San Miguel.

Nervousness coiled like a steel spring in Webb Matlock as he walked toward the Donovan adobe, his hand slick with cold sweat against the gunbutt. The house was still and dark. Webb and Johnny and Florentino leaned against the dry, crumbly wall, listening, holding their breath.

"Florentino," Webb whispered, "you stay out here in the shadows and watch. Don't show yourself unless somethin' goes wrong. Johnny and me, we'll try and take him after he goes in the house."

Florentino nodded. *"Buena suerte." Good luck.*

The front door was open. Theft was rare among the people who lived in these villages because everyone knew everyone else. A thief could not go long undiscovered, or unpunished. This was poor country for a locksmith.

Inside, Webb and Johnny stood a while and studied the dark room until they could pick out the few pieces of furniture: chairs, table, bed. There was not even a stove. Cooking would be done outdoors in a round, earthen oven. A strong smell of spilled liquor clung to the place, liquor that had soaked into the dirt floor in considerable amount. Webb could imagine the raucous drinking bouts that must have been thrown inside these barren walls.

He could also detect the faint lingering of cheap perfume, and he was glad Ellie had remained outside.

Johnny asked, "Webb, do you reckon Ellie can take it when she sees Clabe comin'?"

"Why not?"

"She's acted kind of strange today. Like she was with us but still alone, if you know what I mean."

Webb nodded solemnly. "In her place, would you do different?"

"I don't know; that's what bothers me. Was I her and I saw Clabe fixin' to walk into a trap, it'd be all I could do to keep from hollerin' to him, tellin' him to run like the devil was after him. How do you know she won't?"

"She's come this far. I don't think she'll break down now."

"I hope not. I just wish I could be as sure."

Webb took a chair in one corner, facing the open door. Johnny sat on a bench in the corner opposite the front of the room. They sat in silence, listening. From outside they could hear the quiet life of the village passing the early hours of the night—dogs barking at the edge of town, a cow bawling for a calf, a woman calling her children to bed. Someone strummed a melancholy tune on a guitar, and a voice lifted gently in a melancholy song of love and death.

Webb looked out at one strange noise and saw a lank-bodied, long-nosed old sow walking down the street, her small brood following right along, trying for milk every time she paused a moment.

After a long time he heard someone walking slowly up the dusty street toward the house, feet dragging a little. Webb's heartbeat quickened. He pushed to his feet, the gun ready. In the darkness he could see the dim outline of Johnny Willet, who had done the same.

They waited, their tenseness building as the footsteps drew nearer and nearer the door. Finally Webb thought sure he was about to see the figure of Clabe Donovan framed in the doorway, dark against the starlight. But the man—whoever he was—passed on by the house and kept walking. He began to sing softly to himself in a voice that carried no melody. It was a Mexican song, a Mexican voice. Not Clabe Donovan.

Webb let his breath out slowly and wiped the palms of his hands against his shirt. He sat again in the creaky chair, wishing the tenseness would leave him.

He had the feeling it wouldn't be much longer now. Donovan would be here directly. Clabe Donovan, dead these many years and now back to life again. A different man now than he had been before, a savage, vengeful man no longer possessed of those few good qualities which once had made even his enemies respect him. Enemies like his one-time friend, Webb Matlock.

Webb heard the footsteps. Steeling himself, he pushed up from the chair. He could hear a man's voice speaking softly. The words were Spanish, but even Webb's untrained ear could tell that the Spanish was slurred by a careless *gringo* accent. A woman giggled foolishly.

The pair appeared in the doorway, their silhouettes plain. They were a tall man with a big sombrero and a slender woman whose full skirt almost swept the floor. The man embraced her, then began feeling beside the door for a table he knew was there. He found the table and set down a bottle that went clunk as it fell over. He righted it quickly, both he and the woman laughing. His back to Webb and Johnny, the man fished in his pocket and came up with a match. He struck it on his bootsole and lighted a single thick wax candle that stood in a saucer on the table.

Webb's voice was so steady that it surprised him.

"Hands up! Don't make a move, Clabe Donovan!"

The man stiffened, his hands flat on the table. For

the space of several seconds he stood like that, his back still turned. Slowed by drink, he was plainly too stunned to know what to do.

The girl turned and saw the guns. She shrieked, her eyes going wide as silver *pesos*, her hands lifting to cover her mouth.

Webb said, "Turn around slow, Clabe. Make a single suspicious move and I'll shoot to kill."

Donovan still seemed stunned. "Who is it?"

"Webb Matlock. I've come to take you back across the river."

"You got no authority here."

"I got all the authority I need, right here in my hand. Turn around now, Clabe. Turn slow and careful."

Some sardonic humor seemed to move in Donovan. He began to laugh. Then, slowly and deliberately, he turned.

Webb's mouth dropped open, and he cast a surprised glance at Johnny Willet. The resemblance was uncanny, but this was not Clabe Donovan.

This was Clabe's brother, Morg!

13

❧

"What's the matter, Webb Matlock?" Morg Donovan laughed contemptuously. "Somethin' give you a shock?"

For a moment Webb was speechless. "Where's Clabe at, Morg?"

"Where he's been all these years. In that graveyard over at Dry Fork."

"But we thought . . ." Webb trailed off. "Then we were right, all that time. It *was* Clabe who died that night, breakin' out of jail."

Morg nodded. "Blown to pieces by a shotgun in the hands of an old fool who couldn't have wiped the dust off Clabe's boots." The sardonic humor was gone from Morg Donovan now. A somber chill crept into his eyes. "I swore I'd get even for what happened to my brother. I've made a start."

"But you're through now, Morg. We're takin' you back across the river, and there's no Clabe Donovan to get you free this time."

Donovan said scornfully, "You know how far it is to the river? You'll never get there with me. You may not even leave Arroyo de Lopez. What if I decide just to sit down here and call your bluff? You're not the kind of man who would shoot me in cold blood."

"Wrong, Morg." Webb's voice was bitter. "Balk on me and I *will* kill you, right where you're at. I remember the way you blasted down Uncle Joe Vickers at the wagon-yard in Dry Fork. You didn't give him a chance."

"He's the old devil who killed Clabe. I owed him that shootin'."

"Slow and easy now, Morg, unbuckle your gunbelt and drop it."

All this time the good-looking young Mexican woman had stood frozen, not comprehending the words but grimly certain of their import.

Ellie Donovan was unable to stand the suspense any longer. At this moment she stepped in the door, her face tense. "Clabe?" Morg Donovan turned. She gasped in surprise at the sudden realization that this was not her husband.

Morg—with the quick wit that had always been his brother's—took advantage of the distraction. In one motion he ripped off his sombrero, whirled and snuffed out the candle with a sweep of the big hat. In the darkness he roughly shoved both women aside and leaped for the open door. Webb stood helpless, afraid to fire because of the women.

From outside he heard a sharp thud and a grunt and a body sliding on the bare ground. Webb sprinted across the small room and out the door.

Florentino Rodriguez said, "Is all right, Mister Webb. I hit him over the head as he is come out." He held the shotgun up for inspection against the stars. "I hope the barrel, she is not bent."

The stunned Morg Donovan swayed on hands and knees, shaking his head and groaning.

The Mexican woman came out of shock. She took a horrified look at Morg Donovan, then turned and ran screaming down the street.

Florentino bent and grabbed hold of Morg Donovan's arm. "Mister Webb, this place is pretty quick a hornet's nest."

Webb grabbed Morg's other arm and helped the outlaw to his feet. Donovan's knees were wobbly. Webb turned toward the dark place where the horses were. "Let's haul our freight."

Ellie ran beside them, still looking at Morg. "But, Webb, this isn't Clabe," she protested in confusion.

Webb wished he had time to explain. For that matter, he wished he fully understood it himself. "It never was, Ellie. Clabe is dead."

He thought Ellie was going to fall. She stumbled, caught herself and stood a moment with her hands over her face. Then, recovering, she hurried to catch up with the men.

Morg was still groggy as they reached the horses. Quickly Webb tied the man's hands with a strip of rawhide he had brought for the purpose. He tied one end of the rawhide through the fork of the saddle so Morg could not get loose. From down the street came the rising sounds of a village awakened, the barking of dogs, the cries of frightened women, the wild shouts of excited men.

Two men came running hard around the corner of

Donovan's adobe house. They heard rather than saw the movement of Webb's group in the shadows. One of the men leveled a pistol. The other knocked the gun upward just as it fired.

"You fool!" Webb heard him cry, "you might hit Donovan!"

Webb took a firm grip on Donovan's bridle reins. "Spur 'em!"

The horses clattered out across the bare, packed ground into the moonlight. A chorus went up. Someone fired, but the shooting stopped as abruptly as it started.

Carrying Donovan, the packhorse lagged. Webb's arm was stretched backward to the point that it was painful to hold onto the reins. He pulled his own mount down to get slack, then took a wrap around the horn and touched spurs to his horse. The impact caught the led animal in midstride and almost jerked him to his knees. The groggy Donovan grunted. After that, there was no more difficulty. Donovan's horse stayed up.

The creek lay ahead, its waters murmuring peacefully in the night. Webb and his group spurred into it, shattering its quiet, raising a silver spray in the moonlight. The cool splash of water was refreshing to Webb. In half a dozen long strides his horse gained the far bank. Webb reined up a moment to look back. He could hear horses, the hectic clatter of pursuit.

"The brush yonder," he said, pointing. "We can't outrun them. Maybe we can shake loose from them in the thicket."

Water hitting his face had helped bring Donovan

back to full consciousness. With his hands tied he had a strong grip on the saddlehorn. To fall out of the saddle while tied to it could mean dragging, and many a man had died dragging from a horse, his ribs caved in by a hoof or his head broken against a tree.

"Matlock," he complained, "you're a-fixin' to get me drug to death."

Webb said coldly, "Just stay in the saddle. That part is up to you." He didn't slow down.

Ahead, a heavy stand of mesquite brush and catclaw choked a wide draw that angled back toward the creek. Webb rode into it full tilt, the others right with him. They ducked their heads against the lash of thorny mesquite that scratched at their faces and ripped at their clothes. Morg Donovan cursed because he could not raise his arms for protection as the others could. He could only duck his head and hope he did not lose his big sombrero. Webb did not sympathize with him.

They rode deep into the brush before they stopped to listen. They could hear horses behind them.

"Gettin' closer," Webb whispered. "Don't anybody make a sound."

The pursuers fanned out and entered the thicket. Listening, Webb tried to tell how many there were. It was hard to gauge, maybe six, eight, even a dozen. The outlaws had slowed to a walk, and they pushed with caution through the hostile tangle. Webb bent low in the saddle, trying not to present a silhouette. It was so quiet here he almost fancied he could hear his watch ticking. He could hear the constrained breath of Ellie and Johnny and the two Mexicans above the whisper of brush, the soft padding of hoofs, the squeaking of saddle leather. For a time the pursuit drew inexorably nearer. Then the riders began veering away.

Donovan had sat with a confident air about him, waiting for his men to come. Now it seemed they were going to miss him. He shouted, "Over here, boys! It's me!"

Webb pounced on him, clapping his hands over Donovan's mouth and almost pulling the outlaw from the saddle. Donovan made a desperate grab at the horn to keep from falling. Webb kept his hands over the man's mouth a moment and listened. Once more the riders were heading in their direction.

One of the men shouted, "Where you at, Morg?"

"Just holler again," called another. "We'll find you."

Webb pressed the cold muzzle of his pistol against the back of Morg Donovan's head. He muttered, "Make another sound and I'll blow your damned head off!"

Donovan's eyes rolled. He held his silence.

The riders kept working through the brush, but they missed their mark. They moved on by, the nearest passing twenty yards away. Webb held the muzzle tight against Donovan's neck. The man kept quiet.

Finally the riders were gone, although the sound of their search still continued.

"All right, Morg," Webb gritted, "I didn't aim to do this, but now I will." He pulled a handkerchief from his pocket. "Open your mouth."

"That thing's dirty," Donovan protested.

"Your fault, not mine. Open up."

Donovan opened his mouth, and Webb wadded the

handkerchief into it. He pulled another handkerchief from Donovan's own hip pocket. He ran this one across Donovan's mouth and tied the ends behind the man's neck.

They could still hear the riders working through the brush. Ellie Donovan had pulled up beside Webb as if drawing strength from him. He reached out and touched her hand.

Finally he heard someone far off say, "This is damn foolishness. They could be in this thicket anyplace, waitin' to blast our heads off without us even seein' them."

Webb couldn't make out the reply, but he surmised that it was in agreement. The riders pulled back, leaving the thicket. They congregated on open ground at the edge of the draw. Webb could hear the sharp-edged rise of voices tangled in dispute. He couldn't understand much of it, but he heard a man say finally, "It's a long way to the Rio Grande."

After that the men pulled away. Webb held still until all sound of pursuit was gone. He sagged, some of the wound-up tension slowly loosening—temporarily, at least.

Webb looked at his companions' faces and could feel the anxiety that remained there. "All right," he spoke, "we better be on the move. That *pistolero* was right. It's a long way to the Rio Grande."

Pablo had done his work and more than Webb had ever expected. He sent the young man home to San Miguel with his gratitude.

Riding out then, Webb took his bearings on the north star. Terrain might vary, and a man might ride into a strange land where he had no landmarks to guide his way. But, when all else failed him, there still were the stars, constant and unchanging. In point of miles, the shortest way to the Rio would be to follow the north star. They might come across obstacles that would hold them up, that would force them to detour. But, as long as he could see the north star, they would never really be lost.

They moved carefully out of the brush, taking their time. They knew Donovan's men might be waiting somewhere, listening. In the clear, they paused a bit to listen too. They caught no sound of anyone hunting them, but Webb would bet that someone was. They rode a couple of miles before Webb saw fit to stop and take the gag from Donovan's mouth. "Next time you try another stunt like you pulled a while ago, that gag goes back in," he said roughly.

Donovan was relieved to be rid of the thing. He drew up saliva and spat, cleaning his mouth of the dry and dusty taste. "You're a fool, Matlock. You think them boys of mine went back to town to forget things over a bottle of *tequila*? You think they don't have a good notion where you're headed with me?"

Webb said evenly, "The point is, *we've* got you, they haven't."

"You'll never get me to the river. Ain't no way you can make it before daylight. Come sunup, when the boys can see, they'll close in on you like hounds on a rabbit."

"We're not rabbits, Morg."

"You'll wish you was. You'll wish you could just run down a hole and pull it in after you."

Webb succumbed a while to a burning compulsion to run the horses, to put some quick distance between themselves and Arroyo de Lopez. But he knew the mounts couldn't stand the pace long, not and have reserve strength left. He pulled the horses down to a trot.

Morg Donovan snorted. "Make you feel better to run, Matlock? Run all you want to. You still got to cross that river, and you'll never do it."

Webb's eyes narrowed. His voice was sharp as flint. "You're not gettin' away, Morg, just get that through your skull. Whatever happens to me, I'll have one bullet left for you. And I'll use it!"

For a minute their eyes met, stabbing, and hatred leaped between them hot and keen.

They moved in a steady trot through the darkness, cutting across the rough and rocky rangeland, through the brush, over the cactus-strewn Mexican prairies, across the dry creeks and washes. They were wasting miles, seeking their way through. Webb wished they could strike a good trail leading northward, but he knew it would be risky. Donovan's men would be using the roads and trails, trying to beat them to the river.

Webb stayed in the lead, Donovan's horse trailing half a length behind at the end of the reins. Ellie rode beside Webb, on the opposite side from Morg Donovan. Johnny and Florentino brought up the rear, looking behind them for pursuit.

Ellie kept turning her head, glancing at Morg. Amazing how much Morg resembled Clabe Donovan now.

Webb could remember that there had always been a likeness, but Morg had been somewhat the younger in those times so long past, and the resemblance was not so pronounced as it had become now. Same size, same build, same general features. Only when you looked him full in the face could you readily tell the difference. In this moonlight, with the dark shadow cast by the black sombrero, it was hard to get a look at his face.

After a long time Ellie asked, "Morg, why the masquerade? Why did you want everybody to think you were Clabe?"

Morg Donovan stared at Ellie, his eyes detesting her. "Because Clabe Donovan was somebody! He was a real man, Clabe was. You never appreciated him."

Evenly she said, "I loved him, Morg, you know that."

"Loved him? Then how come you ran off and left him?"

"I couldn't stand the life we were leading. I begged him to quit. He promised he would, but he didn't do it. Just one more time, he always said, just one more time and he would call it quits. But I knew he wouldn't quit until they killed him. I couldn't stand it anymore."

Morg said with an ancient bitterness, "And finally they did kill him, killed him because he was caught tryin' to get me out of trouble. But I swore that wouldn't be the end of it. I swore I'd pay back everybody who had a hand in what happened to Clabe."

Webb asked, "How come it took so many years to start?"

"We needed money, me and the few that was left.

We went down into Mexico and tried to rob a mint. It was a crazy thing to try. I got wounded and caught. One of the other boys was caught with me, and a couple got killed. I spent years in a prison down yonder, a Mexican prison. You know what they can be like, Matlock. The boy that was with me, he died, and dyin' was the easy way out. But I lived because I couldn't afford to die. I still had debts to pay."

Now that Morg had begun, he seemed compelled to tell all of it. His voice was as grim as blood. "I done a lot of thinkin' while I was in prison. I knew how Clabe had died. It came to me that with his face all blasted away, nobody could really swear it was Clabe. Could've been me, for all anybody could prove. Now, Morg Donovan never meant much to anybody, except to Clabe. But Clabe Donovan, he was really somebody, a legend. Shame for him to die the way he did.

"It came to me that maybe he didn't have to be dead after all. He could still be alive, through me. After all, I never had amounted to no hell of a lot. All I had to do was pretend I was Clabe, and Clabe would be alive, all over again. If he'd lasted longer, Clabe Donovan would've been a man they'd write books about, like Jesse James and them. Man like that, he don't ever really die because folks don't ever forget him. I figured I owed that to Clabe. I could be him. I could bring him back to life and make him known the way he ought to've been."

He fell silent, remembering. Webb said, "One thing you overlooked, Morg, you never were the man Clabe was. You didn't have his brain for makin' plans, for gettin' things done."

"I was younger, wilder. I left a lot of that behind me in prison. Time I broke out of there, I was a lot smarter than when I went in. I figured I could use Clabe's name and do proud by it. Prison gave me lots of time to plan. It didn't take me long to round up a couple or three of the old hands and to find some new ones as good as the others had been. Far as the new hands knew, I really was Clabe Donovan. The old ones, they kept their mouths shut. I lined things up with Bronc Tomlin. We started with horses and cattle first because they was easy, and we needed money. From that, I figured we'd work on up to banks, and even trains. Wouldn't be long till Clabe Donovan would be known from New York City to the Pacific Ocean."

Webb said, "You couldn't go on forever, wearin' a dead man's boots."

Morg replied, "A year or two, then I figured I would just fade away. They would always wonder what had happened to Clabe. Makes it even better, don't it, when folks don't really know? They worry over it, and they don't ever forget. They talk about it as long as they live. They'd never forget Clabe Donovan, not in a hundred years."

Webb said, "When we take you back, everybody is goin' to know the truth. They'll know Clabe Donovan is dead."

Morg shook his head. "Who's to tell? Not a one of you is ever goin' back across that river!"

Webb glanced at Ellie, and then back to Morg. "Would you kill a woman?"

Morg said bitterly, "I'd kill *her*. Think I didn't hear about her, gettin' herself involved with the Dry Fork sheriff, the very one who put her husband in jail, the man responsible for gettin' Clabe killed? Her, the only woman Clabe ever looked at twice? The night I shot the old man who killed Clabe, I came within an inch of killin' her too. I stood and looked at her through the window and started to shoot. Then I thought, better to kill the sheriff she intended on marryin'. Make her a widow twice over. Let her live to worry over that and wonder why."

Webb saw that Ellie was crying softly. He remembered the night of which Morg spoke. He remembered how shaken Ellie had been because she had thought she saw Clabe Donovan standing in the darkness. He shuddered now, realizing how close she had come to dying that night.

He said, "Morg, you've let hatred twist your mind until you're crazy. Any man who could even think of shootin' down a helpless woman . . ."

"She belonged to Clabe!"

"But Clabe was dead."

Morg shook his head violently. "No, he wasn't dead. I wasn't goin' to let him stay dead. I was bringin' him back to life, and she belonged to him." He looked wildly at Ellie, his eyes accusing her. "She belonged to him, I tell you. She belonged to Clabe!"

Webb's mouth went dry. Great God, the man *was* crazy! He had almost come to believe he *was* Clabe Donovan.

Webb licked dry lips and tore his gaze from Morg Donovan. "Come on, let's push. We want to get as close to that river as we can before daylight."

They rode as hard as Webb thought they dared,

consistent with saving the horses. He followed the north star and found his way blocked periodically by washouts that they had to circle around, by a creek too deep to try until they hunted and found a natural ford. All this, he realized in a helpless chum of anxiety, was costing them time.

Eventually they came to a road that seemed to head generally northward. They halted at the edge of it. Webb took out his pocketwatch and tilted it so the moon fell full on the dial. "A little past three in the mornin'," he said. Wouldn't be much sign of light for a couple of hours yet.

"How far would you say it is to the river, Morg?"

Morg Donovan threw back his head contemptuously. "Think I'd tell you? Find out for your ownself." He paused, drawing some pleasure from the fact that he was able to withhold knowledge that Webb needed. "I'll tell you this: it's too far to make it before daylight. And come daylight, you won't make it anyhow."

Frustrated by the delays they had encountered in trying to cut across country, Webb was tempted to use the road awhile. Surely the road would seek the easiest way north and save them time. But there was a danger . . .

Florentino said urgently, "Mister Webb, I think I hear something. Listen!"

Webb listened but heard nothing. Florentino's ears must be better than his, he thought, or the Mexican was letting imagination get the better of him. Then the sound came to Webb too.

Hoofbeats, coming up the road.

Webb waved his hand. "Back!" They pulled away from the road, and he was glad they hadn't crossed it, for their tracks might show in the moonlight. The road hadn't been used much. They stepped to the ground.

"Open your mouth, Morg," he said. "The gag."

"Not again!" Morg protested.

"I don't trust you. Open up."

When he had gagged the outlaw, he caught his horse's nose and that of Donovan's mount to keep the animals from nickering. In the night the sound of the approaching riders grew stronger. Presently the men came by, pushing their horses along in an easy lope. Seven riders.

When they had passed, Johnny Willet asked in a nervous voice, "Reckon them was Donovan's men?"

Webb nodded. "I doubt anybody else would have business travelin' this road at such an hour. They were his, all right."

He took the gag from Morg's mouth. Morg spat, face twisting at the dry taste which lingered. Gruffly he said, "Sure, they was my boys. Got any doubt now what'll happen when you start across that river? You got no chance, Matlock, no chance atall."

A prickling sensation explored up and down Webb's backside. His mouth went flat and grim. "Well," he said, "the road's out. We got to keep movin' cross-country. Let's get at it."

He could see the weariness bearing down on Ellie Donovan's thin shoulders. She spoke not a word in complaint but rode in sad-faced silence, her mind probably numbed. Sympathy for her was like an ache in Webb, but he knew nothing to say that would alleviate her misery. He held silent and hoped she knew how he felt.

The eastern sky began to pale, and daylight crept cautiously over this unfamiliar desert land. Webb glanced often toward the deepening red tinge that arose in the east. Usually he welcomed the dawn, but this time he wished he could hold it back. He wasn't ready and wouldn't be ready until they had swum that river and could put Mexico behind them.

Sunrise. Warm light bathed the cactus-dotted prairie and the irregular pattern of the brushlands. Webb sat nervously in the saddle, his gaze constantly working the land before him, studying every object that aroused suspicion, always finding it to be a tree or a bush, or perhaps a wandering burro. The torturing question kept burning in his brain: how far to the river?

A gunshot sent his heart leaping in alarm. He bent low in the saddle, instinctively drawing his pistol. Wide-eyed, he looked around him. He saw dismay in Ellie Donovan's eyes, triumph in Morg's. Two more shots followed.

"Signal," Webb said. "Somebody's spotted us, and he's signaled for the others."

Johnny Willet swallowed, looking for signs of whoever had found them. He saw nothing. With the echoes that rocketed through the cool morning air, it was hard to tell even where the shots had come from.

"We must not be far from the river," Webb guessed. "They fanned out to watch for us." He figured the Donovan bunch would have spread out back from the river far enough that they would be able to gather again before their quarry reached the line.

He saw that Ellie was scared. "Ellie, you feel up to a hard ride?"

She nodded. He said, "All right, then, let's run for it."

He spurred into a lope. The others followed him. The horse's hoofs drummed hard, churning dust from a thin turf of sparse grass. The brush seemed to fly by. They came to a thicket, but Webb never slowed. He ducked his head and threw up his arms for protection and spurred on through. The switchy green mesquite limbs bent and clawed and then whipped back into place. He lost part of his shirt but never looked back.

He heard Florentino shout, "Mister Webb, to the left!"

Webb saw two men riding to intercept them. He glanced back and saw a third, three hundred yards farther away but closing in. To the right came another.

"Let's give them a race," he said. "Stretch 'em!"

He spurred hard, urging his horse to all the speed it had. Donovan's mount had a hard time keeping up, and the animal's reins grew taut on Webb's saddlehorn. Webb saw that Ellie was falling behind. She couldn't hold the pace. He slowed, hoping to give her a chance.

A movement ahead of him caught his eye. Two more riders, directly in their path. These men were waiting to head them off. Webb caught the glint of gunmetal in the sun. He heard a warning shot, fired into the air. He saw suddenly the futility of trying to outrun these men. He raised his hand as a signal and began to rein in his horse.

He was breathing hard as he brought the animal to a stop. Ellie and Johnny and Florentino gathered about him, their eyes asking him what they could do now.

Webb pointed ahead. "Look yonder. The river!"

He could see it now, or rather he could see the meandering line of brush that told him where the river would be. Its waters were hidden behind the green foliage. Not far now, probably not more than a mile. But it could as well have been twenty, for Donovan's men stood like a wall between them and the Rio Grande.

Johnny Willet asked, "We can't outrun them, and we can't count on outshootin' them with Ellie here, so what can we do?"

Webb frowned darkly as he watched the Donovan men warily begin closing in. An idea came to him.

"We're goin' to keep on ridin', Johnny. We're goin' to force our way through. Florentino, I'll swap you my pistol for your shotgun."

The Mexican handed Webb his weapon, taking Webb's in return. Webb turned to face Morg Donovan. "All right, Morg, you ride up here alongside of me. You're fixin' to be our ticket across that river." Morg hesitated. Webb tipped the gunmuzzle up, pointing it right into the man's eyes.

"Now," Webb said, "just calm and easy, let's move ahead, in a walk. Show them we're comin' through."

Seven Donovan men had lined up ahead of them, spreading themselves ten to fifteen feet apart. They stared in astonishment as the little posse started again, moving directly toward them. The outlaws had their guns ready but didn't try to use them. They just sat on their horses and stared.

Thirty feet from the widespread line, Webb lifted the shotgun barrel and placed the muzzle at the back of Morg Donovan's head.

"Spread apart there, boys," Webb said evenly to the men ahead of him. "We're comin' though."

Morg Donovan's eyes widened in fear, for there was a razor keenness to Webb's voice, and the shotgun was cold against Donovan's skin.

The Donovan men stared uncertainly, some bringing up their guns as if to use them, then thinking better of it. Slowly they spread apart and gave the posse room to pass.

Webb hoped his face didn't show the momentary relief that swept over him. He swallowed, resisting an urge to lick his dried lips. For the moment he had tipped the scales his own way. One bad move, one sign of weakness, and the whole bluff might fall in shambles. He held his breath and tried to avoid looking back.

He heard the horses then, and he knew they weren't being allowed to get away so easily. He glanced over his shoulder and saw what he had feared. The Donovan men had split. They were falling in to ride with the posse, half of them on one side, half on the other.

They trailed along watchfully, warily, like gaunt and hungry wolves stalking a little bunch of buffalo.

14

Nearer and nearer they came to the Rio Grande. It would be at the river that the final decision must be made, that the bluff must be allowed to stand or be challenged in a blaze of fire and smoke.

To Webb it was no bluff. Though it cost his own life, he would squeeze this trigger, would kill Morg Donovan before he himself would die.

Webb's gaze searched eagerly ahead to the river and beyond. Sure, there was nothing to stop Donovan's men from following them across the river, to keep waiting for a chance to free Morg Donovan. But Webb doubted that they actually would. To him the river meant sanctuary. It was here that he must either win or lose. Across the Rio it wouldn't be far to help. He was sure that here at the river the Donovan crew would make its move or back away.

The Donovan men rode along abreast of Webb's group, four on one side, three on the other, keeping twenty or thirty feet from the posse. He could feel the eyes of the men watching him, waiting to seize upon any momentary advantage. Webb held the shotgun in a steady hand, the muzzle at Donovan's head.

This was the one chip he had left in the game.

Riding, he let his gaze move from one to another of the Donovan men, weighing them, judging them. His brother Sandy was not among them. Florentino hadn't lied. Sandy wasn't with the Donovan gang, and Webb felt sure he never had been.

But Augie Brock was there. Augie Brock, who had been Sandy's friend. Beside Augie rode another youth of about Sandy's size and age. This, Webb reasoned, must have been the one with Augie in the bank holdup at Dry Fork, the one so many people had taken to be Sandy. Conscience chewed on Webb for having even considered the possibility that Sandy could have outlawed.

He saw nervous stress weighing on Augie Brock. Webb said, "Augie, you've got yourself in awful rough company."

The youth said, "Webb, you can boss Sandy around, but you ain't goin' to tell me nothin'."

"Wasn't tryin' to tell you anything, just want you to take a hard look and see for yourself. You don't really fit in with a bunch like that. Is this the best you had hoped for?"

Augie said, "This company suits me just fine." But his voice carried no real conviction. Webb thought he could sense misgiving.

They were nearer the river now. The ageless Rio Grande flowed ahead of them just three hundred yards, then two hundred, then one hundred. The tension was winding tighter in Webb.

Thirty yards from the river one of the Donovan men—one Webb had taken as Donovan's *segundo*—suddenly spurred his horse up and circled in front of the group, stopping there. He placed himself squarely in Webb's path. "All right, mister lawman, I reckon we'll stop and parley a little."

"Parley about what?" Webb asked evenly. "We're crossin' that river, and Morg Donovan is goin' with us."

Webb didn't stop his horse. The man retreated a little, allowing Webb to move closer to the river. Then, abruptly, the rider seemed to make up his mind that this was as far as it went. He made a quick signal with his hand. The other six Donovan riders pushed in closer. Each held a gun. But then, so did Webb and Johnny and Florentino. With the shotgun pointed at Donovan's head, it looked like a standoff.

The leader declared, "We're callin' your bluff, lawman. We want Morg Donovan."

Webb's eyes narrowed. "Back off. We're takin' him across the river."

"You're forgettin', there's only four of you, and one is a woman. We could kill the whole bunch before you could wink an eye."

Webb said flatly, "But I'd see it comin' soon enough to pull this trigger. I don't aim to see Morg Donovan turned loose on the country again. Before I'd let that happen, I'd kill him like I'd kill a lobo wolf! Back off now or I'll give you Morg Donovan *dead!*"

The outlaw's face twisted in frustration. Looking into the angry eyes, Webb could almost see a dozen ideas flashing through the man's mind and being re-

jected as quickly as they came. Gradually the outlaw's mouth hardened. He flicked a glance at one of
the other Donovan men, a Mexican.

"Juan, you're closest to the woman. Put that rifle
of yours on her, the way the lawman has that shotgun
on Morg."

Webb felt his blood chill. If there was a weakness
in his own group, it was Ellie.

The outlaw said with a new confidence: "Now, lawman, you strike me as bein' a man with a conscience.
Bad as you want Donovan, you wouldn't trade this
lady for him, would you?" He answered his own question. "No, I reckon not. Now we got the same hand in
this game as you have. You'd risk your own life, but
not this woman's."

Morg Donovan gave a long sigh of relief and slumped
a little. His tongue moved across dried lips. "Good
work, Trace." He turned to face Webb. "Told you,
didn't I, Matlock? The boys wouldn't let me down."

Webb touched the shotgun to Morg's neck. "Just
you hold still, Morg. You're still my prisoner. I haven't
turned you loose." Morg had started to grin, but the
grin disappeared. Webb glanced toward the shaking
Augie Brock. "Augie, you've eaten many a meal in
Miss Ellie's place, and some of them when you couldn't
afford to pay her."

Consternation came into Augie's eyes. "Miss Ellie,
what did you have to come down here for, anyway?"

Ellie didn't answer. Her face was ashen, and Webb
suspected she was too scared even to speak. Webb said,
"Augie, she came because it was the right thing to do.
Now you owe it to her to do the right thing yourself."

Augie looked as if he wanted to break down and cry. "You got no right to ask me. I didn't want nothin' like this to happen. I ain't goin' to take no hand in it, no hand at all."

Webb said, "If she dies, Augie, her blood will be on you."

The outlaw named Trace said, "Wrong, lawman. She's your responsibility. What you goin' to do?"

Ellie cried out, "Don't turn him loose, Webb. Not after all we've been through."

Webb looked at the Mexican. Trace said, "If you're wonderin' whether Juan will do it or not, don't bother yourself. Won't be the first woman he ever killed. Slit his own wife's throat because he caught her with another man. Juan ain't got no particular use for women. One looks about the same as another to him."

The held-in breath slowly went out of Webb, and he sagged. He had hoped for help from Augie Brock. From the hard look in the Mexican's eyes, Webb had no doubt the man would kill Ellie without batting an eyelash. Webb swallowed, the strength gone from him.

"You'll let her go if I turn Morg over to you?"

Trace said, "We'll talk about it."

Webb glanced at Morg Donovan. "How about it, Morg? Leave her alone?" He pushed a little on the shotgun to be sure Morg felt the cold rim of the muzzle against his neck.

"All right, I'll let her go."

Webb said bitterly, "To get this close and lose . . ." He grimaced and lowered the shotgun. He glanced at the man named Trace. "All right, Morg is yours."

"Drop that shotgun, then. And make your men drop their guns."

Webb glanced around. "Johnny, Florentino . . ." The two complied.

"Six-shooters too," said Trace. When that was done, the Mexican lowered the rifle he had held pointed at Ellie. Ellie sagged. Weakly she stepped to the ground and leaned against her horse, her hands over her eyes.

The color was drained from Morg's face as he pulled away from Webb. He rode up to the man named Trace. "Here, cut me loose."

Trace took a knife and cut the rawhide that held Morg's hands to the saddle. Morg flexed his wrists and doubled and loosened his fists, rubbing to aid the circulation. Presently he looked back at Webb Matlock, his face clouded in hatred.

"Matlock, I owe you a debt. And if there's one thing the Donovans always do, it's pay their debts."

He held out his hand toward the nearest of his men. The man handed him a pistol. Morg swung the weapon toward Webb.

Ellie screamed, "No!" and leaped toward Morg. Morg's horse shied away at the sudden flare of skirts. Morg's hand flew upward, and his first shot missed.

In the moment of confusion, his own horse rearing, Webb quit the saddle. Morg tried with one hand to curb his mount and with the other to aim at the moving man. He missed a second time.

Ellie had turned back to where Webb had dropped the shotgun. She scooped it up from the hard ground. She cried, "Webb!" and pitched the gun to him. He caught it in both hands. Then, with no time to bring it to his shoulder and aim, he swung it against his hip, brought the muzzle up and squeezed the trigger.

The blast hit Morg Donovan full in the face and bowled him backward as if he had been struck by a sledge. Without a sound he slid off the horse and dropped lifeless to the ground. The shooting had thrown the horses into confusion and panic. The men struggled to bring them under control. Then they sat in their saddles and gazed horror-struck at the sight of Morg Donovan lying face down, the ground slowly reddening around him. The horses began to act up again, catching the smell of blood.

Trace said shakenly, "Just like Clabe. Just like Clabe." He turned to face Webb, who stood with the empty, smoking shotgun slack in his hand. "All promises are off, mister lawman. There ain't a one of you goin' back across that river now."

Augie Brock's voice broke through. "Let them alone, Trace!"

Trace looked around into the bore of Angie's pistol. "What the hell do you think you're doin', kid?"

"I'm stoppin' you. Spillin' their blood won't help Donovan now. Besides, I don't think you'll want to tangle with that bunch comin' yonder on the other side of the river. Look!"

The outlaw's head jerked to follow the sharp nod of Augie's chin. A whispered, "Damn!" escaped him.

Across the river, ten or a dozen men came pushing their horses hard.

Trace said, "We've flushed all the law there is in Texas. Let's get out of here!"

The outlaws swung their horses around and spurred south, forgetting about Morg Donovan, forgetting the little posse in the face of the larger one. All fled but Augie Brock. He held back, his head lowered in shame. He let his pistol slide into the holster. "Miss Ellie, I feel awful bad. I remember all the times you fed me when I was hungry. And there I was, about to back off and let them kill you."

Webb said, "Augie, you might have been slow, but you finally came around. We're much obliged."

Augie wasn't satisfied until he heard it from Ellie herself. "You did real fine, Augie," she said weakly. "And thank you."

Augie looked anxiously toward the river. The first of the riders already were splashing into the water from the other side.

Webb said, "Augie, the fact that you helped us will go a long ways with a jury. Run now and you'll run till the day you die."

Augie said, "I know, but I sure don't fancy none of them jails." He mounted his horse and started to run. He went perhaps fifty yards and pulled up. He turned and came back with his head down. He dismounted slowly. "You promise, Webb?"

Webb said, "I'll help you all I can."

Augie shrugged, accepting the inevitable. "I thought it'd be a fancy life, ridin' with the wild bunch. Truth of it is, I was scared to death of most of them. And that *tequila*, it always made me kind of sick."

The riders reached the near bank and pulled their horses to a stop. Webb looked up gratefully into familiar faces—tall old Quince Pyburn with some of Jess

Leggett's cowboys. And there was Sandy Matlock! Webb's mouth fell open in surprise. The sun struck and flashed against something metal on Sandy's shirt. It was a Texas Ranger badge.

Sandy jumped to the ground and rushed to his brother's side. "Webb, you all right?" He glanced then at Ellie Donovan, who still knelt where she had grabbed up the shotgun. "You, Miss Ellie? How about you?"

She nodded and tried to smile and began to cry softly instead. Webb took her hands, lifting her to her feet. He put his arms around her and held her close against him.

"She's all right, Sandy. We're all goin' to be just fine."

Quince Pyburn dropped stiffly to one knee to look at the outlaw's body. "Clabe Donovan," he said quietly. "Looks like we got to bury him again."

"It's not Clabe," Webb told him. "It's Morg." As briefly as he could, he told of Morg's masquerade, and the reasons for it.

A tall man strode up, a stranger to Webb. "Webb Matlock?" he asked. Webb saw that this man wore a Ranger's badge like Sandy's. The Ranger said, "I'm Russ Talley. Been hearin' a right smart about you from Sandy."

Webb frowned in puzzlement. "I don't understand, Talley. How did all of you happen to be here?"

"Judge Upshaw sent for the Rangers before he . . . before he died. Captain detailed me, and because Sandy knew the country, he sent him along to show me the way. Mister Pyburn there, he told us where you'd gone. We gathered a bunch of volunteers and came to help. We couldn't cross over the way you did, but we scattered up and down the river to be around in case you needed help when you came back. We heard shooting a while ago and came running."

That, Webb remembered, would have been the signal given by the first Donovan man who spotted them.

Looking now, he could see still other riders coming, drawn by the sound of the guns. No telling how many miles of river they had patrolled.

Talley said, "Matlock, that brother of yours is going to make a good Ranger. A little green yet, and rough in spots, but he has the makings. You should be proud of him."

Webb said soberly, "I am."

Sandy had walked over to his friend, Augie Brock. He stood with one hand on the worried youth's shoulder, talking in a voice too quiet for Webb to hear the words. Webb thought he knew the gist of Sandy's conversation, though: that Sandy would stick by Augie and help him all he could.

Presently Sandy came back to Webb, his hands shoved deep into his pockets, his head down. "Webb, I'm sorry if I caused you any worry. I left here mad. Aimed to make myself into a full-fledged Ranger before I came back. Wanted to show you what I could do. Now I can see that I ought to've written you and Birdie a letter." He frowned. "You should've seen the hot reception they gave me in Dry Fork. I hadn't no more than got off my horse till a dozen people was holdin' guns on me. Lieutenant Talley, he had to do a lot of explainin' before they'd turn me loose."

Indignation flared in Sandy's face. "Did you know, Webb, there was folks in town actually thought I'd outlawed? Thought I'd gone off and joined up with Donovan's bunch? Can you imagine anybody gettin' a crazy notion like that?"

Webb turned away to keep Sandy from seeing the sheepish look in his eyes. "It's hard to imagine."

Some of the men had rolled Morg Donovan's body in a blanket and were tying it across a horse. Lieutenant Talley watched the job finished, then said, "We better get back across the river. We've got no real right to be here."

Webb leaned down and took Ellie's hands. "Feel like ridin' again? We can stop on the other side somewhere, and you can get all the rest you need."

She nodded. "I want to put this place behind me." She started to get up but paused a moment. "Webb, now that it's over, I'm almost glad it turned out this way, that it wasn't Clabe."

Webb said, "Ellie, maybe you ought to take a long trip someplace, like San Antonio or one of those other big towns. Do somethin' different a while, put your mind on other things. You'll be surprised how fast you'll forget all this."

She arose, her face turned up toward his. "That sounds like a good idea, Webb, but I don't want to go alone. Will you take me?"

Webb gripped her hands tighter. "I'll take you, Ellie. Anywhere you want to go."

DARK
THICKET

1

The war against the Union lay five weeks behind him, and he had crossed the Sabine out of Louisiana four days ago. Owen Danforth was beginning to feel at last that he was truly back in Texas. Here, until he decided he was ready to return, the war would not touch him.

Until he was ready... A dull throbbing brought his right hand up to grip his tightly bandaged left arm. Not all the fever had left it. He wondered if he would *ever* be ready to go back.

Late in the morning he had broken out of the close and confining piney woods. Now he rode upon the higher, drier prairies that looked and smelled of home. His rump itched with an urgency for getting there, but the afternoon sun was in his eyes, and he knew night would catch him with miles yet to go. The big Yankee horse beneath him no longer took a long and easy stride. The journey had been wearying, and only a couple of times along the way had Owen managed to beg oats or corn for him from some farmer he met, some stranger in whose barn he slept a night. The war had left little enough even for people to eat, and horses must sustain on whatever grazing they could find. The fresh spring grass was yet weak, and so was any animal that depended upon it.

Owen came finally to a wagon trace which seemed to strike a chord in his memory. Turning in the saddle for a different perspective, he thought he recalled using this road when he had traveled eastward two years and more ago with his brother Ethan, eager to join the fighting before it could all be finished without them. He found familiarity in the pitch of the gentle hills, the steeple of a distant church, the lay of a neglected cornfield with a gully started at its lower end, gradually carrying away the fertile topsoil with every rain.

A mile ahead he saw a string of large wagons moving ponderously toward him. They reminded him of the long military supply trains he had seen early in the war, trains that had gradually shortened as the Confederacy found it difficult to keep filling them. These, he saw as he came nearer, were heavy freight wagons paired in tandem, each pair drawn by four spans of big draft horses and mules. He pulled out of the trail to yield them room. A tired-looking middle-aged man on horseback rode up to him. He gave Owen's bandaged arm a moment's study.

"Howdy, soldier," he said pleasantly. "Where you bound?"

Owen said, "Home. I'm Owen Danforth. You'd be Jake Tisdale, wouldn't you?"

Tisdale blinked. "Owen?" His eyes narrowed for a longer, more careful look. "Damned if you ain't.

Wouldn't of knowed you, son. You've changed a right smart."

"So've you. When I left here you was farmin' on the river. You in the freightin' business now?"

Tisdale nodded. "War duty. I was too old to tote a rifle, and they said I'd do the government more service haulin' freight. I take cotton bales down to the Rio Grande and ferry them across to Mexico. Confederacy trades them to French and Englishmen for war supplies. The Yankees can bottle up the Texas ports, but they can't do nothin' about us tradin' in Mexico." He pointed his chin toward the lead wagon, its wide-rimmed wheels raising dust as they labored by. "I come north with guns and ammunition and such."

Owen had heard about the cotton trains. "I been told the Yankees invaded Brownsville from the sea to put a stop to this."

"They did. But we cross the Rio farther west, where their patrols can't reach. Then we travel down the river on the Mexican side and thumb our noses as we go by. Makes them madder'n hell." Tisdale looked at Owen's arm again. "If you're lookin' for work, I believe I can find somethin' you could do with one arm."

Owen shrugged. "Maybe later, after I see how things go with my folks. You seen them, Mr. Tisdale?"

Tisdale shook his head. "I been on the trail too much. It's all I can do to spend a night with the wife and young'uns when I pass through." He frowned. "I hear things, though. Seems like your old daddy's still got notions against the war. There's some fire-eatin' patriots that'd do him bodily harm if somebody was to just lead the way."

Owen grimaced, suddenly not sure he was in a hurry to be home. "I ought to've known he wouldn't see reason."

Tisdale seemed hesitant to speak. "I *heard* you and him had a considerable disagreement when you left for the army."

"I was of age to make up my mind. So was my brother."

"Maybe the Lord's sent you at a good time. You bein' a wounded soldier come home, maybe the hotheads'll stand back and leave him alone. But you watch out, son. Things are touchy. There's been men killed for sayin' less than your daddy has."

Tisdale shook Owen's hand and fell into the dusty wake of the last wagon. Owen watched the train move away in its own slow time, and a sourness settled into his stomach.

Hell of a situation to come home to.

Gauging the position of the sun, he decided he should reach Uncle Zachariah Danforth's farm before dark. The tall bay horse needed rest, and Owen could better face the confrontation with his father if he arrived home fresh. Uncle Zach had been of the same mind as Andrew Danforth on the confederacy question and the war, but at least he could be tolerant of an opposing viewpoint. Tolerance was a seldom thing with Owen's father.

The left arm felt hot beneath the bandages, which had needed changing for the last two days. Now and then a sharp pain grabbed him with the violence of a cotton hook. Odd, he could not remember feeling any pain when the Yankee saber had slashed him. He had been caught up in the shouting fury of hand-to-hand fighting. Something about the fever of battle masked the pain until the excitement had peaked. Only then had he realized his arm was hanging uselessly, blood spilling from his sleeve and running down a dead-numb hand that could not feel its warmth. The first doctor who examined him was ready to saw the bone in two. Owen had fought like a cornered badger until the doctor turned away in his frustration, telling him to go ahead and die if that be his choice. Blood poisoning had nearly killed Owen, but he still had his arm. He could not yet tell whether it would ever be of use again.

He felt no rancor toward the doctor or even toward the faceless Yankee who struck him and rode on. He had no idea, for the excitement had been intense, whether the Yankee had been small or large, young or old. He did not know if the man had survived the fight. Many on both sides had not.

I'll be home tomorrow, he told himself. His mother would know what to do, what would be needed to draw out the fever and the poison. If the arm was to be saved, his mother would know how.

When the fever had been at its worst, the lifeline to which Owen had clung most tightly was an obligation to set things right with Andrew Danforth, to reconcile for careless and angry recriminations flung at their parting. Perhaps tomorrow he would find better words.

The sun was twenty minutes gone behind the great oak trees on the river when a turn of the trail and a clearing of the scattered timber showed him Zach

Danforth's cabin in the dusk. Before he thought better, he touched spurs to the big horse and tried to bully a faster trot from him. He slowed, knowing he had taxed the animal too much already.

Uncle Zach had been a widower longer than Owen could remember. His only child had died at birth, along with its mother. Zach had helplessly watched her die and could never bring himself to put another woman through that jeopardy.

Riding toward the double cabin, Owen kept his eyes on the open dog run between its two sections. He shouted, "Hello the house. Anybody home?"

A gruff voice spoke behind him. "Turn slow, soldier, and show me who you are."

Owen turned quickly, stiffening at sight of a shotgun. Zachariah Danforth stood beside a small shed where he sheltered his harness, saddles and other goods that needed protection from the weather. He raised the shotgun to let Owen see the muzzle of it.

Owen swallowed. "Uncle Zach, it's me."

"Owen?" Suspicious eyes stared from under a wilted felt hat that had been old when Owen was yet a boy. "Come a little closer and let me see."

Owen was drawn thin, and he had not been able to shave himself decently since he had taken that saber wound. He wore a beard that had not felt scissors or razor since he had left the Georgia cotton warehouse that served as a field hospital. "It's me sure enough, Uncle Zach."

The eyes flickered with glad recognition, and the shotgun dropped to arm's length. "Git down, boy. I was lookin' for company, but you ain't what I expected."

Owen dismounted slowly, clinging to the saddle after his feet were on the ground, for his knees threatened to buckle. Zach was about to embrace him when he noticed the bound arm. He still almost broke Owen's right shoulder with a loving squeeze of his big hand. "You been hurt, boy."

"That's why they let me come home."

Zach's long silence and pained eyes spoke of sympathy. He had always provided a sympathetic refuge when Owen had one of his many quarrels with his father. "I'll put your horse up and find him a bait of oats. You look like you've had a long trip on a bad road."

"Looks don't lie," Owen admitted, rueful at letting someone else take care of his horse. That was a job a whole man did for himself.

Relief washed over Owen as he stared into that kindly, beloved face. Zach was a little older than Owen's father, but the eyes were the same, the deeply lined face similar except for Zach's rough, gray-streaked beard.

"Good-lookin' bay you got," Zach commented. "Better than you left here on."

"Turncoat horse," Owen said. "He was in the Yankee army. I caught him runnin' loose after a little sashay against some Union supply wagons. Owner never showed up to claim him."

"Wonder the army let you come home with him. They keep the good ones for the officers and make the boys take the plugs."

Owen frowned. "A lieutenant taken him away from me. The night I left, I borrowed him back off of the picket line."

Zach spat. "I hope you brought home a gun, too. You'll need it, to keep that horse."

"There's a pistol in my saddlebag. I got it the same way I got the bay."

"Carry it in your pants, or in your boot. They won't give you time to fetch it out of your saddlebag."

Owen blinked. "Who? We never had much trouble with horse thieves in this country."

Zach gave him a troubled study. "Things ain't like you left them, son. You've probably got a notion you put the war behind you when you started back, but you didn't. It's here."

"Yankees?"

"Worse. The country's overrun with heel flies."

Heel flies were insects that buzzed around the hocks of cattle in season and drove them crazy. "What have heel flies got to do with the war?"

"These are the two-legged kind. Home guards, they call theirselves." Zach spat again, and Owen could see anger boil into his eyes. "They enforce the *con*script law and make sure everybody says a prayer once a day to Jefferson Davis. They see somethin' they want, they take it in the name of the Confederacy. They see somebody they don't like, they jail him for the same cause, or do worse. It's almost a pity you come home, boy. Now you'll see what you been fightin' for."

Before Texans had cast their votes for secession, Zach and Owen's father had been among several in the county who campaigned vigorously to remain within the Union. Sam Houston had talked against secession, and like many Texans those two old settlers thought Sam Houston had hung the moon. They had embraced the Union flag too long to turn against it.

That had been the source of much friction, some spoken and some swallowed, between Owen and his father.

He could see the years had not tempered Zach's feelings. He knew within reason that his father's would be as strong.

When the bay horse had been fed, Zach took Owen's rolled blanket and his saddlebags under his arm. "We tend the stock-first, *then* the men. I ain't got much in the way of fixin's, young'un, but I'll not leave you sleep hungry."

Owen might have been a *young'un* when he left home, but the war had whipped that out of him. Times he felt as old as Uncle Zach.

In the kitchen side of the double cabin, the old man coaxed a small blaze in the fireplace and hung a pot of beans to warm. He whipped up a batch of bread with stone-ground corn of his own raising and ground a double handful of coffee beans. "Coffee's scarce," he said. "I generally save it for Sundays, but this is an occasion." Lastly he cut thick slices of bacon and laid them in a skillet. It was simple bachelor fare, but to Owen it had the aroma of a feast in the making. He had missed more meals than he had found on the trail home.

Zach said with a touch of sadness, "It's good to have you here, Owen. Been an empty place without you comin' over to see me . . . you and your brothers."

An old ache came to Owen, and he stared at the floor. "I wrote you what happened to Ethan. Did you get my letter?"

Zach nodded. "Died in your arms, you said."

"It was quick. He was gone in a minute after the bullet struck him." He kept looking down, unable to lift his gaze. "I never did hear just what happened to Andy Jr., except that he was killed."

Zach was awhile in answering. He rubbed the corner of one eye. "It was after they started the *con*-script law. Your daddy knowed they'd be comin' after your brother first thing, so he let him and a couple others of the same persuasion light out for Mexico. They got a hundred miles before a home guard patrol caught up to them. Claimed the boys put up a scrap, but you know Little Andy wasn't no fighter. Murdered all three and left them layin' where they fell."

Zach paused. "I went down with your daddy to bring the boys home, but some kind folks had buried them. We never could find just where."

Owen felt a biting anger and the helplessnes of loss. "Dad shouldn't't've let him go. If he hadn't been so almighty set against the war . . ."

Zach's eyes gave no quarter. "You taken one brother to war with you and lost him. Your daddy tried to keep the other at home and lost *him* too. Looks to me like you and him ought to call it even and find a way to get along."

Owen rubbed the hurting arm. "That's what I want to do, if he will."

"Give him time. They was brothers to *you*, but

they was sons to *him*. You can lose a brother and go on. Lose a son, and you lose a part of yourself."

Owen said, "I'm not proud of the way I left here. I said things I shouldn't've. When I get home tomorrow, I'll set myself straight with Dad and with Mama."

Zach looked away, suddenly. "Your mama?" He gave his attention again to the cooking, turning the bacon with a fork. "I reckon where you been you didn't get much mail."

"Been way over a year since Mama's last letter. Most of the mail gets lost."

Zach set the food on the table. Owen tried to remember his manners, but the hunger was too much. He wolfed down the first plateful, then gave more time to the second. Zach ate little, watching him with troubled eyes. When Owen had finished, Zach said sadly, "I didn't want to tell you till you'd had your supper. Your mama died back in the winter. There was a fever come through the country."

Owen had seen so much of death on the battle-grounds that he had thought he was immune to grief, but this caught him unprepared. He walked outside, and Zach let him work out his feelings alone. Much later, when Owen went back into the cabin, Zach sat in an old rocking chair that had been his wife's. He looked at Owen without comment, waiting for Owen to speak. But Owen had no words to say.

Zach stood up, finally, and walked over to look at Owen's bandage. He unwrapped the dirty cloth and frowned at the wound. "Wonder you didn't lose the arm."

"Almost did. Truth is, Uncle Zach, they sent me home figurin' I stood a good chance to die."

"No money in your pocket. No medal on your coat. You didn't get much except experience, did you?"

"I've had aplenty of *that*."

Zach cleansed the wound with homemade whisky, which raised a fire in the raw flesh. He took a drink out of the jug and offered it to Owen. The fire in the arm was too strong for Owen to risk another in his belly.

Zach observed, "Still fevered some, I'd say."

Owen told him it was.

"Well, I know what'll draw that out. I'll fix you a pony poultice."

"A what?"

"You just set here and rest. I'll be back directly." Zach lighted a lantern and went outside. When he returned the aroma came through the door with him. He carried half-dried horse manure in a bucket. He said, "This won't do much for your social standin', but it'll do a right smart for your healin'."

He wrapped the arm lightly with clean white cloth, then applied a liberal helping of the manure and wrapped it over with more cloth to hold it in place. "I'll bet if you asked ten doctors, there wouldn't be *one* tell you about this."

"I expect not," Owen replied dryly.

The arm felt better; that Owen would have to admit, though it was some time before he became reconciled to the odor.

He lay awake a long time, remembering his mother, seeing her face in the darkness, hearing her voice. It seemed to him that he could feel a drawing sensation in his arm, and a sense of extra heat even beyond the fever that had been in it. He slipped away finally into a heavy sleep demanded by his weariness. When he awoke, it was suddenly and in response to a loud voice.

"Danforth! You come out here, Zach Danforth, or we'll come in there and fetch you out!"

Owen sat up quickly, bringing a sharp pain to his arm. He blinked in confusion, not remembering for a moment where he was. He heard his uncle curse softly across the dark room as he dressed and stamped to get his feet all the way into his boots. Zach said, "You just as well get up, Owen. Night's over."

Owen was still putting on his clothes when Zach stepped through the cabin door and a presunrise glow was reflected in his bearded face. Owen let the left sleeve hang free, his heavily wrapped arm inside the shirt. He could hear a belligerent voice.

"We're lookin' for some deserters, Danforth. Tracks showed they was in the river bottoms yesterday. We figured you're the most likely man hereabouts to be hidin' them out. We're searchin' your place whether you like it or not."

"Go ahead and search, Shattuck, and God damn you to hell!"

Owen pulled on his boots and walked through the open door to stand beside his uncle. Against the half-blinding sunrise he saw a full dozen horsemen. He knew the one nearest the cabin. Before the war, Phineas Shattuck had been the kind of dramshop brawler who liked to beat up an occasional stranger smaller than himself but always slipped out the back door if someone bigger came in shopping for a fight. Owen's father and uncle had taken Shattuck to court over a wagonload of acorn-fattened shoats removed from the Danforth river bottom land. They had forced Shattuck to pay, but they had not gotten the man sent to jail as he had deserved. Shattuck was a landowner, even if a small and grubby one, and not to be lightly imprisoned like some luckless hired hand for becoming a little careless in the gathering of livestock. He was given the benefit of considerable doubt. Afterward, Andrew Danforth's barn had burned. Everyone knew who had done it.

Shattuck's hand went to the butt of a pistol in his waistband, and he glowered suspiciously at Owen. "Who are you?"

Owen knew Shattuck would feel no friendlier when he knew. "I'm Owen Danforth. Andrew Danforth is my father."

That name deepened the hostility. "What're you doin' here?" Shattuck stared at what was left of Owen's once-gray uniform. "You desert from the army?"

Owen touched his bad arm. "I taken a saber cut. They sent me home till I get well."

Shattuck seemed to believe, though it was plainly against his will. "You got any papers?"

"In the cabin, in my saddlebags."

Shattuck looked to the two horsemen nearest him. "Jones, Adcock, you go with him. Keep a sharp watch, and be sure there ain't nobody else in there."

Owen had given the other riders no more than a glance. When these two moved so he could see them without the rising sun in his eyes, he was surprised to find that they were boys, probably only fifteen or sixteen years old. One had the rough look of a born schoolyard bruiser. The other was unsure, perhaps even a little frightened. Most of the men from that age up to infirmity were gone to the war.

The older of the boys wrinkled his nose. "What stinks?"

Owen said, "My arm."

"My God," the boy declared, "you must've got the *gan*grene."

Owen's saddlebags lay in a chair. His pistol was in one, but caution told him it was best they not see it. He opened the other and took out the paper he had been given, showing he was free to return home on convalescent leave. He tried to show it to the older boy, the rough one, who gave it only a glance, upside down, and said, "Captain Shattuck's the one to read it."

Captain Shattuck. A lot of rank, Owen thought, for a pig thief.

Shattuck read the paper without comment, then frowned at the two boys. "You look at the other side of the cabin while you're afoot. Make sure there ain't no deserters in it."

He shifted his attention back to Owen. "You sure you got a wounded arm? You sure that ain't just a lie to help you desert from the service?"

Owen held down a quick rise of anger. "You want to unwrap it and see?" He moved closer.

Shattuck's face twisted at the odor, and he backed off. "I'll be lookin' in on you from time to time. If you don't lose that arm, I want to be sure your old daddy and this renegade uncle don't make you forget you're still a soldier."

The two boys returned from the other side of the cabin and reported it clear. Shattuck said to Zach, "You probably got rid of them deserters before we come. We'll look the rest of the place over before we leave. If we ever catch you . . ." The rest went unspoken.

He rode to Zach's pens and observed the horses across the fence. "You, soldier boy, come over here."

Owen caught a half-trapped look in his uncle's eyes.

Shattuck demanded, "That big bay horse yours, boy?"

Owen said it was.

"A man on sick leave don't have use for a horse like that. We'll borry him from you and leave you one good enough for what little travel you'll be doin'. Adcock, turn that black horse of yours into the pen. I'll take the bay, and you can have mine."

Owen pushed forward to protest, but his uncle's restraining hand was firm on his shoulder.

The black horse was old enough to vote, almost, and seemed to favor its right forefoot. Small wonder, Owen thought darkly, that Shattuck wanted to force a trade.

"Come a long ways, ain't you, Shattuck?" he said.

"How's that?"

"You used to just steal *pigs*."

Shattuck drew back his big hand. Zach quickly stepped in front of Owen. "This boy's wounded, Shattuck."

Shattuck slowly lowered his hand, but the red did

not drain from his face. "When you get ready to return to your regiment, soldier, I'll study about givin' this horse back to you."

He saddled the big bay and mounted. He ordered his men—his boys, actually—to spread out widely and sweep the field and pastureland all the way to the river. As they left, Zach said, "There'll be six foot of snow here on the Fourth of July before he lets you have that horse. The only way you'll get him is to take him."

"I'll do that," Owen swore.

Zach watched in silence until the line of horsemen disappeared over a rise and into timber along the river. "Well, boy, you've met the heel flies."

Owen looked at the black horse, the anger still churning. "I'd just as well saddle up and get started."

Zach shook his head. "Wait awhile. Give Shattuck and his boys time to clear the road."

Zach fixed breakfast, about the same as supper except that he did not heat the beans again. He ground more of his precious coffee beans against Owen's protest. Zach said, "We're kin, boy. What's mine is yours; you don't even need to ask. I'd always figured to leave this farm to you and your brothers. Now there ain't but you left. When I'm gone, the place belongs to you."

Warmth came over Owen. He wanted to hug his uncle, but he was shy about it. He could only say, "Please don't be in any hurry to go. I want you to live a hundred years."

"That's my intention."

Eating, Owen noticed Zach straighten suddenly. He asked, "They back?"

Zach motioned for him to hush and strained to listen. Owen heard some kind of birdcall. Zach pushed away from the table and walked out to stand in the open dog run. He looked around, then put two fingers in his mouth and whistled. Owen heard the distant birdcall again. The hair seemed to rise on his neck.

"Stand easy, young'un," Zach said calmly. "It's all right."

Four horsemen rode out of the timber on the river and up to the cabin. A young man looked vaguely familiar, a face dimly remembered from Owen's boyhood though he could not place name or circumstance to it. The man was armed with two pistols on his belt and a rifle across his lap. He appeared severe enough to rush a bear with a willow switch. The other three wore gray uniforms, or pieces of them. Of late, the average Confederate soldier's uniform was whatever clothing he could beg, borrow or get away with.

Zach said, "Mornin', Vance Hubbard. Some fellers was here while ago lookin' for you and your friends."

Vance Hubbard. Owen remembered. Hubbard's father had been a farmer and a fellow campaigner with Andrew and Zach Danforth against secession. He had died, leaving a widow, a daughter and two sons. Hubbard studied Owen with as much suspicion as Shattuck had shown but without the malice.

Zach explained Owen's presence. Hubbard dismounted and extended his hand. Owen said, "I remember you now, Vance, but I had to look at you awhile."

Hubbard studied the stained and fading remnants

of Owen's uniform. He said, "I hope your memory will continue to be just as short, should you be asked if you've seen anyone." A little of a smile came. "The time my father fell sick, your daddy and your Uncle Zach brought you and your brothers to help my brother Tyson and me bring in the crop."

Owen had not forgotten. "I was seventeen or eighteen."

"You did a man's work." Hubbard turned to Zach and nodded his chin at the three riders. "These men have hidden for two days without food."

"Anything I've got, they're welcome to."

Owen stood openmouthed. Zach explained, "There's a lot more people against this war than you might think. There's a bunch of men holed up in the big thicket over east . . . fellers runnin' from the *con-script* law, and some who've taken French leave of the army. The heel flies ain't got the guts to try and root them out of that heavy timber. Vance and some of us do what we can to help."

Owen had heard nothing of this, where he had been.

Zach saw his consternation. "This ain't the only place, Owen. There's pockets of resistance like this all across Texas. Over on Bull Creek outside of Austin, a bunch of the boys are holed up in the cedar brakes just like these here. And out in the German settlements, there's a lot of Dutchmen dead set against Jeff Davis. They've kept troops busy almost ever since the war started."

Zach put his hand gently on Owen's shoulder. "Son, I know how you feel, so I wouldn't ask you to be a party to it. What say I saddle your horse and get you started to your daddy's place? What you don't see or hear, they can't hold against you."

Owen was uneasy, knowing these three men were deserters. By not reporting them he was putting himself in jeopardy, even bordering on treason. But he saw something in Vance Hubbard's determined face that would stop a cavalry charge.

Uneasily he said, "Looks to me like a risky business, Uncle Zach. I wish you wasn't in it."

"Everybody serves, son, one side or the other . . ."

As Owen started to ride away, Hubbard said, "Tell your daddy I'll be by to see him one of these nights."

Owen remained uneasy, for he had a hunch that to associate with Hubbard in these times would be akin to sitting under a lone tree while the thunder and lightning played.

He felt a touch of resentment. Nobody had a right to put his uncle in that sort of danger . . . or his father.

2

Before the cabin came into view, Owen rode upon thirty or so spotted beef cattle that wore the family's D Bar brand, and with them a brindle milk cow heavy in calf. She would be freshening soon, ready to go back into the milk pen. The sight of the cows loosed a tingling of eagerness for home. The black horse, he had decided, was not so much lame as simply aged. The unjust nature of the forced trade still rankled. That bay had been worth a dozen snides of this kind. Phineas Shattuck had probably rejoiced all the way to town.

Owen had removed Zach's odorous pony poultice and bathed himself in the chilling waters of a creek. If pressed, he would have to admit his uncle's treatment seemed to have drawn out some of the fever. But the smell had been intolerable.

He skirted the edge of a field in which he had unwillingly worked from the time he had been seven or eight years old. The sweat used to stream as he stolidly gripped a Georgia stock and followed an equally reluctant team of mules. He had left here hoping never to touch a plow handle again. Now he wished he had two good hands for the work.

The house was a double cabin, built like Uncle Zach's, its two sections sharing a common cypress-shingle roof. Inside the open dog run between them, a narrow set of stairs led up to a sleeping area where Owen had wrestled with his brothers for blankets.

The nearer Owen came to the house, the more he tried to spur faster movement out of the black horse. The spirit might have been willing, but the flesh would not be rushed. Owen's eye was drawn to the little family cemetery, fenced with flat stones his father had hauled down from an outcropping on the hill the winter after he had settled here. The firstborn had been placed in the ground after just two months of a struggling life. Two other children lay beside him, their grave markers mute testimony to the harshness of early Texas. Owen pulled the horse in that direction, for there would be one more marker now than when he had gone off to war.

His throat feeling swollen, he dismounted and opened the iron gate. He removed his hat and stared at the newly chiseled stone that said *Idella Danforth, Beloved Wife and Mother*. The stone seemed to dissolve into a blur, and he did not hear the footsteps behind him until a familiar voice said, "Owen?"

Turning, he saw his father. Andrew Danforth looked ten years older than when Owen had last seen him. But he was still a towering figure, taller than Owen, even broader of shoulder because he had spent a long life at hard labor.

Owen wanted to go to his father and hug him, but

he could not. Andrew Danforth had the same reticence. He stood off at two paces and stared at Owen's bound arm. "It's not . . ."

"I've still got it," Owen said. "I just don't know yet how much use it'll ever be."

"Why didn't you ever write, son?"

"I did. I guess the mail never got through."

The elder Danforth looked as if he wanted to take the long step that would carry him to his son, and Owen waited for him to do so. But the best the two men could bring themselves to do was to stand at arm's length and awkwardly shake hands. Andrew walked to the new grave and touched his hand gently to the tall stone. "You didn't know about *her*?"

"Not till yesterday. I stayed all night at Uncle Zach's."

"I know. Phineas Shattuck came by a while ago with his guards, braggin' and threatenin'." He frowned at the black horse, standing with all its weight on three feet, showing no inclination to go anywhere though the rein was but loosely draped around the iron gatepost. "Not much of a trade, was it?"

"Someday, some way, I'll get my horse back."

Andrew shook his head. "Phineas can't help bein' what he is. Most of what his family ever had, they stole. Nobody would pay much mind to him before the war. Now they've got to, and he's made the most of it."

He looked at Owen's arm again. "Phineas would probably give ten years of his life to have an honorable wound like that, if he didn't have to suffer for it. He probably resents the fact that *you* got it."

"If he went where I've been, he'd have his chance. How come he's *not* in the army?"

"He owns a little land and some cattle. That exempts him. And he knows things some authorities wouldn't want him to tell." Andrew turned away from his wife's gravestone and looked at those of his other children. "There's two missin'," he said quietly.

Owen swallowed, listening for blame. Andrew might not say it, but Owen felt it was there, just beneath the surface. He wished he were still at Uncle Zach's.

Andrew seemed to have trouble bringing out the words. "It's good to have you at home, son, even in this condition. But you'd just as well know before we ever speak on politics: I ain't changed a particle."

Owen said, "Neither have I. But this is home."

He wished he could speak an apology and hear one in return. But he saw the determined set of his father's shoulders and remembered why he had left in the first place.

They walked toward the house, Owen leading the horse. Owen said, "This place looks just like it did the day I left it."

"Time you've been home a day or two you'll know it's not. I run out of day before I run out of things that need doin'. I mortally miss your mama, son."

Owen frowned. "You sure takin' care of the place is all you been doin'?"

Andrew missed a step. "What do you mean?"

"I met Vance Hubbard over at Uncle Zach's. He said he'll be by to see you."

Andrew stopped. "You still a soldier, or did they turn you plumb loose?"

"I'm still a soldier. If I get well enough, I'm supposed to go back."

"Bein' a soldier, there's things you'll be better off not knowin'. If you didn't report them to the government you'd feel like a turncoat. If you did, you'd betray old friends. So if somethin' comes along you don't understand, don't try to. Go off by yourself and try not to see anything."

Uneasiness stirred in Owen. He could guess, from things he had seen at Zach's, what his father was trying to say without putting it into words. "Dad, you and Uncle Zach are sittin' in on a dangerous game."

Andrew looked across the field, the rolling prairie. His jaw was firmly set, "I came here an American, when Texas was still a republic. I worked as hard as anybody to see that we got ourselves into the Union. I didn't stop bein' an American because of a family fight."

"You think that's all it amounts to, just a family fight?"

"That's the meanest kind of fight there is. You ought to know that, as much as anybody."

Owen rested the next couple of days. Most of the fever left his arm. He suspected Zach's pony poultice had helped, but he did not repeat the treatment.

He did the chores that were possible one-handed, feeling a rising of guilt that he could not do more to help his father. He began unwrapping the heavy binding every day and trying to exercise the stiffened left arm. At first it would not move except when forced by his right hand. Then he was able to move it slightly when he put a strong will to the task. He could flex his fingers a bit, though he had little control.

"It's comin' back," he told his father hopefully.

Andrew did not smile. He did little smiling that Owen could see. "Keep workin' at it, but don't raise your hopes. It's a long fall to the ground when things don't work like you thought they would." A little of bitterness was in his voice.

They talked of many things, but some they avoided. Left unspoken were their opposing opinions about the war, which stood like a stone fence between them. Never mentioned were Owen's brothers, who had died far from home. If the conversation threatened to turn in that direction, one or the other would change the subject. Owen began to hope the war might simply leave them alone, and that fence might never have to be climbed.

But the war came to them anyway.

Upward of noon one day, Owen was awkwardly going about the cooking of dinner while his father plowed out a new stand of corn. He heard horses approaching, and he stepped into the open dog run. Across the green pasture came a dozen riders, bathed in the bright sunshine of a Texas spring. They might have been a pretty picture had Owen not recognized the big bay horse and the man riding him. Anger rising, he stepped out of the shadows and looked toward the fields. His father had seen. Andrew Danforth laid the Georgia stock over and strode through the newly cultivated corn toward the cabin. He reached there about the time the horsemen did.

Phineas Shattuck was the first to speak, directing

his attention to Owen. "How's that arm, soldier? About ready to go back to duty?"

Owen grudgingly raised the bound arm as far as it would go. He said, "It's a ways from healed."

His glance swept the line of riders. They appeared to be the same young boys, pretty much, who had ridden with Shattuck the last time. The rough one, Adcock, had pulled his horse up almost even with Shattuck's, but he deferred to another man, an older one, astride a big sorrel that Owen thought might be the finest-looking horse he had ever seen. He compared his bay to that one and thought he would not mind a trade. But of course he would have to get the bay back first.

The man wore a black patch over one eye, and a streak of white whiskers ran like a slash through his dark-brown beard. Owen suspected the beard was an effort to hide a scar. War scar, more than likely; there were plenty of them around.

The man rode closer to Owen. "How did you get the wound, soldier?"

"Yankee saber, sir." Owen had unconsciously added the *sir*. This man had a bearing that identified him as an officer, though Owen had to look hard before he saw the badge.

The man said, "I received mine from a Yankee shell that killed my horse and two men nearby. They said I was unfit for further duty. I trust they have not dismissed you so lightly?" The question had the harsh flavor of gall about it. Clearly, he had not willingly given up the fight.

Owen said, "I'll be goin' back if this arm heals proper."

The man gazed at Owen's father. "And if you do not allow yourself to be influenced unduly by those whose loyalties are not as strong as ours."

Andrew Danforth said firmly, "My son's old enough to make up his own mind, Chance. I'll not tell him what he should do."

Chance . . . *Chancellor*. Owen remembered. Claude Chancellor had been sheriff of this county when Texas seceded. It was said of him that he had read more books than any man in the county, even more than a schoolteacher. He looked different now. The war, more than likely . . . the eye patch, the beard, the wounds seen and unseen. By the tiny badge Owen took it that he was sheriff again.

Chancellor said, "I remember you, Owen. You were working in your father's field the last time I saw you. You are a man now, with a man's responsibilities. Ordinarily there is no one who holds more strongly than I to the biblical injunction that thou shalt honor thy father. In your case, continue to honor him, but I would advise you not to listen to him in matters of duty."

Owen made no reply. He stared at the face and that stern eye. Compared to Chancellor, Phineas Shattuck was a cur standing in the shadow of a gray wolf.

Chancellor spoke to Owen's father in a tone that reminded Owen of their old friendship. Not all things had fallen victim to the war. "You may not have heard, Andrew, but there was some shooting last night. A patrol came upon Vance Hubbard and some of his hideout people from the thicket. The youngest Hubbard boy was seen with them. They got away into the timber without anyone shot, so far as we know. But now there is a price on Tyson Hubbard's head, just as there has been on his brother's. And there will be a price on anyone who helps them."

Owen looked for his father's reaction, but whatever Andrew Danforth was feeling, he kept it bottled up.

Chancellor said, "I felt it only fair to warn you . . . once."

Andrew Danforth said evenly, "We all do our duty, Chance, as we see it."

Shattuck declared, "If I was you, Claude, I'd haul him in to jail right now. You know where his sympathies are at."

Chancellor gave Shattuck a quick glance that showed his annoyance at the uninvited suggestion, or perhaps at the familiar use of his given name. As sheriff, Chancellor once had arrested Shattuck on charges brought by Andrew and Zachariah Danforth. Owen suspected he did not relish riding with the man now, even in the service of the Confederacy.

Chancellor studied Owen's arm, then his face. "Andrew, your son seems to have acquitted himself well in the service of his country. The old can often learn much from the young. I would suggest you seek your son's counsel." He drew away.

Shattuck pulled around to follow him but stopped. A touch of malice was in his eyes. He patted the bay horse on the shoulder. "Soldier, this is quite a mount you've lent to your country's service."

By the time Owen thought of an adequate reply, the guard detail had ridden away. He turned to his father and declared, "Phineas Shattuck would mortally love to catch you at somethin' he could call treason."

"And I know some people who would mortally love to catch Phineas Shattuck over in the thickets, without all those wet-eared kids around to protect him."

"*You* been over in that thicket, Dad?"

"You askin' me as a son, or as a soldier?"

Owen pondered darkly. "I ain't askin' atall. I take back the question." He thought he knew the answer anyway. "That Shattuck's dangerous."

"Only if you turn your back on him. I try to see him before he sees me."

"I wish you'd try not to see Vance Hubbard at *all*. He's liable to get you killed."

"He's the son of an old friend. This trouble won't change that." He obviously did not want to continue the subject. "How long till dinner's ready?"

Owen told him it would be thirty minutes if he did not drop anything, an hour if he did.

Andrew said, "I'll go back to the field. Can't afford to be wastin' daylight."

That night, as was his custom after supper, Andrew took down the big Bible that had been a wedding gift long ago to him and Idella Danforth. He read awhile by lamplight, then went out onto the dog run to sit in a straight-backed chair and meditate in the coolness of the night. He did not say, and Owen never asked him, what he was thinking about . . . the Bible, the war, better days when the family had been together.

Owen sat beside him in silence, flexing his fingers, moving his bad arm up and down as far as he could. He could see a little improvement from one day to the next.

Andrew exclaimed, "Did you see that?"

Owen straightened, alarmed. "What?"

"A little glow of fire out yonder, at the edge of the timber. Somebody lighted a pipe, I think."

Owen frowned. "Your Unionist friends?"

"They'd know better. It's probably some of those home guard kids, come by to take a look at this place."

Dread began to build in Owen. "Maybe waitin' for your friends to show up."

Andrew grunted. "Son, I didn't mean for you to leave one war and find yourself in another."

"You don't *have* to be in this one."

"In a way, I'm a soldier like you are. I'll do what I can to help those who believe the way I do."

"Sooner or later they'll drive you to the thickets. Or maybe worse."

"I'm a hard man to kill. Those home guards are mostly just boys anyway."

Impatiently Owen said, "A *baby* can kill you if you put a gun in his hands. Give these boys a bad model to pattern after and they can be as dangerous as grown men. Maybe worse, because they haven't learned how to think things through for themselves. They follow whoever hollers loudest."

"Like you and Ethan did, when you joined the army?"

That stung. Owen said, "I may've been a kid when I went, but that seems like ten years ago. I know what I'm doin' now."

Andrew nodded grimly. "So does your old daddy."

Nights, Owen made his bed where he had slept

when he was a boy, over the dog run. At first, because he was used to the noise and midnight comings and goings of the military, the relative quiet kept him uneasily awake. His first few nights at home he lay for hours listening to the stirrings of the creatures that moved in the darkness, the birds that sang by starlight. He had to get used to them all over again, as when he had been a child.

One night—he had no clear idea of the time—he awakened to a sound that did not fit. He raised up on one elbow and listened. It came again, a faint birdcall that sounded like one he had heard at Zach's cabin. Heartbeat quickening, he pulled on his trousers and climbed carefully down the ladder, favoring his left arm.

He was not surprised to see his father standing in the heavy shadows of the dog run, pulling his suspenders up over shoulders covered by long underwear but not by a shirt. Andrew said sternly, "If I was you, I'd climb back up yonder."

Owen's voice was just as firm. "I'm not sleepy."

"I don't want you mixed up in this."

"I'm already mixed up in it, just bein' your son."

Andrew seemed inclined to argue further, but something moved in dark shadow by the corral. A cloud covered the moon, and two men hurried to the cabin. An urgent voice asked, "Andrew?"

Andrew said, "Come up onto the dog run, Vance, where it's good and dark."

With Vance Hubbard was a young man about Owen's age. Another runaway from the army, Owen assumed.

Vance Hubbard grimly shook Andrew's hand and turned to face Owen. "Remember my brother Tyson?"

An old memory stirred. Owen had considered Tyson the boy as quarrelsome, trying to dominate. He was well into his twenties now and looked about as always. Owen felt the distrust in Tyson's long stare and did not extend his hand.

Vance Hubbard said, "Would you mind leavin' us, Owen? I've got to talk to your daddy."

Owen demanded, "You fixin' to get him into trouble?"

Andrew said sternly, "We're already in trouble. It started the day Texas threw in with Jeff Davis."

Owen pointed into the night. "There's liable to be some home guards out yonder. If they catch the Hubbards here . . ." He did not feel that he had to finish it.

Tyson Hubbard's voice was like a challenge. "We circled the place real good before we came in."

Vance Hubbard was more conciliatory. "I wouldn't put your daddy in danger."

"He's in danger just *knowin'* you." Owen did not intend the resentment to color his voice, but it had.

Andrew said with reproach, "The Hubbard family have always been our friends, son. You'll treat them with respect."

"And if they get you killed?"

"Lots of people are gettin' killed these days."

Hubbard studied Owen with concern. "It'd be better if you went somewhere and let me and your daddy talk."

"I think it might be better if I stayed."

Andrew said, "I don't agree with my son, but I trust him. What brings you-all here, Vance?"

"My mother, and my sister Lucy. The government's seized our farm since Tyson went on the list. The home guards taken our womenfolk to town."

Incredulously, Andrew asked, "To jail?"

"No, but they've put them in a little house at the edge of the settlement where they can watch them easier. Figure, I reckon, that me and Tyson'll come after them."

Andrew's voice was angry. "Holdin' them hostage. That sounds like somethin' Phineas Shattuck would think of. They been mistreated any?"

"Not that I know of. But sooner or later they're liable to be, just from frustration if nothin' else."

"What do you want me to do, Vance?"

"I've written a letter to my mother. Reckon you could get it to her someway?"

"I'll *find* a way."

Owen interrupted angrily. "You know what'll happen if they catch you tryin' to smuggle a letter in there . . . *his* letter?"

Firmly Andrew replied, "They've got no right to hold a man's family. Where's the letter, Vance?"

Hubbard took it from his shirt pocket. "I never wanted them in the thicket, but now I don't see any other way till we can smuggle them away from here someplace. They're in danger where they're at. I'm tellin' Mama to stay ready. Sometime in the next few nights we'll create a diversion. While the guards are distracted, we'll go get her and Lucy."

"You'll get somebody killed more than likely."

"You got any better ideas?"

Andrew shook his head. "I'll take her the letter. And if there's anything else I can do to help . . ."

Hubbard said apologetically, "I wish I didn't have to put this on you, Andrew. I'm afraid to ask your brother Zach. He'd just wade in there bold as Lucifer, tellin' Shattuck to go to hell. He'd end up in jail, or dead. And all for nothin', because the guards'd get the letter."

Andrew nodded. "Just tell me what house they're in."

The Hubbards were gone as silently as they had come. Tyson had said almost nothing, but his eyes had bored into Owen the whole time he had been there. Owen shivered, and he realized it was not from the coolness of the spring night. He stood in silence with his father on the dog run. At length he said, "The people in town all know you. The minute you get in sight of that house, they'll be on you like chickens on a June bug."

"I promised him I'd go."

Owen clenched his right fist in anger and frustration. "You won't go. *I* will."

Andrew blinked in surprise. "You'd do that for Vance Hubbard?"

"Not for him, for *you*. You're the only daddy I've got."

3

In the fading light of early evening Owen warily studied two boys slumped in boredom on straight-backed chairs behind the livery. Andrew had told him Phineas Shattuck had confiscated the barn and corrals for the keeping of the home guard mounts after Old Dad Wilson, the owner, left town hurriedly in the dark of a winter's night. Like Owen's father and uncle, he had campaigned against secession. Like Andy Jr., he had been overtaken and left where he was caught.

Owen sensed that the two boys were not stable swampers. They had probably been assigned to watch the house where the Hubbard boys' mother and sister had been placed. All the way to town he had devised reasons for visiting the women, excuses he could tell the guards. He had rejected each in its own turn, knowing no better was likely to emerge from a reluctant imagination not used to constructing lies. The longer he considered, the less he expected any story to be accepted. He wore a Confederate soldier's uniform—the badly worn remnants of it, anyway—

and the people in that house were womenfolk of hunted Unionists at a time when it could be worth a person's life to be a bunch-quitter.

A sack suspended from Owen's saddle carried foodstuffs his father had packed—bacon, a ham from the near-empty smokehouse, shelled corn to grind for bread. Andrew Danforth had always shared with people in need, sometimes at the risk of putting himself in the same condition. Carrying food to the Hubbard women was explanation enough, in Andrew's view. Texans could understand compassion for women, even for women of the enemy.

Without explanation Andrew had put a jug of his brother Zach's corn whisky into the sack. Andrew never used it much himself except for medicinal purposes, and he was seldom sick.

Owen had asked with a frown, "That Mrs. Hubbard . . . she's not one of them women that hides and drinks, is she?"

He remembered how she had looked a few years ago. He would not have taken her for a secret sipper. Andrew had reacted with indignation that Owen could even harbor such a thought about a good woman. But he did not explain the jug. "It just may come in handy," he said. "A little corn whisky can answer a lot of questions."

Owen judged that the two boys by the stable were not long from their mothers' apron strings. They might not be difficult to fool, but he felt remorse even before he made the effort. He would never have thought he would one day mislead people of his own side to favor a scalawag Unionist. He drew a deep breath and touched his heels gently to the old black horse's ribs, reining him toward the poor, slightly leaning frame shack that served as a house. He had seen slaves living in better.

He recalled the good, solid log house on the Hubbard farm the time he had gone there with his father and brothers to neighbor-help. The elder Hubbard had broken his leg just as he had begun harvesting his corn crop. A lot of other people had been there, turning an unfortunate accident into a celebration of human kindness. Now some of the men who had labored for Hubbard that long, hot day were enemies of his sons. Others were hiding with those sons in the thickets. More than a few had gone away to fight, and some would never come home.

Where Owen had been, up against the Yankee lines, he had not seen the rancorous divisions which had materialized here in Texas. Perhaps, he thought, it had existed but had not been obvious to a soldier focusing his attentions upon his own survival.

He had chosen to arrive in town at dusk to avoid attracting more attention than necessary. It had been easy to locate the house by Vance Hubbard's description. The authorities had brought the Hubbard women to the poorest end of Poverty Alley, just behind the livery barn and corrals.

Well, he reasoned, if Vance Hubbard had not made his choice to throw in his lot with deserters and the like, he would not be a fugitive, and his womenfolk would not be reduced to this. Given *his* own choice, Owen would not be here to help them. Many a poor Confederate war widow was probably faring worse.

He was fifty feet from the house when the two boys roused themselves from their lethargy and swaggered out to meet him. He recognized the freckle-faced Adcock, who appeared to have assumed the leadership whether assigned it or not.

"Where you goin', soldier?" Adcock demanded. He would probably be a sergeant if he were a few years older, Owen thought darkly, and no credit to the rank. He had all the scars of the town's junior bully.

"I come to fetch some vittles to the Hubbard women," Owen replied.

The boy grunted his disapproval. "Don't you know who they are? A soldier like you, wounded and all, I wouldn't think you'd want no truck with the likes of them."

"I been fightin' against men, not against womenfolks. Mrs. Hubbard was a nice lady before the war. I'd hate to think she was hungry."

"She won't go hungry," Adcock retorted. "We figure the first real dark night that comes along, them sons of hers'll be in to try and fetch her. Then we'll have them." His eyes narrowed. "Or maybe you wasn't really thinkin' about the old lady Hubbard atall. Maybe you was thinkin' about that girl." He quickly convinced himself and broke into a secret-sharing grin. "You been a long time away from the women, I expect."

Owen considered all the lies he had made up and discarded. Now this brash kid guard had furnished him one better than his own. He said truthfully, "I don't hardly remember her."

Adcock clearly did not believe that. The grin remained. "She's skinnier'n I like them, but I reckon she'd look good to a man who's been off to war awhile. We got to search you first. Orders from Captain Shattuck."

Captain, Owen thought sourly. The title still struck him as damned important for a pig thief.

The two boys went over him thoroughly, even feeling his boot tops for a possible weapon. Owen had purposely left his pistol at home. He would have lost it here, had he brought it. He felt a little anxiety that they might discover the letter. Adcock rammed his hand deeply into the sack of grub. His face lighted as he lifted out the jug.

"I'll swun, soldier, you *must've* figured on havin' yourself a time. We'll have to hold this. Contraband, you know."

Owen realized why his father had put in the jug. He felt disappointment in the two boys, for they were much too young to be drinking the kind of liquid fire Uncle Zach cooked up. He asked, "Can I have it back afterward?"

Adcock exchanged a gleeful look with the other boy, probably not a day over fifteen. "If there's any left. Go on, soldier. Them women are welcome to the rest of the stuff, but this is too good for any scalawag family."

Adcock uncorked the jug. Owen led the black horse the short distance to the house, which had not even a fence to prevent loose livestock from wandering up onto the tiny porch. He tied the reins to a splintered hitching post which leaned to the south. As he lifted the sack of grub with his good arm he heard the younger boy begging Adcock to share the jug.

Adcock kept turning away, denying him a drink. Owen frowned. He judged that Adcock would be flat on his back in a little while. The boy sure needed better raising.

Owen stepped onto the porch, which was barely large enough to sleep a respectable dog. Damned poor trade the government had made the Hubbards. Maybe when the next war came they would be a little more thoughtful about their loyalties. He rapped his knuckles against the doorjamb, not entering unbidden though the door stood open for the evening breeze to pass through. "Mrs. Hubbard?"

A girl moved cautiously into the doorway between front room and back. She stopped there, apprehension in her eyes as she blinked, trying for recognition in the poor light. "Who is it? What do you want?"

"Name's Owen Danforth. My dad thought you-all might be shy of vittles. I brought some."

The girl took a tentative step into the room. Her apprehension eased, suspicion taking its place. "You got a soldier suit on. You sure you're a Danforth? Maybe you just come here to spy on us."

Owen was about to tell her of the letter but heard a commotion behind him. The two boys were moving toward the house and wrestling over the jug. They seated themselves on the edge of the porch, Adcock laughing loudly and the other boy protesting that he was not getting his share.

The girl said testily, "I wish you'd tell your friends to go away and leave us alone."

"They're not my friends," Owen told her. It occurred to him that he probably had few friends in this town anymore. Most anywhere near his age had gone off to fight or had fled the country to keep from fighting.

In the fading light he realized he would not have recognized Lucy Hubbard if he had encountered her unaware. He remembered a shy and sun-blistered farm girl of fourteen or fifteen, possessing nothing in the way of looks that would cause him to think about her twice. Now she was grown, or just about. She still looked sun-blistered, probably having done a man's fieldwork since her father's death. She had otherwise turned into a presentable young woman, even *if* a little skinny. Self-consciously he asked, "Ain't your mother here?"

He heard a rattle of pans in the kitchen. Mrs. Hubbard said, "Who is it, Lucy?" and came into the doorway. He remembered thinking her a strikingly handsome woman the time he had helped harvest the Hubbard field. She looked older now. It seemed to him that everyone had aged more than the few years gave call for. "You're really Owen Danforth?" she asked, incredulous. "You've changed."

"Seems to be an epidemic of that," he remarked.

She looked with sympathy at his bound arm. "You're hurt."

Her concern left him flustered. It would be easier to dislike her if she didn't give a damn. "It'll be all right."

"I heard you mention your father."

"He sent some vittles. Heard you-all was taken from your home kind of sudden. He was afraid you might be needful."

Mrs. Hubbard smiled gratefully. "Andrew Danforth was always a kind man. But how did he know about us?"

Owen looked cautiously back toward the porch. He carried the sack into the poor, small kitchen and said in a low voice, "Your sons come by the place last night." He reached deep into the binding on his left arm and brought forth the letter. "Vance wanted Dad to fetch you this."

Mrs. Hubbard glanced at her daughter, then seized the letter. Owen quickly motioned her back toward the small fireplace, away from the door. "Them boys find out about this, I'll go to jail. And maybe you-all with me."

Lucy Hubbard stared at Owen with disbelief. "You're one of Jeff Davis's soldiers. How come you to bring us that letter?"

Owen's pent-up resentment edged into his voice. "If I hadn't, my dad would've. They'd've searched him better than they searched me. No tellin' what they'd've done to him."

"So you did this for him. You don't really care about *us*."

Owen's face heated. "I didn't come here to lecture you about politics. I just come to fetch that letter."

Mrs. Hubbard said firmly, "Leave him alone, Lucy. He's run a risk to do us a favor, and I'm sure he had to search his soul."

Lucy replied stubbornly, "He's one of them. How do we know he didn't read the letter and tell Phineas Shattuck what's in it?"

Mrs. Hubbard studied Owen with patient eyes.

"Because he's a Danforth. The Danforths have always been honorable people." She handed her daughter the letter.

Lucy's eyes widened as she read. "If they come and try to rescue us from this place, there'll be somebody killed."

Her mother raised a finger to her lips and looked quickly through the door toward the boys on the porch. Adcock lay on his back, humming softly. The other boy finally had the jug. From the level to which he raised it, Owen judged that the better part had been put to use.

"I'd best go," he said. "The less I know, the better for all of us."

"Please don't hurry," Mrs. Hubbard said earnestly. "I apologize for Lucy. This has all been hard on her. She had no part in it, but she's paid the same price as Vance and Tyson and me."

He would have felt more sympathy for the girl if she appeared to want any of it. "War ain't easy on nobody." He touched his left arm, for it had begun to ache. The long ride into town, he supposed. He moved toward the door.

Mrs. Hubbard caught his good arm. "You must be hungry. It'd be a poor show of gratitude if we let you leave without feedin' you."

He lied, "I ain't hungry. I don't eat much." He felt as if he were in some alien place. He wanted to get away from it and these women who represented the enemy. But the promise of food stayed him.

Mrs. Hubbard paid no noticeable attention to his

answer. She emptied the sack Owen had brought. "Slice off some of that ham, Lucy. I'll fix up some cornbread. I don't imagine you've eaten too well where you've been, Owen."

Argument was useless. The welcome aroma of the cooking soon broke any harbored resistance. He went into the backyard to a small woodpile, miserable leavings of the house's last tenant. He could not swing an ax with one arm, but he could carry firewood a few pieces at a time. He dumped it into a wooden box beside the fireplace. He remembered that on the farm the Hubbards had had a big iron stove, where Mrs. Hubbard had cooked as well as Owen's own mother.

"That'll be good enough to finish supper," Mrs. Hubbard said.

"I'd just as leave fill the woodbox, anyway."

She shook her head. "We may not stay around to use it."

His mouth tightened. Two women, afoot. He could not see that they had any choice.

It was good dark outside when he sat down by dim lamplight to the ham and cornbread and brown gravy. There evidently was no coffee in the house. At her mother's bidding Lucy brought water in a bucket from the cistern. She watched Owen with distrust. He reciprocated her feeling, but when she moved up beside him to place a tin cup by his plate he sensed her body warmth. It set him to tingling in a pleasantly uncomfortable way he had not experienced in a long time. He tried the water and thought it had a slight flavor of cypress shingles.

Mrs. Hubbard studied him thoughtfully. When he had finished supper she said, "You've done us a great service, Owen. I hate to impose on you for more."

Suspicion arose quickly. "What more?"

"As long as Lucy and I are kept prisoners here we're a danger to Vance and the others with him. Shattuck *wants* him to ride in and try a rescue. That's why we were put here—bait."

Owen nodded. "It looks that way to me."

"They've just kept a couple of boys posted through the daytime . . . don't expect Vance to try anything in the daylight, I suppose. But pretty soon they'll send a heavier guard to watch this place all night. Those boys appear to be dead drunk and asleep on the porch. If we're to get away, now is the time."

"You might get clear of the house. But then what?"

"We'll manage. I'd take it as a great favor, Owen, if you'd look around and make sure there aren't any more guards outside."

"Mrs. Hubbard, I'm a soldier . . ." The look of hope in her face stopped him. His father would have helped her. He would probably still try, when he heard about this. "All right," Owen said reluctantly. "I reckon I can do that much."

Lucy protested, "He'll call up the guards, is all he'll do."

Owen frowned at her. She was not making this any easier.

"Hush, Lucy," her mother said. "Sometimes you have to trust."

Owen walked out onto the porch. The two boys were as still as they would ever be, short of death. The jug lay between them, tipped over, the stopper out. Owen stepped farther into the street, making a long, careful survey. He returned to the house, still watching the sleeping boys.

He told Mrs. Hubbard, "Nobody out there that I can see. But they won't leave boys here long to do men's work."

Mrs. Hubbard looked to her daughter. In moments they had thrown together the few clothes they owned, tying them up in a tablecloth. They had sacked their little bit of food. She said, "Then we'd better not waste time."

Owen protested, "You won't get anywhere afoot. They'll catch you, come daylight."

Mrs. Hubbard said, "We know that. But the guards' horses are in that corral over yonder. We'll borrow a couple."

"*Steal*, you mean. You women don't know nothin' about stealin' horses."

"Do *you*?" Lucy challenged.

He had taken back his good bay horse from the officer who had confiscated it, but he did not consider that stealing. "I know two women ain't just goin' to walk in there and take two horses out of that corral."

"It's a risk," Mrs. Hubbard acknowledged. "But I see no other way." She had the hell-bent look of a drill sergeant.

He chewed his lip in anger, certain they would be caught and that letter found. It wouldn't take the authorities long to realize who had carried it to them. He said, "You-all blow out that lamp, then, and come with me. I'll probably get hung if they catch me, but I couldn't go back and tell my dad I left you in a trap like this."

He gave the two boys another cautious glance as the women followed him across the narrow porch. Not even Gabriel's horn would awaken those heel flies before daylight. His pulse picked up while he moved briskly in the hoof-softened street, leading his black horse so he would not have to come back and get him. He felt that his heart was making enough noise to arouse the guard troop.

The women pressed close behind him. He could hear their footsteps, light and quick. He stopped at the corral gate and felt for the chain latch, careful not to make a noise. He handed the black's reins to Mrs. Hubbard with a silent command to wait. He studied the pen from one end to the other for sign of a guard. He rough-counted a dozen or fifteen horses. Several saddles had been placed upon the top rail, blankets draped across them, bridles hanging. Owen took short, shallow breaths, expecting at any moment to be challenged. He decided no one had seen reason to post a special guard on the horses in the friendly environment of the town.

Lifting a bridle from a saddle, he eased among the horses. Most drew away from him, but he managed to tempt one by extending his hand as if he held some sugar or a biscuit. Somebody's pet, he thought. He bridled that horse and led it through the gate to the women. While they quietly saddled it, he moved back among the horses with a second bridle.

He recognized the Yankee bay which Shattuck had

confiscated. Temptation almost overcame him. He thought of leaving the black in trade, but any such swap would be like painting his name in big red letters on the fence. He took another horse instead.

He half expected someone to raise a holler, and the hair seemed to bristle on his neck as the women finished the saddling. He wondered how they were going to ride astride with long skirts better suited to side-saddles. Lucy Hubbard mounted first, her skirt pulling up. He tried not to look, but he glimpsed an ankle, more than a man was usually privileged to see, short of matrimony. Silently he reproached himself. This was no time to be letting his mind stray into such a direction.

Mrs. Hubbard appeared much calmer than Owen felt. She pointed her chin. "We'll ride yonderway till we're clear of town. We wouldn't want to run into anybody."

Irritably Owen demanded, "You-all know where you're goin'?"

"To your Uncle Zach's. He'll help us."

Owen said, "There's a chance they got people watchin' him."

Mrs. Hubbard showed no fear. "In that case we'll just have to take care of ourselves."

Owen tried to remember how she used to be. He had considered her a typical farm wife, handsomer than the garden run but otherwise not particularly different from most others he knew. She had seemed placid, accepting life as it came, even the time her husband broke his leg and could not harvest his crop. Owen did not recall seeing her show this kind of

stubbornness before. "Even if they don't catch you—
which they will—do you think you could find your
way to the thickets all by yourselves?"

"We'll manage. You've done more than your part,
Owen. You'd best be goin' home."

And spend the rest of his life explaining to his
father, and to himself, why he had gone off and left
two strong-headed women who needed help even if
they didn't believe it . . .

"Damn it," he said, "I'll see you to Uncle Zach's."

Mrs. Hubbard did not argue. Owen glanced at
Lucy and found her trying to pull her skirt down.

They rode in silence for possibly half an hour. Owen
frequently looked back, listening for pursuit. At first he
heard only the night birds and the nocturnal insects
seeking to mate or to feed. He began to hope that he
and the women had traveled far enough to evade any
pursuit. Then he heard horses moving in a long trot,
somewhere behind.

Grimly he said, "Must've found them boys on your
porch." He reined toward the dark shape of a brushy
motte. He dismounted and led the women into the
dark shadows.

The black tried to nicker, and Owen held a hand
over its nose. He would have been tempted to smother
it had he not needed it so badly. The two he had taken
for the women showed little interest in the oncoming
horses.

His heartbeat quickening, he wished he could ar-
range for Phineas Shattuck to be forced to eat this
black horse, raw.

He held his breath as the riders hurried along a

wagon road that skirted the motte. When they were safely past he said, "Looks like they're headed toward Uncle Zach's. Probably outguessed you. You don't want to go there now."

Mrs. Hubbard shook her head. "We'll just have to make the thickets. We'll find Vance and Tyson the best way we can."

Owen grimaced, suspecting the answer before he asked. "Think you know how to get to the thickets from here?"

Mrs. Hubbard said, "They're northeast. Which way's northeast?"

Owen grunted in frustration. "You don't know?"

"Clouds have got the stars covered up. I can't tell in the dark, without stars."

"Then you're bound to ride in a circle till daylight. They'll find you and fetch you back to town."

"Some soldiers carry a compass, Owen. I don't suppose you'd have one?"

He had never owned a compass or even had his hands on one more than a time or two. He had been blessed with a tolerable sense of direction as far back as he could remember.

Angrily he said, "If I'd known how helpless you-all were goin' to be, I'd've delivered that letter and been gone like a shot. Now if they catch you they'll know damn well I was the one got you out of town."

Lucy said, "Looks to me like you're bogged to the hubs just like we are." Owen thought he detected some sense of satisfaction in her tone. Despite his helping her, she still resented the color of his threadbare uniform.

"But I ain't no runaway," he retorted.

"Not until now."

Mrs. Hubbard admonished her daughter to silence. "Just show me the direction, Owen. If we get started right, I think we can stay with it."

"No you wouldn't," he clipped. "You'd go around in circles, like I said. You-all just let me alone to think."

He turned his back on them in irritation. Angry words rose up but were denied expression by a control hammered into him by his stern upbringing. His sense of their having used him did nothing to cool his anger.

"I betrayed my government, just comin' to you-all in the first place. I've stolen government horses for you, and I've sneaked you out of town. They can't hang me but once. I'd just as well go the whole way."

Mrs. Hubbard said, "You don't have to, Owen." But her voice told him she wished he would.

"I'll take you to the edge of the deep thicket. After that, you're on your own."

Lucy Hubbard gave him the first completely civil words he had heard from her. "That's more than we could ever have asked."

Owen sniffed. He suspected this was what they had had in mind from the beginning. He rode in silence, ignoring them when they tried to coax him into conversation. Two or three times Lucy rode close enough to bump her leg against his. He wondered if she was trying to tempt him over to the Unionist side of the fence. It would be a cold night in July . . .

He stopped every now and again to listen, half expecting to hard-luck upon a detail of home guards. He began to fear that daylight would catch them still out in the open. As dawn's first glow began in the east, they reached the first scrub timber that marked the fringe of the dark and forbidding thickets.

He shifted in the saddle and looked behind him. Morning light was not yet strong enough to tell him whether what he saw in the distance might be trees or cattle or horsemen. He thought it prudent to assume the worst.

"We'd better ride into the brush a ways."

They moved perhaps half a mile into the closely grown timber. The heavy growth made passage slow and difficult, briars tugging, Spanish moss hanging down and brushing his face. In a spot clearer than most he said, "The horses need a rest." He dismounted stiffly and loosened the girth so the black could breathe easily. He supposed he should help the women down, but he felt he had already gone the second mile and more. Once in a sortie he had been cut off behind enemy lines for a time. The same feeling of entrapment bore heavily upon him now as he experienced a sense of being in enemy country. He shivered to a chill that had nothing to do with the morning's coolness.

Mrs. Hubbard said, "You've done more than your due, Owen. We can tell our directions now. We'll ride till we come across somebody. We're bound to, sooner or later."

Owen nodded, dull from fatigue. "Sounds fine to me." He would be tickled to be shed of them.

He stretched out on the ground, gripping the aching left arm. The long night's ride had done it no good, and it had not helped the old black horse either. He drifted off into sleep.

He awakened suddenly as something sharp prodded his ribs.

A man stood over him with a long saber in his hand. "Wake up, soldier, and give an account of yourself."

4

Owen decided against rising immediately to his feet. The saber point was near his throat. He did not know whether the red-bearded man threatening him was one of the thickets' hideout people or a home guard. He thought darkly that in his awkward situation it might not make much difference.

"I'm Owen Danforth," he said cautiously, raising his right hand to show he offered no resistance.

"Name don't mean nothin' to me," the man said brittlely. "You've got a uniform on. You run off from the army?"

"No. I was sent home till my arm heals up."

"Then you still fancy yourself a soldier?"

Owen suspected his reply was not the one this man wanted to hear, but he would not lie. "I'll be goin' back when I'm able."

The man moved aside one step, and Owen raised up cautiously to a sitting position. He saw two men on horses in the nearby brush. One held the reins to the bearded man's animal. He betrayed no evidence of being any friendlier than Red Beard. Guardedly Owen said, "I brought these women to the thicket."

Mrs. Hubbard and Lucy had slept a little apart from Owen, in their clothes. The voices had awakened them. Mrs. Hubbard hurried to Owen's defense. "What he says is the truth. I'm Vance Hubbard's mother."

The man looked at her in surprise and tipped his hat. He took another uncertain step away from Owen. "Ma'am, it's an honor to make your acquaintance." He regarded Owen with unrelieved suspicion but nodded at him to get up. "I wonder at you, ma'am, bringin' this soldier with you. He's got no business here unless he's quit the army, and he says he ain't."

"We needed him."

"It don't seem likely he'd bring you out of kindness and him a soldier. Gould be the government sent him to spy on us."

Mrs. Hubbard shook her head. "He was reluctant. I'm afraid we crowded him into it." Evidently more for Owen's sake than to convince the man with the saber, she added, "I hated to do this to him. But I saw no other way for my daughter and me to join my sons."

Owen slowly and carefully pushed to his feet. "Mister, if you're worried about me tellin' what I've seen, I ain't seen *nothin'*. What *is* there to see in all this brush? Times, a man can't hardly make out his horse's ears."

One man grinned, but the Red Beard stared coldly at him.

Owen argued, "This is the farthest I've ever been into the thickets. I expect the home guards've been farther."

The horseman with the grin pushed in closer. He

said, "Ain't been but a couple had the nerve to try. Some jolly boys marked their hides with a bullwhip all the way out. They ever come in here, it'll have to be with a big force."

Red Beard's eyes narrowed. "You might be the lad who fancies showin' that force the way in."

Owen's pulse was drumming. "I don't *know* the way in."

The bearded man turned to the two on horseback. "With all due respect to the ladies, I don't see how we can afford to let him go." He rubbed the butt of a pistol in his waistband.

Mrs. Hubbard interjected fearfully, "I've known this young man for years. His father is Andrew Danforth. He's helped many of the men who are in these thickets. Probably even you, Red Upjohn. I got his son into this predicament, and I'll take the responsibility for lettin' him go."

Upjohn said, "It ain't your responsibility to take, ma'am. It's mine." He turned a hard gaze on Owen. "We got too many lives at stake here to risk them for one. There's been good men shot or hung by the other side on nothin' but suspicion. And I'm *sure* suspicious of this one."

Owen saw madness in the man's eyes, and death. He could not breathe.

Mrs. Hubbard deliberately placed herself in front of Owen and spread her arms protectively. Lucy quickly followed suit. "If need be," Mrs. Hubbard declared, "we'll go back out with him. And if the home guards catch us, *you* can explain to my sons."

Red Beard looked to the other two men for support

but found them against him. The one with the pleasant face said, "No, Red. We owe Vance too much."

"*I* don't owe him," Upjohn declared. "I found my way into this place without help, Banty Tillotson." He pointed the saber at Owen. "It was a soldier boy about like this one who put the rope around my son's neck and hung him before my eyes."

Mrs. Hubbard said, "Sir, killin' another father's innocent son won't put the breath back into yours."

The man called Banty placed a hand on the Red Beard's shoulder. "She's talkin' sense, Red. Come on now, let's take him to Vance and see what *he* says."

Red stared coldly at Owen. Owen's mouth was dry as he awaited the verdict. Red declared, "We dassn't take him in there. He'd see so much we *couldn't* let him go. Jim Carew, you stay here and watch him. Me and Banty'll take the womenfolks to Vance. Whatever he decides, I'll abide by it."

Mrs. Hubbard sighed in relief and turned to Owen. "I'll hurry things as much as I can."

Owen said urgently, "I've got to get home. If the guards go to our house and find me gone, they'll know. I'll be in trouble, and my dad with me."

Red Upjohn's eyes told him he was fortunate to have earned even this much of a concession.

Lucy touched Owen's hand. Her fingers felt cold. "I was unkind to you last night, Owen. I'm sorry."

His resentment arose again. "Sorry don't help much."

He sensed regret in her voice. "If your army is mad at you, you can stay in the thickets with us."

Owen gritted, "If my army finds out what I done,

they'll be more than just mad. They'll probably want to hang me."

"You're makin' too much out of it. They can't really care that much what two women do."

"They care what your brothers do. And they care when somebody helps them."

He imagined he could still feel the gentle touch of Lucy's hand as she rode off into the brush with her mother and two of the men. She was still looking back at him as she quickly disappeared into the trees and scrub brush and briars.

Owen had never had reason to explore the dark, forbidding thicket country, even before the war. He knew the dense growth extended unbroken for miles. As a youngster he had been warned away by stories—probably untrue—of boys and even men who had sought to explore its mysteries and never came out. It was said a man could live in there for years if he learned its ways or become hopelessly lost and starve if he did not.

He silently took the measure of Jim Carew, a small man who deserved the nickname "Banty" more than the man who had it. Owen decided any lack of physical stature was offset by the rifle. It made Carew seven feet tall. Owen asked, "You quit the army?"

Carew eased. Even so, Owen had a notion he would shoot if pressed. "No. I taken my leave when I heard the *con*script men was comin'. They'd done taken my brother and let the Yankees shoot a leg off of him. Looks to me like you've paid *your* price. That arm goin' to stay crippled the rest of your life?"

"I'm beginnin' to get some use of the fingers."

"High price to pay for your slaves, don't you think?"

Owen replied sharply, "We never had no slaves."

"And neither does anybody else I know, hardly. Don't seem right for them to take us poor boys and make us fight so the rich men can have their slaves."

"It ain't just over slaves," Owen protested. "It's over rights and whether those people back east can tell us out here what we've got to do and all . . ." Owen stopped, anger rising. He realized he was falling back into an old quarrel he had lost to his father before he and Ethan had gone off to join the army. Argument with Andrew had been fruitless; why fire his blood again with a stranger? This was a dispute nobody ever won.

Owen said, "My dad sees things like you do. There's a good chance the guards are already at our place, tryin' to make him tell where I'm at. The longer I stay out, the worse trouble him and me'll be in. I wish you'd let me go home."

"And if it turns out you *are* a spy, and you bring the guards or the soldiers in here . . . I ain't takin' a thing like that on myself. So you lay down and get your rest, boy. If you're all right, you'll be home soon enough."

Owen assessed the determination in Carew's face and knew it was adequately reinforced by the power of that rifle. He lay down, but he did not sleep. Each time he opened his eyes just enough to see, he could tell Carew was becoming more and more relaxed. The man had probably stood guard all night. Owen made it a point not to move, not to jar Carew out of the lethargy into which he was slipping.

Carew's chin eased downward. He let his eyes close a moment, opening them suddenly and wildly as he resisted going to sleep. Owen lay still. Presently Carew nodded off again. This time he slumped. Owen waited to see if he might bestir himself, but he did not.

Cautiously Owen pushed to his feet. Standing over the sleeping man, he reached down and grasped the rifle. Carew's hand had opened and let go of it, but the weapon remained against the man's chest. Owen picked it up and stepped back.

Awakened, Carew grabbed at it but missed. He stared at Owen in dismay.

Owen said, "You just sit there. I got no interest in hurtin' you, and I got no interest in betrayin' your people. I just want to get back where I belong."

He tried in vain to think of some way he could saddle the black horse with one hand and not relinquish the rifle. He beckoned with his chin. "You'll have to saddle him for me."

Carew frowned. "I don't think I will. You don't look like the kind that'd shoot a man."

"I've shot at Yankees. Seems to me you're kind of a Yankee, bein' where you're at."

Carew made a step. "I don't think you'd shoot me."

"Maybe I'd just fire this thing into the air, and we'd see who comes first—your people or the home guards."

"All right," Carew grumbled, "I'll saddle him. But I'll catch hell when Red Upjohn gets back here with Vance Hubbard. And that grinnin' Banty Tillotson will hooraw me for a week."

Owen looked with some temptation at Carew's horse, a better-looking specimen than his own. He considered forcing a trade but feared the animal's description might be known to the authorities. It might even be stolen.

I'm in trouble enough already, he thought.

When Carew had finished, Owen swung into the saddle.

Carew complained, "I'm goin' to catch hell for sure."

"You want to come with me?"

"I ain't in *that* much trouble."

"I'll leave your rifle out yonder a ways." Owen touched heels to the black horse's ribs and sought his way through the tangle. He looked back two or three times, afraid Carew might be following, but he saw nothing. At the edge of the brush he paused, searching for a home guard patrol. He saw only a scattering of cows, quietly grazing in the morning sun.

He considered keeping the rifle, but he had made a promise. He wedged it into the fork of a hackberry tree.

He began to wonder if the pursuit had been only in his mind, a product of his fear and his feeling of guilt over helping the Unionists. That group of riders last night might have been nothing more than routine patrol. They might not even have been home guards; they could have been anybody.

A rising morning breeze moaned through the brush behind him. He was reminded that Hubbard's people in the thicket might bring him more trouble at the moment than anybody out in front. He rode across the open prairie in the direction of Zachariah Danforth's. Maybe Uncle Zach would feed him and advise him what he should do next.

A sense of caution bade him approach Zach's place from the timbered side, where he could see before he was seen. He tied the black horse and cautiously walked the last few feet to the edge, stopping in the shadow to survey the ground.

Dark smoke twisted where the cabin was supposed to be. The wind lifted it for a moment, and he saw to his horror that the cabin was down, its roof and part of the walls fallen in, still ablaze. He forgot caution in the rush of anxiety. He grabbed the reins and swung them up over the black horse's head, bumping his own head fiercely on a heavy, low-lying branch as he pushed himself up in the stirrup. "Uncle Zach!" he shouted as he spurred out of the timber, looking anxiously for sign of the man.

He saw him, lying facedown a few feet from the burning cabin. Zach's clothing smoldered from the heat of the blaze. Owen jumped to the ground. The black horse snorted and tried to jerk free of him, fearing the flames. Owen had to wrap the reins around his wrist to keep from losing him.

He knelt and touched his uncle, knowing even before he did that Zach Danforth was dead. He saw the bullet wounds, half a dozen at least. Any one of them would have been enough. Whoever did this had taken out a lot of spite.

Shattuck! It had to be Shattuck. Firing the cabin fitted his style, like the time he had burned Andrew Danforth's barn for revenge. Andrew had not been able to prove it, but he knew Shattuck had bragged about it to some of his cronies. That kind of talk was hard to keep secret, though it had no value in court.

One side of the cabin collapsed with a sudden rush of sparks and flame and smoke. The black horse jerked loose and trotted off twenty or thirty yards before stepping on the reins and stopping himself. Owen got his one good arm beneath his uncle and clumsily dragged him farther from the flames. He turned him over and tried to wipe the dried blood from the face and beard. He knelt then and cried, partly from grief, partly from rage.

Murdered him! Set the place afire and shot him when he came out. Shot him down and went off and left him.

Owen held to his uncle's hand and let the first outpouring run its course. He looked around for something with which to cover his uncle's body but saw nothing. Everything had burned with the cabin. He walked out to the black horse, untied his coat from behind the cantle and used that.

A thought struck him, and his jaw dropped in horror. *They'll be going for Dad . . . if they're not there already!*

He swung up into the saddle, wishing for a weapon but having none. Anything Zach might have had was either stolen by those who had killed him or was destroyed by the blaze. His stomach churning, he turned for one more look at the place where he had known many happy times as a boy.

"Someday, Uncle Zach . . . some way . . ."

He saw the horsemen then, two of them, a quarter

of a mile away and moving toward the smoking remains of the cabin. His heart tripped.

The distance was too great for him to tell if one might be Phineas Shattuck. He clenched his right fist but knew it would be foolhardy to remain here without a weapon. He moved the black horse quickly into the timber to be out of sight, and once in its cover he moved as rapidly as the dense growth would allow, in the general direction of home. He paused once to look back at the riders, to see if they might be in pursuit. They continued to move toward the cabin. Either they had not seen him or they had no interest in him. That, he thought, made it unlikely either was Shattuck. They might be other contingents of the home guards, however, or they might be Red Upjohn with Jim Carew or Banty Tillotson trailing him from the thicket. He had no desire to confront either possibility.

Impatience burned, but he forced himself to remain within the protection of the timber. In earlier years when he had fled a disagreement with his father, he had used this cover to take him to the sanctuary of Uncle Zach's. Zach had always had an easy knack for cooling tempers on both sides so that Owen and his father would ride home together in a spirit of reconciliation. But Zach had not so easily handled his *own* temper. The persuasive powers he used on others he had been unable to apply to himself. Owen could only speculate that some angry confrontation had preceded his uncle's killing. Phineas Shattuck would not have required much provocation, especially if he held all the advantage.

Owen moved occasionally to the edge of the timber

to look for anyone following him, but he saw and heard no one. That only partially relieved his concern. It would not require much imagination for someone to guess he was following the course of the timber and to parallel him, just beyond sight on the rolling prairie.

Late in the afternoon he came to the homeplace, to a point from which Vance Hubbard had emerged that night to visit with Andrew Danforth. There Owen dismounted and walked to the edge, crouching. To his pleasant surprise he saw his father in the field, hoeing weeds from the growing corn. Owen watched briefly, hardly able to believe that Shattuck and his guards had not already come to take Andrew into custody, or to do what they had done at Zach's.

Perhaps, then, there was still time.

Owen remounted and rode out of the timber. His father saw him and leaned on the hoe, relief coming like sunshine into his furrowed face.

"Son," Andrew spoke gladly. "I'd about decided they'd taken you. Come dark I was fixin' to ride to town and see. Where the hell you been?"

"I'll tell you directly," Owen said urgently. "Right now we've got to get away from this place, while there's still time."

Andrew blinked. "Time for what? They didn't catch you, or you wouldn't be here."

Owen's right hand clenched into a fist. "There's no easy way to tell you, Dad. They've killed Uncle Zach."

Andrew sagged as if Owen had hit him. He let the hoe fall. His lips formed the word, "Zach," but Owen did not hear it.

Owen said, "Somebody shot him. Burned the cabin. Shattuck, I'd guess. I thought he'd've been here for you before now."

Andrew's big knuckles went almost white as his hands made powerful fists. "They wouldn't just've shot him without some excuse . . ."

"I helped Miz Hubbard and her daughter get away from town last night. I taken them to the thicket. Shattuck probably figured Uncle Zach had a hand in it. I just can't figure why he hasn't already been *here*."

Andrew stiffened, his gaze hardening on the line of timber down by the river. "I reckon he has. He was just waitin' for you to show up."

Owen turned quickly in the saddle. He heard the heavy drumming of hooves as half a dozen horsemen spurred toward him and Andrew. At the head of the group rode Phineas Shattuck, on Owen's big Yankee bay. Even at the distance, Owen saw a pistol in his hand. He glanced at his father and saw that he carried no weapon.

"Swing up behind me, Dad. We'll make a run for it."

Andrew made no move except to shake his head. "Ridin' that old plug? They'd be on us like hornets. We'd just as well meet them here." His face clouded with outrage as his gaze fastened upon Shattuck.

Owen watched the riders come, and his heart sank. "I'm sorry, Dad. I knew better, all the time I was helpin' them women. One thing just led to another . . ."

"It was my fault for not leavin' you out of it. Just don't say nothin' to Shattuck. Act like you don't know nothin', and don't admit to nothin'."

Shattuck swung his arm. Some of the riders circled to surround the Danforths. Shattuck reined up, victory in his eyes. He held the pistol at arm's length, pointed at Owen's father. "Andrew Danforth," he declared with great solemnity, "I place you and your son under arrest in the name of the Confederate States of America. The charge is treason!"

The words were so careful and deliberate that Owen felt Shattuck must have rehearsed them over and over in his mind.

"Treason?" Andrew asked, his voice firm. "On what grounds?"

"On the grounds that you and your son plotted to aid and abet the escape of prisoners important to the government."

"Prisoners?" Andrew asked. "What prisoners?"

"Them Hubbard women. You knew damned well we was keepin' them in town to make Vance Hubbard show hisself. Your son here, this gallant wounded soldier . . ." his voice went harsh with sarcasm ". . . tempted two wet-eared boys with a jug of whisky and snuck them women out of town. Stole some horses, too."

Owen was about to speak, but his father moved up beside the black horse and leaned a shoulder heavily against Owen's leg. Owen remembered the admonition to hold silent.

Andrew said, "My son reluctantly took some foodstuffs to Mrs. Hubbard because I asked him to. If the women left town afterward, he wouldn't know nothin' about that. He come right on home."

Shattuck's eyes lighted on Owen with a savage

triumph. "Your son's just now *got* home. We been watchin' this place for hours."

"He left again this mornin' early, to go see his Uncle Zach."

Owen marveled at the ease with which his father lied. He never used to have any inclination in that direction. The war, Owen decided. It made men lay aside old moralities and do whatever was expedient.

Doubt flickered briefly in Shattuck's face before conviction returned, and victory. "We was there this mornin'. We didn't see nothin' of him."

Andrew's voice hardened. "He got there after you'd gone. He found Zach just like you left him." Accusation burned in his eyes.

Shattuck's jaw dropped, but he regained his confidence, for he was the one holding the pistol. "We went to take your brother into custody. He put up an argument, and there wasn't no choice. He was shootin' at me."

Owen saw Shattuck's eyes waver. They said he lied. Owen looked at the young guards who sat their horses beside Shattuck. One was the freckled Adcock, who had been dead drunk when Owen had left him last night. One side of his face was blue and swollen. Somebody had struck him, hard. Adcock was hunched in the saddle as if in mortal misery, staring at the ground. That also told Owen that Shattuck lied. His stomach burned with hatred.

Andrew declared, "You've got no evidence, Shattuck. I say my son came home last night. You got any proof that he didn't?"

Shattuck leaned forward, bringing the pistol's

muzzle up to point at Owen. "I know what he done. That's all I need."

Andrew declared, "A court'll want evidence."

"Court? Who said anything about a court?" He turned to young Adcock. "You ain't much on brains, boy, but you can trot up yonder and catch a horse for the old man. Saddle him and get yourself back down here in a hurry. Johnson, you go with him. If he ever slows to a walk, I want you to use your quirt on him."

Despite his own predicament, Owen was able to feel sorrow for Adcock, and a touch of guilt. The boy might be a blusterer and a bully, but Owen had trapped him into this disgrace.

Owen soon had worry enough over his own predicament. As the two young guards led a saddled horse to the field, Andrew demanded, "You goin' to let us go to the house and pick up some clothes?"

Shattuck said, "Them you got on'll do fine."

"Not for long."

"You ain't *got* long."

Owen saw a grim conviction come into Andrew's face. Andrew gave his son a look that expressed regret he could not have put into words.

Owen knew, then, and he shuddered. Shattuck did not intend for them to reach town.

5

ndrew Danforth grimly studied Shattuck, then his gaze drifted over the boys as if he harbored some forlorn wish for help from them. "You're talkin' murder."

"In a war there ain't no such thing as murder."

"My son's a Confederate soldier. He's not your enemy. Kill *him* and it's murder."

"Not when he's done treason."

Andrew gave his son a long look of regret, of silent apology. "Shattuck, treason has got nothin' to do with it. This is for revenge because we put the law on you years ago."

"So *you* say. I say you've both betrayed your country. We're takin' you to town. If you was to try and run, we'd have to shoot you."

Andrew's voice went hard with accusation. "And you'll say we ran, whether we do or not."

"You'll run. Sooner or later you'll see it's the only chance you've got." He smiled coldly. "Take it *now*, if you want to."

Owen saw defeat in the slump of his father's

shoulders. Sadly Andrew said, "I wish you hadn't come home, son."

Dread settled in Owen's stomach like something dead. The boy Adcock looked at him with eyes that told of shame.

Andrew said darkly, "Convenient for you, Shattuck. First Zach, then us . . . all three Danforths in one day."

Shattuck replied, "The fortunes of war."

"The war won't last forever. No matter which side wins, you won't always have the office to hide behind. Sooner or later *somebody*'ll get you. It's just a question of who."

Color surged into Shattuck's cheeks. "You shut up, Danforth, or I'll shoot you right here." He leveled his pistol.

Owen went rigid, expecting the blast.

One of the boys said, "Somebody's comin', Captain." His tone was of relief.

Shattuck's pistol swung around as his head jerked. Two riders skirted the Danforth cabin and moved down toward the field. Shattuck squinted, trying worriedly for recognition. "Who's that?" he demanded. "Who *is* it?"

The boy named Johnson replied, "Looks to me like Sheriff Chancellor."

Shattuck cursed under his breath. "Ain't he got nothin' better to do . . ."

The brown-bearded Chancellor and a younger man rode up in a brisk trot. The sheriff's eye fastened momentarily upon Owen, then upon his father and finally upon Phineas Shattuck. Owen tried to read whatever thought lay behind it, but the good eye betrayed no more secrets than the patch which covered the other. Chancellor said, "We were afraid we'd find these two like we found Zach. We have trailed you all day, Shattuck. Why didn't you let me know what happened in town last night?"

"It was *my* business and no concern of the county," Shattuck said defensively. "There was treason done. It was my place to set it right."

Frowning, the sheriff rubbed one hand along the side of his face, where a white streak through his beard covered a war scar. "Wilkes and I buried Zach in his family plot. How many times do you have to shoot a man to kill him?" Accusation was in his voice.

"You know what him and Andrew've been up to all along. And this boy here, he forgot what uniform he had on."

Chancellor gave Andrew a moment's study, Owen a bit longer. "Zach Danforth was a good man. He was a friend of mine once. I had hoped he would be again, when the war is over."

"He resisted arrest. I was forced to shoot him."

The sheriff turned to the boys for corroboration. None would look him in the eye. His frown deepened. "What's your evidence against these two?"

Shattuck straightened in the saddle as if bracing for attack. "I've got all the evidence I need, and it's not a county matter. We're takin' these traitors to town. You can go on about your business."

Chancellor gazed at him so sternly that Shattuck

had to look away. "My business is in town. So long as you're traveling in that direction, we'll ride along and help you."

"We don't need no help."

"They might try to run away, and you would have to shoot them. With a couple more of us to watch them, they won't run." A hard smile flickered as he glanced at his deputy. The deputy glared at Shattuck with no effort to hide his contempt. Chancellor turned his attention again to Owen. "Soldier, I don't want to believe you would do anything to disgrace that uniform."

Owen said, "I never had no such intention." He hoped his eyes did not betray a lingering of guilt for what he had done. He could lie to Shattuck as his father had, without hesitation or shame. Chancellor was another matter. That one eye seemed to pierce all pretense and seize mercilessly upon the truth.

Andrew pulled Chancellor's attention from Owen. "I'm glad you came along, Chance. I tried to tell Shattuck, but he wouldn't listen. You've got no argument with my son."

Chancellor looked again at Owen, but he made no commitment. "Shattuck, it will be way into the night before we get to town."

Tightly Shattuck said, "It's *Captain* Shattuck!"

"To these boys here, perhaps. I have a longer memory."

Shattuck colored again. "Johnson, lead out!"

Chancellor spoke quietly to his deputy, who positioned himself beside Andrew. Chancellor pulled his horse in by Owen's.

Owen saw his father bow his head and close his eyes. Offering up thanks, Owen thought. And well he might. As the fear ebbed, Owen's anger came back. Some was directed against his father. Andrew's partisanship had put them in this predicament. Texas was Confederate, not Union. If he and Zach could have accepted that . . .

Riding, Owen flexed the fingers of his left hand. They were slow to respond, but at least they showed improvement.

The sheriff watched him. "Considering going back to your old unit?"

"I wish I was already there."

"I don't know how bad a mess you're in. It depends upon how much credence the court places in Shattuck."

"What if they believe him?"

"At the least, prison. At the worst, a rope. You'd better think hard about what you'll say for yourself, soldier."

"I'm loyal to Texas. This wounded arm ought to say that for me."

Chancellor gave him a long appraisal, then shook his head. "Half the men you meet today carry a battle scar."

Bitterly Owen said, "Show me Shattuck's."

The black horse felt as if it would collapse beneath him before they reached town. The animal had been ridden almost continuously for more than twenty-four hours with little time to rest and graze. But for Owen to say so would be to admit what he had done last night. He held his silence and pitied the old horse.

It gave him no satisfaction to realize that the guards' horses had been through nearly the same punishment. The big Yankee bay seemed to hold up better than any. It was too good an animal for trash like Phineas Shattuck.

Owen felt relief of sorts when the lamps and lanterns of town began to glow through the darkness, though he knew well enough what awaited him there. They rode past the darkened little house from which he had taken the Hubbard women. The boy Adcock gazed at the place and mumbled darkly.

The jail was of rough lumber, old and sagging a little atop a foundation of heavy posts which held it up from the ground. It had been built in the Spartan days of the Texas republic when people were few and money scarcer. Owen had considered it a misshapen structure even when he had had no reason to fear it. Now it was an ugly presence brooding in the darkness like some fearful old fortress out of the Dark Ages in stories he had read as a schoolboy.

Shattuck said, "Well, Chancellor, we've got them here. There ain't no need you troublin' yourself any further."

His voice betrayed too much of hope. Owen looked anxiously at the sheriff. Chancellor smiled with a raw irony. "We've come this far. We had just as well see them safely inside a cell. It might strike their fancy to turn back at the door and run."

Owen sighed. He dreaded a cell, but that was safer than being in the open with Shattuck if no outsider was around to see.

Shattuck brusquely ordered the guards to dismount.

He dispatched half of them to lead the horses to the corrals. "Adcock," he commanded, "I want you to brush my horse real good. I want to see his hair shine like a mirror when the sun comes up in the mornin'. You hear me?"

Adcock replied in a small, angry voice, "Yes sir."

"See that you do, or I'll wear out a bullwhip on you." He turned then to Andrew Danforth, shoving him roughly through the door. "Git in there!" He turned toward Owen, but Sheriff Chancellor positioned himself between them.

Chancellor said, "Go ahead, soldier."

Owen stepped through the door. The inside was pitch-dark. He could barely make out the form of his father just in front of him. If there had been any way out except the front door, this would be the time to break and run, he thought. But run where? He listened to the trampling of heavy boots as the rest of the men and boys crowded in behind him.

Shattuck demanded, "Where's that jailer? Why ain't there a lamp lit? Benson, damn you, where are you at?"

Someone struck a light and lifted the chimney from a lamp. Suddenly Owen became aware that more men were in the room than should be. Five or six more, at least. He heard Shattuck's gasp as someone shoved the muzzle of a big Navy revolver to his throat.

A stern voice ordered, "Everybody stand real still!" Owen knew that voice. He had heard it at Uncle Zach's and again at his father's cabin. A man moved into the narrow circle of dim lamplight, a pistol in his hand.

Vance Hubbard.

Hubbard's younger brother Tyson held the shuddering Shattuck at gunpoint. Red Upjohn and Jim Carew and the grinning man named Banty stood just at the edge of the lamplight.

A couple of guards who had made it only as far as the door turned to run away into the night. Owen heard a commotion outside and knew they had been stopped. Vance Hubbard evidently had brought a sizable contingent of the brush people to town.

Firmly but with some semblance of courtesy Hubbard said, "Chancellor, I want you and all these heel fly boys to go back yonder into that cell, where the jailkeeper is at. Real quiet now. I wouldn't want anybody to get hurt."

Chancellor, his hands raised, looked back at Shattuck. With sarcasm he said, "You've given the orders all day, Shattuck. What do you say now?"

Shattuck eyed a pitiless young Tyson Hubbard, whose expression indicated that he would gladly squeeze the trigger. Shattuck rasped, "Do what he says." The guards moved into two open cells, as ordered. Shattuck started to follow them, but Tyson Hubbard stopped him, stroking the muzzle of the pistol against Shattuck's bobbing Adam's apple.

"Not you," he said. "We just might take you with us."

Shattuck's eyes went wild. "What're you fixin' to do?" No answer came. He asked again, fearfully, "What do you want me for?"

"To be sure nobody follows too close. If anything happens, they'll have to stop and bury you."

Shattuck made a noise as if he were strangling.

Andrew Danforth had been silent. Now he said, "You've taken a lot of risk, Vance."

Vance Hubbard closed the cell door on the men and locked it. "No more than you've done, many a time. I'm just sorry we didn't get to Zach's place in time. They killed him."

Andrew looked at Shattuck, and his eyes narrowed in hatred. "I know."

Hubbard said, "I was afraid even this might be too late. I thought Shattuck might never get to town with you."

Andrew said, "Claude Chancellor's to thank for that. He came along just when we needed him."

Hubbard looked through the cell door. "Chancellor, I wish we weren't on opposite sides."

Chancellor responded firmly, "We were not always, but we are now. The only thing that can change it would be for the war to end."

Hubbard signaled for his men to retreat outside. Owen was reluctant to move. "Where we goin'?" he demanded.

"Out to the thickets, amongst our own."

"*Your* own, not mine," Owen said. "I don't belong there."

Tyson put in, "You do now. After what you done for my mother and sister, you can't stay here."

Owen knew Chancellor and Shattuck had heard. Angrily he declared, "I *might've*, if you hadn't said anything. Now you've spoiled that for me."

Andrew gripped his son's right arm. "Come on, Owen, we ain't got time now to argue."

From the cell Chancellor said, "You'd *better* argue, soldier. Once you ride away with those people, you're an outlaw."

Owen protested, "I didn't ask for this." He looked to his father. "Dad, it's already gone too far . . ."

He did not see the fist coming until too late. His head rocked back under the force of his father's hard knuckles, and fire exploded in his eyes. He fell. Strong arms caught and lifted him. He heard his father's voice, dimly. "Sorry, son, but we'll argue later. This ain't a fit time to talk."

He felt himself supported between two men, his feet dragging. His head pounded; his jaw ached. He struggled to pull free but was too weak to fight. He was aware that they were at the livery stable, and he heard his father say, "Put him on that big bay horse Shattuck was ridin'. It's rightfully his."

Red Upjohn argued that the horse was sweaty and tired, but Andrew said it was not that far to the thickets. The horse would have plenty of time afterward for rest. Owen was lifted into the saddle. When he felt himself about to slide off, somebody grabbed him. Vance Hubbard's voice lifted into a shout, and others followed, stampeding the guards' loose horses out into the darkness.

Gunshots racketed and echoed. Shattuck shouted futilely, "Don't shoot! *I'm* here."

But firing continued. Some seemed to come from the town and some from the Hubbard rescue party, shooting back toward the flashes. Owen heard a sharp cry of pain. Tyson Hubbard shouted, "Vance!" Then everybody was spurring the horses into a hard run. Owen held to the saddlehorn to keep from falling. He felt his father's strong arm steadying him.

"Hang on, son. We got a ways to go."

Owen's head gradually cleared. He became able to sit up in the saddle. He was strong enough to grip with his legs and remain astride without help from Andrew. He could see the dark forms of horsemen on either side of him and knew there were seven or eight besides himself and Andrew. And Phineas Shattuck. Someone had bound Shattuck's hands to the saddle.

Owen looked behind him but saw no sign of the town. He judged that the horses had already run a mile or more. Somebody was slumped low in his saddle, two men on either side holding him on his horse.

Vance Hubbard had been hit.

Owen looked back again. Andrew said, "Ain't no use lookin'. They're back yonder someplace, after us."

Owen said bitterly, "I don't belong here."

"You don't belong dead, neither. They'd have you hangin' from a live oak limb by now."

"Maybe not. You didn't give me a chance to choose."

"Between livin' and dyin'? There *wasn't* no choice."

Someone declared grittily, "A boy ought not to talk back to his daddy." The voice belonged to Red Upjohn, the man who had talked about killing Owen in the thicket. He said sternly, "It's on account of you that Vance Hubbard has got a bullet in his back. I tried to tell him, but he said he owed you for the womenfolks."

Andrew Danforth declared, "Don't try to saddle my son down under that whole load. Vance did it for me, too." He pulled over near Hubbard for a better look at his condition. Tyson was holding his brother in the saddle. The look in his face said the situation was grave.

Andrew swore. "Shattuck, you've got a lot to answer for."

Shattuck stared at the ground moving beneath the feet of the horse upon which he was tied. Owen thought he heard a whimper.

Daylight came. Owen glanced back, expecting pursuit. He saw nothing, but he felt it was there. Shattuck turned too, and it seemed to Owen that the whites of his eyes showed large as he studied Vance Hubbard's slumped form. Tyson Hubbard looked at Shattuck, and the look promised death.

The morning sun was half an hour above the horizon when the riders passed over a hill and Owen saw the dense growth of the thicket ahead. No pursuit had shown itself. The horsemen slowed to a steady trot, then to a walk to make the pace easier for the wounded man. In the daylight, Vance Hubbard's face was gray as clabber and just as cold. The riders had stopped twice in the night to stanch the bleeding, but there had been neither time nor light to extract the bullet lodged in his back.

Now, in the edge of the heavy timber, time was taken. Though Owen still felt anger against his father for bringing this calamity upon them, he could no longer resent Vance Hubbard. Whatever Hubbard might have owed him, he had repaid, with interest.

Someone spread a thin blanket. Upjohn and another man placed Hubbard upon it, on his stomach. Hubbard bit his lip to suppress a cry, but a groan came anyway. Tyson cursed the men for not being gentler with his brother. Red Upjohn glared, and Owen felt he would have knocked Tyson off of his feet had other considerations not been more pressing. Andrew Danforth ripped open the blood-soaked shirt and examined the swollen, blue-edged wound. "Bullet's in there deep."

Tyson trembled, touching his brother. "We've got a doctor in camp. A tooth-puller, is all, but he's got some tools. If we try to cut on Vance here we may kill him."

Andrew worried, "He may not make it to camp."

Hubbard spoke painfully, "I can make it. Just put me back on my horse and hold onto me. I'll get there."

Tyson pushed to his feet, his eyes blistering Phineas Shattuck. "Here's *one* piece of excess weight we don't need to be takin' no further. Banty, give me that rope off of your saddle."

Banty was hesitant.

Shattuck cried, "No!" He looked around desperately for help. "Please, I ain't done nothin' but my duty."

Tyson seethed, "And loved every minute of it. Banty, your rope."

Banty just sat there, his mouth open in silent protest. Someone else handed Tyson a coiled rope. He loosened it.

Owen held his breath and waited vainly for someone to stop this. Heart pounding, he looked to his father and saw hesitation.

Shattuck began to weep. "Please, somebody . . ." His gaze fastened hopefully on Owen. "Soldier, I wasn't really goin' to kill you. You ain't goin' to let them . . . Please!"

Tyson shook out a loop and tossed it over Shattuck's head. Shattuck tried desperately to dodge, but his movement was restricted by the thongs that bound his hands to the saddle. "No," Shattuck pleaded in a piping voice, "you can't do this." Tears spilled down his cheeks. "Please, I'm beggin' you . . ."

Owen saw in some of the men's faces that they were not strong for a killing. Upjohn surprised Owen by saying, "You don't really want to do this, Tyson. Hangin' is ugly. I seen my son . . ."

But no one actually moved to stop it. Owen listened to Shattuck's pleading and felt his stomach turn. Remembering Uncle Zach, he tried to tell himself it was justified. But he knew he could not let it happen. He stepped to Tyson's side and lifted a pistol from Tyson's waistband. He maneuvered quickly to put his back to the brush so no one could get behind him. He poked the weapon into Tyson's ribs.

"Take the rope off of him."

Tyson exploded in outrage, "Owen, you've wore out your welcome with me."

"I never asked for your welcome. I said take the rope off."

Andrew put in, "Son . . ."

Owen told him angrily, "You could've stopped it. You didn't."

"I wasn't sure I wanted to. I'm still not."

"*I* am. Dad, cut his hands loose." Tyson seemed about to pull away. Owen shoved the pistol into his ribs, hard enough to bruise. "Tyson, you stand real still."

To Owen's surprise it was Red Upjohn who came

reluctantly to his support, not Andrew. Red declared, "The soldier boy's right for once, Tyson. Kill Shattuck thisaway and they'll call up half the troops in Texas to clear out the big thicket."

Using the saber he had once pointed at Owen's throat, he cut Shattuck's bonds.

A murmur rose among the men. Andrew Danforth looked around fearfully for any move against his son. "Everybody stand easy."

Shattuck, white-faced, slipped the loop from around his neck. He did not wait for a blessing. He drummed heels against the horse's ribs and tore away through the brush.

Owen stepped back from Tyson, but he held a firm grip on the pistol. "Don't anybody go after him."

Tyson's eyes brimmed with tears of anger. "You'll wish you hadn't done that."

"I'm already charged with treason for somethin' I didn't want to do. I won't have you pilin' murder on top of it."

Gravely Andrew said, "Just because you saved him, son, don't think Shattuck'll be forgivin' of you. It'll set hard with him that you saw him whine and beg for his life. If he ever gets you in his hands again there won't be any use in you beggin' *him*."

"He ain't goin' to get me in his hands."

Tyson's fury had not ebbed. "We ought to tie you out here at the edge of the brush and leave you for him to find. Then you'll see how much mercy he'll have."

Andrew stepped in front of Owen. "We don't need any more talk like that. There's your brother to see after."

Owen made a fist and defiantly moved out from behind his father. "I can take care of my own self."

From Vance Hubbard came a quiet pleading. "For God's sake, Tyson, take me to camp. Don't let me die here while you-all fight amongst yourselves."

6

The faint smell of woodsmoke told Owen they were approaching the camp, though he saw but little through the heavy mixed timber, scrub and briars. He could not discern even a horse trail. The people who lived in this deep fastness took care not to repeat the same route in and out so much that the thick ground layer of fallen, rotted leaves would betray the way. Only an expert tracker could trail fugitives deeply into this dense sanctuary.

The men took turns helping young Tyson hold his brother in the saddle. Vance Hubbard seemed more dead than alive. They talked hopefully about his recovery once they brought him under the care of his womenfolk, but Owen had observed too many men wounded in military conflict. Not often had he seen a man look as used up as Vance Hubbard and survive. Regret weighed heavily upon Owen's shoulders.

The irony lay heavily on him, too, the fact that this had all started with his freeing of the Hubbard women so they could be with Vance and Tyson.

Damn this war, he thought with bitterness. *Who wanted it in the first place?*

How the men found the hidden camp was a mystery to Owen, but they drew into a clearing, part natural and part created by axes and muscle. Owen saw a dozen or more tents, some sizable, some only rough shelters rigged with sheets of stained canvas ranging from gray to yellow. Mrs. Hubbard bent over a campfire where a couple of smoke-blackened pots were suspended from an iron bar. She straightened to watch the riders enter the clearing. Her hands went to her throat as she recognized her oldest son slumped, a grim young Tyson holding him in his saddle. She called out and came running. Lucy Hubbard rushed from the largest of the tents, a bucket in her hand. She saw her brothers and dropped the bucket, dumping its water on the ground.

Owen held back out of the way. With his bad arm he would be little help in easing Vance down from the saddle. His father and Tyson Hubbard carried the wounded partisan into a tent. Mrs. Hubbard made one short cry, then gathered her wits and began to direct her son's handling.

A thin-faced little man hurried across the clearing with a small black bag. He would be the dentist Tyson had mentioned. Through the open front of the tent, Owen watched him probe the wound while Mrs. Hubbard held Vance's hands. Her lips were pinched almost white. Lucy knelt beside her brother and took up the blood with a piece of cloth so the dentist could work. Her face was drained pale, but she did not flinch from the task.

Vance lapsed into unconsciousness, or he might not have stood the pain. So far as Owen knew, he had not rallied enough to speak to Mrs. Hubbard or Lucy.

Bitterly Tyson Hubbard said, "I'd like to get my hands on the heel fly who done that to him."

Andrew said, "A price of war, son. Nobody wanted it."

"Somebody must've, or it wouldn't've happened." He looked around belligerently, giving vent to his frustration and anger. His gaze lighted on Owen. "If you hadn't stopped me, that Phineas Shattuck'd be dead now, like my brother's fixin' to be."

From inside the tent came Mary Hubbard's firm voice. "Don't be talkin' foolishness, Tyson. If you've got to blame somebody, blame *me* for wantin' out of that town. That's where it started."

Andrew placed his big hands on Tyson's shoulders. "Shattuck's got a lot to answer to the Lord for, but he didn't fire the shot that brought your brother down." He glanced at his son. "I know it helps when you can find somebody to blame for a thing like this, but nobody is, and *everybody* is. This war could've been stopped before it ever started if enough people had stood up and said their say. We let ourselves slide into it a little at a time till we couldn't climb up out of the hole anymore. In a way, we're all to blame for what's happened to your brother."

The men of the camp, including those who had participated with Hubbard in the Danforth rescue, stood around quietly, solemnly. They waited as Owen had so often seen soldiers do between battles, waiting for life, or for death, or for God knew what. It struck him that this clearing resembled a hundred military encampments he had seen at one time or another. Yet these were not soldiers so much as refugees. In that moment, though they represented a side against which he had fought and against which many of his friends had died, he felt pity for them in this austere exile.

A coldness came upon him as he considered that he had unwillingly become one of them. He did not know how he might ever return to his own side in this war. He looked to the heavy brush which seemed to press in against the rough clearing from all around. Even the wind could not properly move through the dense growth that surrounded him. He felt somehow choked, somehow imprisoned.

Red Upjohn moved up beside Owen as the operation continued in the tent. Owen saw an anger in the man that was hard to fathom. Upjohn growled, "If you'd never come home from the war, there wouldn't've been no need for us to raid the jail."

Owen had no wish to be drawn into a fight, but he could not let the remark pass unanswered. "If it hadn't been for some damnyankee's saber, I wouldn't've had to."

The little man named Jim Carew had seemed subservient to Upjohn before, but now he displayed an indignation that surprised Owen. "Red, this is a time to hold your silence. If you've got to exercise your mouth, go say a prayer for Vance."

Upjohn gave him a challenging stare, but Carew stood up to it. Upjohn backed away and went to see after his horse, which he had left tied with the saddle on.

Owen said quietly, "Thanks. I didn't want to fight him."

Carew gave Owen a look that said he was no happier with him than with Upjohn. "I almost had to fight him myself, after you run off from me yesterday. You left me in a tight place."

"I was in a tight place too. I told you I had to get home before Shattuck came lookin' for me. I didn't make it."

Carew nodded. "We followed you. We wanted to just ride in and pull you and your daddy out of that trouble a lot sooner, but Vance said surprisin' Shattuck at the jail wouldn't be as dangerous." He stared gravely toward the tent. "Even Vance Hubbard could be wrong."

Owen heard a metallic thump as the dentist dropped a lead ball into a tin pan. He heard the man telling Lucy to let the wound bleed and cleanse itself. "We seem to have more blood around here than medical supplies."

Mrs. Hubbard asked quietly, "What are his chances?"

The doctor was a moment in answering. He shook his head. "Ma'am, a lie would be a disservice to you."

Lucy reached quickly to grasp her mother's hand. Mrs. Hubbard did not look up. Andrew Danforth placed his hand on Mary Hubbard's arm, expressing with a touch what might not be said in words. Tyson Hubbard put his arms around his mother and his sister.

A raspy voice spoke, "Mama." Mrs. Hubbard bent over her son. "I'm here."

Owen had to strain to hear Hubbard say, "Mama, I wish . . ." The voice stopped there.

Mrs. Hubbard said, "I know. I know." She leaned her head down against him.

Vance asked, "Where's Andrew Danforth?"

Andrew replied, "I'm with you, Vance."

"Andrew, watch out for my family. You and your boy, please see after them."

Andrew assured him, "We will." Andrew looked up at Owen, his eyes asking. Owen could only nod, wondering how he could help anyone else when right now he could hardly help himself. He found Lucy watching him through eyes that brimmed with tears. Probably wishing she could trade him for her brother, he thought.

He clenched his fist against a feeling half anger, half helplessness. If the two women had been content to remain in town, Vance Hubbard would not be dying. Owen would not be a fugitive from his own people, and most certainly he would not be a semicaptive here in the midst of this interminable thicket. But as he watched Mary and Lucy and Tyson Hubbard standing strong in their grief, he could hold no anger against them. This seemed not the time, not the place. There was blame enough, he thought, for everybody.

He wondered, as he had wondered many times on one dusty, red-spattered battlefield and another, how people so recently friends, Americans together, could have allowed such a madness to come about. He wondered if Andrew was right, that the people could have stopped it had they tried harder. Surely if they had known then what they knew now, they would have.

Vance Hubbard proved stronger than the camp had thought. He lived through the afternoon and most of the evening, seeming at times to drift away into unconsciousness but responding when spoken to. His family remained by his side. Andrew Danforth never strayed far, though once he came out to suggest that someone fix a meal for the women so they would not have to leave Vance. As darkness came and no one took it upon himself to post guards, Andrew called the men together and assumed that responsibility. Most of the men accepted without seeming to question the propriety or Andrew's right. Red Upjohn grumbled something about a newcomer taking over without even waiting for Hubbard to die, but he stopped when Carew angrily whispered an answer no one else could hear.

Andrew studied his son. "You willin' to stand your share of the duty?"

Owen made no effort to suppress his resentment. "What duty? If it was up to me, I wouldn't be here. If it hadn't been for you, I *wouldn't* be."

Red Upjohn declared, "You wouldn't put him on guard, would you, Danforth? He may be your son, but he's a Confederate. If any of his side was to show up, he'd join them against us."

Owen tried to think of a response. All that came was anger.

He heard Mary Hubbard's stern voice behind him. "Mr. Upjohn, Owen Danforth is here because he went beyond duty to help my daughter and me. None of us wants to be in this place, Owen least of all. But he *is* here and I'll expect you to make the best of it or leave my son's camp."

Taken by surprise, Upjohn touched his fingers to his hat brim. "I've got nothin' but respect for you, ma'am. I'm just thinkin' of the good of the camp and wonderin' if we can stand the risk of this soldier boy. His sympathies ain't changed."

"That makes him the most unfortunate of us all," she said firmly. She looked back toward the tent where Vance Hubbard lay. "Except for one."

"Yes ma'am," Upjohn said deferentially. But as he turned away his parting look told Owen he was simply being kind to an unfortunate woman. He had changed his mind about nothing.

Andrew Danforth shrugged. "All right, son. I *won't* put you on guard duty. You've got a bad arm anyway."

Owen snapped, "I watch with my eyes, not my arm. Since you've gotten me into this mess, I'll stand my share of the duty. But Upjohn is right about one thing. If any of *my* people come along, I won't shoot at them."

Banty Tillotson grinned. It seemed to Owen that he grinned most of the time, whether there was anything to grin about or not. Banty said, "You don't need to worry, Owen. Anybody gets this far into the thicket by himself is lost anyway. He'll be beggin' you to shoot him."

Owen flexed the fingers of his left hand and found them less stiff than yesterday. He raised the arm gently until pain stopped him. Healing was lower than he would like, but it seemed to be coming. One of these days he would not have to let a woman take up his fight.

Andrew Danforth studied him worriedly. "I don't know what it'll take for Red Upjohn to have confidence in you."

Owen shook his head. "I don't give a damn. I just want him to leave me alone." He looked around the little camp, which in the dusk seemed even more hemmed in by the brush. "I wish *everybody* would leave me alone."

Andrew's eyes narrowed. "Me included?"

"You had the most to do with me bein' here. I've got a lot of things to sort out in my mind, and that's one of them. Another is what I'm goin' to do about it."

"I don't know what you *can* do about it. All the bridges seem to've been burned."

"With somebody else holdin' the torch."

Vance Hubbard clung to life until after dark. Owen heard a little cry from Mrs. Hubbard and knew the waiting was over. He saw the two women holding one another. Tyson stood with his arms around both. Owen removed his hat and stood slumped outside the tent. Even more than before, the camp seemed a cold and brooding place, sad beyond measure. He wanted to get away. But how? And where could he go?

It was impractical to herd the horses in the heavy brush, but a military-type picket line was not appropriate either. The grass was sparse, and keeping the horses so close together gave them little chance to graze. Instead, they were scattered, each staked on a long rope that gave it an opportunity to find sustenance, poor as it might be. To fetch hay or other feed into this thicket in any meaningful quantity was clearly out of the question.

Owen walked to the big bay, which stood at the end of a rope. The horse seemed already to have cropped off whatever grass might have been available to him. Or perhaps other horses had done it before. This was no place, Owen thought, for either men or horses to remain very long. He ran his hand along the heavy neck and down the shoulder. Temptation chewed at him. It would not be difficult, while everyone's attention was on the death of Vance Hubbard, to saddle the bay and ride out of here. But he had no personal knowledge of what lay beyond this brush except in the direction of town and home. In that direction, he could not go.

He felt in his shirt pocket for the paper which had given him permission to come home on convalescent leave. He was reassured to find it still there. It would have been easy to have lost it. He tingled to a sudden realization. Phineas Shattuck had scarcely looked at it. He probably had no idea to what military unit Owen belonged. It was unlikely the local courthouse had any record, either, for Owen had enlisted in San Antonio. If he could but get out of this place and escape capture until well beyond Shattuck's influence, the document should provide him safe passage through any checkpoints. He could rejoin his old outfit without anyone there knowing the trouble he had encountered at home.

A rough voice said, "You wasn't figurin' on leavin' us, was you?" He knew before he turned that the man was Red Upjohn.

Owen sagged in disappointment, for he had waited too long. "I suppose you'd put a bullet in my back if I was to try."

Upjohn grunted. "I'll bet if you offered to lead Shattuck and his guards to this camp, he'd drop all charges."

Owen could not deny the thought. But he had not permitted it serious consideration. "My dad's in here."

"Seems to me like everything ain't too pleasant between you and your daddy. Seems to me like you might even be mad enough to turn him in."

Owen demanded, "What kind of a Judas do you think I am?"

"How many kinds are there?"

The exchange had caught the attention of Tyson Hubbard. He came out and listened, then said evenly, "Owen, don't you get any notions about slippin' away tonight . . . or any other time. I'll be watchin' you."

Upjohn turned on Tyson with almost as much animosity as he had shown Owen. "You Hubbards brought him here. If it was up to me he'd already be dead."

Tyson flinched under the unexpected attack. "*You* can leave any time you take a notion, Red."

"And I will, if *I* decide to. Ain't nobody can tell me what to do. Especially no wet-eared kid too big for his britches." He stalked away like an angry old bull after a fight.

Banty Tillotson had followed Tyson. He managed

an infectious smile that lifted a little of the tension. It seemed to Owen that Banty was the only perpetually good-humored man in this somber camp. "Don't you-all fret over what Red Upjohn says. Poor feller's got a rail or two missin' out of his fence."

Tyson grumbled, "We ought to run him out of this place. Seems like he's always startin' trouble in camp."

Banty said, "Ignore him. It ain't worth the worry."

Tyson jerked his head at Owen. "You come too. From now on, you stay away from the horses until one of us is with you."

Owen was not angry so much as disappointed over the idea that he had let an opportunity go by. But he realized Upjohn had probably been watching him all the time. Had Owen so much as reached for his saddle, he might have taken a bullet in his back. His gaze followed the bitter Upjohn, and he reflected that war's cruelties seemed to kill some people without making them stop breathing. Upjohn had been wounded deeply, in a place that showed only through the madness in his eyes.

Because the horses had eaten out all the grass within practical reach of the clearing, a decision was made to move camp a couple of miles to a place where a small seep would provide water enough for people and horses. Vance Hubbard was buried at the edge of the old camp, the place marked by a crude cross cut of hackberry limbs. That would have to serve until a better day, when something more appropriate could be done.

Lucy and Tyson Hubbard looked back as the small brigade put the clearing behind them and pushed into the brush, but Mary Hubbard forced herself to keep her gaze forward. Andrew Danforth rode beside her, a quiet sympathy in his eyes.

He had buried dreams of his own. Many of them.

Presently Andrew moved up to the front of the column, assuming by his nature a leadership that death had vacated. No one questioned the fitness of his doing so; the men seemed to accept. At one time or another he had helped many of them to reach the sanctuary of this great thicket. Despite his personal resentment, Owen could see in his father what he had seen in many officers he had served, a strength and confidence that others sensed without the requirement of noise or show.

Movement through the tangled brush was slow and tedious, the riders falling into several more or less parallel tracks, single file, ducking low branches, weaving a crooked pattern. Owen became aware, after a time, that he had lagged to the rear. A persistent notion came to him again. This might be his chance to pull away. By the time he was missed it would be too late for anyone to backtrack and find him.

A stern voice put an end to the notion. "I can read what's runnin' through your mind, Owen. I'd drop you before you could go twenty feet."

Tyson Hubbard had worked in behind him. And behind Tyson rode Red Upjohn. They had little use for one another, but Owen thought they had more in common than they realized.

He found to his surprise that he had unconsciously

made a fist with his left hand. *That*, at least, was an improvement.

The brush thinned a bit. Lucy Hubbard slowed her horse until she fell back even with Owen. She turned in the saddle and glanced at her brother with challenge in her eyes. "Mind if I ride with Owen?"

He shook his head, figuring she would do what she wanted.

She said, "Me bein' here might help keep you out of trouble with my brother."

"I'm in no trouble with him."

"Looked like it to me. Are you so anxious to leave us?"

Owen was surprised that it showed so plainly. "I don't belong with this bunch. You know that. My dad knows it."

"What if he hadn't carried you out of that jail? You'd probably be dead now . . . like my brother." Her voice caught.

He let a little of his resentment return. "I doubt that'd make much difference to you."

"It'd make a lot of difference, Owen." She touched his hand. He started to pull it away but did not follow through. Her touch stirred him.

She said, "We owe you."

He glanced back toward her brother. "If you figure you owe me, talk to *him*. All I want is to get out of this place. I've got no interest in betrayin' anybody."

She nodded. "It wouldn't do any good right now, but give him some time to get over losin' Vance. And give *me* time too, Owen."

"Time for what?"

"I don't know yet. Just time." She went silent, looking toward the riders ahead. Owen stared at her, his blood oddly warm.

He could think of nothing which would make his position here more uncomfortable than to become involved with a Unionist woman. But the tingling sensation from her touch remained with him.

The site selected for the new camp was brushier than the other and required much ax work to clear places for the tents. Owen decided to try the growing strength of his left arm. He had been taking it from its crude sling and exercising it regularly, finding a little more flexibility from one day to the next. The hand still allowed only a weak grip, but at least he could hold an axhandle; the right hand and arm did most of the work. The first few times he swung the ax, the left arm protested with a stabbing of pain. He gritted his teeth and dared it to stop him. It did not.

His father watched him in silence. Owen paused to allow the weak arm to rest. He demanded, "Any advice?" His tone said he solicited none.

Andrew shook his head. "You'll do what you want to anyway. I'm glad to see the arm is better."

Owen spoke with gravel in his voice. "I just wish it hadn't waited so long. I wouldn't be here."

His father's eyes did not waver. "I don't know any more ways to say I'm sorry. I won't try again."

Owen gradually became aware that the group's isolation was less complete than it might seem. Always, men from camp were out scouting the thicket, watching for signs of intruders, patrolling the edges to help men who legitimately sought a way in, harassing and turning back any attempt by the authorities to penetrate this fastness. There were places where men like Banty Tillotson and Jim Carew and Red Upjohn sometimes rode to meet at night with collaborators on the outside, men who could tell what was happening in the rest of the world, who could advise them on the activities of Phineas Shattuck and his home guards. Andrew and Zach Danforth had performed that duty for a long time. Now Andrew was the successor to Vance Hubbard's leadership, and he depended upon others' eyes and ears.

This information seemed not to travel in just one direction, however. At times the reports indicated that the authorities were more aware of what was happening inside the thicket than they had any right to be. They seemed to know that Vance Hubbard was dead, which might be explained by Shattuck's having seen him shot. But they seemed also to know that Andrew Danforth had assumed the leadership, loose though it was. That might or might not have been just a good guess, Andrew said worriedly when Jim Carew brought him the report.

Owen perceived that his father began studying the men in camp more closely than before, and that the lines in his face seemed to darken with the passing days.

Upjohn's leaving always lifted the spirits of the men in the clearing, though their morale inevitably sagged again when he returned with his brooding eyes, his scowling ways. In contrast, Banty Tillotson's jaunty manner was a tonic to the somber encampment. It was a joy to see him riding in, that grin like sunshine through the trees.

Andrew's worry deepened when Red Upjohn came in a day overdue from a lone foray, taken on his own volition, into the open countryside. Upjohn made it no secret that he harbored reservations about Andrew's right to give orders in the camp, but he reported to him nevertheless. He said he had been discovered and almost caught by a heel fly patrol. He had taken refuge in the brush near the Danforth farm. The kid guards cautiously probed the edge of the timber but did not risk venturing far into it.

While he was there he had seen something else. Someone was working not only Andrew's farm but Zach's.

"Who?" Andrew demanded sharply.

Upjohn shrugged. "If I was to hazard a guess I'd say that Shattuck confiscated it for the government. And around here, he considers *hisself* to be the government."

Andrew reacted as if Upjohn had punched him in the stomach.

If Red Upjohn's news was disturbing, Carew's a couple of days later was worse. The man's horse was flagging badly as he pushed him into the little clearing. Banty Tillotson met him with a smile. "You look like you been on a two-day drunk, Jim, and your horse with you."

Andrew Danforth went to confer with Carew at the

edge of camp, where he was unsaddling. Carew said, "I'm cold sober. You'll quit that silly grin too, Banty, when I tell you what I heard."

He had ventured all the way to town in the darkness to watch, to listen. His face was grim as he turned to the waiting Andrew.

"They're comin' to the thicket, Andrew. And this time it won't be just Shattuck and a few of them kid guards. This time he'll have two or three full companies of army troops. He's swearin' around town that he'll bring us in or kill us all."

7

ometimes Andrew Danforth reacted suddenly to news, and sometimes he took a while to chew on it. This time he chewed. He gave first Owen, then Carew a long, quiet contemplation. He turned to Banty Tillotson, who had walked up in time to hear.

"You've been out too. You hear anything like that?"

Banty's reaction was characteristically nonchalant. "Nope. Anyway, they've tried before. They ain't taken a man out of these thickets yet."

Carew said earnestly, "They've never tried it in the kind of force they're talkin' about." His manner showed he placed stock in what he had heard. "Always been a few kid guards or a bunch of bigmouths like Shattuck. Never been soldiers in strength ever tried an honest-to-God push through here."

Banty smiled condescendingly. "You're always lettin' your imagination run away with you, Jim. Sounds to me like Shattuck braggin', is all. I wouldn't lose no sleep over it."

Red Upjohn scowled at Owen. He said nothing,

but Owen thought he read Upjohn's mind: *The trouble started when you came here.*

Mary Hubbard emerged from her tent, carrying a long-handled spoon. Andrew thoughtfully watched her stir a pot of beans suspended over a low-burning open fire. He turned his gaze to young Tyson Hubbard. Tyson seemed almost cheered by the news. Andrew asked, "What do you think your brother would've said?"

The young man's eyes were full of fight. "I don't know what he'd've said, but what *I* say is, let them come. We can rag them like a terrier. We'll hit them where they're not lookin' and scatter out through this brush like quail through tall grass. Not much risk they'd catch us."

"Not much," Andrew pondered. "But *some.*"

Tyson declared, "I'm willin' to take my chances."

Andrew frowned. "Are you willin' for your mother and sister to take them with you?"

Tyson sobered. He looked at his mother. She stopped stirring the beans. Concern came into her eyes as she studied her son and Andrew.

Tyson asked, "What're you gettin' at, Andrew?"

"Even if we did what you're talkin' about, which I don't favor, there'd be too much danger here for the women."

Mrs. Hubbard did not suffer her curiosity to remain unsatisfied. She let the long spoon sink into the pot and walked up to the men, her arms folded. "I get a feelin' somethin' has come along which concerns me, Andrew."

Andrew looked to Carew, who told her what he had heard. Mary Hubbard's gaze fastened solemnly upon her son. She said, "I suspect, Tyson, that you want to go out there and fight them."

Stiffly he said, "We owe them that for Vance."

She replied firmly, "We owe it to Vance to stay alive until this war is over. That's what *he* was tryin' to do."

Andrew put in, "Mary, is there someplace you could go where Shattuck and his bunch wouldn't look for you? Kinfolks, maybe, that he wouldn't know about? Somebody not carryin' the name of Hubbard?"

"Over east, in Austin County ... my brother, Ed Bradshaw and his wife Vi. Might be a problem to get there without somebody catchin' us, though."

Andrew's gaze lighted upon Owen. Owen was uncomfortable under the stern appraisal. Andrew said, "Son, you've been wantin' out of this thicket. How'd you like to take Lucy and her mother to their kinfolks?"

Owen's eyes narrowed. "That's how I got *into* this thicket."

"You haven't talked much since we've been here, but I know you've itched to get back to your outfit."

"I've wanted to get away from *here*," Owen admitted, glancing at the belligerent Red Upjohn.

"You still have your leave papers. They'd take you anywhere, once you got clear of Shattuck's country." His voice fell. "I'd hope you'd go someplace besides that damnable war. But I couldn't stop you the last time. This time I won't try."

Owen's pulse quickened at the thought of putting

this thicket behind him. Even the battlefields seemed better, though he knew only time and distance made them so.

Tyson declared, "I don't like it. Owen's still a rebel. Come to a showdown, I'm not sure he'd pick my mother and sister over ol' Jeff Davis."

Andrew's eyes were unreadable. "He did once before. That's how come he got in all this trouble. But you can watch him yourself, Tyson. You're goin' with them."

Tyson's mouth dropped open in protest, but Andrew raised his big hand. "Look at your mother, boy. She's lost one son. I know how she feels, because I've lost two. If you stayed here she'd keep lookin' back over her shoulder, worryin' about you. She might even turn back and fall into Shattuck's hands. You'll go for *her* good, not for yours."

Mary Hubbard gave Andrew a look that spoke of gratitude. Owen was startled by the thought that she might feel something more than simply gratitude.

Tyson shot a resentful glance at Owen. "I belong here, fightin' with the rest of you. That's what Vance would've done."

"We're not goin' to fight them," Andrew said. "We're goin' to evaporate in front of them like a dew in July. *That's* what your brother would've done."

Tyson stared at the ground. Andrew placed a hand on his shoulder. "There's more to it than just your mother needin' you. One of these days—pretty soon, likely—this war'll be over with. A lot of the people we're callin' enemy will be our friends again. You don't want to have to remember that you killed some of them. Best thing you can do is stay out of the fightin' till that time comes." He looked at Owen. "That would be the best for all of us."

Any reply would have courted argument. Owen made none. If he could not leave his father with good feelings, at least there was no point in leaving him with the internal scars of another fight between them.

Andrew forged ahead as if both Owen and Tyson had agreed, though neither actually had. He turned to Mary Hubbard and called Lucy from the tent. "You'll want to do your travelin' at night, at least till you're well past anyplace where people have heard of the Hubbards, or of Shattuck."

Relief was in Mrs. Hubbard's eyes. "I'll be glad to get Tyson away from here. Once we're with my family we'll keep him out of sight." Her voice turned worried. "I wish *you'd* go with us too, Andrew."

Andrew shook his head. "There'd be suspicion. I'd draw attention to you. Here I can at least slip out now and again and keep an eye on my farm."

A sadness came over her, mixed with a little of anger. "They've confiscated your farm, just like they've taken ours."

"For now," Andrew said evenly. "But when the war's over there'll be regular courts again, no matter how it turns out. Then we'll see who owns that farm, and yours."

Mary Hubbard suggested that a start be made as soon as possible, though the four might have to wait a time for darkness at the edge of the thicket before venturing into the open. She feared that the longer Tyson was given to study on the matter, the more argument he would raise. Once on the way, he would find it difficult to turn back. The noon meal finished, Red Upjohn watched as Owen threw his saddle on the big Yankee bay.

"I'd like to trade you out of that horse," he said. "He'd serve me well if the heel flies ever give me a run."

Owen replied, "I've got a long ways to travel before I get back to my outfit. It'll take this bay or somethin' as good to carry me there."

Owen's intentions had rankled Upjohn from the beginning. Owen considered that understandable in view of the man's politics, his story about being forced to watch the lynching death of a son. Upjohn turned to Tyson, who was saddling a horse for his mother. "You may not be the man your brother was, but it's a good thing you're goin' too, boy. Wouldn't surprise me none if this one was to turn your womenfolks in. He'd like to get himself pardoned for helpin' them the first time."

Tyson gave Upjohn a startled glance. He was used to nothing except abuse from the man. He turned a hard stare on Owen. "He might *think* about it. But he'd find himself shakin' hands with the devil quicker'n a dog can swaller a biscuit."

Owen choked down a surge of animosity. It was useless to argue. Upjohn was a bitter, driven victim of the war, and Tyson was a hotheaded young fool trying to be a man but not knowing how. Owen was determined to make allowances, no matter how difficult. Lucy helped by walking up and standing quietly beside him. He asked which horse she wanted. She pointed to a black, which Owen considered a sound choice for traveling the night in secret.

She remained close beside him as he put the blanket and the saddle on her horse. He said, "Lucy, I've got no intention of lettin' the heel flies catch you."

"I know that."

"I wish you'd tell your brother. The suspicions he's got, he's liable to shoot me if I even sneeze."

"He'll be better when we get him away from this place." She held the black horse's reins while Owen cinched up. "I'm glad *you're* goin' with us. I've felt guilty for what me and Mama did to you. We played on your sympathy, you know. We knew what we were doin'."

"I never had any doubt of that."

"You could've ridden off and left us any time." She reconsidered. "No, I guess you couldn't. That's where we had you. But maybe you *should* have."

"Could be. Just don't give me any trouble this time."

She told him earnestly, "I'll never do anything like that to you again. I wouldn't have before if I'd known you." She touched his hand, and the touch was warm. "I know you now."

Owen turned away, wondering uneasily if he knew *her*.

He realized he should have told his father good-bye in a proper manner, but they had only stared at one another. The ghosts of two dead young Danforths stood between them, even at parting.

As Owen expected in view of the early start, they reached the eastern edge of the thicket while the sun was still two hours high. Owen and Tyson dismounted and led their horses cautiously to the fringe, studying the rolling, mostly open country beyond.

Tyson said impatiently, "I don't see nobody out there. We could sure use the daylight for travelin'."

"So can the heel flies. For all we know, there could be twenty of them just over that rise."

"Or there might not be any for twenty miles. I feel like a coward brushin' up this way, waitin' for dark so we can go sneakin' out."

"Your brother must've spent a lot of time brushed up, waitin'. I never heard anybody call *him* a coward."

Tyson said no more about his impatience, though he continued flexing his hands nervously.

Tyson's dun horse had a temperament to match his rider's. Baring its teeth, it stretched its neck and attempted to take a bite out of the big bay horse's hide. The bay squealed and whipped around to defend itself, almost jerking the reins from Owen's hand.

Owen asked irritably, "Is that the best horse you could pick?"

"Nothin' wrong with him. He's a good judge of character."

Owen pulled aside to keep the bay out of the dun's reach. "We ought to rest awhile. We'll likely ride all night."

"I ain't rested since the night Vance was shot."

"Then at least quiet down so your mother and sister can." Owen was surprised by the command he put into his voice.

Tyson said resentfully, "Now you're givin' orders like your daddy. But at least he's on *our* side."

"I'm on the side of not gettin' caught. You stay here if it suits you. I'm goin' to tell the women they'd ought to rest. And I figure on doin' the same."

He left Tyson by himself. In a little while Tyson came to where the others' horses were tied. The women lay on blankets. Owen had stretched out on the ground beneath a big hackberry tree. He opened his eyes just enough to see Tyson without betraying that he was watching. Tyson looked around irritably, as if tempted to voice his objections, then seated himself near his mother. He did not lie down. He took out a pocket-knife and began whittling on a long stick, taking out his frustrations with the blade. By dusk the stick had been reduced to a toothpick, and he was surrounded by a pile of curled shavings.

Owen pushed to a sitting position and said, "It'll be dark pretty soon. I favor us eatin' a bite."

They ate jerky and cold bread brought from the camp. *Poor fixings*, Owen thought, but he had done worse many a time, back where the real war was. They saddled. Figuring Tyson would disapprove of any choice he made, he said, "One of us had better ride out in front and the other stay close by the women. Which'd you rather do?"

Tyson made no secret of his distrust. "Reckon I'll scout. Anyhow, I know the way to our kinfolks'."

"Suit yourself," Owen said, knowing he would in any event.

They skirted the edge of the brush at first because the thicket continued a couple of miles more, parallel to their intended direction of travel. That would allow them a quick retreat back into cover. But soon the thicket fell behind them, and only an occasional dark motte of timber offered shelter. Should they encounter travelers on the open road they could only pull off out of the way, dismount and hope darkness would prevent their being noticed. For a time nervousness goaded Owen like a sharp spur. Every bird which trilled in the distance sounded like the jingle of a curb chain or a spur rowel. He could not sustain that level of agitation indefinitely, however. Eventually he eased.

"You-all doin' all right?" he asked the women, trying to force confidence into his voice.

Lucy replied, "We're well protected. What do we have to be worried about?"

Owen wished he shared her faith.

He watched the stars for time and direction. He judged they had ridden a couple of hours when Tyson turned the dun back in a long trot from his position fifty yards forward. "I hear somebody comin' down the road," he whispered urgently.

There was no motte, but a short way out from the wagon ruts stood a stone fence upon which some settler had invested years of hard labor in off times when he could spare the hours away from his plow. The fence stood about chest high and looked black against the sliver of pale moon.

Owen said, "Let's get over against that. If we stay low, maybe they won't see us."

The women moved quickly, and Tyson followed. The four dismounted and crouched. The horses' heads would show above the fence, and in Owen's agitated imagination the dun color of Tyson's mount seemed to glow in the dark. Owen hoped whoever was coming would regard the horses as loose stock and pay no particular attention.

He listened to the hoofbeats, still at some distance. He heard a low murmur of conversation, a sloshing sound as if one of the horses had drunk too much water. He held his hand over his bay horse's nose to prevent its nickering a welcome to the others. His mouth turned dry as old leather.

Tyson muttered. His mother shushed him.

Owen thought, *I'm glad you weren't in any army outfit with me. You might've gotten us killed.*

There were two riders. One sang in a rough, off-key voice, stopping only to tilt his head back. A bottle caught the moonlight and reflected a silvery light. Owen heard the other rider say, "I want a little more of that before you finish it all." The voice was middle-aged, or older. The horses looked to be long in the tooth too, from what Owen could tell by their shapes and tired manner of movement.

Farmers, he decided with relief. They had not even noticed the four horses against the stone fence.

When the travelers were safely past, Tyson said with some resentment, "Just a couple of old codgers. Look at the time we've wasted. We could've just ridden on by them and they wouldn't've paid us no mind."

Owen said, "But if somebody stopped them farther down the road and asked them, they'd remember they saw us."

Tyson said, "I'm lookin' forward to the day when we can ride up and down these roads without havin' to hide. When the Union wins the war . . ."

Owen interrupted him testily. "You fixin' to lead the way, or do you want me to?"

Tyson's dun took a parting bite at Owen's bay. Tyson seemed to take pleasure in that.

They came across no one else that night, though they suffered a few anxious minutes when Tyson spotted something on the road ahead and feared it might be a patrol. Half a dozen cows were bedded down for the night in the broad ruts worn by hoofs and wagon wheels. The sleepy cattle pushed up hind end first and moved warily aside for the horses. A calf trotted off in fright, then bawled for its mother.

As dawn began to bring light in the east, Tyson pulled out of the trail and pointed to a heavy stand of timber perhaps a quarter mile from the trail. He disappeared around a hill while Owen accompanied Mary and Lucy Hubbard toward the trees. Tyson reappeared, pushing his horse into an easy trot. He caught up at the edge of the timber.

"Farmhouse on the yonder side of the hill," he said. "Wasn't nothin' comin'. We could make a little more distance if you-all feel like riskin' it."

Owen said, "No use pushin' our luck."

"I just want to get back where I belong," Tyson declared to his mother. "And that don't mean hidin' out with kinfolks."

She seemed disposed to meet his challenge, but she was startled by a loud snorting and a clatter in the timber. Owen reached for the pistol in his belt, stopping when he saw three half-wild hogs that had wandered upon the riders unexpectedly and had whipped back to escape. It was common practice for settlers to turn hogs loose in the timber to fatten on acorns. They became so wild, sometimes, that the grown ones could be brought down only with bullets. The easier-caught shoats made good eating, cured and left their appointed time in the smokehouse.

"Damn!" Tyson exclaimed. "I thought the heel flies had us. That spotted one looked kind of like Phineas Shattuck."

Mary Hubbard reproached her son. "That kind of language is not necessary in front of your sister."

Lucy smiled. "Let him be. I've heard a lot worse. Even said worse myself." She turned the smile on Owen. "That shock you?"

Owen shook his head. "I've always had my suspicions." He pointed his chin. "We ought to go a little deeper into these woods before we make camp. I'm thinkin' there's apt to be a creek in there somewhere. Me and Tyson can take turns sittin' out here on watch."

Tyson said, "If we could catch us a shoat, it sure would beat the cold bread and jerky and stuff we brought with us."

Owen reminded him, "Shattuck's the one that used to be a pig thief. I don't care to join his class."

The women were tired, and Tyson looked worse. After they had eaten the little that passed for breakfast, Owen said, "You-all get some rest. I'll watch."

For once Tyson offered no argument. He unrolled a blanket beside the little stream they had found, doubled it and flopped down as if he had been knocked in the head by an axhandle. Lucy gave her brother a look of compassion but said, "Don't you take the whole day on yourself, Owen."

Owen warmed at her show of concern. "I'll be all right."

He judged it was near noon when he saw a movement far back along the road. Six horsemen rode at a trot, spurring into an easy lope for a time, then dropping back to the slower pace, sparing their horses. They had just enough amateurish military manner to make him suspect they were heel flies. His mouth went dry again. He half expected them to turn off and investigate the timber. They remained on the road, passing over the hill, disappearing in the direction of the farmhouse Tyson had told about.

Owen's pulse slowed to normal. But the horsemen were still riding through his mind when a noise made him turn quickly, hand dropping to the pistol.

Lucy Hubbard said, "Don't you shoot me, Owen Danforth, or I may never speak to you again."

"What're you doin' here? You're supposed to be restin'."

"Tyson's still asleep. I thought I'd come and spell you awhile . . . let *you* rest."

"You're a woman. I couldn't let you stand watch."

"Why not? My eyes are as good as yours, I expect. If I saw somebody comin' I'd wake you up. That's all *you'd* do, isn't it, wake us up to travel in a hurry? You sure don't figure on havin' a fight with anybody."

"I don't figure on havin' one with *you*. Guard duty is a man's job."

"Well, I'm here. You can either go back to camp and rest or you can lie down where you're at."

"I couldn't sleep with you here."

She smiled thinly. "I'm not askin' you to sleep with me. That'll come later, if I decide to marry you."

He felt as if nettles burned his face. "I'm tryin' to be serious with you, Lucy."

"So am I, Owen. When this war is over, I may want to be *real* serious."

She showed no sign of leaving, and any sleepiness he might have felt had abandoned him. She seated herself on the ground beside him. The closeness aroused him in a way he found unnerving. On the one hand he wanted to get up and leave, quickly. On the other he fought a strong wanting which said to reach out and take her, to throw himself upon her. He sensed that she knew his conflicting emotions and that she intended him to feel them. He wanted her here, yet he resented her manipulation.

She touched his hand. "I didn't mean to upset you, Owen. I'll go if it'll make you feel better."

She started to push herself up from the ground. He caught her wrist and pulled her back. "No. Stay."

She looked at him, smiling, and kissed him.

A faint smell of woodsmoke drifted to him from back in the timber. He told Lucy, "You better go warn them not to let that fire get any size to it. It's liable to draw visitors."

Lucy said, "They know that," but she went anyway. In a while she was back with a cup of coffee. "Mama said she stood it as long as she could. Here, this'll give you strength."

"I've *got* strength. What I need is to be out of this trap and back to where I don't have to worry about anything except Yankee soldiers." He accepted the cup, however, blew across it a few times, took a long swallow and sighed. "You can tell your mother she sure knows how to make coffee."

"So do I," Lucy responded. "You'll find that I'm a pretty good cook myself. I'll show you someday, when we're all back where we belong."

He frowned. "You ever goin' to quit raggin' me?"

"Someday, when I've got you."

"Some Yankee soldier or some heel fly may get me first."

"You won't let that happen. It wouldn't be fair to *me*."

Tyson Hubbard came out eventually, carrying his rifle at arm's length. He looked suspiciously at his sister. "It take two of you to watch?"

Lucy replied, "Owen watches the road. I just watch Owen."

"Don't you be forgettin' that he's still a Reb soldier. It was his kind that killed our brother."

Owen said tightly, "Those people aren't soldiers. They're not even a good imitation."

"They're good enough to kill somebody." Tyson went rigid, staring toward the road. He brought up the rifle, cradling it. Owen turned. From around the hill came a man riding bareback on a heavy-boned old plow horse, plodding deliberately toward the timber. Tyson leveled the rifle.

Owen raised his hand. "Wait. He don't look to me like a heel fly, much less a soldier."

"I ain't fixin' to shoot him, unless he gives me cause."

But anxiety in Tyson's face showed he would need little cause.

Owen motioned Tyson and Lucy back into the timber. "It's probably the man who owns the place. Maybe he's huntin' his hogs."

"And maybe he's spyin' for the government," Tyson said, walking backward, unwilling to turn away from the oncoming stranger.

They retreated farther back into the woods. The rider stopped, finally. "Howdy in there!" he shouted. "You folks in yonder, I'm fixin' to come in. Don't you-all shoot me."

Owen gave Tyson a quick glance to see that the rifle was not aimed at the figure he could see vaguely through the foliage. "He knows we're here. We'd just as well talk. Lucy, you go back yonder with your mother."

She made no argument, turning and walking briskly through the trees. Tyson said, "If he makes one wrong move . . ."

Owen called, "Come on in, mister, but keep your hands where we can see them."

The farmer pushed the big horse a little way into the timber, his hands at chest level. "I got no weapon on me," he said evenly. "I ain't come to make trouble. I come to give you warnin'."

Owen walked cautiously around the farmer and his horse, looking for a firearm and seeing none. The man was large and muscular. He reminded Owen of his father and Uncle Zach. Every deep line in that craggy face had probably been graven honestly by the hard work and constant worry that is forever the farmer's lot. The big hand the man extended in friendship bore the calluses and scars of ax and hoe and plow. Owen accepted the hand and winced under its crushing grip.

Tyson took the hand with reluctance, and then backed off in distrust.

The man said, "I'm Heck Frazier. My place is around the hill yonder. This is my timber you-all are takin' your rest in, and welcome to it, I might say. My milk cow got out last night. I was lookin' for her about daylight when I seen you folks turn off of the road and come up here."

Owen felt foolish. "You saw us?"

"You-all ain't too experienced at the outlaw business, I reckon. I would've just figured you were soldiers takin' French leave if I hadn't seen the womenfolks with you. There's been more'n a few stopped in this thicket to catch their breath. Then, when them heel flies come by the house and asked if I'd seen two men and two women . . ."

Owen swallowed. "You didn't tell them?"

"I'm sixty-two years old, sonny, and I didn't get there by pokin' my nose in where it wasn't wanted. I just told them I'd been workin' all day and wouldn't've seen a train of elephants if they had happened to pass by." He gave Owen and Tyson each a moment's study. "One of you'd be Hubbard, I reckon, and the other one Danberry."

"Dan*forth*."

"Them heel flies know you-all by name. Asked me if I know anything about a family by the name of Bradbury or Bradshaw or somethin' like that over in Austin County."

Tyson cursed softly. "That's Uncle Ed. We was goin' to his place."

The farmer shook his head. "If I was you, I wouldn't. They seemed to know an awful lot about your plans."

Tyson's eyes were angry. "How could they? Unless they caught somebody from the camp and made him tell."

Owen felt his stomach churn. "Or maybe they didn't have to. Maybe they've had a man of their own in there all along."

"A spy? But I know them all," Tyson protested. "There ain't a one of them . . ." His face clouded as he reluctantly accepted the reality. "If I ever find out who he is . . ."

Owen turned back to the farmer. "We're much obliged, Mr. Frazier. Only thing I wonder is, how come you told us?"

Frazier shrugged. "I don't care for them heel flies. Don't mistake me: I got two boys in the Texas army. I mean, I *had* two. Lost one of them the first year of the war. Other one I ain't heard from in a long time. Don't have no idea where he's at." Sadness was in his eyes. "We was all Americans once. I pray God for the day when we'll all be Americans again." He cleared his throat. "You-all probably need fresh meat. If one of my shoats comes to hand, feel welcome. I'll bid you God's blessin', and good day." He remounted and rode back out of the timber.

Owen turned to Tyson. "Your mother and sister have to go somewhere else now."

Tyson agreed, but Mary Hubbard did not. Her jaw set hard as Owen and Tyson repeated the farmer's story. She declared, "We're goin' on to Ed's and Vi's."

Owen argued, "But the heel flies'll be there."

"You think I could leave this country without knowin' if they did somethin' to my brother and his wife?" She shook her head stubbornly. "You can leave us if you want to, Owen, but us Hubbards'll see about our kin."

Owen looked at Lucy and shrugged. They were his kin too, almost. "I'm come this far," he said. "I'll stay with you."

8

It had always seemed to Owen during his military experience that the worst predicaments came from his company's being led into a situation for which officers had no proper plan but up and went anyway. That seemed the situation now. He had pondered for hours on the way and had come up with no idea that did not offer more hazard than promise.

From the brushy knoll where he stood in darkness with Tyson and Mary and Lucy Hubbard, the Bradshaw house three hundred yards down the slope was vague in shape, menacing in its blackness beneath a smothering dark canopy of large trees. In the quarter hour or so they had watched, they had seen no lamp or lantern. There had to be a sentry, perhaps more than one. Owen had seen horses standing loose in a corral— too many, Mary Hubbard said, for her brother to own. They must belong to the heel flies.

Her voice was tense. "If they've hurt Ed or Vi . . ."

Tyson said, "The only way we'll know is for me to go down there and have a look."

Owen had always admired nerve, but he deplored

rashness. "How do you figure to see without *bein'* seen?"

Tyson pointed. "There's a strip of brush yonder that stretches almost to the barn. I can use it for cover."

"I doubt they've got your aunt and uncle in the barn. They'd be in the house. And whatever heel flies aren't out on guard are probably in there with them."

"Once I get to the barn I ought to be able to spot any lookouts they got and work around them. I can sneak like a wolf when I've got to."

"Sounds to me like the wolf is fixin' to sneak into the trap. They'll swallow you up."

Logic was no deterrent to Tyson. "I'll figure that out when I get there."

Owen had known Tyson's kind in the war, supremely confident in their ability to do anything imagination might invent. He had seen a few win medals. He had seen more of them buried with honors. He said as much.

Tyson demanded, "You got any better notion?"

Owen admitted he did not. "Maybe I'll get one while I go down there with you."

Mary Hubbard said, "I don't want you boys takin' chances."

Owen resisted the temptation to declare that he had already taken the biggest chance, agreeing to fetch them here. "I can't promise you anything, Mrs. Hubbard, except that we'll try. If we don't come back in an hour or so, you and Lucy better be puttin' some miles behind you before daylight. Go to some kin that the heel flies wouldn't know about."

Lucy caught Owen's hand and held it fearfully.

Mrs. Hubbard said, "We won't talk about such as that. You boys are comin' back."

Owen grunted some kind of answer and mounted his horse. He and Tyson rode cautiously, ducking the low, raking limbs as they worked their way through the long strip of brush. For all of her expressed concern, Owen knew Mary Hubbard had left them no alternative. They had to go down to the house for a look. He wished for all of Tyson's confidence and twice his common sense.

That family was a single-minded lot, he thought, from the late Vance Hubbard to his mother and Tyson. Lucy was probably just as hardheaded. He wondered if he had implied any commitment to her that he might come to regret.

He followed because Tyson knew the place and the way. An old, too-familiar dread built in Owen's stomach, as it always had before any fight he had known was coming. He had never understood people who showed none of it or claimed they never felt it. He had always regarded them as fools or liars.

Tyson dismounted within the cover of the brush. He did not look back, taking it for granted that Owen would follow his lead without question. Owen *had* questions, but he held them.

Tyson pointed and whispered one word, "Barn."

I can see that for myself, Owen thought with a quick irritation. The barn was a swayed log structure twenty or thirty yards beyond the fringe of scrub timber. Beyond that extended the aging corrals, and beyond the corrals the log house with its traditional two sections under one roof, an open dog run between.

Owen judged it to be fifty or sixty yards away. It might as well be fifty miles for all the chance he could see of reaching it undiscovered, unless all the heel flies had forsaken their duty and gone to sleep. That was a possibility if no mature and responsible man had come with them on this mission to impose discipline.

Tyson whispered, "Let's make a run for the barn."

Owen grabbed his arm firmly enough to give pain. "Let's not. Let's watch awhile."

Tyson wrested his arm free. He was about to go anyway when something moved beside the barn. Owen caught Tyson's arm again. Tension had brought Tyson's muscles to steel hardness.

The figure seemed no more than a shadow at first, slowly taking form as Owen concentrated on it. Moving out of the pool of darkness beside the barn, it took on the shape of a man walking slowly and without evident purpose, loosely carrying a rifle at arm's length. The guard rounded the corner, took a long and uneasy look toward the house, then lowered himself to the ground and rested his back against the barn's tough wall.

Not much of a sentry, Owen thought. Probably one of those half-grown buttons of the type Phineas Shattuck liked to boss around. Away from Shattuck or other authority, it was natural for boys of that self-asserting age to do as they pleased. It pleased this one to rest.

Tyson whispered, "If he nods off to sleep, we can sneak up and hit him on the head."

"He's just a kid. I don't want us hurtin' him if we don't have to."

"He's a damned Confederate."

Owen bristled. "So am I. I'm here to help your womenfolk, and that's all. I didn't come to hurt my own people."

"Heel flies ain't people."

"They're just kids, most of them. Whatever quarrel we've got is against people like Shattuck. They tell them what to do."

The sentry sat with arms folded across his knees, head against his arms. Presently the rifle slipped from his fingers and slid slowly down the boot tops that covered his shins. It came to rest across one foot. The boy did not move.

"He's gone," Tyson said.

He was not, altogether. Tyson's dun horse chose that time to bare his teeth and take a bite at Owen's big bay. He was tied too far to reach him, but the squeal of equine anger brought the sentry's head up. He reached down for the rifle and looked around in confusion. Tyson moved to quiet the horse, but the boy was already aroused. He pushed warily to his feet, the rifle up and ready. Owen realized the boy did not know from what direction the sound had come. He seemed, after a minute, to conclude that it had been made by the horses in the corral. He walked to the fence, grumbling at the animals to quit making a fuss. He succeeded only in stirring them up.

When no other sentries appeared, Owen whispered, "That must be the only lookout they've got." It stood to reason. Boys sent on a man's errand remained boys.

Tyson said, "Now's our chance to make it to the barn."

Owen had no clear idea what advantage that might yield them, but Tyson was not burdened by Owen's doubts. He sprinted from the brush to the heavy shadow of the barn. Owen took one more look to be sure the sentry had not seen, then followed him, talking under his breath about what happened to people who leaped first and looked afterward. He flattened himself against the barn.

The sentry came slouching back, rifle again at arm's length. He was looking over his shoulder, muttering about fool horses. He almost bumped against Tyson.

Tyson touched the cold muzzle of a pistol against the young man's throat. He whispered, "I'd be obliged if you'd give me that rifle, real careful and quiet."

Astonished, the young man simply turned loose. The rifle fell to the ground with a light clatter. Eyes wide as dollars, the guard raised his hands. Owen stooped to pick up the weapon and took a good look at the face. "I know you. Name's Adcock, isn't it?"

This was one of the boys Owen had caused to drink himself into a stupor on the Hubbards' porch, a boy he had seen Shattuck chastise unmercifully afterward. Adcock moaned, "You're that soldier Danforth. You've done it to me again. Shattuck'll have me shot."

Tyson threatened, "Make any wrong move and we'll do it for him. We want to talk to you a little bit."

He motioned toward the brush. "Let's go out there where nobody's apt to come up on us unawares."

The boy lamented, "Oh Lordy, he just won't understand this at all. He'll have me court-martialed and shot." But he went as Tyson indicated with a motion of his pistol barrel. Adcock looked apprehensively back over his shoulder.

When they reached the brush Owen turned to survey the barn and house. He half expected to see other sentries come running, but even the horses had gone quiet in the corral.

Tyson kept the pistol under young Adcock's chin. "Now, what've you-all done to the people who live in that house?"

"We ain't done nothin' to them," Adcock protested. "Johnson, he's in charge. He just told them not to go outside or nothin'. Said there wouldn't nothin' happen to them if they followed orders." He stared fearfully at Tyson or at Tyson's pistol. "They *are* your kinfolks, ain't they?"

"What did they tell you?"

"Said their names was Bradshaw and they didn't have no kin by the name of Hubbard. We'd about decided the informer was mistaken."

Owen demanded, "What informer?"

Adcock stiffened. "I done said too much. I ain't tellin' you anymore."

Tyson angrily grabbed Adcock's shirt and jerked him against the muzzle of the pistol. "By God you will!"

Owen caught Tyson's arm. "Hold off. Don't hurt him. I think we ought to be able to make a trade, us and him." Tyson eased back, releasing his hold. Adcock whimpered, plainly afraid he was breathing his last. Owen felt sympathy, remembering his own vulnerability at that age.

Owen tried to make his voice reassuring. "We can help each other, boy. You've got a choice. We can leave you tied up, and they'll know we caught you. You already said Shattuck's liable to shoot you. Or we can leave you to go back to your post without anybody ever knowin'. The only way they'd find out would be if you told them yourself."

Adcock glanced hopefully from one captor to the other. "You'd do that, and not get me in more trouble than I already am?"

Owen nodded and looked as honest as he knew how. "You just tell us the truth. Nobody ever needs to know you went to sleep on the job."

"Tellin' you anything would be like treason."

Owen shook his head. "Not when you can't help it. You're in a trap, same way I was. All we want is to keep Shattuck from catchin' our people. We're a thousand miles from the fightin', and what happens here won't make any difference to the real war."

Tyson pressed, "Who told Shattuck we figured to come to this place?"

Adcock shrugged. "All I know is that Shattuck's had somebody in the thickets with you people for a good while now, slippin' him information about who's in there, and what you-all're up to."

Tyson cursed. "If you don't know his name, tell me what he looks like."

"I can't. I ain't never seen him that I know of. That

was officer doin's. They never told me none of that stuff."

Tyson caught Adcock's shirt again. Owen pulled Tyson's wrist away. He was surprised, suddenly, to realize he had used his left hand. The wounded arm had gained more strength than he had realized. "No use hurtin' him." He turned to Adcock. "We heard Shattuck intends to invade the thicket in force."

Adcock nodded. "He's got a bunch of regular soldiers on the way. Time comes, that spy'll slip out of you-all's camp and lead them in there. Shattuck figures them he can't capture, he'll kill. Them he captures, he'll hang."

The dread came again, stronger than Owen had ever felt it. His stomach seemed weighted, cold as December. "Dad wouldn't figure on that, somebody guidin' the soldiers in."

Tyson Hubbard grimaced. "Vance wouldn't've either. He always figured his protection was the Confederates not knowin' their way through the thickets." He stared bitterly at Adcock. "For all we know, this'n could be the one shot him that night as we were ridin' away from town."

Adcock cringed from the threat in Tyson's eyes. "It wasn't me. I never drawed a gun." Desperately Adcock told more than he had been asked. "It wasn't none of us that shot your brother. It was the informer done it. He taken advantage of the confusion and all the shootin'. He got behind Vance Hubbard and put him out of the way."

Tyson swore. "I'm goin' back there, Owen. I'll find out who he is and kill him!"

"We may not go anywhere if we rouse up the rest of Adcock's bunch. Settle down." He gazed sternly at Adcock. "Anything else you can tell us about that spy?"

Adcock held his fearful gaze on Tyson Hubbard. "I already told you more than I know."

Owen unloaded the youth's rifle and handed it to him. "You go back to your post. Act like nothin' happened, and Shattuck won't ever know the difference. If you don't peach on us, we won't ever have to peach on you."

Adcock walked hurriedly across the open space to the barn. It obviously took a strong effort on his part not to run.

Tyson said between clenched teeth, "I never seen a heel fly I could trust."

"You can trust his fear. He's scared to death of Shattuck." Owen moved toward the horses. "Let's get back to the women."

Owen recounted to them briefly what he and Tyson had learned. "I feel like Adcock told us the truth; they haven't hurt your kinfolks at the house. When we don't show up here the boys'll finally decide the whole thing was a mistake and go home. Adcock sure won't tell them any different. And while they're waitin' here you-all can be ridin' on to other kin that Shattuck doesn't know about."

Mary Hubbard frowned. "Owen, are you still figurin' on goin' back to your army?"

Owen nodded. "That's been my intention all along."

Her eyes were more severe than he had ever seen

them. "I know you and your father have had your disagreements. But he's a good man. That boy put a whole new complexion on everything. If you ride away from here now, Owen, you're not the man I thought you were. Your father and the others . . . they've got to be warned."

Owen's eyes met Tyson's. "They will be. Me and Tyson are both goin'. I don't know the thicket well enough to find the way by myself."

Tyson argued, "Ain't no use in that. You see Mama and Lucy to where they're goin', then head on back to your damned army. I can tell your dad about the informer."

"You can't tell him everything I need to. There's been a wall between me and him. After this, we may never see each other again. I don't want to remember that we parted in a strain."

There was more, a fear that Tyson would do something rash and never reach the men in the thicket. But he saw no use in speaking that concern and rousing Tyson's indignation.

Lucy leaned to Owen, her arms spread for him. She said, "Don't you worry about Mama and me. You just watch out for yourself and Tyson. When this is over with . . ."

Owen kissed her. "I'll come huntin' you."

"I'll be easy to find."

Tyson stared incredulously at the couple, then looked to his mother for an explanation. She did not attempt one. Mary Hubbard hugged her son and beseeched him not to let himself come into harm's way. Then she and Lucy were riding eastward, and Owen and Tyson spurred west. In a moment, looking back, Owen was unable to see the women. A sense of loss settled darkly over him, and it stayed a long time.

He and Tyson rode faster going back, taking risks. They traveled by day as well as by night, though they avoided the main trails where traffic would have increased the hazard of discovery. At one point they dismounted behind a tall stone fence and watched a troop of cavalry moving on the road. Except for the officer who rode in front, the men had no military uniforms. The Confederacy lacked the resources to clothe its army in style; this late in the war it did well to furnish weapons.

Tyson said, "Reckon they're on their way to join Shattuck's invasion?"

Owen shrugged. "Might be." He felt a little of anger. "Seems like with the fightin' to be done against the Yankees, they oughtn't to waste all this effort on a harmless little bunch of dissidents hidin' out in the brush."

"Dissidents hell! We're patriots. You damned Rebs are the dissidents."

It was an old argument fought too many times and never won. Owen said, "Come on, let's go." He climbed back upon the bay and spurred off, letting Tyson labor to catch him.

As he rode, he reviewed in his mind all the men he had met in the thicket. That one of them was an informant to Phineas Shattuck he could not doubt, given Adcock's story and the fact that the heel flies had known where the Hubbard women were going. He had no reason to doubt that the informant had shot Vance Hubbard in the back. He suspected from the grim purpose in Tyson's face that this was gnawing relentlessly at the young man's innards.

If Owen had spent long enough in the camp to become better acquainted, he might have an idea who now was about to betray the men in the thicket to Shattuck and the soldiers.

Tyson slapped the palm of his hand soundly against the horn of his saddle. "Red Upjohn!"

"Hunh?"

"Red Upjohn. He's the one. I know it."

Owen's mind raced as he tried to remember details. "What makes you think he's the informer?"

"I never liked him in the first place, always a troublemaker in camp, never satisfied, stirrin' up first one and then another to be dissatisfied. He never did really like Vance."

"I reckon he had reason to be that way, seein' a son lynched as a Unionist."

"He *said* his son was lynched. His word, was all. I don't remember anybody in camp ever sayin' they knew anything about it except what he told them. I don't remember anybody ever sayin' they even knew him before he come into the thicket. They taken him on his own say-so."

Owen thought back on the morning Upjohn's saber had punched him none too gently awake. He had had a feeling then that Upjohn would have killed him simply out of suspicion, had it not been for Banty Tillotson's intervention and Mary Hubbard's pleading.

Later he had accepted the explanation that Upjohn was bitter against all soldiers because of what had happened to his son. He remembered other allowances he had made.

Owen said, "I'm tryin' to remember just where he was ridin' the night you-all took us out of that jail, the time your brother was shot."

Tyson replied crisply, "You had to be held in the saddle, so you wasn't seein' anything very clear. But *I* can remember. Upjohn was somewhere behind us."

"So were a bunch of others, I expect."

"But I remember Upjohn hangin' back, shootin' at the ones that was shootin' at us . . . so he said. And when Mama told your daddy about Uncle Ed and Aunt Vi, Red Upjohn was standin' there listenin'."

"It wasn't exactly a secret in the camp."

"It was him," Tyson declared. "It was him. And he'll lead Phineas Shattuck and the soldiers into the thicket . . . if I don't kill him first."

They were within a short distance of the thicket when they rode over a hill and came suddenly upon a troop of soldiers taking their rest, cooking their supper. Pulse racing, Owen looked for a way to run, but there was none. They would be overtaken or shot before they traveled a quarter of a mile.

Tyson reached for the pistol in his belt. Owen grabbed his arm. "Don't be gettin' us killed. Keep your mouth shut and let me do the talkin'."

A tall man wearing a gray coat, the only remnant of a once-proud uniform, stepped out into the trail and raised his hand. "You men hold up there. Identify yourselves and state your business on this road."

A bar on his shoulder identified him as a lieutenant. He was backed by enough soldiers to make any order nonnegotiable. Swallowing his doubts, Owen saluted and once again tried to be a good liar. "We're from B Company, sir. They're up ahead of us, on their way to join a home guard outfit and somebody named Shadrack."

"Shattuck," the lieutenant corrected him. "How is it that you have fallen behind the rest of your unit?"

"Our horses went lame, and we had to recruit a couple of replacements. Captain said if we didn't catch up by dark, he'd nail our hides to the fence." It seemed a plausible enough story. Owen modeled it after an experience six months ago back east.

This lieutenant believed it or said he did. "It will be dark shortly, and you are not about to catch up that soon. You men will join my company for the night. We are all traveling the same direction."

Owen argued, "The captain is real particular."

"I'll explain to him when we catch up to your company. I feel he would not want you men to become lost and find yourselves in some tavern instead of your appointed place." His firm manner indicated he expected unconditional obedience. Any further argument might arouse his suspicion.

Owen glanced at Tyson, trying to tell him with his eyes that this was no time for doing something foolish. "We're obliged to you, sir. Just as long as you'll make sure our captain understands . . ."

The lieutenant accepted easy victory with grace. "You men attach yourselves to a likely mess. At least you shall not miss your supper."

A familiar voice spoke. "I know these men, Lieutenant. I'd be pleased to have them join me."

Owen's heart sagged as a man stood up from his seat on a rolled blanket beside a campfire. He wore a black eye patch and had a streak of white in a dark beard.

Sheriff Claude Chancellor!

9

Shaky himself, Owen feared the sight of Chancellor might cause Tyson to run. Tyson glanced toward his horse and a stand of scrub timber three hundred yards away, evidently weighing his chances.

Chancellor said in an easy manner, "I don't have much in the way of fixings, but I'd be proud to share with you boys."

Owen swallowed. "We'd be obliged." He wondered why Chancellor did not draw the revolver from his belt and place them under arrest. But when the sheriff moved his hand it was a friendly gesture, reaching out. Owen accepted with wariness. Tyson spoke not a word. He hesitantly took Chancellor's hand, though his eyes said break and run.

The lieutenant asked, "You'll vouch for these men, Sheriff?"

Chancellor nodded. "Their fathers have been friends of mine."

Dismay turned gradually to puzzlement for Owen, but he asked no foolish questions.

Chancellor looked at Owen's arm. "It appears that wound of yours has about healed."

Owen moved the arm for demonstration. "It's come a ways."

Chancellor told the lieutenant, "The Yankees gave him a remembrance, just as they did me."

That seemed to settle any lingering doubts the lieutenant might have had. "At least you men have been granted a chance to face the enemy and test your mettle. I have been relegated to this backwater to chase after deserters and ragtag Union sympathizers skulking in the thickets. Hardly the proper opportunity for a man to discover what stuff he's truly made of."

Chancellor's voice grated with irony. "The deserving are often overlooked, while others are blessed by opportunity."

The lieutenant missed the bitterness. "Spoken truly. Now I leave you gentlemen to your supper and attend my own." He walked across the camp to a fire where a black servant knelt stirring a pot. At least, Owen thought, the lieutenant was suffering in comfort.

Chancellor turned to his own fire, giving attention to a blackened tin bucket, its contents simmering on a small bed of red coals. "Beef stew," he said. "The remnant of a dinner which a kind old lady fed me at noon. She insisted I bring along what was left so I would not languish at nightfall."

Owen looked around apprehensively. "How come you didn't tell that officer who we are?"

Chancellor gave both young men a long, silent study. "I am not Phineas Shattuck. I remember you

boys from better days. And I remember your fathers."
He gave Tyson his quiet sympathy. "I heard what happened to Vance. I've heard also that Andrew Danforth
took his place in the thicket."

Tyson said sternly, "Nobody taken Vance's place."
He glanced at Owen with defiance. "Somebody had to
hold things together, is all."

Owen said nothing.

Chancellor declared, "I'm surprised to find you-all
traveling openly on this road. It's foolhardy, to say
the least."

Owen replied, "We found out there's been a spy in
camp. He's fixin' to lead Shattuck and the troops into
the thickets."

Chancellor nodded, a grim set to his jaw. "Did you
find out who this spy is?"

Owen shook his head negatively, but Tyson said,
"We know."

Chancellor stared into the heating bucket of stew.
"If you should confront him, I hope you'll remember
that he regards himself as a man of duty, the same as
yourselves."

Tyson demanded, "Was it his duty to kill Vance?"

"We do things in war that we would not consider
at any other time. We kill our enemies."

Tyson's voice was edged with hatred. "Well, I know
who *my* enemy is."

Chancellor said, "This war is like a dying horse,
dragging to a pitiful end. We'll soon be able to put this
insanity behind us and seek after friendship again.
There'll be no need to call any man an enemy."

Owen nodded. "That's what my father said." It struck him odd to hear the same thought expressed by a man who represented the opposite side.

Chancellor stirred the stew. "I tried to dissuade Shattuck from this big drive into the thickets. I told him there was no need, that to have the people holed up in the thickets is as effective as having them in jail. They can do no real harm there, and we don't even have to worry about feeding them. He said he wouldn't feed them; he'd *hang* them."

Owen grimaced. "He hates almighty hard."

Chancellor grunted. "For a purpose. He's taken your families' farms in the name of the Confederacy. If everybody who had any claim is dead, nobody can challenge Shattuck's rights. He'll buy those places from the government for a few cents on the dollar."

Owen blinked in surprise. That thought had never occurred to him. Tyson cursed softly.

An ironic smile came back to Chancellor's face. "You boys are young and innocent. You see patriotism in its pure sense. A man crafty enough can work patriotism for his own gain. The Confederacy means no more to Shattuck than it means to the lieutenant's pack mule."

Owen gritted his teeth. "Shattuck's a damned pig thief."

Chancellor shook his head. "He *used* to be a pig thief. He has advanced his family's name to major larceny." He shoved the long handle of a spoon beneath the bail to lift the bucket from the coals. "Sorry I have no bowls or cups. We'll have to pass the spoon between us."

Supper was lean and finished in little time. Chancellor nodded for Owen and Tyson to follow him. He strode to the army officer's campfire. "Lieutenant," he said, "since I have company now, I have decided to ride on to town before I sleep. I'll take the responsibility for these young men."

The lieutenant had no quarrel with that, and the three were quickly in the saddle. Owen looked back nervously, watching the several flickering campfires recede in the distance. He still puzzled over Chancellor's intentions.

Tyson Hubbard said suspiciously, "Chancellor, if you're figurin' on turnin' us over in town, you better think some more. We've still got our guns."

Chancellor gave him a look that bespoke a strained patience. "If I'd wanted your guns I would have taken them as soon as you entered that camp. Too many good men have died for no reason. I want you-all to go into the thicket and warn everybody to pull out while there's time. Scatter like quail. Let the pig thief find an empty sty."

Tyson's suspicions would not let him believe. "You ain't just lettin' us go."

"I am, as soon as we are safely beyond sight of camp. The invasion won't start until that company makes rendezvous with Shattuck and the others."

Owen asked, "Will you be with them when they come in?"

"It would be taken as strange if I did not go along. And how else would I be able to see the look on Shattuck's face when he finds himself holding an empty sack?"

Presently the trail came near to the heavy, brooding mass of the thicket, blacker even than the darkness that surrounded the three horsemen. Chancellor said, "This is a good place."

Owen extended his hand. Tyson did not. Owen said, "Mr. Chancellor, I won't forget what you've done for us."

"I hope you will, at least until this wretched war is over. It would not do for the wrong people to know. Godspeed."

Tyson spurred off in a lope toward the forbidding blackness of the timber. Owen did not call after him; the sound might carry back to the soldiers. He struggled to catch up because he would have difficulty finding Tyson once he entered that dense thicket. To his relief, Tyson reined in and waited for him, angrily admonishing him to hurry up.

Tyson said, "I don't trust that sheriff. I want to put as many miles between us and him as we can."

"Chancellor's an honest man."

"I don't trust any Confederate. And I'm rememberin' that you're one. If you want to ride with me, you'd better keep up." Tyson began picking a course through the tangle of brush in the poor light of a rising moon. Fortunately for the horses, he was forced to a walk, often a slow one. Keeping pace with Tyson presented no challenge to Owen now. He suspected Tyson had only a vague idea where they were, but after daylight his familiarity with the thicket would bring him to the dissident camp. For now, the main concerns were to travel in the right general direction and not break down the horses.

A couple of times during the night Tyson dismounted, loosening the cinch to let his mount rest. His voice, when he spoke at all, was curt. Owen harbored an uncomfortable feeling that sooner or later he and Tyson were due a confrontation, that would leave one of them—maybe both—bruised more than a little and leaking blood on the ground. He smiled grimly when Tyson rode headlong into a heavy, low-lying branch and cursed at the bite of the thorns.

Maybe that'll drain a little of the contrariness out of him, he wished. But anger and grief had eaten too long at Tyson. They would not be easily dispelled.

Daybreak found the two men in a small clearing, resting their horses and waiting for enough light that Tyson could determine where they were. One place in this thicket looked the same as another to Owen. He realized anew how helpless he would be here by himself. Difficult or not, Tyson Hubbard was a necessity. Tyson walked restlessly around the clearing, peering into the brush. At length he returned to his horse and tightened the cinch. He said nothing, but his manner indicated that Owen had better do the same or be left behind. Tyson set out toward the southeast.

Owen queried dubiously, "You know where you're goin'?"

Tyson replied crisply without looking back, "If you don't like my direction, there's aplenty of others."

Owen knew he must follow or soon be lost. He must trust to Tyson's familiarity with the thickets and, beyond that, to Providence.

At length Tyson reined up, looking around first with hope, then with certainty. The relief in his face revealed that he had secretly worried he might not find his way. "We ain't far off," he said. "I just hope your daddy ain't taken a fool notion to move camp."

Defensively Owen replied, "Anything he's done, I expect he's had a reason."

Tyson glanced back, surprised. "Kind of changed your tune about him, ain't you?"

"Don't get the wrong idea. I haven't changed sides."

They came upon the camp with a startling suddenness. A lean, ragged sentry stepped out in front of Tyson, rifle hanging at his side. He asked needlessly, "Hey, boy, you back?"

"You damn betcha," Tyson replied tightly. "Where's Andrew Danforth at?" He did not wait for the reply, which followed after him in an exasperated tone. "You'll find him over yonder at his tent, if he ain't somewhere else."

Andrew Danforth was sitting on the ground in the sunshine, oiling a rifle. He looked up quickly, then pushed to his feet with alarm. "You boys are supposed to be a long ways from here. Where's the women-folks?"

Tyson said, "They're all right, but this camp ain't."

Andrew Danforth stared past Tyson at his son. Owen stiffly climbed down from the horse and clung for a moment to the saddle, the weariness heavy.

"Son," Andrew said, taking a couple of tentative steps toward him, "I sent you away from this place. I sent you back to your own outfit where you said you belonged."

"I still belong there," Owen replied. He moved

toward his father but stopped short. "Somethin' come up."

Tyson put in bitterly, "There's a spy in camp. He killed my brother. Now he's fixin' to lead Phineas Shattuck and the soldiers into this thicket. They're figurin' to hang every man they can catch."

Danforth took a long breath. He looked first at Tyson, then at his son, wavering between doubt and belief. "How'd you-all come to find out?"

Tyson told it. The account spilled from him with anguish and anger, leaving him atremble.

Andrew Danforth accepted with evident reluctance. "And who is this spy? Did the kid tell you that?"

Tyson's eyes were narrowed as they restlessly searched the camp. "He didn't tell us, but we know. Where's Red Upjohn?"

Danforth looked quickly to Owen for corroboration. Owen shrugged. "Upjohn seems the most likely."

"The most likely? Then you don't know for sure . . ."

Tyson's fists were clenched. "Sure enough to suit me. Where's he at?"

"He's on lookout down below the thicket with Banty Tillotson and Jim Carew. They'll let us know when the soldiers come and where they are."

Owen declared, "With Upjohn for a guide, Shattuck'll comb this thicket. There won't be any safe place to hide. It's best everybody to leave it and scatter." *Like quail*, Chancellor had said. Tyson had not mentioned Chancellor's part in helping them. Owen considered telling, for his father would be pleased in light of their old friendship. But he looked at the anxious men quickly gathering around to listen. If anyone here were to be captured and forced to talk, word of Chancellor's act might reach Shattuck. That would be poor thanks for a great kindness.

Andrew did not need to repeat Tyson's story or to give any orders. He stared solemnly at the threadbare, hungry-looking men around him. He said simply, "There's no more sanctuary. Each man had best follow his own inclinations."

The mood was more of disappointment than of fear, or even of anger. One man said, "There's other thickets. I've got kin in the rough country way out on Bull Creek. They've stood off soldiers ever since the war started. I expect they'd be glad to take in anybody that wants to go with me."

Another said, "The soldiers can't be everywhere at once, even if Red Upjohn *does* help them. I'll just keep movin' in this thicket and take my chances." That was the decision of many, to scatter in twelve directions and offer the troops no concentrated target. A half-blind dog might stumble upon a covey, they reasoned. It took a hunter to smell out a lone quail.

In minutes the camp began breaking up. Andrew Danforth watched with sadness as the men packed their few belongings and saddled their horses. He told Owen, "I don't expect that every one of them can get away. The soldiers would have to have the worst kind of luck not to catch a few."

Owen asked, "What about you, Dad? You're not goin' to stay here and take a chance on bein' amongst them?"

Andrew frowned. "They've become my responsibility."

"Not after they split up. I came back to make sure Shattuck doesn't catch you."

Pride came into Andrew's tired eyes. "You were free and clear, son, and then you turned around and came back for *me*."

"We've had our arguments, but us bein' on two sides of this war don't stop you from bein' my father."

"Or stop you bein' my son." Andrew put his arms around Owen.

Owen swallowed. The barrier of old angers that had built between them seemed to fade like a morning mist. He felt toward his father now as he had not since he had been twelve or thirteen.

Andrew faced south. "There's three men down yonder, standin' watch. You-all say one is a spy. Maybe he is, and maybe he's not. But at least two of them aren't, and I've got to give them a chance."

Owen said, "We might run right into Shattuck's soldiers."

"Not *we*, just *me*. I don't aim to risk you boys."

Owen said, "I didn't come back to see you go off and leave me."

Tyson declared, "And I want to see Upjohn. Over my sights."

Andrew's voice went stern. "If he's with the soldiers, we'll know he's the one. If he's not . . ."

Tyson's eyes pinched with impatience. "We goin', or we just goin' to stand here and talk about it?"

Andrew said, "If you're goin' with me, you keep

your hands away from that gun." He looked to Owen as if to ask his help in controlling Tyson. Owen could only shrug. There was but one way to control Tyson—to sit on him.

They rode southward, most of the time in single file. Andrew led. Owen watched his father's back, remembering other times, happier times, that he had followed . . . to the cattle, to the field, into the timber to hunt meat for the table. He had followed with pride in those days. That pride had returned, and he warmed himself in the glow of it.

Considering the density of the thicket, Owen wondered how his father expected to find the missing men. But Andrew seemed to know where he was going, and he held firmly to his direction despite the turns and switchbacks made necessary for negotiating a path through the brush.

Owen turned often to look at Tyson, who followed closely yet seemed strangely alone. Tyson's eyes held grimly to the horsemen ahead of him, but his mind was elsewhere.

In time they came to the edge of the thicket without having encountered anyone. Andrew's face betrayed his worry. He said, "They figured to scout beyond the edge, to get a little more of a lead when the soldiers come."

He looked to the east, then to the west. He arbitrarily reined his horse westward, just outside of the timber. There being no need to ride single file, Owen pulled up beside him. Tyson continued to hold himself apart, trailing. They rode in silence, Owen's tension building as he watched the rise and fall of the hills in the direction of town. Sooner or later, probably sooner, Phineas Shattuck would come riding over those hills with enough soldiers to invade Mexico.

Andrew pointed. "Yonder's somebody."

Owen blinked, and he saw one horseman. The rider evidently saw them at about the same time. He hauled up for a minute, studying them with suspicion, then spurred into a long trot toward them.

Tyson cursed in recognition. "Red Upjohn!" He drew the pistol from his waistband.

Andrew pulled over beside him and laid a big plowman's hand on the barrel. "Put that thing up, boy. We don't know for sure."

"*I* know."

"I said put it away!"

Tyson swore under his breath but gave to the compulsion in Andrew's stern gaze.

When Upjohn was sure of their identity he put his horse into an easy lope. He reined up, giving the two young men a moment of surprised attention. "I thought at first you-all might be Banty and Jim. You seen them?"

Andrew's manner was calm. "No. We've seen nobody except you."

Upjohn glanced back over his shoulder. "We split up. We was supposed to meet in the woods over back of the old Baxter farm, but neither one of them ever showed up." He pointed. "The soldiers are on their way, Andrew. They'll be showin' up over that hill yonder pretty soon now. I'm afraid they may've caught Banty and Jim."

Tyson seethed. "Or maybe somebody handed Banty and Jim over to them."

Upjohn's red-bearded jaw went slack. He was taken aback by Tyson's sudden show of hatred. "What're you talkin' about, boy?"

Tyson drew the pistol. "I'm talkin' about *you*, spyin' on us, tellin' Shattuck everything we done. I'm talkin' about you shootin' my brother in the back. If the soldiers are comin', it's because you've pointed the way."

Upjohn blinked, incredulous. He looked at Owen, then at Andrew. "I don't know what put a notion like that in the boy's mind, Andrew, but he's wrong. You know what happened to my son. I wouldn't help the people who done that to him."

Andrew said, "I know what you *said* happened to your son. Now that I think on it, I don't remember anybody ever sayin' he knew it to be true."

"But it *is* true," Upjohn insisted, color rising. "And I sure ain't never spied on the camp."

Andrew gave him a moment's hard study. He turned to Owen and Tyson. "Boys, I believe him."

Owen was not sure, and he said so.

Tyson was beyond reasoning. His knuckles tightened on the pistol. Owen pushed up in the stirrups and threw himself upon Tyson. The pistol fired, and Tyson's horse jumped. The two young men plunged to the ground. Tyson landed on his back, Owen on top of him. Breath gusted from Tyson, but he struggled to bring the pistol back into line. Owen managed a grip on Tyson's wrist and twisted his arm.

Andrew stepped down quickly and wrested the pistol from Tyson's fingers. Tyson struggled and cursed beneath Owen's weight.

Andrew said, "Red, I'm givin' you the benefit of the doubt. But I can't guarantee how long we can keep this young hothead under control. You'd better go, and stay out of his sight."

Upjohn replied, "Andrew, I swear . . ." He stared down at Tyson. "Boy, I never done none of them things you said. As for your brother, I disagreed with him some, but I never knowed a better man." He looked back at Andrew. "Except maybe this one."

Owen said, "You better go. I don't know how much longer I can hold him." Pain drove through his arm. He feared Tyson's struggling had undone some of the healing.

Upjohn pointed. "Somebody's comin' yonder, Andrew. You all better not stay in the open." Then he was gone, swallowed by the heavy brush.

Tyson cursed Owen and tried desperately to throw him off.

Andrew said, "Better let him up. There *is* somebody comin'." He squinted. "It's Banty Tillotson."

Owen turned Tyson loose and stepped to his feet. He tried to look at the incoming rider, but Tyson staggered him with a hard fist. Owen threw up his arm in defense, blinking, trying to dispel the blinding flashes that whirled before his eyes.

Andrew threw his arms around Tyson and pushed him back. "Stop it! The fight's over."

Banty Tillotson drew rein, studying the angry scene with amazement, then amusement. He broke into his familiar grin that Owen had found to be like morning sunshine in the somber camp. "You're the last people I expected to find here. I don't suppose you've seen Red Upjohn?"

Andrew nodded. "We've seen him. That's what this ruckus is all about. Tyson's got it in his head that Red's a spy."

Tyson spat. "And I'd've shot him, but they stopped me."

Banty asked, "Where'd you get a notion like that?"

Andrew put in urgently, "There's no time to be talkin' about it now. The soldiers are comin'. Where's Jim Carew?"

Banty replied, "There's no need to be lookin' for Jim. The soldiers have already got him." His hand went down to his hip, and it came up full of pistol. "They'll be here directly, and then they'll have *you*."

Andrew's mouth dropped open. "Banty . . ."

Banty said, "You-all just stay on the ground, where I can watch you. It won't be but a few minutes."

Andrew expelled a long breath. "It wasn't Red who was the spy in camp. It was *you*."

Banty nodded. "I never taken no pride in it, but they said it was my duty, and I done it."

Tyson choked for breath. "Did you . . . did you really shoot my brother in the back?"

Banty said regretfully, "He was a good feller, but he was my enemy. I seen a chance to put him out of the way with everybody figurin' some heel fly done it. I'm sorry, boy, but that's the fortunes of war."

Andrew seemed more sad than angry. "And now you're fixin' to turn us over to Phineas Shattuck."

"I never liked him much, but he's on *our* side."

Owen's gaze was drawn to movement at the top of a low hill. He saw what he took to be perhaps a hundred horsemen. His stomach knotted. They were his soldiers, his side. But they would hang him as if he had been a Unionist all along. In their eyes he was a traitor. The fighting he had done back east, the wound he had taken, would count for nothing now.

Andrew said, "My son is still a Confederate soldier. You know how he come to be caught up in all this. Let *him* go. Let both boys go."

Banty shook his head. "I wish I could. But I've got my duty. If it's any consolation, I'll be sorry about it."

Owen looked back toward the troops. They were coming at a steady pace, only a few hundred yards away.

Banty said, "If you've got anything you want to say to your Maker, you better be at it. Shattuck won't give you time."

"Did he give Jim Carew any time?"

Banty shook his head gravely. "None at all." He turned his horse half around to glance back at the oncoming soldiers.

The slap of a rifle shot startled Owen. Banty jerked in the saddle, then dropped to the ground, limp as an empty sack. His horse danced in fright, almost stepping on him. Andrew strode quickly forward and picked up the pistol where it lay near Banty's twitching fingers. Owen's mouth was dry as powder. He licked at his lips, but his tongue was dry too.

Red Upjohn rode out of the brush, black smoke curling from a rifle in his hand. "Them soldiers are almost on us. You-all better get mounted in a hurry."

Nobody had to be told twice. Owen gave the riders one glance as he swung into the saddle. He guessed them to be three hundred yards away.

Upjohn looked down on the fallen Banty. The eyes were open, but they showed no life. Upjohn said with a touch of regret, "I always liked ol' Banty. But I reckon he won't be leadin' them soldiers anyplace." He touched spurs to his horse. Owen and Andrew and Tyson followed him into the brush.

They rode hard, weaving, dodging limbs. Briars and thorns tore at Owen's clothing and gouged his flesh, but that was far preferable to what awaited if they did not outdistance Shattuck and the troops. They came in time to a stream that meandered through the thicket. They rode in it, finally moving out upon a mass of fallen, rotting leaves that would not betray sign of their passing.

When they felt safe enough to stop in a small clearing and rest the tired horses, Andrew said, "Thanks, Red. If it hadn't been for you and that rifle, we'd be dead now."

Upjohn shrugged. "If it hadn't been for your boy jumpin' on Tyson when he did, I'd've been dead before you."

Tyson's face flushed. He seemed silently mustering nerve to speak. At length he said, "Red, I don't know any way to tell you how sorry I am."

Upjohn gave him a long, angry study. "Boy, I don't even want to talk to you!"

10

Owen was alone when he left the thicket in the pitch black that preceded the moon's rising. He followed the stars in a northeasterly direction, listening intently because he could see so little. It stood to reason that the soldiers would throw a picket line of sorts around the edge of the brush because their attempt at invasion had been crippled by Red Upjohn's rifle. The thicket was too immense for an adequate blockade by whatever soldiers the regional command could muster. Still, Owen could remember from his boyhood an awkward, stumbling pony that used to have a way of finding and falling into the only badger hole within a mile and a half. His own luck might be no better.

He rode all night without encountering anything more threatening than a few sleeping cattle. These moved aside but made little commotion that might attract attention of anyone standing watch in the darkness. Once the moon was up and Owen could see his way, he moved easier across country, skirting fields, hugging the timber where he found it, avoiding roads and trails where a patrol might wait. By daylight he judged he had put twenty or twenty-five miles behind him. He did not know how far Phineas Shattuck's authority and influence might extend. To maintain some edge of safety, he watered the bay horse in a creek just at daylight and rode into a grove of trees. The grove was within sight of a trail he had traveled with the Hubbards. He watched, but the only movement he saw was a couple of wagons, one laden with freight, the other with kids and chicken coops. Neither looked warlike.

He gave the bay several hours to rest and graze; he had been ridden long and hard the last few days. Owen felt no urgency beyond his wish to see Lucy again before he returned to that other war.

Toward noon a distant jingling brought his eyes open. A dozen horsemen moved down the trail in what he supposed was meant to be a military formation, though it was strung out and ragged, the men tired and listless. Owen's heartbeat quickened. He saddled the bay horse to be ready for a run should the soldiers make a move toward the grove. They had probably been part of the force that made the abortive push through the thicket and had come up empty-handed. Owen did not intend to give them cause for celebration.

They passed on down the wagon trail. Owen's pulse slowed, but he was nagged by a residual uneasiness. The bay could rest again when he had put more miles behind him. Owen gave the riders a while to be well beyond sight, then rode out the opposite side of the grove and around the hill, holding to his northeast-ward course.

Not until his second full day did he come upon another potential for trouble. It happened so suddenly that he had no choice but to play his hand for luck. Two horsemen rode from a motte of moss-strewn oaks. One raised a hand, signaling Owen to stop. The other balanced a rifle across his saddle.

Owen swallowed. To hesitate or to turn and run would almost certainly result in capture, or worse. At such a range the rifleman would have to be blind in one eye and nearsighted in the other to miss him. Owen hoped his face did not betray his anxiety. He forced a shallow smile, holding his right hand well away from the pistol in his waistband. "Howdy," he said.

The man who moved toward him wore a badge so small that Owen did not see it until it caught the sunlight for an instant. "You look like you're of an age to be a soldier."

"I am," Owen replied, trying hard but having to abandon the smile. He reached into his shirt pocket and brought out the leave paper given him at the camp hospital. It was becoming tattered along the edges. The lawman quickly scanned the page, frowning. "Owen Danforth, private. That you?"

"Yes sir."

"Says here you was given leave to recuperate from a wound. Where's it at?"

Owen raised his left arm. "It's still a little stiff, but I figure it'll be all right by the time I get back to the company."

The lawman still frowned. "Danforth. Seems to me I've heard that name lately." He glanced back at the other man, who only shrugged.

Owen swallowed again. It was probable that Shattuck had sent word about the Danforths beyond his own county borders. "We're a sizable family. There's aplenty of us around. None in jail, though, that I know of."

"Not everybody's in jail that ought to be," the lawman observed. He handed the paper back to Owen. "I've always been a man of faith, and I'll take it on faith that you're the man this paper talks about. You go on back to your company, soldier. You better hurry, though, if you want to get in on any more war. Talk is that it's about over with."

Owen did not have to feign surprise. "It's got that bad?"

The lawman nodded sadly. "We've run out of everything except cotton. The boys are about down to chunkin' rocks at them Yankees."

Owen's shoulders sagged as he remembered the ordeals he had endured, the friends he had seen die. He folded the paper and put it back into his pocket. Because it had bluffed him through the roadblock, it would probably pass him through others he might encounter as he moved even farther from home. To that extent, he felt relief. To the news about the war, he felt only regret over the sacrifices he had witnessed, terrible sacrifices now clearly wasted.

The lawman said, "Couldn't nobody blame you much, soldier, if you just laid up someplace and waited. I reckon you've already given your share."

"I'm still alive," Owen observed. "I've known a good many who aren't."

"Been too many paid too much. Don't get yourself killed on the last day of the war."

Owen came, in time, to the Bradshaw house where he and Tyson had been bringing Mary and Lucy Hubbard and where the waiting heel flies had changed their plans. He watched from the brushy knoll. He thought it likely the heel flies had given up and gone home before now. He saw a woman hoeing a garden and a man plowing a field of tall corn. He considered riding down to talk to them but regarded that as too much risk. The less these people knew, the better for them and for everybody else. He turned the bay horse away and left the Bradshaw place behind him.

Tyson had told him in a general way how to find the farm where Mary Hubbard's sister lived. Her husband's name was Josiah Wilbank, and it was said he raised some of the finest mules west of the Sabine River, or had until the Confederate army took them all for the war, paying him in scrip that would probably never be worth a secondhand chaw of tobacco. Owen found when he reached the vicinity that Tyson's directions had been too sketchy. He stopped at a farmhouse to inquire and found himself face-to-face with half a dozen young home guards who seemed of about the same caliber as Shattuck's. Their faces had known no introduction to a razor and needed none. But maturity was not a requirement for pulling a trigger, so Owen handled them with deference and showed them his document of leave. One of the youngest boys burned with curiosity about Owen's wound and pestered him to show it. An older boy had a greater sense of propriety and freely gave Owen directions to the Wilbank farm. "Anything to help out a soldier boy," he declared. "I'm goin' to be one myself, pretty soon."

Owen reflected on what the lawman had told him earlier about the poor state of Confederate arms but chose not to dampen the eager youngster's dreams of glory. "You'll make a good one."

He thought it high time the war was over and done with, before any of these boys became old enough to go.

The boy's directions took him to the Wilbank farm. It was richer-looking than he had expected, the road winding among great and ancient oak trees from whose branches long beards of Spanish moss moved gently with the wind. Nearing the large frame house, however, he could see marks of poverty induced by the long war, the old paint faded and peeled, the long wooden fences leaning one direction and another because there was more work to be done than men to do it. As he had observed in the heart of the old South, the larger the fortune, the farther the fall.

He came upon the women gathering vegetables from a garden just south of the big house—Lucy, Mary Hubbard, another woman he judged to be Mrs. Hubbard's sister, and a girl of twelve or fourteen. The two Hubbard women set down their baskets and hurried to the gate to meet him. Lucy was first, eagerly throwing her arms around him though half a dozen people watched. Her mother hugged Owen, then stepped back with worry in her eyes.

"Where's Tyson? And I thought your father might come."

Owen explained the failure of Shattuck's invasion. "They scattered out and tried to make a sweep, but they didn't have Banty to guide them. It was easy to stay out of their way, then cut back around them to where they'd already been. Dad decided to stay and try to gather up the men who didn't leave the thicket. Tyson stayed too. Decided if he was to come here he might draw attention, maybe get your folks in trouble."

Mary Hubbard frowned. "You sure they're safe?"

Owen told about seeing soldiers on the road. "Looks to me like the troops've pulled out and left Shattuck no better off than he was. Maybe worse, because the soldiers probably figure he put them to a lot of trouble with nothin' to show for it."

Mary Hubbard stared thoughtfully at Owen, then at Lucy. "You left Tyson in good health? And your father?"

"They're fine." He did not tell her about Tyson trying to kill Red Upjohn. She probably knew enough of her son's shortcomings without Owen adding to the list.

Lucy clung to Owen's hand. "And you? Would you stay here with us?"

He dreaded the look that would come into her eyes when he told her. "I'm goin' back to rejoin my company." Lucy's face was as sad as he had expected. He wanted to take her in his arms, but too many people were watching.

Mrs. Hubbard showed the couple a gentle smile.

"Lucy, I would expect he's starved half to death. Why don't you take him in the kitchen and fix him some supper? We'll be in when we've finished here."

Lucy led him by the hand. When they were alone, behind the door, she turned to him with love, and wanting, and despair.

He stayed the night, for the Wilbank family assured him there was plenty of room. Their own sons had gone off to the war, their chairs vacant at the big table. One chair would remain forever unused. The young Wilbank girl stared into his face with shameless curiosity, giggling and turning away each time he looked at her. After breakfast Lucy followed him to the barn for one last embrace after he saddled the bay horse. The Wilbank girl was there, watching, paying no heed to her mother calling from the front gallery. Owen rode away, looking back until the great oaks hid Lucy from his sight. He continued northeastward, crossing the Sabine, setting out upon the muddy ground of western Louisiana.

He had been on the trail two weeks when he learned of Appomattox. He had quit dreading the soldiers. Occasionally, late in the day, he would come upon a detachment, show his leave document and spend the night in their camp, sharing whatever rations fortune might have vouchsafed them, and sometimes oats for the horse. Almost always, someone would try to trade him out of the big bay, arguing that if he was going into battle the animal would probably be killed anyway, and it was a shame to see such a one wasted.

One night he saw a campfire in the dusk and fell into the company of a dozen soldiers who looked as if they had just been sentenced to hard labor on the gun emplacements at Galveston. They were silent and morose, barely greeting him as he rode up. When he asked if he might join them, a hollow-eyed one who had not shaved in a month said with a shrug, "You'd just as well. Thirteen can't be no unluckier than this twelve. Whichaway you headed?"

Owen told them he was returning to his company. It would probably be somewhere back in Georgia, the best he could judge. The one who had spoken stared at him, his expression somber. "There ain't nothin' for you to be agoin' back yonder to. Ain't you heard? It's all over with."

"The war's over?"

The man nodded. "They didn't *whip* us. Ain't nobody can ever say that. They starved us out and run us out of anything to fight with. Lee's surrendered, but *I* ain't. I'm just goin' home. We're *all* agoin' home."

Owen clenched both fists. He was able to make almost as much fist with his left hand as with his right. "Two weeks I been tryin' to get back to my company. Now I find out I wasted all that."

"We've wasted a lot more than two weeks, friend. We've wasted four years. You'd just as well's to turn around. Whoever ordered you to go back, he ain't in authority no more."

Owen's gaze roved over the rest of the men. Their faces told him it was as the lawman had predicted to him, back in Texas. One of the men motioned for Owen to help himself to coffee. "We've brewed up the last we've got," he said bitterly. "Just as well drink your share and help us celebrate."

Owen accepted, for he had not tasted coffee since the Wilbank farm. He pondered what the men said and felt the infection of their dark mood. He turned to the bearded man. "You said somethin' about losin' authority. Who *has* authority now?"

"Nobody that had any kind of rank with the Confederacy. That's all gone. The Yankee soldiers'll be comin' along behind us . . . a few days, maybe a few weeks. *They'll* decide who's got authority. Won't be none of *us*, you can bet."

An idea brought a tingling to Owen. "What about home guards . . . people like that? They still have any say-so, you reckon?"

The bearded one shook his head. "They'll be lucky if the Yankees don't throw them all in jail."

Shattuck. Whatever legal authority he might have had was gone now, Owen realized.

The bearded one frowned at him. "You look like you're smilin'. What you got to smile about?"

Owen sipped the coffee and let the smile widen. "I was just thinkin' about a pig thief."

Strangely, as he started west again it seemed that almost everyone he met had heard the news before him. He wondered how he had missed it for so long. He stopped at first one place and then another, offering his work for a little food to see him on down the road. He found a dismaying number of hungry women and children who obviously had no food to give him, and he asked for none. Some of the women were bitter over the war and its failure. Others were only thankful that their menfolk—those who had survived—would be coming home.

At sunset, after crossing the Sabine into Texas, he came upon a little cabin badly in need of repair. Two small children watched bashfully from inside a sagging picket fence marred by broken and missing boards. Their faces were pinched and sallow. He knew by the look of them that food was scarce in this house, and he determined to pass it by.

A young woman stepped out onto the narrow little porch, shading her eyes against the glare of the fading sun. She watched him until it was clear he intended to ride on by. She hurried down off the porch and out to the gate, which hung by a single leather hinge. "Mister! Mister!"

He turned around, riding back to her and the two children. He took off his hat. "Yes, ma'am?"

She studied him with wide eyes. "You're a soldier, I'd take it by the look of you."

"I have been," he acknowledged.

"You seen anything of the Yankees? You know how long it's liable to be before they get here?" Fear was in her voice. It was not the first time he had heard the question, from men as well as women. It was usually asked with apprehension.

"No, ma'am, I got no idea."

She looked past him at the road, as if she expected to see the invaders just behind him. She asked quickly, "You got someplace you're ridin' to before dark?"

He admitted he was still several days from home.

The woman said, "Then you'll be needin' a place to sleep. There's room in the house."

There couldn't be much, he thought. Four or five paces would take a man from one side of the cabin to the other. And if there was any food in the place, it had to be miserably little by the looks of the woman and the two children who clung to her skirt. "I'd be puttin' you to too much bother," he said, looking for a graceful way to keep riding.

"It'd pleasure me . . . *us*. You go put your horse in the pen. If the Yankees was to come, I'd feel a lot better havin' a man around here."

"You got no man of your own?"

"He went off to the war. Ain't heard from him in over a year." Her tone carried a sense of desperation. "Please, mister."

He looked toward a small picket shed that served as a barn. "I wouldn't want to crowd you-all. I'll sleep out there."

He found a barrel in the shed but no oats in it. He led the bay horse out some distance and staked him in grass. Then he sought the woodpile and chopped wood until the young woman called him into the cabin for supper. It wasn't much, mostly greens she had gathered in the wild, and a little salt pork. He had looked in the smokehouse and found it empty.

A tallow candle burned on the table, making a valiant struggle against the gloom of the little cabin. She apologized for not having bread. "We run out of corn early in the spring. We'll be havin' some more pretty soon, out of the field. It's makin' good ears."

The children stared at Owen. He doubted that the

smallest, a girl, could even remember her father. He did not want to voice his suspicion that the man of the house would never come home. The woman volunteered the possibility. "He wrote to us at first, and I reckon he wouldn't've quit writin' if he wasn't killed. My old daddy-in-law taken care of us awhile, but he died just after he done the spring plantin'. I don't know what's to become of us without a man on the place." He saw the wish in her eyes and looked away.

She said, "Ain't no tellin' what them Yankees might do, findin' us alone here thisaway." The fear came back into her voice.

He said, "They ain't goin' to hurt women and children."

"I don't know. I never seen no Yankees. But if they wasn't bad we wouldn't've been warrin' agin them, would we?"

At full dark she put the oldest child, a boy of three or so, into a crudely built bed softened by a cornshuck mattress. She rocked the little girl until she fell asleep, then placed her beside the boy. She tucked a cotton quilt around the children, then turned to Owen.

"This is a pretty good little farm. With a man on it, it'd make a fair livin'."

"I expect it would," he said uneasily, sensing where the conversation was leading.

"You ain't a married man, are you? No, I'll bet you ain't. You got a farm like this to go home to?"

He mumbled something that was not really an answer. She touched his hand. When he tried to pull it away, she held it. "You could stay here. You'd soon

get to likin' this place. I'd see to it that you liked it."
She drew closer, then was standing against him, body
atremble. She said, "It ain't meant that people always
be alone."

He wanted to pull away from her, and at the same
time he did not want to. Her lips were parted, and he
felt the warmth of her breath upon his face. A powerful temptation swept him, a hunger that demanded
to take what was offered. He gripped her arms and
felt the rising of blood in the woman as well as in
himself. He sensed that she wanted him whether he
stayed for the night or forever. But he sensed also
that she might have wanted almost any man who
happened upon this place at this time of fear and
loneliness and vulnerability. He looked at the sleeping children in the edge of the flickering candlelight
and forced himself to draw away from her.

"I'll be goin' to the barn," he said, not really wanting to. He hurried outside, afraid if he lingered the
heavy urgency of their wanting might change his mind.

Were it not for Lucy, he might have stayed.

He heard the woman crying softly as he walked
briskly away from the porch. He slept little, half expecting her to come out to him in the night, and
wondering what he would do. He might not send her
away.

He was up before daylight, saddling the bay. He remembered seeing a couple of deer dart from the edge
of a field to the nearby timber as he had approached
the evening before. He rode back the way he had
come, working into the woods and riding slowly, look-

ing toward the open ground beyond the trees. Soon
he saw two does browsing amid scrub brush in the
last short while before the sun's rising. They would
take a bite, then look quickly around, ready to race
the little distance back into timber at any sign of danger. Owen wished for a rifle but had only the pistol.
He tied the bay horse and advanced slowly toward
the deer. He used the trees for cover, moving only
when the deer browsed, freezing his movement each
time one jerked its head up. One seemed to look directly at him, and he feared it had spotted him. But it
would turn its head away to nibble at a bush, and he
would move forward a step or two. When he was as
near as he thought he would be able to go, he braced
the pistol against a tree. He aimed for a point behind
the shoulder and fired. The doe jumped straight up,
fell, kicked for a minute and went still. The other
bolted.

He gutted the doe where she lay. As he was finish-
ing he watched a rider on a black horse moving toward him in the pale light of sunrise. The stranger
hailed him at some distance to assure him he presented no threat. As he neared, Owen could tell he
was a young man, wearing the tattered vestiges of a
once-gray uniform.

The horseman halted, smiling. "You goin' to need
any help eatin' that venison?"

"Maybe," Owen replied. "Where you headed?"

The young man shrugged. "Damned if I know.
Somewhere west. Ain't no use goin' back to Georgia.
Yankees burned everything, from what I hear."

Owen smiled. "You hungry?"

"Last thing I ate was a slow-movin' rabbit, the day before yesterday."

Owen said, "There's a cabin down the road yonder, just around that timber. I was fixin' to take this deer meat to the lady who lives there, but I'll let you take it for me. I'll bet she'll fix you a good breakfast with it."

"You ain't comin'?"

"I got business on down the road. You'll save me some time if you'll deliver her this."

"I'll consider it a privilege."

Watching the soldier ride away, the doe tied behind his saddle, Owen thought of the woman and remembered the hungers which had ached in him last night. He could not truthfully have said that he turned away without regret. But he did turn away.

He came to the Wilbank farm late the following day, his heartbeat picking up at the anticipation of seeing Lucy. The fires kindled by the other woman had not quite burned out. Josiah Wilbank, working in the field, unhitched an old workhorse and rode out bareback to meet Owen on the road. "Been lookin' for you to show up," he said jovially.

"Lucy at the house?" Owen asked without taking time first for conventional niceties, beyond a hasty handshake.

Wilbank shook his head. "She and her mama left here three days ago, soon after we heard the war was over. They was anxious to get back to their own place."

"Their place was taken away from them," Owen worried, "same as ours was."

"But it was taken away under the powers of war. I expect the courts'll give it back to them easy enough, if it even has to go that far."

Disappointed, Owen said, "I figured we'd all go home together. I'd even figured maybe . . ." He broke off. He had entertained some notion of having the Wilbanks' minister marry him and Lucy before they started back. He saw no gain in telling Wilbank. No use telling anybody until he first asked Lucy. "I'd best be ridin' on, then."

Wilbank would not hear of that. He prevailed on Owen to spend the night, his young daughter plying Owen with all manner of personal questions from supper until bedtime. At daylight Owen was on his way.

He purposely avoided the town, for he had no way of knowing the political situation there, the dangerous resentments that might still be lingering from a war fought and lost, the opportunities for getting himself embroiled in some painful unpleasantness before he even got home. He skirted the great thicket and rode to the Hubbard farm.

To his surprise he found it deserted. He found no tangible sign that Lucy and her mother had even been there. It was plain enough that the place had been worked. The fields were cultivated, the corn plowed out. Phineas Shattuck had probably been responsible for that, expecting the fruits of the harvest for himself. He was going to feel mightily let down that the

Confederate army had not adequately protected the spoils he had considered his own.

The hell with him, Owen thought. The Hubbards could well use whatever crops those fields would provide. He could see poetic justice in Shattuck's having done the work on stolen property, or having paid someone to, then losing it all.

Owen was vaguely troubled over not finding the Hubbards, for they had had time enough to have arrived here well ahead. But his disappointment about not seeing Lucy was soon lost in the excitement he felt over riding freely and without fear across land he had known since boyhood, land he considered home. He avoided the thicket, for he had never spent a comfortable moment in it. He had felt somehow choked by the closeness of the heavy growth. He had felt stifled, cut off from fresh air, from the open sunshine.

He came, finally, to the hill that overlooked the home-place. He paused, looking down upon it, enjoying the sight of the green fields, the open pastureland where the Danforth cattle quietly grazed. He saw a thin gray wisp of smoke rising from the chimney, and his heart felt warm. He touched spurs to the bay's ribs. "You're fixin' to finally get some feed and rest, boy. You're home."

From a motte of trees a rider moved out to intercept him. A momentary flair of apprehension gave way as he remembered that the fighting was over; there was no reason any longer for fear.

Red Upjohn quickly disabused him of that notion. His horse was in a long trot as he rode toward Owen, his hand raised for a halt. Upjohn looked cautiously down the hill toward the house. "Come on, boy," he said urgently. "Maybe you ain't been seen."

"What's the matter?" Owen demanded. "The war's over."

"Everywhere else but here, maybe," Upjohn said, blocking Owen's path, motioning him back up the hill. "Phineas Shattuck ain't fired his last shot."

11

Reluctantly, looking back over his shoulder toward the cabin that was home, Owen followed Red Upjohn in a retreat to the other side of the hill. Upjohn said urgently, "You've got younger eyes. Anybody comin' after us?"

Owen saw no activity around the house. "Who's down there?" he demanded.

"Some of Shattuck's crowd. They're layin' for you to come back, like they laid for your daddy and the Hubbards. Shattuck's got all them folks in jail."

Owen's eyes widened. "My dad?"

Upjohn nodded gravely. "Along with Mrs. Hubbard and her daughter. And that hotheaded Tyson. Charged them all with sedition."

Owen protested in disbelief, "But the Confederacy is dead. He's got no authority."

"He's got the guns. *That's* authority. He's still got a few home guard kids with him. Recruited some toughs that don't mind grindin' their bootheels on other people's necks. Promised them a share, more'n likely, if they'll help him hold onto what he's taken."

"When the Union soldiers get here, they'll set things straight."

"Not if everybody who might contest him is dead."

Owen swallowed. "Dead?"

"Dead. He confiscated the Hubbards' land, and your uncle's, and your daddy's. Then he bought it all from the Confederate government for the price of a few good saddle horses. Unless you Danforths or the Hubbards take him to federal court, he'll keep what he stole. You're the only one still runnin' loose. That's why he's got to get ahold of you. Then he's got to see all of you dead before the federals come."

Owen shivered. "You're talkin' about murder. They'd hang him higher'n the Union flag."

"Not if there was some big, terrible accident nobody could blame him for. I'm guessin' he has all that figured out."

Panic threatened to overpower Owen. "I've got to bust them out of there . . ." He reined the bay horse half around.

Upjohn leaned down, cursing, and grabbed the reins. "Hold on, boy, and think a little. Don't make it easy for him. You're all that's kept them other people alive."

Owen's chill came back. Anger followed it. "What's Claude Chancellor done about this? He's the *real* law around here."

Upjohn's eyes pinched. "Way I heard it, he tried to stop Shattuck from throwin' your daddy in jail, and Shattuck bent a gun barrel over his head. Charged *him* with sedition too."

"There's got to be some good people who wouldn't stand by and let a pig thief get away with such as this."

Upjohn shrugged. "They're figurin' like you did, that the soldiers'll set everything right. But they ain't seen Shattuck from our side of the fence. They don't realize what he's capable of."

Upjohn pointed his red-bearded chin toward a thicket, then reined his horse into it. Owen followed, a dozen wild ideas racing through his mind. Most were akin to suicide.

Upjohn said critically, "That horse of yours looks like he's run out his string. You oughtn't to ride him so hard."

Damn it, Owen thought, *this is no time to be talking about horses.* But Upjohn was right. Without a good horse, he could do little to help anybody. He pictured Lucy in that miserable jail and clenched his fists. "I'll break them out of that place!"

"Sure you will," said Upjohn, "but not by ridin' in there like a big dumb calf to the slaughter. We got to think." He stepped down from the saddle and loosened the cinch so his horse could breathe easier.

Owen's hands trembled as he followed the example. "You said *accident*. What kind of an accident could kill everybody without Shattuck standin' the blame?"

Upjohn grunted. "Your daddy told me what happened to his barn after he tried to get Shattuck jailed for stealin' pigs. And I seen for myself what happened to your uncle's cabin."

"Fire!" Owen exploded. That *would* be Shattuck's way.

Upjohn gave him a moment to let the terrible picture take its full shattering effect. "As I recollect that old jail, it's built of lumber, dry as powder. Stands up high on wood posts. Wouldn't take nothin', hardly, to touch it off. It'd go up in a minute, with all them folks locked in their cells. There couldn't nobody prove Shattuck done it himself."

Owen shuddered in cold dread. The grisly logic was inescapable. It was just the kind of plan to take root in a mind like Phineas Shattuck's. It occurred to Owen that Red Upjohn also had such a mind, warped by bitter experience. Perhaps it took a man like Upjohn to understand a man like Shattuck and anticipate what he might do.

Upjohn said, "We'll rest these horses till dark. Then we'll slip into town and figure out what to do."

A stranger riding across country in the night could easily have passed the settlement without noticing it. Lamps cast a dull light through a scattering of windows, and lanterns glowed dimly on a porch here and there. Otherwise, the town was dark and devoid of welcome. Owen and Upjohn sat on their horses at the outer edge, watching and listening to the oppressive silence. A horse nickered, a baby cried. A dog barked somewhere, and a couple of others briefly relayed the message. Owen heard no music, no laughter. Life had turned Spartan and bleak here as the war had dragged on. Few people had either the money or the disposition to indulge themselves. Now he sensed that the psychology of defeat had laid a cold hand upon the place. Like other towns he had passed on his way home, this one waited in silent dread for the federal soldiers and an unknown future.

"Ain't much town," Upjohn observed. He had never lived here.

Owen shrugged. It was small and backward, judged against cities he had seen during his soldiering. Growing up miles out in the country, a rough-handed and unread farm boy, he had always suspected the townspeople looked down on him. He had been uncomfortable here. But never before had he felt like an enemy, infiltrating hostile lines.

He pointed for Upjohn's benefit. "That yonder's the livery stable and wagonyard. I heard Shattuck confiscated it when Dad Wilson tried to run off to Mexico. They caught up with the old man and shot him."

Upjohn grunted. "Convenient for Shattuck. I don't reckon Wilson left any relatives to take up his fight?"

"No." Owen knew what was on Upjohn's mind. His stomach felt cold.

Upjohn pointed with his chin. "Let's ease down yonder on the dark side of the street and take a look at the jail."

Owen rode as near the buildings as possible, noting the alleys for a possible quick escape. He stopped opposite the jail. From the open front door, a lamp cast a dim orange light upon the sagging wooden walk. A movement caught Owen's eye. A man stood in the doorway, blocking the light. He was no more than a silhouette, but Owen recognized the slouch. His breath came short.

Upjohn brought up his rifle. "This'll be easier than I thought."

Owen laid a shaking hand on the barrel's cold steel. "No. I won't do it thisaway."

Upjohn reconsidered. "You're right. You've got to live here; I don't. Tell you what to do: you ride on down yonder and go into that dramshop so people will see you. Then, when I shoot him, nobody can say you done it."

"You don't understand. I can't shoot him from ambush or have you do it either. I saw enough of that in the war. Maybe we can bust in and surprise him."

Two more figures came to stand in the doorway. Upjohn said, "We'll play hell surprisin' *three* of them."

"We'll figure somethin'. Let's move away from here before their eyes get accustomed to the dark." Owen pushed the bay into a narrow space between two buildings, half afraid Upjohn might fire the rifle anyway. But Upjohn followed him.

Presently they were at the back side of the corrals, behind the livery barn. A dozen or so horses stood in the pen, most at rest, a few tugging at hay piled in crude racks built of branches tied together. At the corner of the corral a hay shed sagged with age. Owen remembered that Dad Wilson used to keep extra saddles there for protection from the weather.

He said, "When we get the folks out of that jail, our best bet is to run for the thicket and wait there till the soldiers come. We'll need horses for everybody."

"*When* we get them out?" Upjohn shook his head. "You mean *if* we get them out. Best let me do it my way. Kill Shattuck and that'll be the end of it."

"Been too much killin' already."

The corral was not guarded; Shattuck evidently had seen no reason it should be. Owen and Upjohn quietly caught and saddled four horses. When Owen caught a fifth, Upjohn said, "We've got all we need."

"Claude Chancellor's in there too," Owen told him.

Upjohn grumbled that jail was the proper place for a Confederate sheriff. Owen told him of Chancellor's part in sending a warning to the people in the thicket. Upjohn reluctantly acknowledged that he might have redeeming qualities, even if he *was* a Confederate.

"*I'm* a Confederate," Owen reminded him.

"But you got a good daddy."

When the five horses were saddled, Owen opened the gate and eased the others out into the town section, careful not to stir them to more than a gentle walk lest the sound of their running draw attention. He looked back at the hay shed. "When we wanted to surprise the Yankees we used to pull a diversion and draw their attention away from what we were fixin' to do."

"Shootin' Shattuck would be diversion enough. It would surprise the hell out of *him*."

Owen knelt and pulled some dry straw together. He took a flint and a steel from his pocket and struck sparks until one finally ignited the straw. When the blaze was large enough that the breeze would not blow it out, he kicked the burning straw into a pile of hay.

"Shattuck won't stay at the jail when he sees a fire at his livery barn. Let's move up yonder and be ready."

The blaze was quickly climbing into the shed as Owen and Upjohn led the saddled horses away. Upjohn grunted in dark satisfaction, looking back. "Shattuck'll squeal like a pig caught under a gate."

They tied the horses to a rack in darkness between two buildings, then hurried afoot to a corner where they could watch the front of the jail. Already, a red glow was building behind the livery barn.

From somewhere in that direction a voice shouted, "Fire!"

A man stepped into the door of the jail. Owen heard him declare, "Phin, it looks like your stable's burnin'."

Shattuck rushed out the door, cursing. He wasted but a moment in looking. "Come on," he hollered, "or I'll lose the whole damned thing!"

He struck an awkward run down the street. Two men followed him. From all directions, Owen heard shouting as more people discovered the fire.

"Now!" he declared. "We got to be quick." He sprinted toward the jail door, pistol in his hand.

Though he had seen Shattuck and two others leave, he stopped by the door to listen. Hearing nothing inside, he rushed in, Upjohn a step behind him. His gaze swept the lamp-lighted room for another guard. There was none. In his haste Shattuck had left no one to watch the jail.

"Dad? Lucy?" Owen called excitedly.

Lucy's voice responded from behind one of the iron-barred doors. "Owen?" He saw her in a cell with her mother.

He looked quickly for keys but saw none hanging on the wall. He began pulling drawers from the desk.

Lucy shouted, "The bottom one, on the right."

Keys jingling in his hand, Owen fumbled at the first lock and forced himself to slow down. He swung the door open. Lucy threw her arms around him. He almost crushed her.

Upjohn stood watch by the door, rifle in his hand. "You-all better put off the lovin' till a better time."

Mary Hubbard yanked the keys from Owen's hand and hurried to another steel door. Owen said, "Dad! Tyson! We got horses waitin'. We'll make a run for the thicket."

Mary Hubbard said soberly, "Your dad can't be ridin' anywhere. He's shot."

Owen's breath almost left him. He saw his father lying on a cot, making only a feeble move to get up. His chest was swathed in bandages splotched red. Claude Chancellor lay on another cot, his head wrapped. He made no move at all.

Lucy said, "Mr. Chancellor can't travel either. His head's broken. Doctor Levitt says it wouldn't take much to kill him."

"Won't take much if Shattuck comes back. We can't stay *here*."

Andrew Danforth reached up for Owen. Owen squeezed his hand, hard. Andrew said weakly, "You oughtn't to've come here, son. We'll be all right when the soldiers arrive."

"You won't be *alive* that long if we don't get you-all away from this jailhouse!"

Mary Hubbard knelt beside Andrew and pressed her lips gently to his forehead. "Let's leave it to Owen this time."

Owen asked her, "You know somebody in town who'll take them in and not tell Shattuck?"

"Doctor Levitt would. He's been here twice a day to see after Andrew and Mr. Chancellor. He's got no love for Shattuck, or fear either."

Tyson Hubbard and Red Upjohn stared silently at one another, old grudges still bubbling near the surface. Owen said, "Tyson, you and Red fetch Mr. Chancellor. I'll get my dad."

He blew out the lamp, plunging the jail's interior into darkness. Lucy and Mary Hubbard helped Owen bring Andrew Danforth to his feet and walk him haltingly to the door. Owen stopped a moment for a look outside. The blaze at the livery grew larger and redder, the flames leaping high enough that they reached over the barn. "Let's go," he said.

Upjohn and Tyson bore Chancellor between them, the man barely conscious enough to move his feet. They moved out of the jail and around the corner, every step strained and painful. Lucy cried, "Owen, we can't keep carryin' them this way."

"We can carry them to the horses and then hold them in the saddle to Doc Levitt's. Keep comin', before somebody sees us."

Somebody already had. In the dancing red light from the spreading stable fire he saw two men hurrying toward him. Heart tripping, Owen drew the pistol from his waistband.

Claude Chancellor's deputy declared, "You won't need that. We come to help you." He got an arm around Chancellor. The other man motioned for the women to let go of Andrew, and he brought his own broad shoulders to the task.

Owen said distrustfully, "You wouldn't tell Shattuck . . ."

The deputy spoke Shattuck's name like a curse and spat. Owen knew the other man then, the teamster

Jake Tisdale, whom he had met on the road when he had come home wounded from the war. Upjohn glanced questioningly at Owen, but Owen could only shrug. They had no choice except to trust Tisdale and the deputy.

Tisdale said, "This town's had a gutful of Shattuck. We just been waitin' for the soldiers to come and pull his teeth."

They struggled to lift Andrew and Chancellor onto the horses. Owen mounted the big bay and put his arm around his father to keep him from falling. Tyson and Upjohn rode on either side of Chancellor, who seemed not to grasp what was happening. The two volunteers walked ahead of the horses. Tisdale raised his hand once and motioned the riders into the shadows as people ran toward the blaze.

They arrived in a few minutes at the back of the doctor's frame house. Levitt stood on his little front porch, watching the hay shed flames. Wind-driven brands had spread them to the main barn. Jake Tisdale hurriedly fetched Levitt to the rear of the house. The doctor, a bent-shouldered old gentleman with white hair and a goatee, recognized Chancellor and demanded, "What're you people trying to do, kill that man?"

Owen said, "No sir, tryin' to keep *Shattuck* from killin' him."

The doctor offered no further argument. "The back door," he said quickly, trotting to open and hold it.

Gently they placed Andrew and Chancellor on two beds. Mary Hubbard stayed close by Andrew, holding his hand while the doctor explored the wound to determine if movement had restarted the bleeding. Levitt said, "He'll be all right, I think," and turned his attention to the groaning Chancellor. "Lucy girl, you'd best pull those curtains so nobody can see from outside."

The fire at the barn was crackling, leaping wildly. A couple of dozen people had formed a bucket brigade in a vain attempt to save the structure. Now they abandoned that effort and shifted their attention to nearby buildings, trying to keep them from catching. Shattuck stood in the dirt street, yelling for them to come back and help him. His shouting was to no avail.

Standing just back from the front door to lessen the risk of being seen, Owen watched the barn collapse in a great explosion of flame, flinging sparks high into the air to fall again in a blistering shower. Any building within a hundred yards stood in some jeopardy of catching a firebrand. Men ran in all directions, seeing after their own, leaving Shattuck to watch helplessly as his buckled barn went into the final contortions of destruction.

Owen thought bitterly, *That's one piece of plunder that won't do you any more good.*

Tisdale and the deputy helped the doctor examine the sheriff. Owen heard Tisdale assuring Chancellor, "It's us, ol' Pete and ol' Jake. We'll stay right here and see that nobody hurts you."

Upjohn warned, "We got to do somethin' about them horses. Somebody'll see them."

Owen forced himself away from the pleasure of watching Shattuck stomp in wild frustration. "Right. When Shattuck finds the cells empty he'll probably figure we ran for the thicket. We'll want him to keep thinkin' that." Followed by Upjohn and Tyson, he hurried outside. He unsaddled his bay and threw his saddle into the doctor's small buggy shed. "I wish you-all would lead these horses out yonder a ways. Hide the saddles in the brush and turn the horses loose."

Upjohn cast a grudging glance at Tyson. He was still unable to put aside what young Hubbard had tried to do to him. "Come on, boy. I reckon you've got sense enough for a simple chore like this."

The horses were almost instantly swallowed up by darkness. Owen turned toward the house, then flattened himself against the fence. He saw the dark figure of a man hurrying down the alley, carrying a firebrand in each hand. The flickering light touched upon the face just long enough for Owen to recognize him.

Phineas Shattuck!

Shattuck looked furtively to one side and then the other but did not see Owen pressed into the shadows. He moved in a trot, his manner making it plain that he did not want to be seen.

A prickling ran up Owen's back as he realized Shattuck's intention. He followed, holding to the shadows so the dancing light of the stable fire would not betray him. He froze in place each time Shattuck stopped. At the jail, Shattuck looked back a final time, then thrust one firebrand beneath the floor. Almost instantly, flames began to spread among old dry tumbleweeds blown under the jail, trapped against the foundation posts since last winter. Shattuck hurried around the corner. Owen did not follow, but he knew Shattuck was firing the other side.

This was what he had expected of the man, but the

reality struck him like a sledge. *You cold-blooded bastard! You think your prisoners are still in there!*

Shattuck trotted back, watching over his shoulder. Owen pressed himself against a building, but not quickly enough. Shattuck stopped dead in his tracks, drawing his pistol.

"Who are you?" he demanded. "Come out here where I can see you."

Owen drew his pistol, then stepped into the open. The fire licked its way up the jailhouse wall behind Shattuck. The man's features were in shadow, but Owen knew the light of the flames revealed his own face.

Shattuck exclaimed, "You!"

"Me, Shattuck. And I saw what you did."

"Who you goin' to tell? You'll be dead, like them people in that jail are fixin' to be." Triumph was in Shattuck's voice. In his excitement he seemed to take no notice of Owen's pistol.

"But they're *not* dead. We already taken them out."

Shattuck wavered. He tried to look back at the jail without taking his eyes from Owen. Owen could imagine the thought that must be racing through Shattuck's mind. If anybody *was* trapped in the jail, he would be hearing cries for help by now. The only sound was the crackling of the fire, rapidly sweeping the old frame structure.

Shattuck seemed to realize something else. "It was *you* set fire to my stables."

"Not *your* stables, Shattuck. You stole them, same as you figured to steal our land. Now you've got nothin'. Wait till the soldiers get here. And wait till this town finds out you fired your own jail to get rid of your prisoners."

Shattuck's weapon blazed. Owen stumbled as a slug seared a streak across his ribs and knocked some of the breath from him. He gripped the pistol with both hands and tried to hold it steady upon Shattuck. The darting flames half blinded him. He squeezed the trigger once, then again, and he kept squeezing until the hammer snapped on a spent cap.

Shattuck was gone, disappeared into the darkness. From somewhere Owen heard hoofbeats, a horse running. He heard men shouting, rushing toward the jail. Someone yelled, "There's people in there! We've got to get them out!"

Owen staggered to the front of the blazing jail, blocking the men rushing at the door. "No," he told them, "don't get yourselves killed for nothin'. Nobody's in there. We already got them out."

Somebody said a flying brand from the stable fire must have been carried on the wind all the way to the jail. Owen declared, "No, Shattuck set it afire. He wanted to get rid of the prisoners. I shot at him, but he got away."

A merchant ran up to report that Phineas Shattuck had just taken a horse out of a pen behind his store and had spurred away.

Some of the men called angrily for a posse to ride after him, but calmer heads counseled that pursuit in the darkness was futile. Owen realized that, as Jake Tisdale had said, the town had simply been tolerating the man, confident that he would be put in his place when the soldiers came.

He pressed his hand to his burning ribs and felt his fingers go sticky with blood. But the bullet had done no more than cut a shallow furrow.

Red Upjohn and Tyson Hubbard spurred into the street. Upjohn jumped to the ground, fighting to hold the reins as his horse reared and squealed its fear of the flames. Owen told what had happened. Upjohn swore, then looked off into the darkness. "Shattuck probably lit out for the thicket. Well, he forced other people to stay in it. It's only justice for *him* to have to hide there."

Lucy Hubbard came running up the street, calling anxiously for Owen. She threw herself against him and pressed her head against his chest. "I heard the shots, and I was afraid . . ."

His ribs burned fiercely, but he held her and said nothing that might make her turn him loose.

Upjohn stared into the darkness. "Come first light, I'm goin' to the thicket and hunt for him."

Tyson said, "I'll go with you."

Upjohn pondered, his doubts strong. "I'd rather have a broken leg. But I suppose you'd trail behind me anyway. Better to have you where I can watch you than behind me doin' God knows what."

12

Impatient for the sight of home, Owen trotted the bay horse ahead of the wagon to the top of the hill. His eyes followed the curve of the trail through the curing grass to the double cabin. No one was there, so far as he could see. Jake Tisdale and several townsmen had ridden out yesterday to call upon the guards Phineas Shattuck had left and invite them to vacate the county of their own accord before a less courteous committee escorted them to the line.

He pulled the bay horse out of the trail and waited for a determined-looking Mary Hubbard to bring the wagon even with him. Lucy Hubbard was beside her mother on the spring seat. She said, "At least they didn't burn the place down."

Owen glanced again at the cabin, glad it had not followed Uncle Zach's into a pile of ashes. "Shattuck wasn't here to help them think of it." He looked in the bed of the wagon at his father, lying on several thicknesses of blankets. "You all right?"

His father declared, "I *will* be when you-all get me home."

They pulled up in front of the double cabin. Owen looped his reins over a wheel and leaned across the wagon's sideboards. He helped his father rise to a sitting position. "Slow now."

Andrew Danforth waved his son away. "I can make it to the ground all right. Nobody has got to carry me."

Mary Hubbard declared, "You'll do nothin' foolish, Andrew. We'll help you, and that's that."

Owen caught a smile in Lucy's eyes and could not restrain his own. Mary Hubbard would not be a silent wife to Andrew. Owen suspected that when he was able to rebuild the burned cabin on Uncle Zach's place, he would not find Lucy silent and subservient either.

He had not asked her yet, but she was waiting. Her eyes had told him that.

Andrew let Owen and Lucy help him down from the wagon, then shrugged them off. Mary Hubbard took his good arm and led him to the dog run.

Owen said, "I'll go put the horses away." He turned back toward the wagon and stopped short. A horseman emerged from heavy brush by the creek. A couple of grazing cows were startled by his sudden appearance and moved in a half circle to get around and behind him. Owen squinted but could not recognize him. The rider slumped over the horse's withers, his head bowed so that his hat hid his face.

"Company," Owen said warily to Lucy, motioning for her to retreat to the open space between the two sections of the cabin. "Might be a Shattuck man comin' back." He drew his pistol.

Lucy said, "It's not. It's Shattuck himself."

Owen blinked, not certain. As the rider neared he knew Lucy was right. He swore under his breath and stepped back into the dog run, his hand nervous on the grip of the heavy pistol. Lucy hurried to the wagon, ignoring Owen's call for her to stay where she was. She grabbed a rifle they had brought from town. She turned, waiting for Shattuck. In her face was the same ungiving resolve Owen had seen at times in her mother.

He said, "If anybody has to shoot him, let me be the one. I've already got a war on my conscience."

"You may miss," Lucy declared. "But I won't."

Owen saw no belligerence in Shattuck. Approaching, the man remained slumped, barely raising his head. Owen saw blood, dried and stiff, almost black upon the shredded remnants of a shirt. Shattuck held one arm tightly against his chest, as if it might be paralyzed.

The horse stopped a few paces from Owen. Shattuck wheezed, "Help me, you-all. They're comin' after me."

Hatred burned like a slow fire in Owen's belly. "Why should *we* help you . . . you of all people?"

Shattuck tried to steady his gaze, and Owen realized with a start that the man could barely see. Shattuck's face was the color of clay . . . the gray of death.

Shattuck seemed confused, frightened. "You ain't the ones I left here. Who are you?"

"I'm Owen Danforth."

"Danforth? The soldier?" Shattuck lowered his head as if he were on the verge of giving up. "*You* done this to me, boy. It was you put these bullets in me. Now them other two, they want to finish what you commenced."

"What two? Who's after you?"

The voice quavered. "I don't know. Never seen them close. But they've dogged me like bloodhounds."

Red Upjohn, Owen realized, and Tyson Hubbard. They had not come back to town since the night of the fire.

Shattuck asked plaintively, "You fixin' to shoot me again?"

Owen said bluntly, "I'm studyin' on it. You got it comin'."

Shattuck's voice rasped a weak effort at argument. "It was war. The war's over now."

"It was over before you tried to burn my dad and all them others to death."

"You wouldn't kill a helpless man, not in cold blood. I can't even hold my gun." Shattuck broke into a spasm of coughing and seemed about to slide from the saddle. The sound was painful. Owen tried not to feel sorry for him.

Andrew Danforth's voice came from the dog run. "Don't torment the man, son. He's dyin'. Help him down."

Owen looked back at his father leaning against the doorjamb. "After all he done to you?"

"He's finished. He won't hurt me anymore, or anybody else. You'd help a sick dog if he came to you like this."

"Or put him out of his misery." Bitterness roiled like tainted meat in Owen's soured stomach. But he placed the pistol in the wagon seat, out of harm's way, and took a position beside Shattuck's horse. "All right," he said grudgingly, "ease down. I'll help you."

Shattuck's remnant of strength left him as he brought his leg over the cantle. He tumbled. Owen grabbed him. The stench of the wounds struck him like a stinking wet blanket slapped across the face. Shattuck cried out in pain.

Andrew said, "Better put him in the wagon and get him to town. Maybe Doc Levitt can do somethin'."

Owen doubted that. He had seen too many in this condition. "He'd be dead before we could get him halfway there."

Andrew's voice was determined. "You'll wake up nights wishin' you'd tried."

Lucy laid down the rifle and came to Owen. "I'll help you."

Shattuck dragged his feet as the two young people supported his move toward the wagon.

A voice hailed them from the direction of the creek. Two horsemen spurred out of the timber. Red Upjohn was shouting, but distance and the wind muffled his words. Owen thought he knew the gist of them. He said urgently, "We'd better put him in that wagon quick. We're apt to have our hands full."

Shattuck groaned as they placed him upon the blankets which had been a pallet for Andrew Danforth. He was not too far gone to hear Upjohn's voice. He pleaded, "They're here. Don't let them have me . . . please!"

Lucy promised, "We won't."

Owen wanted to warn her not to make rash promises she might not be able to keep. He turned away from the groaning Phineas Shattuck to face the grim-eyed pair who rode up within spitting distance of the wagon. Both looked haggard, but they also looked like hunters who had treed a long-sought quarry.

Upjohn said, "It's a handy thing that you've got him in that wagon, boy. Me and Tyson, we'll just haul him down to the timber yonder and finish the job you started."

Owen forgot that he had had the same notion himself, not ten minutes earlier. "We're takin' him to town, to the doctor."

Upjohn snorted, "He won't need a doctor. Step aside if you ain't got the stomach for it. Me and Tyson, we'll do what's to be done." Upjohn moved his horse closer. His pistol was in his hand.

Owen remembered his own, lying on the wagon seat two paces away. It had as well have been two miles. "He's mine, Red, not yours. I shot him."

"Then do it yourself, and make a better job of it this time. But if you don't, I will!"

Owen placed himself between Upjohn and Shattuck. "No. My dad said it, and he's right: the war's over. It's time for the killin' to be over too."

Upjohn's eyes were almost shut, hiding whatever lay behind them. He leveled his pistol on Owen. "You're in my way, boy. I come to kill him. Don't make me kill you too . . ."

Owen swallowed. He wondered what everyone else was doing but could not take his gaze from Upjohn . . . from Upjohn, and from the awesome muzzle of that pistol. Owen raised his arms away from his sides, as if they would shield Shattuck from fire. "I'm not givin' him to you, Red."

He thought he saw Red's finger tighten on the trigger. He took half a breath and held it.

Tyson Hubbard had sat silently on his horse all this time. Now he said gravely, "Better pull back, Red. If my sister don't shoot you, my mother will."

Upjohn looked at the girl, giving Owen a chance to cut his eyes toward her too. Lucy had the rifle trained somewhere about the second button on Upjohn's shirt, and her eyes were like flint. Upjohn glanced then at the dog run, where Mary Hubbard stood beside Andrew Danforth. She held a pistol in both hands. Upjohn stared at her, clearly agonizing over his decision. Slowly then, and carefully, he shoved his pistol back into his belt and brought his hand clear enough to show he presented no further threat.

"Hubbards!" he declared with frustration. "If the boy don't kill me, the women will." He looked from Mary to Lucy and back again, perplexed. "I thought you'd all want what I come to do."

Mary Hubbard said, "You're welcome here, Red Upjohn, so long as you come in peace. But if you're set on violence, you'd best keep movin'."

Upjohn shook his head. "I never knew there was so damned many crazy people anywhere." He swung down from his horse and said to Owen, "Go on, then. Take him to hell, if that's your pleasure." He turned toward the dog run. "Mrs. Hubbard, would there be anything here to eat? Me and your boy ain't put nothin' down in three days."

Owen and Lucy moved together. He touched her

arm and found her trembling a little. So was he. He stared at her, wondering. "Would you really have shot him for Phineas Shattuck?"

She shook her head. "Not for Shattuck, but I'd've shot him for *you*. The state he was in, I was afraid he might shoot you first. I wasn't about to let him."

Owen put his arm around her. He did not know how to tell her what he felt, and he did not try. He turned to the wagon. "We'd better hurry and get started."

Lucy climbed up the wheel and onto the spring seat. Owen leaned over the sideboard to rig a shade that would keep the sun from Shattuck's face. The eyes were open, but he knew with a sudden terrible certainty that they did not see and never would see again. Shattuck had probably already been dead when Owen had faced Red Upjohn and that pistol. A chill shuddered through him.

Owen closed the sightless eyes, and he pulled a blanket over the man's stilled face.

Quietly he said, "There's no hurry about anything now, Lucy. We've got all the time in the world."

Forge

Award-winning authors
Compelling stories

. . . .

Please join us at the website
below for more information
about this author and other great
Forge selections, and to sign up for
our monthly newsletter!

. . . . www.tor-forge.com . . . .